Islands in the Fog

by Jerry Autieri

ISBN13: 978-1490460109

CHAPTER ONE

"This is my last offer. All you need do is place your hands upon my blade and swear loyalty. Save your life and the lives of your men." Hardar Hammerhand squinted at Ulfrik from behind the cheek plates of his helmet and tipped the hilt of his sword forward. His gray-streaked beard wagged as he continued. "Go on, lad, and do what is right."

"The next time you call me lad, old man, will be through broken teeth." Ulfrik's lip curled in a snarl. The parley was the waste of time he had expected. Hardar's men stretched into a thin line behind him, outfitted for war in furs or mail coats. They idled nervously with their backs to the sea and their faces to the sun. Their beached ships hid behind them, gangplanks down for a quick retreat. Ulfrik estimated fifty men, a slight numerical advantage over his own force.

Hardar chuckled and elbowed the hirdman at his side. "Did you hear the threat, Dag? The lad plans to break my teeth."

"He's a foreigner, after all, lord. He doesn't know your strength," said the man called Dag.

"Enough of this," Ulfrik interrupted. He swept his arm across the background of grassy plains and blue mountain peaks. "These lands you claim, well, I'm here now. The families living here are sworn to me. You can threaten all you want. But like I told your messenger, Ulfrik Ormsson is no bondsman."

"And as I warned, refusal to swear loyalty while on my lands makes you my enemy." Hardar glared at Ulfrik, then at the two men with him. Both his second in command Toki and his oldest friend Snorri flanked him. "I have been patient, until now. Your refusal means you must meet me in battle."

Ulfrik laughed, shaking his head. "When did you last fight a battle? You are as fat as a walrus. Your men are farmers and boys. Look behind me, Hardar Hammerhand, and look upon the men whose swords clashed with Harald Finehair and his elite warriors. We are fresh from Hafrsfjord; the blood of battle still clings to our weapons. We are hungry for blood, still hot with killing fever. The lucky few of your men will crawl away with a limb or two intact, while we make chum of the rest. Return to your line and order the retreat, or die. Your choice."

Ulfrik slung the shield off his back and turned toward his line. Toki and Snorri fell in as they stalked away. No one spoke as their feet swished through the tall grass. The summer sun struck Ulfrik in the face, and he smiled. An attack into the sun conferred advantage to him, yet another sign from the gods he belonged in these lands.

Having fled High King Harald Finehair, he had gathered his men and their families and sailed in search of a new home. Ari, his old lord's navigator, told him of these remote islands in the oceans at the top of the world. Here was a place a man could be free, he believed. As the

3

eldest son of the Jarl of Grenner, Ulfrik expected to inherit his father's title. In these treeless lands of grass and sheep, he established a hall and raised Grenner's standard. Ever since his brother dispossessed him of a home, flying the black elk antler standard had been Ulfrik's dearest dream. Though he flew it at Hafrsfjord, it was as a bondsman to Thor Haklang and his father, Kjotve the Rich. But Thor perished at Harald's hands and Kjotve died in a last stand on a surrounded island. Never again would he swear loyalty to another man, and especially not to one as base as Hardar.

Forty men, hard-faced men in mail coats and dull iron helmets, regarded him as he arrived before them. Precious few had bows or throwing spears, and Ulfrik feared he would not be able to whittle down Hardar's numbers during their advance. He barred the concern from his face.

"Listen. It's a hard thing to kill boys playing with swords, but that's what we do today. Hardar the whoreson thinks to push us off this slope and off our lands. But we will shove him and his boys into the sea and drown them in blood. Remember who you are: men of Grenner, heroes of Hafrsfjord!"

The rasp of swords torn from sheaths mingled with the defiant shouts of his men. Ulfrik folded into the front rank, both Toki and Snorri joining him. Without being commanded, his men formed into a tight block and joined shields. Down the gentle slope, Hardar arrayed his men in a line. He appeared to dither, his line starting and stopping its advance as he shouted.

"They're going to hit us flat. We'll roll them back down the slope." Ulfrik laughed.

"Keep them off our flanks or we'll get lapped and minced up."
Snorri touched his shield to Ulfrik's, and the two shared a glance. The
cuts on Snorri's face had not healed since Hafrsfjord, leading Ulfrik to
wonder if he would ever stop fighting.

"Hold your spot in the line and slice a few bellies, and the
bastards will flee. One look and you'll see they've no heart for this."

"If this slope were higher and we had more bows, that line
would make a fat target." Snorri spit on the grass, while Ulfrik watched
Hardar begin his march behind tightly drawn shields.

Ulfrik raised his sword. "Join shields, bows fire now."

A line of archers drew off the back rank and aimed down slope.
Most of Ulfrik's bows were lost when he abandoned his ship at
Hafrsfjord, but enough remained to provide harassing fire. The archers
released and arrows shrieked along either flank, angling into Hardar's
line. Shafts popped into shields, and a few men crumpled to the grass. A
second volley hissed after the first, and Hardar's advance stuttered as
more arrows cracked into shields or thumped into flesh. A few men at
the rear ranks fled back toward the ships.

"Archers back in line," Ulfrik ordered. As he guessed, Hardar
commanded his own line to charge the remaining distance. Though old,
Hardar sprinted with surprising speed and his roar defeated the battle
cries of his men. Ulfrik braced his shield, and the man behind bucked
against him to hold the charge. A shining spear point lowered over his
shoulder, the back ranks ready to weave death into the attacker's line.

Shields collided in a hollow shudder of wood and metal. Men on
both sides groaned. Ulfrik slipped back, but his heels dug into the soft
ground and the shallow grade of the slope proved enough to stall the

5

charge. The man behind shoved and a spear slashed over his head into the enemy. Battle cries turned to screams of agony as blades lanced under and between the shield wall. Men staggered, some unable to fall for being pressed onto their opponents.

Ulfrik plowed his blade under his shield, shoulder to shoulder with Toki and Snorri who stabbed with equal vigor. The enemy faces contorted in pain. Hot blood followed screams. The enemy line already buckled, and Ulfrik shoved into the weakness. He flexed the line at the center, calling Hardar's name.

"Fight me, you coward! Fight me before all your men are dead!"

Hardar pushed with his head ducked behind his shield, too far along the line from Ulfrik to meet him in battle. Ulfrik's pulse throbbed in his neck. Victory was at hand, and enemy bodies piled like a tide mark at his feet. He roared laughter, shoved again, and found himself stumbling into the open. Hardar's line broke.

Men streamed down slope, Hardar running with them. Ulfrik's men hounded them, but he called them back. "Don't spread out! Stay together!"

The two ships Hardar had beached were now rolling onto the waves as men splashed alongside, helped aboard by their companions. Those who could not reach the launching ships turned back and flung their weapons into the grass.

"Hostages," Ulfrik said to himself. Warm blood leaked over his leg where the cut he had taken at Hafrsfjord had reopened. Otherwise, he sustained the usual nicks and bruises of battle. He counted it a good day, despite knowing several of his men had fallen. Hostages meant ransoms.

Hardar's ships rocked into the current, long oars extending like limbs into the sea. Toki and his men herded prisoners at the edge of the surf. The captured men staggered and wobbled, eliciting a derisive snort from Ulfrik.

"Farmers and boys wasn't far off the mark," Snorri said as he joined Ulfrik.

Ulfrik scanned the scene. Battles were like summer storms, all wind and thunder and fury. But once the fury passed only stunned silence and destruction remained. The detritus of battle lay all around: broken shields and spear shafts, bent swords and lost helmets. Blood watered the grass, glistening in red beads. The wounded and dying sprawled twisted and intertwined, friend and enemy alike.

"So much death for a few moment's work." Ulfrik wiped his brow with the back of his hand. "We're an efficient crew."

Snorri nodded. "He'll be back. Thought we were an easy mark, fresh from a battle and sea voyage. Now he'll fetch help before returning."

"So I guess. We won this battle, but more battles will come. Ari has scouted lands south of here, a place with better natural defenses and good pastures."

"We're running again?"

Ulfrik watched Hardar's ships diminishing on the horizon. Toki ordered the prisoners seated on the grass with their hands on their heads. "We're not running. We're repositioning." Ulfrik pointed with his sword to Hardar's ships. "He's running."

***

7

Five years later, Ulfrik stood in the fields surrounding Hardar's hall. In the same fields, the majority of jarls from all the Faereyjar clustered in small groups, greeting or avoiding each other as alliances permitted. Ulfrik had learned firsthand how cliquish the jarls of these islands behaved. The twilight sun would not set until well into the night, and the sky was a luminescent blue backdrop to the gathering. Orange lights from Hardar's hall, Trongisvagur, winked in the small windows. The sea breeze was chill and briny, the springtime still young. Ulfrik gathered his green cloak tighter and faced Toki.

"Hardar knows we're here?"

"If I assure you a seventh time will you listen?" Toki scanned the clusters of jarls waiting with their trusted men for Hardar to emerge and open the meeting. "I spoke directly to his second, Dag the Sword-Bender."

"Well you didn't mention Dag before." Ulfrik sniffed and kept his face open and smiling as he vied for eye contact with others. "Hardar is in for a shock tonight. Come, let's stop hiding like two serving maids and ensure we have the support we need."

No longer the desperate newcomer, Ulfrik counted himself among the greatest jarls in the islands. Five years he toiled, built halls, ships, and a forge. Men fleeing Harald Finehair came seeking the hero of Hafrsfjord and Ulfrik's army swelled to twice its size. They bought families and raised farms, and paid shares of silver to Ulfrik's already sizable horde carried from Norway. Traders sought the wealthy jarl of the Nye Grenner, and wood and iron flowed in while wool and hay flowed out.

This night, at the springtime meeting of jarls, Ulfrik intended the rest of the islands to witness his success.

Ulfrik hailed Jarl Ragnvald, a slender man with a handsome smile more suited to skald than a jarl. Ragnvald met him halfway. "Jarl Ulfrik, I feared you would not show tonight."

"And why not? It's time Hardar recognize his closest neighbor. Besides, it would shame me to not show after seeking your support."

Ragnvald nodded a greeting to Toki, then guided Ulfrik away from the others. "I think your idea is good, and your reasoning sensible. I've spoken to a few of my friends, and they are open to new ideas. But you will have to persuade them; you'll need to persuade me, for that matter."

"I've no doubts." Ulfrik glanced back across the field, searching for other faces he recognized. "And I've spoken to others as well. We are all agreed Hardar does not dictate the location of the festival. It is for all freemen. I hope he will be reasonable."

"If you carry the majority, he will need to be. I only hope this settles the peace between you."

"There has been five years of peace between us. After we clashed, he never followed me south. I think that speaks to our relations."

Ulfrik smiled, but Ragnvald guarded his expression. "He is proud and the summer festival has always been his to hold."

"We shall see. There is one more person I must meet before Hardar begins." Ulfrik clapped Ragnvald's shoulder, confident of his support. He now sought another influential jarl whom he had traded with before the start of winter.

"Jarl Hermind," he called as he strode back towards the center of

9

the groups. The jarl turned, his protruding belly seemingly weightless. Men called him Hermind the Fat with good cause.

"Jarl Ulfrik, so you have come. I was worried."

Ulfrik drew close and embraced the jarl. He was hardly a friend, but Ulfrik's words were not for the crowd. "I have your support along with the others?"

The two separated, and Jarl Hermind patted the gold armband Ulfrik had given him at their last meeting. "You certainly do. Make it easy for us, please."

Shortly after speaking to Hermind, Ulfrik saw Hardar emerge from his hall. He came with a retinue of men, and his wife and daughter escorted him. At this sign, a hirdman threw a torch upon a bonfire and the expensive touchwood blazed immediately. The jarls and their companies gathered closer to the fire.

Hardar appeared much the same as when Ulfrik last met him. Without his helmet, his snub nose gave him a boyish look for his age. The yellow firelight glowed in his eyes, and made his carefully braided hair gleam alongside the gold and silver he had adorned about his arms, hands, and neck. A few sycophantic jarls clapped at his arrival, though the majority simply assumed their spots in the circle.

"His daughter has grown into quite a woman," Toki whispered into Ulfrik's ear. He had glanced past her, but now looked more carefully. In fact, she seemed past a marriageable age, though still pretty enough to have attracted suitors. Her hair was as white as her mother's but her nose was Hardar's.

"My son is only five," Ulfrik whispered back. "She's a bit old for him."

Toki stifled his laugh. "Wasn't thinking of Gunnar."

Hardar welcomed the group, his eyes gliding across Ulfrik and Toki without a flinch. Ulfrik admired the facile charm and control he exhibited. He anticipated testing the limit of Hardar's abilities.

Having never attended such an event, Ulfrik studied the others. Each stated their names and heritages and Hardar welcomed them as guests. At Ulfrik's turn, he proclaimed his name. "Ulfrik Ormsson, Jarl of Nye Grenner."

The smile trembled slightly on Hardar's lips, but he managed to hold it. "Be welcomed, Jarl Ulfrik. We are glad you've finally chosen to join us rather than hide from us."

Ulfrik laughed, overloud and out of place. No one smiled, but it suited him. "My intention has never been to hide. You might remember something of my arrival here, and why I've been guarded about joining these meetings."

Hardar's smile tumbled from his face, but he continued around the circle until all were formally introduced. His wife, Ingrid, spoke a few words Ulfrik ignored, wrapped up on how to position his request to this assembly. Her perfunctory comments over, she departed with her daughter. Now Ulfrik expected the true work of the assembly would begin.

Discussion covered matters of law, trade, and news. Ulfrik sat with his hand over his mouth, allowing all the various issues pass without comment. At last Hardar clapped his hands for attention.

"Now that business is done, time for more pleasant discussion. Summer is here, and time for feasting and games. The gods were generous again this winter, and deserve our gratitude. Like every year, I am pleased to host the festival."

Hardar's face beamed and he shared his smile around the circle. He drew breath to continue, but Ulfrik stepped forward.

"Nye Grenner wishes to host the festival this year."

Faces turned to him in the yellow firelight. Ulfrik glanced at Ragnvald, who gave away nothing of his thoughts, and then the others. Wide eyes and raised brows met him, and a few gave approving smiles. Settling on Hardar, Ulfrik pressed his request.

"My people are new, called foreigners by more than a few of you. But we have settled here, raised strong families and farms. Our flocks thrive and my hall is rich. We want to be part of these lands and be one with the people here."

Hardar stepped into the circle as well, close to the cracking fire snapping at the center of the ring. "The festival is tradition of the old peoples of these islands. Trongisvagur has been home to the festival for years. I don't think you are a suitable host."

"So Hardar Hammerhand decides who is suitable and who is not? Are you high king here?"

"Do not insult me," Hardar said, forcing the words through an empty smile. "You could not understand the traditions we hold in high value."

"Nye Grenner has been isolated too long from the rest of you. My people want to marry within these lands, make connections to others. But you would deny us that."

"You are welcomed to the festival here."

"Now you insult me," Ulfrik said, his smile genuine. He enjoyed Hardar's efforts to conceal his rising temper. "Only my men would come, and then not all. That is not what we seek. We have young women who want husbands, craftsmen who want trade, and I have a hall worthy of all of you. But most importantly, Hardar Hammerhand, it is not you alone who decides."

Ulfrik paused, then turned to the rest of the assembly. "Only one man gets the glory of hosting these festivals, and it is always Hardar. Does that sit with you? Only one man speaks to the gods for you? And you bring gifts each year to the same man?"

"Enough!" Hardar checked himself as he stepped forward. Ulfrik whirled, a wicked smile on his face. "Hosting the festival is a terrible burden and expense. I do it each year as I have the means others lack. It is for their benefit."

"And your glory, and your sly way of placing yourself over others."

"No more slander on my lands! You are a poor guest." Hardar's hands shook, and Ulfrik noted he seemed to want to reach for his sword.

"Let the assembly decide," Ulfrik said. "The jarls vote, and if a majority choose Nye Grenner, then you live with it."

Hardar's eyes drew to slits and he folded his arms over his belly. The two stood locked in a stare until Hardar nodded consent. "A vote then. All in favor of Nye Grenner hosting the summer festival, give your sign."

Ulfrik watched Ragnvald and his allies raise their hands. Hermind the Fat raised also raised his. "Jarl Ulfrik has some good points. I'd like to see what he has done with the southern pastures."

Others followed, raising hands and nodding until Hardar waved

13

his arms overhead in defeat. "Very well, then Nye Grenner hosts the festival. But don't look to me, lad, when you've spent all your silver and all your food."

"I am aware of the costs, old man." Ulfrik had not wanted to rise to the bait, but he could not resist. Hardar flashed a brief smile at Ulfrik's lapse.

"Old man? Perhaps we should wrestle at the games, eh lad?" Approving grunts and lusty laughter greeted Hardar's suggestion.

"Most certainly, we will. It will be the best moment of the entire festival."

***

The last blow staggered Ulfrik, and then he collapsed to his knees. Bloody spit hung from his lips, globules pattering on the long grass beneath him. Screaming voices echoed from every direction. His head felt stuffed with wool. He braced himself longer than he thought prudent. Two booted feet appeared wide-set at the edge of his vision. Words started to become clearer now.

"Get on your feet!" someone yelled.

"You've got him, Lord Ulfrik! Up now!" another voice trumped the others.

The two feet remained planted before him. Ulfrik touched his aching ribs, then shoved up. He sat on his haunches and regarded Hardar. The big man was resolute, waiting with fists balled at his sides. Hardar smiled, a crack beneath a pug nose that drizzled blood over his thin lips and beard.

"Do you yield, Ulfrik? I think you're done for, lad." Hardar kept his tone congenial, but his fighting stance did not shift.

"Not yet. Not if I'm still talking."

The men's cheering overpowered Ulfrik's words. The ring of on-lookers flexed with the combatants. Now they crowded the small space, eager to see their favorite win. Ulfrik staggered to his feet and Hardar backed off, wiping the blood from his mouth. They nodded to each other and dropped to a circling crouch.

Ulfrik ignored the crowd, focusing on his opponent's next move. Hardar's hair may have been silvered and thin, his gut bulging and soft, but his reflexes were keen. Ulfrik silently vowed to not allow the same feint to dupe him again. Hardar smiled, his left eye blinking closed from where Ulfrik had jabbed it.

Hardar burst into motion. His massive body sprang as if he weighed nothing. Ulfrik scrambled aside, on-lookers dancing away as he did. He slipped out his foot and pushed Hardar over it. He crashed face-down into the grass. Cheers and curses mingled together in reaction. Ulfrik leapt upon Hardar's back, seeking to finally pin his opponent and end a match he thought had lasted too long.

Hardar expelled a gust of breath. Ulfrik drove his knee into the small of his back, then seized his arm to wrench it behind.

"Yield, Hardar," he hissed into his ear. "You are subdued."

Hardar shook his head and flipped over. Ulfrik lost grip on his arm.

"They look like lovers!"someone shouted. The crowd laughed and jeered as Ulfrik squirmed over Hardar's body while trying to pin his arms.

Ulfrik looked into Hardar's face for a moment. Then his vision

15

turned white and he sloughed to the ground. He vaguely realized Hardar had head-butted him. Again sounds dulled as he lay dazed for the second time. He was limp and ready to vomit. Hardar's arms worked roughly about his trunk, flipping him over. His sight melted from white to brown, and the crowd around him appeared smudgy and indistinct. A tang of copper filled his mouth.

He realized Hardar had clamped his neck in the crook of his arm and his other arm squeezed Ulfrik's windpipe shut from behind. Instinctively Ulfrik's arms flailed, grasping desperately at the hold on his throat. His vision again faded. He tried to turn into the hold to break it, but was too weak.

Ulfrik wanted to concede. He stopped resisting to demonstrate it. Yet Hardar maintained his lock. His head pounded as his sight collapsed to a small circle. Through that hole in the veil of gray, Ulfrik spotted Runa. Her face was tight in horror, and her hands hovered over her mouth. Hardar was strangling him and Runa knew it.

She's watching me die, he thought. *My wife. She can't see me like this.*

He knew the thoughts were foolish, but it gave him power. He took control of his flailing arms, a difficult feat under such duress. He lashed back over his head. Ulfrik grabbed a handful of sweaty hair and yanked as if pulling the tiller of a ship. Hardar rewarded him with a scream. Ulfrik's other hand found Hardar's face, and he worked his thumb into the eye socket.

He thrust with enough strength to touch the back of Hardar's skull. The gouge had its effect, and his arms snapped free.

Ulfrik fell forward, swooning from the rush of air and blood returning to his head. The crowd clamored for him, many chanting his

16

name. But he ignored whatever praise broke into his deadened hearing. He got to his feet and turned to face Hardar.

Now Hardar knelt in the grass with his hand clamped over his eye. Blood ran from beneath his hand. Ulfrik knew he should demand him to yield. But he was no longer inclined to courtesy. Hardar had nearly killed him.

He took a running kick that landed on Hardar's side. The thud elicited sympathetic moans from his supporters. The old jarl toppled and remained flat. Ulfrik turned to the crowd to roar his victory. But when he opened his mouth a stream of vomit ejected instead.

Ulfrik collapsed beside Hardar and he heaved again, the world growing dimmer. The crowd's cheering poured over him and men rushed to his side. Hardar's men did the same. He felt hands trying to raise him. He thought he heard Toki proclaiming the match a draw. Ulfrik wanted to protest. Then he sunk down and knew no more.

CHAPTER TWO

"Is everyone having a good time?" Ulfrik sat up suddenly, his stomach churned and head spun; he fell back onto his bed. He didn't remember how he had got in bed.

He panicked when he awoke to silence and the murkiness of his bedroom. A cool and delicate hand touched a damp cloth to his face.

"Everyone is having fun. Don't move." Runa wiped the cloth over a cut on his cheek and the sting made Ulfrik wince. "Now, you need to rest, but stay awake. Many men don't wake after getting hit in the head like you did."

Runa plopped the cloth into a wooden bowl, then leaned forward to kiss his cheek. He smiled, and gently held her arm. A pale column of light from the lone window broke the darkness. Blue light bounced off the gentle curves of Runa's face. She wore a concerned smile, and Ulfrik felt the bloom of gratitude for her care. His eyes drifted across to where his mail and helmet glinted in the low light, hung on a rack. Beyond the walls of his room, he could hear the occasional shouts of his guests at play.

"I'm like a boy being tended by a nursemaid. I can't be stuck in here, not with Hardar out there."

Runa frowned, withdrawing her arm from Ulfrik's hand to place it across his chest. "You need to recover from that so-called wrestling match. Besides, Hardar is not out there. You nearly blinded him."

"But the bastard was choking me to death."

"So I noticed."

Ulfrik faced his wife. Her smile had vanished and her eyes glittered with concern. His stomach clenched, knowing he had subjected her to her greatest fear. "I am sorry, wife. We jarls are a competitive lot. We just got carried away."

Runa didn't reply. She held his gaze then leaned out of her stool to lie over his chest. "You mustn't ever come to harm, Ulfrik. I need you. Your son needs you. Nye Grenner needs you. Please don't get carried away again."

"I promise." He had learned that a few simple words meant more to Runa than long explanations. He stroked her hair, so lustrous and full that she did not wear a head cover like other married women. He let her rest in silence a moment, the dampness from her tears penetrating his shirt.

At last she sat up and laughed. "Now I'm being foolish. It's just that I'm always worried."

"Do not worry," Ulfrik said as he struggled to his elbows. Dizziness still plagued him, but he determined to shove it aside. "Fate has not seen us this far to kill me in a friendly wrestling competition. I have survived worse. We have survived worse. Take heart, wife."

"Strangulation is hardly friendly. Don't take me for a fool. Five years ago you wanted to kill each other, so why would he have changed?"

"Much has changed in five years." Ulfrik's throat pulsed and he absently rubbed his throbbing temple. The match had gotten out of hand, he knew. Runa clucked her tongue at Ulfrik's words. But he spoke over whatever she wanted to say. "And so where is my boy?"

"Gerdie took him to watch Snorri at the ax-throwing contest. He was scared to death seeing you carried in here covered in blood and vomit. I sent him out to distract him."

Ulfrik nodded silently, ashamed for needlessly frightening his son on what should be a time of happy memories. Ulfrik's own father would not have cared. He wanted to be different, though he often caught himself speaking his father's words.

"You are going to lie down." Runa stood and pressed both of his shoulders back. Ulfrik resisted.

"I am going to the contest. Thank you for cleaning me. Now fetch my cloak while I prepare."

Runa stared at him, her mouth bent into a half-smile. She finally shrugged and turned to get a new cloak. Ulfrik placed his feet on the hard-packed dirt floor, stood off the bed, and wobbled. By the time Runa offered his cloak, he was steady and smirking. She threw it over his shoulders then fished a silver pin from her skirt pocket. "Take it slowly and don't hit your head anymore."

Ulfrik laughed and let Runa pin his cloak. She kissed him again. "Avoid Hardar for now. You've worked too long and hard to waste this festival on your arguments with him."

"Of course, you are right." Ulfrik took a few staggering steps, then exited his bedroom into the main hall. Women and children fussed and scurried in preparation for the feast. Ulfrik paused and reflected on how far he had come since arriving here five years ago. Runa appeared behind him as he stood in the doorway.

"I'll prove to everyone that I am a better man than Hardar Hammerhand. Let the others see what he's really like."

From behind, Runa sighed. Ulfrik didn't think much of it, and left to rejoin the games.

***

Within moments of Ulfrik reappearing to the crowds, Hardar also rushed from his tent. His eye had swollen shut and his face was puffy. Ulfrik turned away to mask his laugh. Hardar had fought well. But he wore his beating far worse than Ulfrik. Men from all the different islands cheered and applauded them equally, though some favored one over the other. Ulfrik, keen to show himself the gracious host, went straight to Hardar with an outstretched hand.

"You are a skilled wrestler, Lord Hardar. You put me to the test." Ulfrik's arm dangled in the air as Hardar, with two hirdmen flanking him, ignored it.

"I won that match." His expression spoke no pleasantries. His

21

swollen eye and face made Ulfrik think of something dredged from a fisherman's net. He pushed ahead without another word, the two hirdmen giving Ulfrik blank looks as they passed.

Ulfrik's face grew hot, but he was still weak and unsteady. He watched in irritation as Hardar strolled over to a knot of men who welcomed him to their conversation. The he glanced around to find others turning away in embarrassment.

"Forget about him." Ulfrik startled at the closeness of the speaker, then turned to find Toki approaching. "He's used to wrestling men who roll over on command."

Ulfrik shook his head. "Then he misjudged when he challenged me to the match. How's Gunnar doing?"

"He's being a boy. Gerdie is herding him while he finds as much mischief as he can. He nearly ran out into the ax throwing contest, if Gerdie didn't cuff him good. He wanted to throw."

They both laughed and Ulfrik leaned on Toki, both in greeting and to steady himself. Together they walked to join the other of the visitors. The gods had provided clear skies, dramatically framing the blue-green mountains of the western ridge of his island domain. Spread out in the knee-high grass fields were clusters of simple tents. Men from all about the Faereyjar Islands had gathered on his land to celebrate the start of summer. Finally emerging from the long night of winter, the summer of never-ending sunlight was celebrated with games and feasting. Hardar had traditionally hosted this, being the richest and most powerful jarl in the southern islands. But this year, citing his age, Hardar offered Ulfrik the honor of doing it for him. For the first time in most men's memories, the summer festivals were held elsewhere.

Gunnar ran screaming toward Ulfrik, delighted. Ulfrik swept up his son, then wobbled with dizziness. "Are you making trouble again, boy?"

"No," Gunnar said as he threw his small arms about Ulfrik's neck.

"You say, No, Father," Ulfrik corrected, and Gunnar nodded solemnly. Still feeling his weakness, he passed Gunnar into Toki's arms. "Go with Uncle Toki now. I have important business. Be good."

Gunnar again nodded as Toki accepted him with a mock expression of pain. "How heavy you've become. You should carry me instead."

Ulfrik laughed. "Thanks for watching Gunnar. He looks more like his mother every day. Looks more like your brother than nephew."

He left Toki to entertain Gunnar, and he sought the company of the other jarls. Runa had been right, he realized. He had not used the festival to mingle and risked losing the real opportunity of hosting the festival: to become another key player in the informal politics of the islands.

So as men raced, threw spears, hurled rocks, wrestled, and dueled, Ulfrik moved among the groups of on-lookers. Hardar walled himself behind a clique of men from the northern islands. While not hostile, their faces were closed to Ulfrik. He realized they could not be won over, so ignored them.

As the day drew on, he noted that Hardar finally regained his jovial manner. But Ulfrik also noted that Hardar followed up wherever Ulfrik had visited. At first he thought it was coincidence. Yet soon it was obvious. *Is he following behind to check what I said or to smear my name*, he wondered.

Though the sun would not set for many hours, the evening feast was soon. Ulfrik cast an eye down the gentle slope to where the buildings of Nye Grenner clustered. Without a single tree on any of the Faereyjar Islands, timber was an expensive import. The locals had shown him how to build with stone and turf roofs. It made for solid homes, if strange ones to Ulfrik's mind. He had built his hall with imported birch wood and stone. It chugged hearth smoke, scents of roasting meats making him hunger. Beyond the rectangles of green roofs the ocean glittered.

Snorri found him staring at his hall. He stood next to Ulfrik and shared a smile with him, then turned to face the hall. "You've done well. In just five years, you've built a thriving home."

"Still can't believe it. I never thought I'd own two sticks, never minds ships, a hall, and a forge. Fate has been kind to me."

"Your father would've been proud to see this place."

Ulfrik nodded silently. Suddenly he felt an unmanly lump in his throat. Snorri was an old man now, over forty years of age. He was the last link Ulfrik had to anyone from his youth. Snorri had stood beside him in his first shield wall. He was the last of what Ulfrik considered to be the heroic, old breed of warriors. His thoughts and opinions counted heavy in Ulfrik's heart.

"We should gather in the guests for the feast. It's going to be the best thing these men have seen, better than anything before."

"Aye, my wife Gerdie and Runa have got to be the best cooks in the world. The poor fools haven't really tasted good food until they've eaten from our table."

They laughed together, and started for the hall. "Let's make sure all is prepared. I can't wait to see Hardar's expression once he tastes my hospitality."

***

The hall reverberated with carousing and merriment. Ulfrik had built his hall large, but tonight it filled with so many men it seemed a hermit's cottage. The hearth pit glowed orange, casting laughing faces in a golden hue. Two women fed it dried juniper branches to keep it burning. Smoke from the roasting lamb whorled at the ceiling as it sought the hole in the roof. The doors were thrown wide, allowing a sea breeze to freshen the room. So many had come to sample Ulfrik's hospitality that they had to sit outside the hall. The women of Nye Grenner squeezed between the revelers, bringing them mead and food, laughing at jokes, fending off wandering hands, and settling friendly debates.

Ulfrik beamed from the high table. Runa sat at his side, radiant in a fine dress and a jeweled pin at her shoulder. Gunnar squirmed on her lap, equally confused and excited by the crowds in his normally quiet home. More tables had been set upon the stage of pounded earth to accommodate the other jarls and their families. Ulfrik wanted to ensure his guests felt respect for their status. They had spent half the night toasting each other, and Ulfrik began to grow dizzy.

"Your mead is the best I've ever tasted, and I've tasted much!" Jarl Hermind the Fat patted his belly, drawing laughter around the tables. "Do you keep your own bees?"

"We do. Only started a few years ago. One of my men comes

25

from a line of beekeepers."

"Then you should trade this mead with me! I cannot wait another year to drink such nectar again." Hermind slapped the table and chortled, spit flinging from his mouth. Others laughed again, only Hardar refrained, barely fitting a trite smile on his swollen face. Ulfrik realized the assumption of his holding the festival again rankled Hardar. He pressed Hardar's sore spot.

"Indeed we should. But if you wait until next year, we will have perfected the brewing of it. Next year when you return it will be even better."

"Truly a fine feast. I am humbled by the skill of your people." Hardar spoke overloud. "Let me toast your wife's skill at the hearth once more."

Everyone raised a mug or horn to Runa, who smiled demurely. Ulfrik put his arm about her waist as he raised his own. "To the best cook I've ever known!"

Hardar and Ulfrik watched each other over the rims of their mugs. Hardar's wife and daughter sat beside him, shrinking into his shadow. They had not spoken the entire night, unlike the wives of other jarls. Hardar's wife Ingrid, her skin still clear and tight for her age, had seemed outgoing when they first arrived. But now she fluttered like a ghost vanishing from sight. Hardar's daughter behaved the same.

"You have made yourself rich in a land where sheep outnumber men. It's no small feat." Jarl Ragnvald now turned the conversation down a new track. He sat opposite Ulfrik. Both he and his wife were soft and gentle folk from the northern islands. Ulfrik had liked him the moment they met. "Your name as a hero of Hafrsfjord has brought you many followers, even to these distant rocks."

"Men follow success, don't they?" Ulfrik sent his words straight at Hardar, glanced at him, then laughed. Runa elbowed him gently for his immodesty, which drew polite laughter. Hardar wore a smile like a day old corpse.

"As I know it, King Harald destroyed all his foes at Hafrsfjord. Odd to call utter defeat a success." The quip came not from Hardar, but from the morose and unfriendly Jarl Vermund sitting at his side. It was the first Ulfrik had heard from this man since his arrival.

Faces of those who could hear above the celebration glanced at each other, then expectantly turned to Ulfrik. He held his smile as he chose his words. "I escaped with my life and the lives of my sworn men. I made no claim for glory on that bloody day. The success I referred to, if Jarl Vermund had been listening, was the rebuilding of Nye Grenner on this island."

Ulfrik held Vermund's gaze, but knew Hardar was studying him closely. Vermund, for his part, gave the faintest smirk. "I apologize, Jarl Ulfrik. I must have misunderstood."

Ulfrik nodded, still holding Vermund's gaze until he finally turned away. It seemed a signal for Hardar to interject his thoughts. "This is an interesting point, though, Jarl Ulfrik. You arrived here with a ship full of men and their families. The freemen of this place got you started on the path to your current happiness."

"I owe the free families who dwelt here everything I am. I feel my work here has bettered their lives. Wouldn't you agree?"

"Certainly," Hardar picked a bone from his plate and turned it over in his hands. He swept his gaze over the other jarls. "But I wonder if they feel that way?"

Small conversations halted, and smiling faces froze. Ulfrik straightened himself, peering at Hardar with slit eyes. "And why would you wonder such things? Do you not see the prosperity here?"

"When you arrived, you were but a few boatloads of people. Now this island is filled with fighting men. Warriors who make claims on the land, desire their own fame and wealth. We people who have lived in the Faereyjar all our lives value the peace of our island homes. It is why we stay here."

"And peace has remained. I still don't understand your question, Lord Hardar."

"Perhaps Lord Hardar has drank too much tonight and is tired," Ragnvald interjected. "Surely the question was just ill-framed."

"What Lord Hardar means," said Vermund, as his smile spread on his gaunt face, "is that Lord Ulfrik has built an army of occupation. In five years, under our noses, he has constantly added hirdmen. His forges spit out weapons and mail fashioned from imported iron. What for, Lord Ulfrik? Peace?"

"Well asked," Hardar agreed, dropping the bone to his plate. His wife murmured to him, and he held up his arm to her face. "Why are you building up such military power? None of us have done as much."

Ulfrik sat back on his bench, short of words. He looked into the expectant faces of the other jarls, most were blank, others shocked, but all waited on his answer. Runa inhaled to speak, but Ulfrik clamped his hand atop hers, pressing it to the table. He did not look at her, but gave a reassuring squeeze.

"Men have come to me of their own will. Many have fled the

oppression of Harald Finehair. Others still seek lords to serve after being scattered at Hafrsfjord, even to this day. It is right that I should arm them, house them, and reward them for their oaths. Can you question that?

"I have traded honestly with my neighbors. Been fair with fishing grounds. Never has one of my men wandered into another jarl's lands to make trouble. We are at peace here. My men take up spear and shield to raid the dog-shit King Harald and take back what he stole from us. Maybe your people, Hardar, have not felt the sting of oppression like the folk of Nye Grenner. But we know the worth of a strong army to protect our homes and freedom, especially after how you greeted us."

Ulfrik's arms trembled. He only now cast his gaze to the other jarls. Ragnvald smiled in admiration, while Hardar and Vermund were predictably unmoved. The other jarls appeared mollified. No words passed at the high table, the carousing from within and without the hall more than covered the silence. The merriment behind Ulfrik contrasted with the coldness before him. He finally withdrew his hand from Runa's and relaxed into his bench again. But Hardar was not done.

"Fine words, but we shall see. How long can an army be entertained raiding sheep? How long before they seek new lands? Our lands!"

Ulfrik shot to his feet. Hardar smirked triumphantly as his wife hissed at him and other jarls turned disgusted faces at him.

"You insult me in my own hall? I will defend my name and honor! Your face is already swollen like a rotting fish. Do you want me to show you what more I can do? "

Hardar tried to get to his feet, but Ingrid and his daughter held

29

him down. Runa stood, Gunnar in her arms. "Ulfrik, calm yourself! He is clearly drunk, and you are too."

Others stood, though they seemed confused as to why they did. Ragnvald and his wife nearly leapt over the table to intervene. "Please, let us not soil a wonderful festival with drunken threats. Lord Ulfrik, Lord Vermund, please sit. Forget these things, I beg you."

Ulfrik glared at Hardar, whose puffy face reddened as he struggled with his wife and daughter. He turned his threatening gaze at Vermund, his oily smile unmoved. Then he looked at Runa, her eyes wide and pleading. Gunnar had fallen asleep over her shoulder. His son's peaceful repose brought an unexpected chuckle to him. *How can he remain asleep through this?* Finally he acknowledged Ragnvald with a nod and sat.

Hardar wrested free from Ingrid and stood alongside Vermund. "I need air," he proclaimed. He stalked off the high stage and pushed his way through the drunken crowd for the hall door. Vermund followed without a word. Ingrid and her daughter sat stricken.

Ulfrik was sorry for them, and shook his head. "We have all drank too much tonight, Lady Ingrid. Please forgive me."

A wave of murmured agreement rippled around the tables. Ingrid simply bowed her head in shame and studied the table before her.

Ulfrik then turned to glimpse Hardar and Vermund exiting the hall. A tiny smile showed on his face. He had become strong enough to elicit jealousy. Ulfrik was drunk, but the part of his mind that remained sober told him that this was nothing to celebrate.

CHAPTER THREE

Toki stood upon the shore staring down the row of beached ships. Each one had its own story, some glorious, others shameful, but most would be ordinary. The dawn colored their hulls yellow and behind them the expanse of the fjord glittered. Sea birds circled above, and the squawking of the puffin colony in the cliffs faintly reached him. Up the slope and across the grass, Nye Grenner's squat buildings still reverberated with the festival.

He stared at his own ship, *Raven's Talon*, bobbing at the dock. She was the smallest of Ulfrik's four longships. She had always been his, though, and he her lone pilot. He smiled, recalling a time before Ulfrik had captured her. *Raven's Talon* had a glorious story, one Toki knew outshone any of the other ships.

His smile faded. The morning chill lingered and he drew his wool cloak tighter. He ambled along the row of unattended ships, their guards still recovering from the night's drunken feast. Toki appraised each one as he passed. He wondered at the seaworthiness of a few. The gods themselves would have to carry these ships over the water. With no timber for repairs or construction, ships decayed and left their crews forever bound to the land.

He shuddered at the thought.

Hardar had taken his flagship, a high-sided and haughty vessel that had weathered the years better than many of the others beached astride it. Toki examined the freshly caulked strakes. One was a lighter color, suggesting a recent repair. Hardar either fixed the strake overseas or traders had sold him the timber. The job, he noted, was also well done. He patted the strake in admiration.

"Don't hit it too hard or it'll spring a leak."

Toki startled, his hand recoiling as if he had damaged the ship. He stepped back and turned to face the voice. Around the opposite side of the prow emerged a delicate woman. Toki immediately recognized her as Hardar's daughter. She wore a cream blouse and forest green skirt. Her platinum hair framed a girlish face that wore vulnerability and confidence in equal measure. Toki's surprise faded, but he remained speechless. Her lips turned in a wry smile, and one brow lifted.

"I was joking. She's old but not in that bad of shape."

"Well, yes, you're right to say so. I was admiring the repair. It's well done. Did you do it?" Toki was not a man for humor, and he had no idea what made him attempt it.

To his relief, the girl giggled and covered her mouth with a pale hand. "I would have liked to try, though."

"What's her name?"

The girl's brows drew together. "Not interested in my name? The ship's name first, is it?"

"Well, no. Not like that. I just, well ..."

The girl laughed now, genuine and from her eyes. "Halla Hardarsdottir, from Trongisvagur."

"Toki Sveinson, from far away."

"A mysterious man, then? Your accent is strange."

"I could say the same for yours." Toki smiled confidently, and Halla's elfin face became serious. Momentarily blinded by her beauty, he now regained himself. He turned back to the ship and thumped the repaired strake, a thud echoing in the hull. He continued to examine it, waiting for Halla to become uncomfortable with the silence. He didn't wait overlong.

"*Thor's Breath*," she said, touching the prow. "That's her name."

"A fine name for a far-sailing ship." He stepped around Halla to conduct his mock inspection. Halla wavered, he saw from the corner of his eye, then followed him. He ran his hand along the hull as he walked. "Got to scale off these barnacles. Creates drag on the ship, which is bad in a chase. A slow ship could mean life or death for the crew."

"Life or death? I'll warn my father."

"Do. I like the high sides, good protection from arrows. What's the deck like?"

"I haven't paid attention to it. I'm not allowed on the ship."

"So your father made you swim here? Do you swim?"

"No I don't, and stop being ridiculous." She shifted onto her

33

back leg and folded her arms, but smiled. Toki flashed his smile back.

"I'd like to inspect her deck. Do you think I can get up on her?"

"What? No, of course not. My father would have me skinned."

"That's unlikely. Let's have a look." Toki pulled himself aboard with the grace of a man long accustomed to life at sea. He stood easily on the deck, despite the sharp slant from being beached. Halla's protests were muffled, and he smiled. The deck was like any other deck. He had no real interest in it, other than to tease Halla. When he judged she might be at her limit, he leapt back onto the beach. "A fine ship!"

She remained entrenched in her spot, arms folded and face blushing. Her smile was unfriendly, sharp as a new blade. "I'm glad you think so. Now why don't you go inspect these others?"

"Because I've already found the best one." He held her gaze a moment, then looked at the ship. "No sense in looking at any others."

Halla unfolded her arms, finally shifting her stance. "Well, you can leave now anyway. Go on."

"Why are you out here alone? Weren't you at the feast last night? Shouldn't you be with your parents, or at least have a man to guard you?"

"If you were at the feast last night, then you'd know why I'm here."

"I was not at the high tables. Too little room for me. Did something happen?" Toki omitted he had grown tired of the same songs and same boasts with the same people, and left the feast early to sleep alone. Now he hoped he hadn't been gone when Ulfrik might have needed him.

Halla studied him, then turned aside. "It's nothing. Just my father being his foolish self. His pride overwhelms these lonely islands. He got drunk and insulted your lord. He went off in a huff, leaving mother and me to sit like two stupid children. I just wanted to leave the whole mess."

"I'm sorry to hear that, Halla. If I had known, I wouldn't have teased you. Please take my apology."

A quick smiled poked in the corners of her mouth. "No harm done. I was too quick to anger. I just wish to go home now."

"Tomorrow you will sail for home. Then this whole land," Toki's hand painted the stripe of purple mountains on the western horizon, "will be behind you and poorer for your leaving."

"Your flattery is a bit heavy handed."

"Out of practice, as you can tell. But I sympathize with you. I had anticipated hosting the summer festival. Now that it's here, it's not what I expected. Escaping it is also what brought me to the ships."

"I've seen you with Lord Ulfrik's son. Babysitting is a dull task."

"Not at all. Gunnar is my nephew, one half of my surviving family. It's not that."

Halla looked at him quizzically. "You don't like bragging all day then drinking yourself stupid all night?"

"Not this time, at least. Look, you leave tomorrow, and you have not been this far south before. Am I right?" Halla nodded. "Then let me show you some of the fairer parts of this land."

"I'm not sure about that."

"Do you really need an excuse to leave the festival? Please, allow me to enjoy one small part of the festival in your company."

Halla's smile broadened, Toki's growing along with hers. She

35

searched his face and Toki held his breath. Finally she agreed. "I can't imagine there's much difference between the north and south of the same island. But I will go with you. Though my father mustn't know. Where shall we meet and when?"

"Just meet me here after the sacrifices this morning. I will show you the southern cliffs. If you need to take someone with you, that will be fine."

"No, I'd much rather it be just the two of us."

Toki grinned, exactly the answer he wanted. He thanked her and left, not looking back. As he trotted up the slope toward Nye Grenner, he knew his life was about to change.

***

Toki had not felt such excitement in years. His pulse beat in his neck. His mind was dizzy with thoughts of Halla. Everyone he met that morning mistook him for being drunk. After pointless wandering, hailing visitors like they were lifelong friends, he strolled into the main hall. The doors hung open as if the hall was gasping for breath.

Toki met Runa inside, her eyes bleary and face haggard. Stray revelers snored in drunken slumber in the shadowy hall. The place smelled of smoke, stale mead, and sweat. Gunnar crawled on the floor, exploring beneath the tables. Runa rolled her eyes at Toki. "The boy is into everything this morning, and I'm exhausted. Can you take him for me?"

"Let him run with the other kids. Or Gerdie will watch him. I've got a lot to prepare for this morning, too."

"Can't you let him follow you for a while? I've got cleanup to do." Runa yawned and rubbed her eyes. Gunnar crawled out from beneath a table triumphantly holding a knife he found. Runa removed it without a word, though Gunnar whined in protest. "Ulfrik's led the rams to the sacred stone. Snorri's giving a hand, but he'll want you there too. And where did you go this morning?"

"Checking on the ships. Come on, Gunnar. I'll take you to see your father."

Runa bent to give Gunnar a kiss on his head. The she paused and regarded Toki, breaking into a coy smile. "Checking the ships? Really? Your smile hasn't been this stupid since we were children."

"You're still drunk, Sister. Good luck with this mess. Looks like the place was ransacked."

He led Gunnar by the hand, his nephew obediently running beside him. Gunnar rambled about how he hoped to see the gods fetch their sacrifices. Toki normally would've corrected Gunnar, but he kept thinking of Halla. She had been receptive to his clumsy advances. The whole encounter was amazing to him. He had feared he would spend his life alone, or with a hag given to him in his old age. Now, he hoped for more.

People were indistinct blurs as he hustled past them. In the same field where Ulfrik and Hardar had wrestled, a large pit had been dug. Dried branches had been piled in to make a fire. Two men finished erecting a spit for roasting the sacrificed rams. He spotted Ulfrik, standing awkwardly in the shadow of the sacred stone that passed for their temple in these treeless lands. He wore white woolen robes and the thick silver arm ring. Sprawling out behind him, sweeping into the fog-shrouded foothills, ran an emerald plain of grass.

"Is that where Odin will eat?" Gunnar asked, pointing at the fire pit. "He can't be burned, can he?"

"I don't know about that, boy. Now be good and stay with me."

"So you didn't walk off a cliff. Where have you been this morning?" Ulfrik stood with hands on his hips. The mention of cliffs surprised Toki, making him fear he had been discovered. Ulfrik waved his hand and shook his head. "Well, you're here now. Do I look foolish in this robe?"

Snorri stood beside him, and clapped his back. "Truthfully, you look foolish out of the robe. I just never told you." They laughed and Toki let Gunnar go to his father, who greeted his son with a brief hug.

Having arrived late, not much remained to do other than assemble the jarls for the sacrifice. As the men began to converge on the pit, Ulfrik turned Gunnar back to Toki's care. Gunnar protested and dropped himself to the grass, as it made him too heavy to lift. Toki swept the boy over his head and then planted him gently at his side. Gunnar laughed and forgot his argument. Toki glanced up to see Hardar had arrived, and Halla stood behind him. She had been observing Toki, and gave the faintest smile when their eyes met.

His return smile fled when Hardar caught Toki's eye. Hardar's flat expression shifted to disgust and he looked away. His eye was still swollen and red from Ulfrik's gouging. Toki knelt to Gunnar, straightening the boy's tunic, and ignored Hardar and his small group. He didn't want to signal too much interest in either him or his daughter.

"So Hardar shows his face this morning without an apology," Ulfrik said, keeping his voice low.

"I heard he insulted you. I'm sorry I wasn't there to stand up for you." Toki stood again, releasing Gunnar to inspect the rams.

"It's better you weren't there. Your hot head would've made things worse."

"Are you saying I would've acted on impulse?" Toki feigned shock.

"You hardly act any other way." Ulfrik and Snorri both chuckled. "He'll have to apologize sooner or later, or he'll look like a fool. I'll show him who the more gracious lord is. Now let's get this done."

Toki guided Gunnar away from the animals, as Snorri led the first one to Ulfrik. Gunnar patted one on the head before he left. "Will it hurt him?"

"Don't worry what an animal feels," Toki advised. But he saw the concern in Gunnar's young face. "Well, they're going to the gods. They'll be happy. Don't say things like that in front of your father."

"Yes, Uncle Toki. Father doesn't care about animals, does he?"

"He cares about his people. That's a jarl's first responsibility. Now be a good son and watch. And be silent. This will be your duty one day."

As Ulfrik assumed his position before the bowls, the people gathered closer. Toki strained to focus on the sacrifice, but his eyes wandered to Halla. An ember fell into his gut. Another jarl, the bony faced Vermund, hovered next to her. He was whispering to her while she stifled her giggles. He stood close. Very close. He could read Vermund's desire as easily as the stars in the night sky.

Ulfrik had started his invocations to Odin, Freyer, and Thor. Everyone turned their attention to him. But Toki lingered on Halla and Vermund. If she noticed him, she gave no hint. Finally Toki faced

Ulfrik, hearing but not listening to what he said. His mind buzzed with his own thoughts. Vermund had traveled with Hardar, and was unwed. Pieces snapped together for Toki. He had competition.

The first ram screamed when Ulfrik sawed open its throat, snatching Toki's attention. Snorri and another man held the other two rams at bay. The ram's blood poured bright and steaming into a wooden bowl. It slumped as its lifeblood pumped away. Two other men hauled it aside as Ulfrik took the bowl in his hands and held it to the sky.

"May this sacrifice please the gods. May it show our gratitude for surviving another winter."

He placed the bowl aside, and repeated the sacrifices two more times, filling two more bowls. When finished, he implored the gods again to favor everyone for another year. Then he unclasped his silver arm band and dipped it into each bowl for each god. He gently shook off the excess blood, then showed it to the crowd.

"The oath ring is reddened again. Swear your oaths upon it, now while the blood is hot, and the gods will know your resolve." Ulfrik held out the oath ring, he would wear it year-round. Many believed the most powerful oaths were made on fresh blood, though any oath given on the ring any time was equally sacred.

"I give my oath," Ulfrik intoned to the crowd, "to protect and provide to those sworn to me, to bring glory and honor to all the people of Nye Grenner."

Toki felt Gunnar's hand squeeze his own. He glanced down and the boy dutifully observed his father, giving no sign to the agitation Toki guessed he felt. Toki again glanced at Halla. *I should learn something from Gunnar. The boy is better than me at hiding his thoughts.*

Toki realized he was tapping his foot, waiting for the rams to be bled and the offerings completed. A few men came forward to swear on the ring. At the finish, gore had spattered Ulfrik's white robes. The gathered visitors nodded in satisfaction, a happy murmur spreading through the crowd. Then the clouds parted for the sun and Ulfrik momentarily blazed like a white flame. It drew expressions of awe from the crowd.

"There's a good sign," said one of the jarls; Ragnvald was the name Toki remembered. Many agreed. But Toki noted two who did not. Hardar and Vermund left without a word, dragging Halla in tow. She did not look back as her father led his small group across the waving grass to a line of bobbing tents. Toki worried she would not keep their date.

"So the gods are happy now?" Gunnar asked, looking at Toki with his lip trembling.

"That they are. You're father pleased them greatly, it seems."

Gunnar nodded and was silent a moment. Then he tugged Toki's arm. "Do the gods always need blood to be happy?"

"I suppose they always do, boy." Toki was not looking at Gunnar, but watching Hardar and Vermund stalk down the grassy slope.

***

Toki and Halla stood at the edge of the northern cliffs. The green sward ran down to the ocher rocks of cliff faces. The cliffs layered back in serried ridges, shading into the blue haze. The purr of the ocean traveled up the walls, filling the silence between them. In the middle distance, birds darted in and out of the cliffs' shadows.

"When I was a girl, I played beside cliffs like these," Halla said.

41

Loose clouds had broken up and the sun hit her eyes, making her squint. "I used to see faces and shapes in the shadows of the rocks."

"Do you see anything now?" Toki peered at the cliffs, imagining the face of a wolf in one. *People born here have never seen a wolf,* he mused. Halla shook her head in answer to his question.

"The puffins live further on. Do you mind the walk?" They had already come far, unobserved. Despite Toki's fears, Halla had slipped her father's attention while he brooded in his tent. Nye Grenner had disappeared behind the folds of the island, vague streamers of hearth smoke placing the village.

Toki did not wait for Halla's answer but resumed walking. She followed in silence.

"I saw you with your nephew today," she said. "He seems well behaved."

"True, though he didn't get that from my family. Must be his father's blood."

"Lord Ulfrik seems a fair and generous man. His people love him."

Toki stopped and faced her. He nodded in answer. Halla clutched her hands over her stomach. The sunlight turned her hair to white fire. She searched his face for something, and Toki found himself suddenly holding his breath.

"When I was younger, I thought everyone loved my father. That everyone respected him." She dropped her hands and faced the sun again. "But as I got older I realized people feared him more than loved him. I remember once, a man had broken an oath to my father. I don't know what for, but he had the man thrown from a cliff while his family watched. Just like this one."

"Sometimes a broken oath deserves death." Toki grimaced at his words. "But I don't have the details of the story. Sorry, I didn't mean to stir bad memories."

Halla raised a hand and smiled. "No. Please, forget what I've said. I shouldn't speak of sadness. I hardly know you."

Toki checked his urge to make a trite reply. "If you prefer to go back, I'll take you."

"No, I have to see these puffins you are so fond of."

"They are a unique bird, if you've never seen them. We're almost there." Smiles again returned and Toki led the way.

He walked a few paces ahead. Wanting to appear confident, he clasped his hands behind his back and casually scanned the blue cliffs across the fjord. In fact, his hand was clammy in his palm. Polite conversation was not his strength. He could stand at the front of a battle line and scream into the face of death. But a willow of a girl one head shorter than him set him trembling.

Not expecting to get this far with Halla, he lacked a plan to advance his desires. Aside from her beauty, her rugged independence intrigued him. He experienced a twinge of shame, realizing that his sister had a similar character and it might be part of Halla's charm. But Runa's confidence could overwhelm a man, whereas Halla's masked vulnerability.

They continued in silence, Toki desperate to ask his questions but unsure of the best way. Halla solved the problem for him.

"What do you think of Jarl Vermund?"

"I think he stands too close to you and you don't like his sense

43

of humor."

Halla burst out in laughter, revealing her strong teeth. "How true! He's an evil old man, one of my father's dear friends. He's used to men laughing when he laughs, and it shows in what he thinks is funny."

"Vermund is fond of you; that's obvious. But so am I."

"Which is also obvious," Halla finished for him. She flashed a honeyed smile. Her expression showed confidence, but hesitation wavered in her eyes.

"Nothing wrong with honesty, right? You suspected my intentions coming out here with me. Alone." She nodded, her smile melting away. "And my guess is you feel safer alone with me than with Vermund."

"So you know about him, then?" Toki shook his head. "Oh, well, to tell it would be spreading rumors."

"Vermund is on my lord's land, within arm's reach of his neck. If there's something to tell, say it." His tone carried more force than intended. The hint of danger to his family triggered it. Halla leaned back, eyes wide. But she answered without hesitation.

"It's said he murdered his wife and his son. That he strangled her in their own bed, and when his son found out Vermund had him thrown into the sea."

"That's a grave accusation to make against a man. Why would he do it and how would you come to know?"

"I don't know why. Some say his wife was a shrew, that he married for her status and family. Maybe she grew too old or was unwilling to please him. He claims she died in her sleep and his son washed overboard in a storm. But many believe otherwise."

44

"And you believe otherwise?"

"It is safer to be wary of him than it is to assume he is a victim of gossip."

"And how do you know? Certainly your father doesn't believe it?"

"I heard it from one of Vermund's men who swore he saw the son thrown overboard. He warned me to be careful of Vermund, on the day we arrived here. I've known this man since I was little girl. I believe him."

"I already didn't like him. I don't mind having another reason. Thank you for your honesty."

Resuming the walk, Toki began to think ahead to how he could progress with this woman. She was only five or six years younger than him, too old to still be a virgin. He hoped he could verify that point on his own.

"I think my father wants us to marry." She blurted the words. Now Toki stepped back in shock. Halla regarded him, brows knitted in worry and eyes wide.

"Well, then, that's complicated. I was afraid you were too good to be true."

She put up her hands in protest. "It isn't a formal arrangement. But I know my father, and he wouldn't let even an old friend like Vermund get close to me if he disagreed."

"Then we must meet when your father is elsewhere. Halla, I confess, I want a chance to know you better. We can visit the puffins, but I merely sought privacy to ask if we might continue to meet. Am I a fool?"

She didn't smile or answer. Toki's face burned, his stomach soured. *So I am a fool*, he thought. *Not half the ladies man you thought, eh Toki? Well, I do live most my life at sea.* Halla folded her arms, her eyes appraising and calculating. She cocked an eyebrow. The wind picked up, blowing her hair across her face. She at last ended the silence.

"Not a fool. And I think you're a fine man, Toki. You serve a good lord, have a beautiful and royal sister, and you are gentle with your nephew. You've got wit, more than most men on these islands. I think I could become fond of a man like you. But I leave tomorrow. If I come back, or we meet again, I will be another man's wife. I'm too old to remain unwed, and many want my hand just for my father's wealth."

"I'm not interested in your father's wealth."

"Obviously not, or you wouldn't have chosen the one way to court me that would ensure my father's anger. Another reason you interest me, Toki."

Halla's worldly insight contrasted with Toki's naive thinking and left him wanting. He had only focused on wooing a pretty girl, forgetting she was the daughter one of the richest men in all the Faereyjar. She was royalty, and he was nothing but a freeman. He bowed his head. "I understand your meaning. I would be nothing more than a distraction for you. Eventually you will marry according to your station."

"No," she said, as forceful as Toki had been moments ago. "I am a free woman, not a piece on my father's game board. I will choose my own husband. Other women choose for love, so why not me?"

"Noble words, but I think your father would not hear them."

"He is a difficult man, vain, arrogant, ambitious. But I am his lone surviving child. He would be hard to convince, and maybe he would never accept my choice, but I will prevail."

Toki stared at Halla, her determination only enhancing her charm. She stood poised with the cliffs and ocean behind. A sea bird climbed into the sky, soaring like Toki's confidence. "I am chastened. Then, will you allow me the opportunity to further impress you?"

Her smile returned and the hardness fled her eyes. "If you can figure a way for us to meet privately, I would enjoy it. I would encourage it, in fact."

Toki's heart fluttered and he felt giddy. He tried to flatten his voice as he spoke. "We have plenty of ships, and I'm at sea often enough. If you have a secret place we can meet, I will find it. But how will you slip away?"

"I have slipped my father's notice for years. Don't worry for me. I have a slave who will help. She can explain to you where we shall meet. Let's plan for one week hence."

"Sounds wonderful," Toki winced at his gushing words. Halla giggled, and he assumed it was for his outburst. He straightened himself and continued. "Now about the puffin colony. It's just ahead as I mentioned. We can still visit it and return in reasonable time. Shall we?"

Halla giggled once more and stepped to his side, offering Toki her hand. He took it, hoping his palms were dry. They walked north along the cliffs, Toki wondering if this was nothing more than youthful foolishness. He thought of Hardar and Vermund again, and shoved away the fear he might be starting a conflict that would end badly for him and everyone else.

CHAPTER FOUR

Hardar pinched his chin, tugging the hairs of his gray streaked beard as he thought. He stood outside his tent, a fresh sea wind bringing its cleansing scent to his nose. He drew it in and held it. The assembled jarls and their hirdmen milled about the fields outside Nye Grenner, forming jovial clusters that broke apart and reformed like clumps of sleet on an iron plate. Hardar snorted out his breath.

"They're having such a fine time for themselves. Damn them." Hardar muttered, one of his own hirdmen looking expectantly at him. Hardar dismissed him with a frown, then entered his tent. It was the largest of the visitors' tents, brilliant white with red stripes. It had served him well in his younger days when he raided overseas in Northumbria and Frankia. Despite fifteen years of storage, it remained in fine condition.

The inside of the tent glowed with diffuse light. Ingrid sat on a stool, hands patiently folded on her lap. Dana, a slave girl from Ireland, combed Ingrid's platinum hair. He gestured her out with a flick of his hand.

"Where's Halla?"

"I sent her with an escort to tour the land. All of these games and arguments bored her."

Hardar stared at Ingrid. She had been a rare beauty in her day, and was still better than the toothless hags most men endured for their wives. But she was older now. Lines creased her eyes and brows. Her hair had thinned. Her eyes were still stunningly clear, cheeks still full. But she could not compare to a young woman, not like Ulfrik's wife.

"Just as well she be gone. I am in a foul mood." He looked expectantly at Ingrid, who simply cocked an eyebrow. He waited, but only distant laughter and the snap of the tent in the wind made any sound. He shrugged and turned away, dropping his sword on his fur bedding. "And I see you are in a foul mood, as well."

"After what you put me through last night? I was humiliated." She kept her tone even, and her gaze on an indistinct point of the tent.

"You should have left with me. I am the one humiliated."

"As you say."

Hardar lowered himself to the bedding. Ulfrik's beating had left him sore. His face was puffy and his eye still wept. But nothing bothered him as much as Ingrid's pat response. He wanted to roar in her face that it is as he says, and will ever be that way. If this were his own hall, he would. But here, even in his tent, he was in public. He had a reputation

49

for calm and generosity. Blaring into his wife's face would damage that reputation, especially considering his actions of the prior night. So he pinched his chin again and closed his eyes until the urge passed.

"Tell me what was said after I left. What did the others think?"

"I cannot claim to know their thoughts. Some appeared shocked."

"But others agreed with me, am I right? They must see what Ulfrik is doing here?"

"No one agreed, but for your friends who left with you. No one dwelt on your words once you had left. In fact, your exit was like a wind that disperses a foul smell."

Hardar's eyes snapped open, and Ingrid remained perched upon her stool. But now she fixed her eyes on his, anger bobbing up in two hazel pools. Ingrid rarely came into such anger, and Hardar had learned caution when she was vexed. But like every misstep he had taken during this festival, he felt helpless to do otherwise.

"You would do well to mind that wicked tongue of yours, woman, or ...,"

"Or? Are you going to put my head on a spear? Throw me from a cliff? I'm interested in knowing what you will do, husband. We've not had such a discussion before."

Hardar felt his temples throbbing, the heat emanating from his face. He kept his voice low, mindful that only plain cloth separated him from the people outside. "Then maybe it's time we did. You are supposed to be my beautiful wife, supporting and ever at my side. But you're cowering in here with a slave girl, doing your hair. And for what? If you're not seen with me, what good is finely dressed hair? People need

50

to see us united and happy. But you did not follow me when I left. You did not go with me to the sacrifices. You sent my daughter away on a tour. People could mistake this to mean you don't agree with me."

"Maybe I don't agree with you."

His limit reached, he sprung to his feet. Hardar was a barrel of a man, thick and rough, but he moved with the speed of a young deer. Ingrid's eyes widened and her mouth dropped open, apologies tumbling out like broken teeth. He seized a hank of Ingrid's fine hair and jerked her head back. He thrust his face into hers as he hissed.

"You better fucking agree with me from now until the end of time. You better show your pretty face at my side whenever I'm in public, and fucking smile. You think because you're away from home that I won't teach you a lesson?"

Hardar wound his grip tighter into her hair, down to the roots, and twisted. Ingrid's face contorted with the pain. But she did not cry out. He pulled again, a stifled squeal escaping Ingrid's gnashed teeth. Then he released her with a shove, dumping her from the stool to the grass. He hovered over her, his hands flexing, itching to strike her for her insolence.

"I will suffer no more humiliation on this trip. Stop sniffling and straighten up again. I'll come back for you when I'm ready."

Ingrid's defiance had vanished and she cowered meekly on the floor. Hardar smiled, satisfied that his woman had returned to her proper spot. He wagged Ingrid's hairs out of his hand, then turned to leave. But she apparently had not finished.

"You are so possessed with glory and status. But you forget your roots. Until you married me, until you took my family's gifts, you had

51

nothing. My father made you rich."

Hardar paused, turned back to face Ingrid. "That was half a lifetime ago. You know that wealth didn't last until today."

Ingrid coughed out a laugh. "No, but you managed to get all of it, didn't you? And my father went to his grave thinking he hadn't given you enough. You're the greatest jarl in all the islands now, Hardar. What a disgrace for all of us."

In one bound he was upon her, his hand striking out. Ingrid's head snapped back with a meaty crack and she sprawled sideways. She didn't scream, having braced herself. She lay with her face in the grass, convulsing with sobs. Hardar had endured her complaint often enough, and had beaten her for it every time. Yet the fool woman never learned. He regretted striking her now; the blow would leave a mark and others would judge what he had done. It angered him even more. Ingrid was normally obedient after a beating, and this obstinate display was both confusing and a surprise. He knelt beside her, but only so she could hear his whispers.

"This place has even turned you against me. I swear this land is cursed. Ulfrik must have a witch in his company, weaving spells on the minds of his guests. Only I see clearly. I will forgive you this time. But don't dishonor your father's memory with careless words. And don't dishonor me for what I achieved with your father's gifts. I made us a great name in these lands."

Ingrid continued to tremble with her stifled crying. Hardar reached to stroke her shoulder, but his hand stalled and withdrew. He lumbered to his feet and exited the tent. Ingrid would understand her place once she had time alone to think.

***

"That roasting meat smells delicious. I could eat one of 'em all for myself!" Dag the Sword-Bender patted his stomach and smiled.

"Go fall into the fire pit!" Hardar shot back. He had wearied of the praise for Nye Grenner. His own hirdman now even seemed taken with Ulfrik and his lands.

Dag dropped his head, folding his chin into his thickly braided beard. "Forgive me, lord."

"Be useful and find my daughter. Jarl Vermund and I need privacy."

Dag nodded, his creased and broad face eager to please his lord. He trotted off across the grass. Hardar watched him go. The lines of beige tents soon hid him. Beyond the tents, the sky was marbled with clouds that tumbled down to the horizon. He turned away and sneered at the smoke rising from the field behind Nye Grenner's new buildings. The shoulders of the mountains rose tall and purple in the distance.

"This place is cursed, Vermund. A witch hides here and weaves a spell over the minds of the guests. Even my wife is not immune. There is nothing great about this place, and Lord Ulfrik is a whelp who has overstepped his station."

The wind whipped around them, filling Hardar's ears with noise. He and Vermund observed the guests, most of them already drunk and falling over each other. Two men had started a wrestling match, which attracted a crowd that gambled on the outcome. A mass of children suddenly broke into a run, squealing and laughing and waving wooden swords overhead. The guests of his festivals had never shown as much camaraderie.

"How many drunken brawls have I had to end?" He waited for Vermund's answer, but his companion only gave a quizzical look. "I mean during the festivals. Gods, every year a new feud is kindled. But this year, nothing but peace! The whelp Ulfrik doesn't even understand what this festival means. He's not one of us, truly. He's a foreigner."

Vermund shifted uneasily. Hardar gave him a sideways look, judging his old friend to be of a different opinion. "What? Not you too, Vermund!"

"Not at all." Vermund's voice was shark-skin rough. Of an age with Hardar, Vermund wore the years just as heavily, showing not only in his voice but in the falling lines of his face and the gray streaks of his tightly braided hair.

"Then what? Ulfrik and these people of his, they're crawling over our lands like ants on a bone. Every year more come from Norway, settling here and taking what they will. It's disgusting."

"Several have settled in my lands. They've been good people."

"Well that's just it! You guide them and show them how to cooperate! You make them one of us. But here I see warships and mail and weapons. And an arrogant boy gloating over me like he rules these lands."

"But he does rule these lands. That is, these lands were free lands to be settled."

Hardar grumbled in his chest, folded his arms and returned to scanning the crowds. He had this final day to endure before he returned home. He spotted Ulfrik, now changed out of his robes. He stood at the center of a large group, apparently entertaining them with some wild, made-up story. Hardar felt his eye throbbing, as if just looking upon him injured it again.

"Vermund, this trip has given me much to consider. When this festival is done, I need to know who my friends are. Look at this upstart, taking this festival that I allowed him to host as an opportunity to build alliances. For what? He has the largest fleet, the most warriors, the greatest fucking people in the whole fucking circle of the world!"

Hardar stopped, realizing he had started yelling. Nearby people glanced in his direction. Vermund remained silent, squinting as the sun poked from behind a cloud. Hardar nervously smoothed his beard and smiled again. "This place is getting to me."

Vermund nodded and started to walk off. Hardar followed, hands clasped behind his back. They headed nowhere, just to leave the scene of Hardar's outburst. Once out of sight from others, he renewed their conversation.

"If Ulfrik is smart in building his alliances, he could cause me trouble. Ragnvald is nearly in bed with Ulfrik, if you can't see that yourself."

"I see it. You haven't said a thing I've not thought of myself. I don't like the whelp either, or his rat-eyed companions. The one called Toki is a spoiled child. As far as I'm concerned, you have my support if it comes to removing Ulfrik. All these weapons and men so close can't be any good for us. A true danger, it is."

"Good to count you as a friend. With all this foolishness," Hardar swiped a hand across backdrop of Nye Grenner, "I can't know who has been duped."

They walked further, headed toward the rocks of the shore

where the visiting ships were beached. He gazed out along the sparkling water. Gray green cliffs across the fjord spread like a stripe on the horizon. North beyond those cliffs his home awaited. He started to think on his own hall, so dark and empty compared to Ulfrik's. But before his mood could blacken further, Vermund broke into his thoughts.

"Hardar, I have a matter to discuss with you. I've been meaning to ask since arriving here. There hasn't been a moment until now."

Hardar felt a smile growing on his face, and his mood lifted. "Go on, old friend. I believe I know your question. But I'll hear it from you."

He turned and regarded Vermund. He stood lean and proud, a strong jarl of the old families of the islands. His hairline had crawled back, and his eyes were now ringed with dark circles. Time's wretched hand clawed all men. But Hardar could still see the strong war leader of decades ago. Vermund straightened himself, a faint smile on his wide mouth.

"I have long been alone since the terrible events that left me as an heirless widower. This past winter was cold and lonely. I took a woman to my bed, but she is nothing to me. Not a woman for starting a new life. Your daughter is unwed, a lucky thing for me. I would ask your permission to court her."

Vermund asked with all the confidence of a man who already knew the answer. He smiled, and Hardar mirrored it. He could hardly consider a better match, tying his family ever closer to the old families with their connections across the islands. Vermund was also wealthy, and maintained a core of fighting men. Hardar's smile continued to stretch across his face.

"I would grant that permission, and wish you much luck."

"Thank you, old friend. She is a charming woman, as beautiful as her mother."

"But more spirited. Be warned there."

Vermund chuckled. "I know it well. I remember when you tried to marry her to Erp."

"I thought she would kill me, and she was only twelve! Now she's a woman and twice as headstrong. But you will be a good match for her, Vermund."

Both men laughed and turned back toward the celebration. Hardar only had to endure one more feast before escaping Nye Grenner and start plotting its downfall.

***

The jarls, their families, and their men assembled along the rocks at the shore, standing in dark clumps before their ships. Their murmuring voices mingled with the gentle rumble of the waves and the call of seabirds. The sun hung fat and yellow in the west, throwing half their bodies into the sharp shadow of the ridgeline. Ulfrik stood up the slope from them, his own shadow a deep triangular blot that stretched before him.

"Have you prepared everything?" he asked Toki as he scanned the assembled guests once more.

"Listen to my answer this time. Yes, I've seen to everything you've said."

Ulfrik shot Toki a scowl. "Have care with your words in public. And I was speaking to the men and the gifts."

"Aye, I was speaking to the same. Just relax, Ulfrik. You're a better man when you're not pretending to be lord of the world."

Ulfrik flinched at the truth of the words. He turned and gave a sheepish look to Runa, who stood silently at his side. She smiled, holding Gunnar who was falling asleep on her shoulder. "Am I that bad?"

"Listen to my brother. He's right for once."

The departure of the guests was as important as their arrival. Ulfrik knew their final impressions would carry long after the event. As such, he arranged for a send-off unlike anything he had ever seen Hardar do. Ulfrik knew he was deliberately outdoing Hardar, and that it was unnecessary. But after Hardar's outburst, Ulfrik wanted to ensure his rival felt humbled.

Ulfrik thought on Runa and Toki's advice, and nodded to himself. "I hate it when Toki is right. Let's see off our guests and return to our lives, eh?"

"Never better words spoken," Toki agreed. Runa nudged Gunnar, who fussed and tried to get comfortable.

Ulfrik called the jarls together, which was also Snorri's signal to march out the men and parting gifts. Ulfrik turned to watch his men, dressed in mail and helmets scoured to a bright finish, file out from behind the hall and down the slope. Snorri led them, two men behind carrying a chest of gifts to bestow upon his fellow jarls.

Surprise rippled through the ranks of the guests. The jarls of the islands had all given gifts upon their arrival, as was customary. But it was unheard of for the host of the summer festival to bestow gifts of his own. The sacrifices and costs of the celebrations were considered enough.

Ulfrik moved down slope, gesturing for Runa and Toki to follow. Gunnar now stood on the grass, staring at the massing of the armored warriors. The jarls were also impressed and left their ships to draw together. Ulfrik saw Hardar and his family hover at the back. His swollen face was pulled into a frown.

"Friends, your company has been most enjoyable. The people of Nye Grenner will ever remember these days. I've prepared some small items for each of you. Tokens to commemorate this year's festival. But also as thanks for the support we have seen from all of you. Many of us are strangers here. You have welcomed us to the lands, and helped us flourish."

Appreciative nods circled around, many men agreeing with the honor shown them. All men seek honor, even if not truly earned. Ulfrik knew he stretched the truth; many of the jarls had never offered help. Some had even ignored him. But those men now smiled and waited to extend their hands for whatever Ulfrik would place in them.

His men formed a semicircle behind him, three ranks deep. He had eighty fighting men, twice the number of any other jarl. They stood with arms clasped behind their backs. Ulfrik wanted a show of force but not one too intimidating. Snorri and his son, Einar, placed the chest beside Ulfrik. He gave an appreciative look to all the gathered jarls, then opened the chest. Some of the less refined men craned to see what had been revealed. Ulfrik smiled and began to call forward each jarl to receive his gift.

Most of the jarls were appreciative. Some lacked fine words, caught by surprise. The gifts were not trifles, Ulfrik having selected

59

pieces from his personal horde. Snorri had warned him not to show too much wealth, fearing it would draw trouble. But Ulfrik felt the eighty men in mail coats counterbalanced it.

He left Hardar for last, both to draw out the suspense and to ensure others would be distracted with their own gifts. But when he called Hardar, many paused to watch the exchange.

Hardar stirred as if he hadn't been paying attention. He looked at his wife, Ingrid, who stared blankly at him. Then he drew a breath and came forward, as if curiosity had stirred him to action. Ulfrik smirked. *This is a worm tearing at your gut, Hardar,* he thought. *I bet you can't beat this next year.*

The crowd watched as Hardar lumbered to stand before Ulfrik. He studied Hardar, trying to make his own expression open but cool. There was still the matter of Hardar's accusation, and the required apology. Ulfrik wanted to seem the better man in this conflict.

Hardar's eyes were two gray stones set into fleshy pouches, searching Ulfrik's face and betraying as little of his thoughts as possible. Ulfrik held that gaze, letting the rest of his vision turn to a blur. Hardar shifted, glancing across to Runa and Gunnar at his side. Ulfrik decided he did not like that, though did not understand why. A tiny sneer curled on Hardar's lips, his pug nose making him look like a leering pig. Finally he spoke.

"Your thoughtfulness and generosity are boundless, Lord Ulfrik. Truly you are a credit to your people." He paused, as if waiting for Ulfrik's response. Ulfrik inclined his head, but withheld his words. Hardar shrugged and continued. He raised his voice so others could hear. "I spoke rash words at the feast. Drink clouded my mind, and I was exhausted from our wrestling match. I apologize."

Ulfrik peered at him. Hardar's eyes did not meet his own but ranged about the men behind him. The words were insincere, he did not doubt. But he forced his smile. "Let us put it up to drink and forget unhappy memories."

Many men agreed, though some held their faces cold. Jarl Vermund smiled wickedly, enough to distract Ulfrik a moment. Then Hardar moved in front of him, breaking Ulfrik's sight. "Well said, Jarl Ulfrik."

"Now I have a gift prepared for you." Ulfrik reached into the box and removed a golden cloak pin. Hardar's own pin was only silver, and had two settings of which one had lost its jewel. Men who could see gasped at the value. Even Hardar stepped back in surprise.

"I cannot accept a gift so precious," he said stiffly.

"I'll not hear of it," Ulfrik said. "You are my closest neighbor, and the first in honor among us all. It is only in accordance to you station. Please accept it."

Hardar paused, regarding Ulfrik with a hard stare. Ulfrik suppressed a smile, enjoying the discomfort he inflicted on his rival. To refuse would shame him, and to accept would make reciprocating a great expense. At last he held out his hand to receive the gift. But he whispered as he did. "You haven't bought me, nor the others."

"I buy no man, but win their loyalty through my own merit," Ulfrik replied, matching the whisper.

The two men separated, and a few of the more naive in the crowd clapped. Hardar stepped away with a smile that did nothing more than show his black and yellow teeth. No warmth came from it.

Ulfrik spoke more fine words, and many of the jarls gave their own speeches. But soon the guests set sail. One by one they launched their ships into the gentle waves of the fjord. Oars poked out and dipped into the water. Hardar had the largest ship, and remained the last to depart. He assisted his wife and daughter up the gangplank and followed without a glance back. Once the ship lurched to sea, only his bright-haired daughter came to the stern to wave once more. Ulfrik and Runa both waved back.

"You've done a fine job ensuring you've made an enemy of our closest neighbor," Runa mumbled.

"He's just full of himself. Someone had to wake him up from that daydream. We're the new power in this land, ife."

The men were already breaking up under Snorri's direction. Toki had disappeared and Gunnar begged to be picked up again. Ulfrik smiled at Runa, who tried to smile back.

"That is just what I'm afraid of, Ulfrik. Men covet power."

CHAPTER FIVE

Toki stood upon the black rocks, careful not to slip into the sea. He wore his sword, and carried an unstrung bow and leather quiver of arrows. Otherwise, he dressed in simple clothing and wrapped himself in a gray wool cloak. He leaned forward into the small boat to get his pack of supplies from Bork. The waters of the cove were as calm as Halla's slave had promised. But Bork jostled the boat as he handed over the pack.

"Careful now," Bork said. "Don't want to be wet all day. Nothing dries in this weather."

Toki nodded, snatching his pack. "I'm fine. Count your time carefully, and return here tomorrow."

"I've got five fingers on this hand," Bork said as he held up his left hand. "And four more on this one. Fucking Irish got the fifth one." He wiggled the stump of his index finger and laughed. "So don't ever stay gone more than nine days and I'll always know when to find you."

"Gods strike me dead if you can count that high. Just remember what we planned."

"No one saw us leave, and no one's looking for poor old Bork. You're fine here, and you paid me enough to not know where you went."

"Good. The silver was for using your boat. And you still owe me, Bork."

Bork cackled, his scraggly beard wagging. Then he used an oar to shove back from the rocks. "Isn't my business where you go. I'm your man, and you know it. Have fun with that lass, but be smart."

Toki smiled and waved to his friend, who sat at his oars and rowed out of the cove. Fog roiled as Bork faded to a dark stain, soon vanishing. Toki turned to the black rock face behind him, searching for a way up. He took several frustrating missteps before finding purchase up to the grass. He sat a moment to rest. His body still ached from six hours of rowing.

Like the south, Hardar's lands were rolling plains of grass that tumbled from blunt mountains and ran down to cliffs. Settlements formed in the flats of the coasts. The plains spread out into the fog, making the perfect cover for Toki. The fog would resist the sun for hours. Though he couldn't see far enough to note the landmarks described to him, he knew to travel east and down slope. He stood again and started out. The grass swished at his feet as he walked. The fog made him feel as though he moved on a disk of green hanging in a cloud.

Toki's excitement heightened now that he had come so far. The week had dragged since Halla had left. Every moment he anticipated this meeting, and fretted over keeping it secret. Fortunately, after the festival everyone was wrapped up in their own concerns. He only worried that Halla had changed her mind. *Otherwise it'll be a long day hiding in a hole*, he mused.

A sheep bleated at him, and Toki leapt back in surprise. Three more resolved out of the dense white. All four looked at him with the dumb expression of all herd animals. Toki had no rapport with animals, not even dogs. These four bleated again and began to run.

Tossing about for a place to hide, he heard more sheep skittering away through the grass. "Odin's balls!" he cursed under his breath. If a shepherd was near he would be discovered in moments. The safest retreat was the way he had come. He jogged along the trampled grass until he judged he had a safe distance. Only birds screeched in the distance, and no sounds of pursuit came. He let his breath run out and restarted his journey.

He searched for the rock outcropping landmark to show him where to turn. Instead he stumbled upon two small shadows in the fog.

Toki's first impulse was to draw his sword. His hand fell to the hilt, but better judgment stayed him. The two shadows stopped, and one voice hissed Toki's name.

"Halla! It's Toki. Thanks be the gods you found me." Stepping into his circle of vision came Halla and her slave, an Irish girl called Dana.

Halla smiled, pausing at the edge of the fog. "You came after all.

65

I waited this morning and didn't find you. I thought you wouldn't show."

"The journey here took longer than I guessed with only two sets of oars."

Halla looked as radiant as he remembered. Her hair was woven into two tight braids hung over her shoulders. She wore a summer dress of green and brown. He noticed the hem of her skirt had been soiled from dragging over the wet grass. Her slave, Dana, looked as though she could have been Halla's sister but for her shorter chin and wider face. She wore a dress of raw cloth, dirty but not tattered, and her hair was cropped short to mark her as a slave.

"Lucky we found you. You're going the wrong way. Homes are just over those rises. I thought I told you to travel down slope?"

"I wasn't going down slope? This fog is more confusing than I thought. But we are together now, and you can show me where we were supposed to meet."

Halla giggled and walked up to Toki. Her closeness quickened his pulse, and her smile led his mind to imagine her laying back in the grass for him. She took his hand into her cool, smooth grip. "I'll be glad to show you. Dana, follow us but not too closely please."

Toki ignored the slave, and simply stared at the young beauty holding his hand. She started forward, giving him a gentle tug. He followed, anxious to get to Halla's secret location.

They traveled in silence until Toki saw the standing stone he had searched for earlier. No runes marked it. It appeared out of the fog like a giant sentinel in a lichen vest. They both stopped in the weak shadow of the stone. "What is its purpose?" he asked.

"No one knows. It was here before my family. Maybe the Irish monks placed it. Or maybe giants."

"Giants more likely. The monks are still here and would've told you about this old stone."

They moved on in companionable silence, then arrived at the secret place Halla had described. She had not overstated the beauty of it. A slender path folded down into a steep drop. Peering through the fog, Toki saw a large basin shimmering with seawater. He guessed an underground cavern fed it. The water lapped a thin strip of sand that yielded to lush emerald grass. As they descended the path, the earth rose around them. Once at the bottom, the air was cool and smelled of sea salt. Toki imagined he was at the bottom of a gigantic well.

"My brother showed me this place when I was a small girl. I've never forgotten it, and come here often."

"Your brother?"

"Dead many years. A fever."

Toki gave a curt nod. "So you came here earlier and didn't find me? I admit that I hadn't expected you to come."

"We must trust each other from now on. I was cursing your name this morning." Halla covered her laugh and walked further into the grass. "Mind the water. It is deep and I fear a current could suck you under. There is a crack in the wall over here. If you can squeeze through, it leads to caves."

She released his hand and walked to where she had pointed. She turned sideways to demonstrate how to fit into the crack. But Toki instead studied how squeezing between the rocks pulled her dress tight against her curves. She stepped back out, her face blushing. Toki smiled, his breath growing hotter. "So where is your slave now?"

"Dana's up there." She gestured toward the steep path. "She will be a lookout. If we are found together, my father will probably kill you."

"He'd have to catch me first." He extended his hand and she accepted, then he pulled her to him. He had long been without a woman, and now he had chosen the most dangerous one to bed. The danger fueled his lust.

"You are a handsome man," Halla said as she drew into him. "I've been watching you since you came to my father's hall."

Toki pressed his lips to hers, pushed his hands beneath her blouse. Urgency and need drove him, and words and thoughts had no place in his mind. Halla recoiled, as if hesitating, but he gently drew her back. He guided her to the soft grass, and prepared to slake his long thirst.

***

On the evening of the next day, Toki and Halla sat together in their secret meeting place. Sunlight skipped across the open mouth of the basin, spilling ochre light halfway down the damp rock walls. The bottom remained in cool shadow. The ambient light gave Halla an ethereal cast to her cream colored blouse and her platinum hair. They sat by the water, its lapping sound echoing through the basin in a serene rhythm. Halla leaned against him, warming the both of them. Neither had spoken for a long time, knowing this was their final meeting before Toki left.

"I am going to miss you, Toki. Fate has been kind in joining us. Time passed quickly."

"Let's think ahead to our next meeting. This cannot be all?"

Toki had never met a finer woman. She made him feel sharp and alive. She was independent, smart, and quick-witted. None of the eligible women in Nye Grenner could match Halla. He resolved to court her with all this strength, dismissing any thought of another. Jarl Vermund's face flashed in his mind, but he thrust it aside.

"This is only the start. Yet my father is possessed with jealousy of Ulfrik. He has not stopped ranting about him since we've returned home. He insists Ulfrik plans to conquer the whole island."

Toki pulled away and looked at her. "We would still meet? Like this, in secret, yes?"

"My father will never accept us, so secret meetings are all we can plan for now." She placed her hand upon Toki's and squeezed it.

"The reward is worth the risk," he said with a laugh. "You will have to consider leaving with me of your will, when the day comes."

She shrugged, leaning away from Toki. "In time. That is what I have been thinking all along, but have not had many choices until I met you. But I need to know you better first. When I do leave home, I can never return."

"I'd say you've seen much of me already."

Suddenly Dana called down the slope, trying to suppress her voice. "Lady Halla, I've spotted men from your father's hall. They've gone out of sight behind the hill. You must leave or they'll discover you here."

Halla's posture slumped. "My parents wonder why I suddenly enjoy outdoor life. I think they've sent men to either fetch me or spy on me. Either way, I must go."

Toki placed his hand upon her shoulder. "Be careful, and calm your father's suspicions. How will I know when to return?"

"I can't think of an easy way. I am not like a man who may travel freely or dispatch messengers." Halla rubbed her hands and frowned. Dana hissed her name again.

Toki glanced at the spindly slave in irritation. "Let's try this. I will return one week hence. If you cannot meet me, send Dana or leave sign of your passage and I will go home. Otherwise I will wait one day for you, and if you do not show I will leave a sign. I will try again the following week on the same day."

"What of your boat?"

"I saw places suitable for mooring it. Now go, before you're found here."

Toki opened his arms and Halla stepped into them. They embraced and he kissed her forehead. Then she dashed up the path, turning back to wave before disappearing over the top. Toki watched a moment longer, as if she might run back to him. She did not, and he started gathering his belongings into his travel sack. Within the hour he was ready to meet Bork and return to Nye Grenner, though his only thought was to return here.

CHAPTER SIX

Ulfrik kicked the grass in frustration. He scanned the ring of men assembled around him, their faces hard and eyes set. A sea breeze tousled hair and tugged at cloaks, but otherwise none moved. Ulfrik paced, his hands clasped behind his back, his brows taut in concentration. He glanced at Snorri, who sat just inside the circle and wrapped himself in a faded red cloak. He slowly nodded at Ulfrik.

"As your jarl, I am sworn to defend and protect you. I will take the matter of disputed fishing grounds directly to Hardar. As for the claim of sheep raiding, I need more proof to accuse him of that. So few sheep could've strayed."

"My flocks are not so large that I'd lose track of them," said Egbert Longneck. He stood again, shaking his fist at the sky. "If

71

Hardar's ships were nearby, then three of my flock go missing the next day, what am I to think?"

Many murmured agreement, but others told Egbert to sit. Ulfrik waved down the excitement. "We've been through this already. No one witnessed Hardar's crews stealing your sheep, Egbert. But Darby and these others have had run-ins with Hardar's fishermen. That's something I can address."

Egbert stomped back to his place in the ring. Ulfrik sighed, weariness straining his voice. "Before we close this meeting, is there more to discuss?" Men glanced from face to face, and no more voices were raised. Ulfrik seized his opening. "Then we are finished. What we have decided today let no man defy."

The assembled freemen rose, dusted off their pants, and broke up. Groups drifted to every direction, many heading over the grassy horizon. As was customary, Ulfrik waited at the center of the ring for everyone to go. Snorri struggled to his feet, bracing his leg and barring his teeth.

The sky was a sullen gray sheet, draining the green expanses of color. Snorri's red cloak was dazzling against it as he approached. "Hardar's nipping at your heels. Wants to see how tough you really are."

Ulfrik wiped his hands on legs, and shook his head. "The sheep raiding doesn't make sense. Why only three? That's got to be coincidence. But what are his fishermen doing this far south?"

"Already told you the answer to that one," Snorri said, putting his arm around Ulfrik's shoulder. "Let's get back to our wives and see what's left in those cooking pots. During the whole meeting I kept smelling that delicious soup."

Snorri drew an exaggerated sniff, while Ulfrik chuckled. "You're getting hungrier with age; I thought old men ate less. What does Gerdie feed you?"

"Anything I ask for, and more." They laughed and ambled down slope to the clustered dwellings of Nye Grenner. A lone sheep wandered between two buildings, bleating at them. He heard Thorvald clanging at this forge in the distance. A new shipment of bog iron had arrived with traders a few weeks ago; Thorvald had been ceaselessly working it into tools, mail, and weapons.

Life in Nye Grenner had settled back to normal after the festival. It had taken several weeks to restore the daily patterns and to replenish depleted food stores. The arrival of the traders had solved most of Ulfrik's problems. After the festival, he heard complaints that men cannot eat gold and glory. Now they had salted meats, wood, iron, and traded their wool and hay. People were satisfied. Up until today.

Ulfrik and Snorri tramped into the hall, Snorri leaving his long knife in the front room as was customary. Ulfrik, being the jarl, had no restriction. The windows and smoke hole were open and the wan light filled the main room. Gerdie and another woman tended the fat iron pot over the hearth, while Runa and two girls worked at the loom in the back. Ulfrik heard Gunnar squealing with delight but didn't see him. He was in a pile of boys who wrestled and played about the hall while the women worked.

"Was I ever that happy?" Ulfrik asked Snorri as they entered the main room.

"Nothing wrong with a happy kid, unless he's simple. But that boy of yours, he's got his mother's wit." Snorri slapped Ulfrik's shoulder

73

and moved to the cooking pot, sniffing at the rising steam. "Is it ready now? Those damn assemblies make me hungry."

Gerdie hustled him to a table, and Ulfrik picked his way back to Runa. She set aside her distaff and basket while the two other girls worked the loom. "Welcome home. How was the assembly?"

Ulfrik embraced his wife, then moved to a bench where he lowered himself with a groan. "It went fine. I settled grazing disputes, kept Thorkel Two-Toes out of his neighbor's pasture. For the third time. Of course, there's the fishermen's troubles with Hardar." Ulfrik mumbled the last statement, knowing how Runa would react. She did not disappoint.

"You were too heavy-handed during the festival. Your friendly competition, as you called it, started a larger fight. Now we've got an enemy to the north." She folded her arms, looking away. Ulfrik glanced after her and saw Gunnar emerge from the dog pile, his smile shining bright through the dirt on his face.

"The festival was over a month ago. I admit, I had fun showing off to him. Can't he let it go? I never insulted him the way he did me, and I'm fine."

"Well, you'll have to ask him. Seems he's sending his fishermen to start trouble. So you'll meet with him, then?" Ulfrik nodded, but stood from his bench.

"Gods, woman! Can I have peace? I will handle matters with Hardar. Before you say it, I will do all I can to renew good relations with him. If he'll be sensible enough to listen to me."

"You must not be hasty with him, Ulfrik. I think he wants a fight."

74

"He had no trouble attacking me without a reason five years ago. So the man needs no reason. Stop telling me what I know to do. I will arrange for travel tomorrow." Ulfrik had shouted, and he now felt foolish as Gerdie and Snorri both pretended not to hear. Runa gave a lame shrug and turned back to her loom.

Ulfrik stood like a man left ashore after his ship had launched. He realized his pulse had quickened and shook his head to clear his mood. "Where has Toki been? I haven't seen him in days."

"Wasn't he doing something for you? Teaching boys about sailing or something?" Runa sat at her stool, her two companions working in silence and seeming to ignore the conversation. She gestured to one of the girls for a basket.

"Teaching boys about sailing? I never asked him to do that. He said he was ... Snorri!"

Snorri was upending a wood bowl to his mouth. He peered at Ulfrik over the rim as he slurped down his soup.

"Did you ask Toki to teach boys about sailing?" Snorri extended his bowl to Gerdie for a refill, then shook his head. "Have you not seen Toki, either? I thought I was just lucky."

"Not at all. He told me he had repairs to make on *Raven's Talon*."

Now Runa dropped her basket and regarded Ulfrik. He stared back at her, and saw the thoughts moving behind his wife's eyes. He chewed his lower lip, knowing that Toki had lied but not knowing why. Ulfrik suspected Runa had guessed. "What's he up to?"

"I don't know, but," she paused and touched her chin, "he has been strange since the festival, whenever he has been present. I am certain he's found a woman. But he hasn't told me so, or anyone else it

75

seems."

Ulfrik folded his arms and made the connections Runa did not. "If he's keeping it secret, it's because I wouldn't approve. And if I won't approve, it's because the match is either below him or with someone he knows I would forbid."

Runa covered her mouth when she realized what Ulfrik was saying. "Hardar's daughter?"

"It's either her or a slave from a neighboring land. And few slaves came to the festival. Hardar is the only jarl with an eligible daughter that I would be unhappy about."

Snorri and Gerdie joined Ulfrik at the high table. The two girls with Runa blushed deeply and she waved them away with an apologetic smile. As they shoved their items into their baskets, everyone waited quietly. Only the laughter and screaming of the boys interrupted the silence. Once the girls had left, Ulfrik punched his fist into his left hand.

"Of all the damn people to pick! If it's true, then he's dancing with Loki." Ulfrik spun back to his bench and dumped himself on it. He pinched the bridge of his nose. His mind's eye filled with an image of Hardar's rage contorted face as he relived their wrestling match.

"Well, it's not ideal," Runa offered. "She did seem like a sweet girl, I mean, at least what I saw of her."

"They all seem sweet at that age," Snorri said. "But I suspected she was hunting for a man. She made eyes at a lot of the younger men. And those eyes probably caught a lot of men too. Only they'd take one look at her father and know to piss off the other way."

"Only my dear friend Toki would not see that." Ulfrik sighed and shrugged. "He would charge straight in and let the plan work itself out."

"You don't know if it's true yet." Runa joined Ulfrik at his bench. She laid her gentle hand on his leg. "And if it is true, what is the harm in it?"

Ulfrik wavered a moment, wondering if he wasn't exaggerating the issue. He looked at Snorri and read the flat expression on his face. "There's much harm in it, wife. Hardar fancies himself the greatest jarl of all time. His daughter should be wed to another jarl of suitable station, one he thinks will increase his power and glory. Toki doesn't fit those demands. At best, Hardar's mood for cooperation is worsened. At worst, I don't want to think of it. You saw how he took to losing a wrestling match."

Runa withdrew her hand, dropping her gaze. Ulfrik scanned Snorri and Gerdie, both regarding him gravely. Silence dominated for long moments. Then Ulfrik let go a drawn-out breath before speaking again.

"I will assign men to watch for his return. We will know the truth of what he's doing. If he is visiting Halla, then he will understand and show good judgment."

Runa laughed and rolled her eyes. "You're talking about my love struck brother?"

Ulfrik bowed his head, and would have laughed if he could see things ending as he hoped. But Toki was as stubborn as Runa and less sensible. "He must understand, or we could have a larger problem than quarreling fishermen."

***

Ulfrik expected meeting outside the hall would make his conversation with Toki less confrontational. He was wrong.

Toki paced over the grass, hands gripping his curly hair. Ulfrik and Runa gave him space. The sky had turned indigo, the closest it would be to darkness during the summer months. A strong wind carried earthy scents and promised a storm. Scattered golden lights twinkled from Nye Grenner up the slope behind them. Toki muttered to himself as he circled.

"Toki, I appreciate your honesty," Ulfrik said, "but you can't be caught in secret meetings with Hardar's daughter."

"I haven't been caught, have I." He stopped pacing long enough to snap out the words, then resumed. Ulfrik looked a Runa, who shrugged and raised her brows.

"Hardar hasn't caught you yet. But I caught you. And Hardar will catch Halla. It's only a matter of time." Toki stopped pacing, putting his back to Ulfrik and Runa. He trembled, as if either to explode in rage or collapse in tears. Ulfrik rubbed his face then covered his mouth with his hand. Runa stepped into the pause.

"In any other circumstance, we would be happy for you. Please reconsider your actions. Hardar would deal harshly with you, and Ulfrik would have to defend you. Think of how that will affect all of Nye Grenner. Please, brother."

The wind gusted, flattening the grass and cracking their cloaks. Toki's shaking subsided, and he faced them. Ulfrik read the pain in his friend's face, and wanted to avert his eyes. But the situation required a firm stance. Toki swallowed and gritted his teeth.

"Neither of you understand. Of course I know what's at stake.

78

It's why I have kept this secret. But Halla is not a passing distraction for me. She is beyond compare. Fate has put us together, can't you see that? Like you and Runa." Toki spread his hands to emphasize his words.

"Gods, Toki, the two situations couldn't be more different. You put yourself together with Halla, not Fate. Let's be honest."

Toki's face collapsed into a frown and Ulfrik's neck tensed. He opened his mouth to continue chiding Toki, but Runa seized his arm to stop him. "Your love is fresh," Runa said, strained patience beginning to show in her voice. "You believe Freya's hand is upon the two of you. It is a hard time to think clearly. But you must."

"We will be married," Toki said. He set his jaw and peered at Ulfrik and Runa.

Ulfrik nearly laughed; he looked so much like his wife when she hit her stubborn moods. He glanced at Runa, her mouth agape and eyes wide. *How do you enjoy seeing yourself*, he thought. *Not so easy being on this side of that stubbornness.* He suppressed a smile, but Toki misread him.

"You think I'm foolish? Halla is her own woman, and she will not be a piece on her father's game board."

"Toki, she is not free to make that choice. Her father and mother will marry her to another of her station. Even if I made you jarl, Nye Grenner is not Hardar's choice."

"Listen, at first I was only after her body. But over this month, we have grown past that and have found something more. I am in love with her."

"So you are. And I forbid you from meeting her again."

Wind filled the silence. Toki's face fell slack, his posture slumped. Runa removed her hand from Ulfrik's arm and turned away.

79

Ulfrik hated what he had said, and wished he had never been in this position. But no other choice existed.

"You are clear on my orders?" he asked as Toki stood staring at him. "You are forbidden from visiting Hardar's lands on your own. You are not to send others in your place. You will not risk getting caught sniffing around Hardar's hall."

Toki remained still but for a fluttering cape. His eyes glistened in the blue light. He swallowed again, then finally lowered his head. His voice was weak and ragged. "She is the finest woman in the circle of the world. I could never find another like her."

Ulfrik glanced at Runa, who rolled her eyes. Ulfrik felt the same way. He knew Toki would be hurt and angry. He might not speak to him for weeks. But soon memories would fade and life would return to normal. Ulfrik needed to be patient and remain firm. But Toki had also not yet committed to his demands. So Ulfrik reached to the silver armband clasped to his bicep. He had worn it especially for this. He worked it off and extended it toward Toki.

"You will swear your oath to break contact with Halla. Put your hand upon the ring and swear before the gods."

"Really, Ulfrik, is this needed?" Runa wheeled to him, a frown creasing her face.

"It is. An oath sworn to the gods is beyond question." Ulfrik saw Toki's expression morph from surprise to horror. The ring flashed white as he held it forward. "Make your oath, Toki, then we will put this matter out of mind."

Toki regarded the ring as if it were an adder foisted on him. But Ulfrik kept it out, and smiled. He had no intention of wearing it again without Toki's oath. The air thickened between them. Toki stepped forward and reached toward the ring. His fingers hovered over it. He licked his lips. Ulfrik pushed it at his hand, encouraging him to grasp it.

At last he snatched the ring from Ulfrik, and held it over his bowed head. "I give my oath to break contact with Halla."

He lowered the ring and raised his head. His face was contorted in pain. Ulfrik had hoped for a stronger oath, but Toki had done all that could be expected. Ulfrik accepted the ring and embraced Toki. "Your sacrifice will not be forgotten, my friend."

When they parted, Runa stepped in and kissed her brother's cheek and cupped his face in her hands. "You have done well. You have put others before yourself, the mark of a great man."

Toki nodded, wiped his nose with the back of his hand, then turned to stride up the slope. Ulfrik stared after him, putting his arm around Runa. "Do you think he will be mad for long?"

"I don't know. But my brother is stubborn, and rarely surrenders his desires. This may not be over."

"But he swore to the gods." Ulfrik looked down at Runa, but she merely bit her lip and watched Toki disappearing into the gloom of the short-lived night.

CHAPTER SEVEN

Halla stood below the high table, watching her father squatting in his prized foreign chair. The air was thick enough to choke her. Though a typically balmy summer evening, she was cold. The night sun filtered through the high windows and broke the hall into dusty columns of straw-colored light. Her father bounced his leg beneath the table, all the while smiling at her. He kept glancing at her mother, who seemed to disappear next to him. She kept her head lowered and folded her hands on her lap.

The final hirdmen had left the room. The door thudded shut at the far end of the hall. Only Dag the Sword-Bender remained, a wispy visage in the shadows behind Hardar.

"Now that we have our privacy," Hardar began, "we can talk."

Halla raised her chin and crossed her arms. But her stomach clenched and a hundred different disasters flooded her mind. She felt abandoned before her father. Even Dana had been dismissed. She only had her mother for support, and she would not look at her.

"I will be direct with you, daughter. You are nineteen years old, well past the age to be married."

An ember dropped into her gut. She started to tremble and her throat dried out. Hardar said a few more things before he paused. Instead of listening to him, she predicted his next words. *Now he forces Vermund on me. That wretched man, that murderer.*

"Jarl Vermund is my old friend, a wealthy and important man. He has expressed an interest in courting you, and I've approved."

Halla's head swam. She was being given away to an old man, no doubt to be his prized possession along with his favorite ring and sword. For a moment the room sounded as if it were filled with a cloud of flies. She touched her head, hoping to clear her mind.

"You're very reserved," Hardar said, one brow cocked. He glanced at Ingrid, who still refused to look up. "Nothing at all like the last time. I suppose you've matured. Good!" He slapped the table as if matters were settled.

"What if I don't find Jarl Vermund suitable?" She had found her voice, weak and thin and disgustingly timid.

Hardar fell back in his chair, face stuck in a half-smile. "Your thoughts don't matter. As long as Vermund is pleased, then you shall be his wife. I wonder where you get this notion of independence?" Hardar frowned at Ingrid. "Your role in this family is to increase its status by marrying well. That's been the whole purpose of feeding you all these years. Do you understand? Produce grandchildren, boys, and you will have done the work Fate has set for you."

Balling her fists, she infused as much iron into her voice as she could summon. "Then I will see to it that Vermund be displeased. I will not be wed to a monster."

Hardar pushed himself straight in his chair, his meaty hands loosening his collar. His eyes drew to slits as he peered down at her. "You are too old to play this game. Vermund is my choice for you, and a fine one. You can make it difficult on yourself if you'd like. It won't change my mind."

"He's a murderer! How can you send me to him? He strangled his wife and threw his only son into the ocean. What will happen to me?" Halla leapt forward, ferocity replacing the timidity. Tears flowed over her cheeks. "I am your daughter. You should protect me."

Shooting up from his chair, Hardar knocked the table forward and set the mugs tumbling to the floor. Both Ingrid and Halla jumped as he roared. "I'll not tolerate vile slander spoken in my hall. How can you even think this? Vermund had differences with his wife, but he did not kill her. He is a victim of Fate's weaving. Where did you hear this filth?"

Halla fell silent, not wanting to name a man who had tried to help her. Hardar stood glowering at her. When he realized she would not reply, he supplied his own guess. "Was it from your mother? We've already discussed this matter and she agrees with me. It wasn't from her, then, was it?"

Ingrid looked up and Halla covered her mouth in shock. Her mother's face was red and swollen, and her left eye hid behind puffy and blackened flesh. Both eyes glittered with tears. Halla immediately understood the so-called discussion she had with her father. Whenever his mother had defied him, he ended the disagreement with his fists. Halla winced with a sympathetic pang, but also felt emboldened. Her mother had stood up for her. She could do the same for herself.

"It only matters that I've heard it, and I believe it. You cannot force me to love a man like Vermund."

Hardar clapped his hands and fell back laughing. He toppled into his seat, his belly rippling with his laughter. Halla felt her face redden. At last Hardar wiped a tear from the corner of his eye. "I will have to remember that one. I'll never force you to love him. May Freya strike me blind if I ever do."

"You are blind already." She wanted to say more, yet even in her anger she had more sense.

"Mind your words, girl! There is no more to discuss. I've arranged for you to meet Vermund here in two days. Get yourself together and prepare to charm him. The future glory of my name depends on a good marriage. Now leave me."

Halla shook, her mind running over a hundred things to say. But she bit back her anger. Instead she gave him a sharp bow and strode out of the hall. She did not look back.

Outside the air hung still and muggy. She stalked away, going nowhere. Dana appeared from a shadow, asking if she was all right. Halla waved her hand to show she wanted to be alone. She followed the slope down to the where grass gave way to rocks and the sea. Waves purred on the beach as she stood looking out to the blue gray waters.

She thought of Toki. He could protect her from Vermund. Despite enjoying the constant sex and attention he paid her, she had not decided on what part he played in her future. The thrill of secret love-making with a handsome and confident man had been enough for her. But now she began to consider him more than a romantic diversion. He could save her from the trap her father had laid. Her father would not dare seek her in Ulfrik's lands, not with all of Ulfrik's warriors to oppose him. Eventually, her father would have to accept defeat and allow her freedom to choose her own husband.

A smile came to her lips. Toki was due to meet her the next day. She would ask Dana to prepare them to leave. Toki also would have to rescue Dana. She did not doubt he would take them both; he had talked often enough about it. Her only regret would be leaving her mother. But Halla had to be practical, or else she would end up worse than her mother. Brushing a strand of hair from her face, her smile broadened. By tomorrow, she would be away with Toki and have left her old life for freedom.

***

Toki and Bork rowed the choppy waves north. Neither had spoken much, but both grunted with the hard work. Bork complained when Toki shortened their rest breaks. Toki did not tell him what he planned. He barely understood it himself, following his instincts to meet Halla a final time.

The skies had threatened foul weather. Toki quailed at the winds gusting off the water. He feared the gods would drown him for breaking his oath. Clusters of gray clouds traveled above them, and both he and Bork stole glances skyward the whole trip.

Now they glided into the secret landing in the crevice. The water sloshed their ship back and forth. Toki's feet were sopping with seawater washed over the low sides of their boat. They angled for a series of flat rocks to make their landing, but an urgent voice called his name from the darkness. Both he and Bork pulled in their oars and searched for the source. Toki spotted Dana's slender form waving from an outcrop. "Lord Toki, please listen. Come closer."

"What's this?" Bork asked in a low growl. "Do you want me to stay?"

"I do. She seems afraid. Wait for my word after I've spoken with her."

Bork opened his mouth to reply, but rain drops started to patter on their heads. Both men scanned the clouds again, and Toki dreaded the storm he saw forming. A raindrop hit his eye and he jerked his head back. Dana hissed his name again.

He picked a path to the slave, and reaching her he noted she held several sealskin bags. She held them out. "Take these to your boat. Lady Halla and I will be leaving with you. Now that you have arrived, I will fetch her."

"You will what? Leave with me? That won't be possible. I mean, well, what's going on?" Toki felt his face grow hot. He had fantasized about running away with Halla, but now the promise of it brought him confusion rather than joy.

"You must speak to Lady Halla." Dana's voice was final, then she dashed up the rocks like a mountain goat. Toki opened the two bags, finding clothing, combs, jewelry, and other personal items. He cinched them shut and bore them down to Bork.

Bork had dragged the boat onto a wide, flat rock. But the sea grew rougher and he fought to keep the boat from sweeping off. "Damn this wind, Toki. I think I'll be staying with you until this blows over. We need to get this boat up on the grass or we're facing a long walk back over the mountains."

"Halla and her slave are leaving with us." Toki's tone was lifeless. He was so preoccupied with his thoughts, he didn't try to help Bork. "We are leaving as soon as she arrives."

A large wave sloshed the boat toward the water, and Bork nearly lost his footing. "Gods, Toki! Some help, please!"

Together they heaved the boat back onto the rocks and held it against the rising wind and waves. The rain started to fall stronger, and soon the storm would hit in force. They decided to carry the boat onto the thin strip of rocks against the cliff sides. If the storm worsened, they had to get it up the cliff or surrender it. Toki didn't like either option.

They waited in nervous silence as the rain held to a drizzle. Toki pumped his leg restlessly waiting for Dana's return. If Halla truly needed help, he could not refuse. She would not flee her home without cause. He decided Vermund had to be the trouble. His arms trembled at the thought of that thin face hovering close to Halla's. The man was a murderer, and a danger to all he loved. He could not let Halla be his next victim. Finally Bork spoke up.

"Why don't you tell me what's going on?"

Toki hung his head, water running into his eyes. "I'm sorry, my friend. I have been poor company." He explained how he had been caught and forbidden from meeting Halla. "But I needed to tell her myself. Now it seems she's in trouble."

Bork smiled and wiped the rain from his face. "That's why old

Bork has kept himself a single man. Life is less complicated."

The reappearance of Dana at the top of rocks interrupted their shared laughter. She called Toki's name then paused for a breath. "Get the boat on the water. Lady Halla is close behind, and is pursued."

"Pursued? What is going on? Is she in danger?"

"We're all in danger. Please, prepare the boat."

"On these waters, my boat will struggle with four people. Can your woman swim?" Bork didn't wait for an answer, but flipped the boat onto its keel. Toki helped him with it, slipping down the thin ledge as he did.

They fought to hold the boat steady against the slapping waves. Toki used a free hand to toss in Halla's bags while Bork replaced the oars. Once they finished, Dana was helping Halla down the steep path. She was covered in a sealskin cloak. Her pale hair splashed from the shadows of her hood. Dana walked backwards, holding both of Halla's hands. Lightning flashed in the gray skies behind her. She slipped with a squeal, then managed herself down to Toki's level.

"You must save me from my father. His men are right behind. Take me to your home, protect me!" She lifted her gray skirt with one hand and ran into Toki's embrace. He crushed her to his chest, and all resolve to honor his oath vanished. He felt her trembling under his arms and knew she needed him. The reasons did not matter to him, only that she had to be defended.

"I will protect you, Halla." She glanced back up the cliff, then Toki guided her to Bork who struggled with the boat. "Get aboard first and hold the sides. Dana, you go next."

The two women slipped easily onto the short benches, their

skirts sucking up the seawater that already puddled in the boat. Bork jumped in and gestured Toki do the same. The women sat between them as they dipped oars into the water.

Lightning flashed again, and this time thunder rolled in the distance. The small boat flopped on the waves like a leaf spinning on a pond. The two women screeched. Toki pulled hard on the oars and tried to point the boat toward the exit, though the incoming waves fought them.

"My father's men!" Halla pointed up the cliff and Toki saw the shapes of three men appear on the ridge. Their cloaks flapped and hair blew in the wind. One man started down the slope while another unslung his bow. One man cupped his mouth and shouted.

"Turn back! You are kidnapping Halla Hardarsdottir. You'll be hunted to the edge of the world!"

"Kidnapping?" Bork shouted over the women's head to Toki. "This is a bit more serious than I'd hoped."

"Row, you dog! They've got bows!"

The men on the ridge took their shots. Toki knew it was a waste of arrows, as the wind would blow them down and the rain would swell their bowstrings. It was an idle threat but he didn't want to be close enough for a lucky shot. Whatever they let loose did not reach the water.

"Does your father know you're with me?"

Halla shook her head. "I think he had someone following me. Only Dana ever knew about you."

Toki felt relieved, hoping he could evade Hardar's suspicion. The men were distant enough to make recognizing him difficult. Only his direction would give them a weak clue.

They finally broke out of the crevice and caught the open sea. The waves would shove them toward the rocks, and so they pointed farther out to safety. Hardar's men ran along the ridge, but soon they would be out of sight.

The first gust nearly capsized the boat. The rain began slashing down in strength. Everyone screamed as waves slammed into them. Toki spit the seawater onto the deck. He looked up and Dana covered Halla with her body. Bork was shaking his head like a dog coming out of a lake.

"We only have to get ahead of them. There's a shingle we can pull into not far from here. Wait out the storm there," Toki shouted across to Bork. "I think we made it away from them."

Bork nodded with a smile. Then Toki spotted a black shape emerge behind his shoulder. The man who had scrambled down the slope had fought to the mouth of the crevice, and now clambered up a rock. Waves crashed all around him, threatening to sweep the fool to his death. Toki saw him line up his bow. The wind and rain would foil the shot, even though he was not too distant. Toki nearly laughed.

Then the wind died. The bow twanged.

Bork's smile never faded as he fell sideways out of the boat. His oars slipped into the water. The wind gusted again, and without Bork's strength Toki fought to keep the vessels under control. He wanted to scream, but rain and spray hit him in the face. Halla and Dana both cried out. He looked again and Bork was gone, swallowed into the thrashing, foamy waves. They were already being blown around a bend and beyond sight of their enemies.

He rowed but was still driven to the rocks. He had to put Bork out of mind and focus on saving themselves. They were blown into a shallow cove, filled with only rocks and cliffs. But they were shielded from the wind and waves. Toki hoped to idle in this spot until the storm passed.

He searched once more for Bork, hoping that against all reason he would pop out of the water. He knew his friend had paid Fate's price for helping him. Toki shuddered, knowing the gods had only just begun to exact their vengeance.

CHAPTER EIGHT

The hall sat in leaden silence. Ulfrik drained his mug, savored the last mouthful, and swallowed. He carefully set it on the table. He folded his hands and wrenched a smile to his face. An insincere smile was better than expressing the rage beating at his temples. Nothing would be achieved in rage.

The hearth fire was at a low burn. The twilight beyond the hall could not penetrate within, so the flames danced a weak yellow light over the gathered men. Ulfrik scanned their faces around the table: Snorri, Ari, and Thorvald, all his closest men and confidants. None smiled. Toki huddled in a dry cloak beside the hearth, his head bowed and his bedraggled hair covering his face. His wet cloak dried by the hearth. Ulfrik heard Gunnar squealing outside in the distance where

Gerdie entertained him while Runa went to Toki's home to care for his two women.

"Friends," Ulfrik began, "we have important decisions to make. All of Nye Grenner might be affected by what we decide tonight."

"Too late for leaving us out of it," Thorvald said, casting a scowl at Toki from the high table. "He's already done the deed, and one of our own is dead for it."

"Don't you think I suffer for that?" Toki twisted to face them. "I will take that guilt to my grave."

"Before this is done you'll have more than one to think about in grave, that's for certain."

"Mind yourself," threatened Ulfrik. Of all the men he called together, only Thorvald had never sailed with Toki. He was the least inclined to understanding, though Ulfrik valued his opinions. "None of us agree with what Toki did. He broke an oath to the gods. That will be repaid as the gods deem fit."

Ari rubbed his face with both hands. His gnarled and thin form filled with shadow, making him appear carved from wood. "He broke an oath to you, too."

"And you broke your oath to Jarl Kjotve to serve me," Ulfrik replied. "Let's not throw spears at each other tonight. I gathered you to help decide the best response to this crisis. Hardar will consider this kidnapping his daughter. Toki sees it as rescuing a woman from a cruel man. What is the best response?"

His words echoed around the hall. Ulfrik smiled again, otherwise he wanted to scream. Toki had broken an oath, and oath-breakers were scum. But Toki was an old friend, a brother-in-law, and a good person.

Ulfrik knew him to be a man of high passions, guided by his sense of honor and duty. But his passions too often ruled him. Combined with the thrill of lust and danger, Ulfrik understood why Toki had been unable to resist Halla.

"Do you think it's a plot?" Snorri broke the extended silence. The thought hit Ulfrik like a hammer. Others sat up straighter at Snorri's question. Ulfrik faced Toki, and the others followed.

Toki shot to his feet, throwing his unbound cloak to the dirt floor. "Then it would be some piece of work! I saw Vermund pursuing her at the festival. She told me at the festival about her fears. Halla is innocent of a plot."

Thorvald snorted at Toki's protestations. But Ulfrik held up his hand. "I believe Halla to be innocent of guile. But that does not rule out Snorri's suspicion. Maybe Hardar planned this to ruin my reputation, or worse."

"He will be searching for his daughter," Snorri said, running his fingers through his gray beard. "He will come to at least ask for your help. The sensible thing is to turn her over immediately."

Ulfrik stared at Snorri, and could no longer force a smile. "And Hardar will demand justice. And justice for kidnapping his daughter would be Toki's life."

Everyone exchanged glances, but soon all turned to Toki. He stood trembling, pale and eyes wide, his mouth working soundlessly. Ulfrik felt a derisive laugh bubble in his throat, but swallowed it. He suspected Toki had never considered where his actions would lead. He stood from the bench and stepped down from the high table.

He gripped Toki's thick arm and squeezed. "I should hand you

95

over. But there is another way, and one I think Hardar much prefers: gold. It will be the second time I buy this fool's life for him."

Toki turned his head away and closed his eyes. Ulfrik released his grip with a shove. Thorvald drank from his mug, standing to challenge Ulfrik. "And what if Hardar won't accept gold?"

"Then it's war."

"War because this one wants a tumble with a jarl's daughter?" Thorvald jabbed his finger at Toki. "Don't we all want to fuck a princess? Should every man's blood be spilled for that?"

"Silence! I asked you here for your clear thinking and all I'm getting is poison. If Hardar refuses gold, he is being unreasonable. That shit of a man has been courting a fight since the festival. If that is his wish, then I will nail his head to my mast and sail it around the islands until it rots off. Like all of us, I pray the gods it will not come to that."

"Hardar is not alone. Others desire our wealth and will join him to steal from us. It's more than a fight between you and him. It's us against everyone else." Thorvald's voice was low and grave.

"I have allies as well, Ragnvald for example. You exaggerate the threat."

Ulfrik folded his arms over his chest. His head throbbed as he glared at Thorvald. The blacksmith's gaze faltered and he sat down again. Snorri and Ari both nodded in approval. Ulfrik then turned to Toki.

"I'm sorry, old friend. We cannot interfere in a father's plans for his daughter. And I can't accuse Jarl Vermund of being a murderer without better proof than third-hand rumor. The life of a jarl's daughter is a difficult one, particularly with a jarl like Hardar. I am going to return

Halla to her family, and again I forbid you from ever seeing her again."

Toki looked at him and swallowed. He nodded and clasped Ulfrik's shoulder. "I'll not defy you again. I have been chastened."

"I sincerely hope you are," Ulfrik said, his expression flat. "For if you defy me, you may never set foot on my land again. I will declare you an oath-breaker and outlaw. I have to protect my people, Toki. All of them."

***

Hardar arrived within a day of Toki pulling ashore with Halla and Dana. Ulfrik never doubted he would show, but he hadn't expected such dire news. The man before him wrung his hands, eyes darting around the hall. The exertion of frantic rowing had matted his hair flat. He repeated himself when Ulfrik did not respond. "All three of Hardar's ships are coming. Beast heads are mounted and shields are off the rails. We could see the gleam of their mail. Do you hear, Lord Ulfrik?"

Ulfrik watched the sweat trickle over his twisted nose. Runa sat next to him, frozen over her breakfast of salted whale meat. The hirdmen lining the tables held still and silent. Warm sunlight from the smoke hole framed the hall in a bright block.

Blinking away the shock, Ulfrik regained himself. "Gather the people to the hall. Summon the rest of the hird to the slope."

Ulfrik's wooden voice lacked power, but men snapped to their duties. Meals were abandoned and drinks spilled as they rushed to retrieve their weapons. Already a horn sounded. Ulfrik closed his eyes at the sound. "War again. How far must a man travel to escape it," he spoke to himself, rubbed his face, then faced Runa and Gunnar.

97

"What's happening, Father?" Gunnar's eyes were wide behind his dark bangs. He sat on Runa's lap, watching the hirdmen rushing from the hall.

"You will stay with your mother." Ulfrik looked into Runa's eyes, her face taut with fear. He brushed her cheek and whispered to her. "It may only be a show. Do not worry, wife. He is eager to embarrass me."

"I hope that is all he is eager for," she replied.

Ulfrik had no more time to spare. Snorri was behind the last of the hirdmen squeezing out of the hall. Ulfrik heard shouts and hurried voices. He pulled Snorri's arm. "Hold on. You need to get Toki and those two women. Bring them to the slope as fast as you can. I will stall Hardar, provided he isn't seeking battle."

Snorri nodded. "He didn't waste any time getting here. Do you think he knows already?"

Ulfrik shook his head. Snorri jogged off while a line of women and children queued at the entrance. Ulfrik returned to his room to wear his mail and helmet. He snatched them off the rack, toppling it in his haste. He gave the hall to Runa, who was organizing and calming the confused people cramming inside. Nye Grenner had never been raided, and many had never experienced that terror before. Ulfrik hoped they wouldn't experience it today.

Outside, his men formed a loose block of gleaming helmets and sparkling mail. Thorvald's talent as a smith was unparalleled, and it showed in the state of the hirdmens' gear. A crew of men were pulling Ulfrik's ships up slope to protect them from capture. On the sparkling turquoise water, three square sails of red and white billowed in the distance. Men crowed the forecastles, spear points flashing. Ulfrik joined

Thorvald at the front rank beneath a pole flying Nye Grenner's standard, a flag of green with black elk antlers.

"Looks like Toki's adventure brought us a fight after all." Thorvald smiled without mirth. Ulfrik ignored him and addressed his men. He felt a swell of pride at how fast they had assembled.

"You know those sails. You know those men. They are Hardar's folk. You may have drank with them, sung songs with them. But if they step foot on our land intending murder, then you kill them. We protect our families, protect our lands. We are for Nye Grenner!"

Ulfrik pumped his fist to the sky and the men roared back and stomped the ground. Eighty men in mail coats raised a massive din aimed at cowing the approaching foe. Ulfrik turned to face Hardar as his sails trimmed and the ships glided to the thin strip of beach. He stood out on the prow of his ship. Despite his size, he gracefully leapt into the shallows to wade ashore. His crews piled out of their ships, dragging the vessels onto the beach. Ulfrik squinted at him down the slope.

Hardar's men huddled behind him like boys behind their mothers. They stood in the rolling surf for reasons Ulfrik did not understand. Seals barked on distant rocks, and the creak of leather and crunch of mail were the only other sounds. Ulfrik inhaled the sea air, waiting.

Snorri and Toki joined the front ranks. Ulfrik leaned forward to see Toki, his face haggard and drawn. "Your woman's father has something to say to us, and I doubt it's about hosting your wedding."

Everyone's attention turned back to Hardar. His men moved out of the surf but halted while he and two other men continued up the slope. Ulfrik raised his fist, and his men answered by stomping their feet and banging their shields in time. The thunderous sound stopped Hardar halfway up. Ulfrik held his chin high as the rhythmic beating intimidated Hardar's untrained men. He tapped Snorri and Thorvald. "You two come with me to witness what he has to say. Toki, you best remain here."

Thorvald planted the standard in the soft ground, then all three approached Hardar. He waited with his hands on his hips, standing before his two men. He wore freshly scoured mail that bulged tight around his middle. His breeches were white with red stripes, his personal colors. A scowl contorted his pale eyes as they searched Ulfrik's face.

"Just thought you'd bring the men by to say hello?" Ulfrik asked, then smirked.

"Where's my daughter?"

His stomach burned at the question, as he hadn't checked if she had accompanied Toki. He hoped Snorri would reply, but he remained mute. "She's ready to travel home. You can take her now."

Hardar's bluster faltered, but he scanned past Ulfrik and his scowl returned. "Then where is she?"

"She's coming, as soon as your men board their ships. You shouldn't have come with an army at your back. I might think you want to start a fight."

Hardar held his belly and laughed. Ulfrik shifted his weight and folded his arms, waiting for Hardar to regain himself. "Your wit is better than the last time I was here. Of course I come to fucking fight! You kidnapped my daughter and sent spies into my land."

Ulfrik frowned. "You misunderstand, Hardar. Your daughter ran away from you, and one of my men was love struck enough to want to save her. You have my word it was nothing more."

"Your word, eh?" Hardar flashed an evil smile, then tapped the man next to him. "Dag, give me the sack."

Ulfrik watched a black cloth sack that hung full and heavy pass into Hardar's grip. He plunged his hand inside while addressing Ulfrik. "Seems there is a misunderstanding. But it's yours. We found this man creeping around my hall."

Hardar yanked out a severed head, holding it by the hair. Ulfrik did not flinch, not a twitch. The face was slack and white, its features soft and distorted. But he knew it was Bork without having to study it. Poor Bork's milky eyes were rolled back and his tongue swelled to fill his open mouth. Both Thorvald and Snorri sucked a breath, and Ulfrik's men protested and shouted from behind. Ulfrik held up his open hand to silence them.

"I know the man, and he drowned at sea if the arrow hadn't done him already. The body must have washed up on your shores. You're playing a dangerous game, Hardar."

Hardar raised Bork's head higher. "Am I? You steal my daughter, hide her from me, and freely admit your men were spying in my lands. Yet I play the dangerous game." Hardar dropped the head into the sack and thrust it back to the man named Dag. "Turns out the arrow didn't kill him. We found him clinging to a rock, begging for help. He wouldn't cooperate even after saving his life. So we made him confess. He told us he was collecting information for you."

"That's a lie. You tortured him into a lie."

"That he was to report everything he could learn directly to you."

"Another lie, pig."

"So that when you invaded ..."

"Enough, you fucking swine!" Ulfrik's sword sprung from its scabbard. The blade hummed and flashed white in the sun. Hardar held still, the point of the blade inches from his neck. His hirdmen reached for their weapons, though Hardar raised a hand to stop them.

Snorri pulled down Ulfrik's blade. "You're letting him bait you. You're better than that. This is a parley, not a fight. Not yet, anyway."

Ulfrik licked his lips then rammed his sword into its scabbard. "You killed one of my men. You know the truth of what you did. Bork was innocent. That I ever admired you is the most disgusting error of my life. You'll take your whore of a daughter and be gone, never to return. If you even face south to take a piss I'll gut you."

Hardar's eyes drew to slits and he straightened his back. "I'll have my daughter and the bastard who kidnapped her. I'll have his head in the sack with the other one. Then I can say justice is done."

"How much do you want for his life? You know I can pay."

"I know you can pay. But his life is what I want. It's the only way I know my daughter is safe from him."

Ulfrik and Hardar stood with eyes locked. Ulfrik's hands began to tremble; the desire to draw his sword on Hardar was a maddening burn in his hand. But a chance for peace existed, and duty demanded he push for it. "Twenty pounds of silver is more than fair. It is a fortune."

Hardar slowly shook his head. The longer he resisted the more he seemed a pig to Ulfrik.

"Thirty pounds of silver. It's near all I have."

"Dumb as he is, the boy's head is probably only a pound. I'll take that and my daughter."

Ulfrik bit his lip. He repeated his offer, and Hardar did not respond. Ulfrik closed his eyes, a bead of sweat streaked down his temple. "If you are not back on your ships by the time I reach my line, I'll fill you with arrows. Return when you are prepared to reason."

Ulfrik spun on his heels, not waiting for Hardar's reaction. He stalked up the slope and barked his commands. "Rank up! Archers ready on my order!"

Grim as his mood was, Ulfrik smiled at the efficiency of his men's response. Shields clacked together into a wall. Spears bristled from behind. Then a block of archers stepped off the back ranks and placed arrows to their strings. The endless drilling and real-life raiding had forged true warriors of them.

Ulfrik reached his line and turned. Snorri and Thorvald fell in with him. Hardar's men were rushing to their ships, though Hardar lingered on the beach. He raised his fist. "I came alone this time, Ulfrik. But I will be back with others!"

Ulfrik ordered one of the archers to pass his bow and an arrow over to Snorri. Hardar continued to curse him as his ships were launching. "Snorri, put an arrow between his feet and give him something to think about."

Snorri smiled, took the bow and aimed. Hardar saw the shot lining up and stumbled back. Snorri released and the arrow arced down the slope to stick at Hardar's feet. He danced away, falling backward into the surf. A wave broke over him and Ulfrik and all his men burst into laughter.

Hardar staggered to his feet and slogged to his ship. Once aboard, he came to the stern and hurled more curses as the ships' oars dipped into the water, pushing them out to the fjord.

"What happened?" Toki asked.

"We just went to war with the strongest and most popular man in all the Faereyjar Islands."

CHAPTER NINE

Hardar craned his neck forward, straining to see against the rosy light of evening. All three of his ships bobbed and drifted with the rolling tide. Gulls screamed above as if daring him to sail. "This is unbelievable," he muttered to himself.

"They don't look hostile," Dag offered, standing below Hardar in the prow.

"Six ships beached on my shore with crews ranked up look friendly to you, Dag? Save me the strength and throw yourself overboard."

"Lord Hardar, they could've burnt the whole place to cinders by now. And those are big ships. Why not capture us and have done with it? They could do it, I think."

Hardar grunted at Dag's words. He jumped down to the deck and surveyed his men. *The fools shit themselves when Ulfrik's warriors threatened*, he thought. They stared at him with wide eyes and slack expressions. He had to speak before one of them started crying for family left behind.

"All right, I don't know where these ships came from or what's waiting for us ashore. They obviously see us, and they're not attacking. Yet. So let's get ashore and learn what these dogs want." He added under his breath, "As if I don't already know."

Hardar waved his hand overhead to signal the other ships. He strode between his men back to the tiller, each watching him as he passed. Ignoring them, he grasped the tiller and bellowed. "Row, you dogs, or I'll put the whip to your backs!"

Their ships nosed toward the shore, and the line of invaders shifted to face them as they approached. The invaders were as well equipped as Ulfrik's men, though they didn't display the same crisp discipline. Despite their numbers, Hardar felt less threatened than he had been by the control Ulfrik exerted over his warriors.

He leapt from his ship to meet an enemy for the second time that day. His ships landed down the rocky beach, out of enemy bow range. He shouted orders as his crews hauled their ships aground. As they formed up behind him, Hardar strode toward the invaders. "Dag, with me."

The leader was a giant wrapped in animal pelts. He detached from the dark line of warriors, who disappeared into the brilliance of the low sun. Only then did Hardar realize the crafty enemy had positioned him to fight into the glare. It made his stomach roil. He stopped halfway and set his feet wide and folded his arms. The enemy would come to him. He wasn't giving another inch.

The giant man lumbered forward with two other men. He halted a spear length away from Hardar. Muscle rippled beneath leathery, tanned skin. His hair and beard were shaggy and gray. He looked like he hadn't washed in a month.

"I want to talk to your leader, not a trained bear," Hardar said.

The giant man smiled with his few yellow teeth. A white scar danced on his cheek as he did. "I am Jarl Kjotve the Rich, King of Agder. You must be the famous Jarl Hardar Hammerhand."

"The bear speaks, too. That's also a famous name you use. Harald Finehair spilled Kjotve's guts and took his kingdom. So give me another name before I lose patience."

The smile fled the man's face and his dark, animal eyes flashed. "You think me a liar? Were you at Hafrsfjord, Hardar Hammerhand? Harald slew my son, enslaved my family, and stole my land. But he did not kill me. Now you know the truth. A man a hundred times more royal than you has paid your shit-pile village a visit, and you call him a liar. This is not what I expected from you."

Kjotve bore down on Hardar and scowled. Hardar felt like a mast was about to fall on him, and stepped back. Shame burned on his cheeks when he realized that he had given ground. "Then forgive me, Jarl Kjotve. News is rarer than trees in these lands. But you can hardly expect my hospitality, not with a hundred men and six ships laid out on my shore. Have you blown off course?"

Kjotve's smile grew and he stood straighter. Hardar looked past him at the blurry line of men. Errant flashes rolled off their helms, but none stirred or indicated attack. He looked back at Kjotve, who folded his arms loosely across his chest. Gold and silver armbands glinted under the sleeve of mail. "I've placed my men in the open and not in the most strategic spot. I wanted you to know we have no ill intent."

"That's why you're all readied for war then?"

"We have to be prepared for anything from you. Besides, I could've plundered your home three times over since you left this morning. I've been to visit your wife, Ingrid. She is a charming and beautiful woman."

"If you touched her, I'll have your balls." His hand reached for his sword; a vision of Ingrid welcoming this brute to their bed flashed in his mind. Kjotve's two companions grabbed their own sword hilts. But Kjotve laughed.

"I may have brushed her hand when she gave me a horn of mead. But otherwise, I've been a behaved guest. Let's come to the point, Hardar. I am here because I think we can help each other."

Hardar's gut tightened and he raised his chin. "Meaning that you can use me before turning on me. You've come for my treasure, haven't you?"

Again Kjotve laughed, a bark from the deep of his throat. "You trust no one. That is good! Trust should be as rare as gold and just as seldom given. Aye, you are useful to me. You are the greatest jarl in these lands, yes?"

Hardar peered at him, holding his words. Kjotve continued, his smile fading.

"But you are troubled by another. You have a rival."

Hardar scratched his beard. "You seem to know much about me, too much for my liking."

"I know a great deal. I will share something with you now. Your rival owes me a debt. Your rival is an oath-breaker and a coward. Your rival is a man I wish to destroy. Do we have a common interest, Jarl Hardar Hammerhand?"

Hardar's eyes grew wider with each word. His mouth nearly watered at the possibilities he imagined with Kjotve's help. "If you are speaking of Ulfrik Ormsson, then we share that interest."

"Let us stand down our men and return to your hall. We have much to discuss." Kjotve's smile furrowed lines into his cheeks. Hardar found himself matching that smile. He scanned the ranks of Kjotve's warriors, and saw how Ulfrik would die.

***

Hardar shoved Ingrid aside, "For the last time, I did all that could be done. An attack would've been disaster."

He peeked out of his room into the main hall. Kjotve and his warriors appeared content to drink his mead. The smoky hall glowed orange with the blazing hearth, sparked to life so Hardar could host a feast to welcome his guests. His own men had to wait outside, so full was the hall with Kjotve's crews. A thin man stood on the table, recounting a tale that drew raucous laughter from his audience.

"I don't care about disaster," Ingrid said with a sob. "My little girl is gone, and you didn't save her."

"Gods woman, she fled by her own free will. She's happier there. I just hope she won't hike her skirt for that ass-dropping she ran off with. Vermund expects a virgin."

109

The slap did not hurt as much as it surprised Hardar. He turned into it, about to push Ingrid back into their room. Stunned, he put a hand to his cheek while she cursed him. "How can you know? Why would she be happier away from her family?"

"I know because she told me. Now don't worry for her. Ulfrik thinks he can scare me, calling her a hostage. He'd never harm her, especially with his brother-in-law besotted with her. She's safe. Now hide yourself and sit on your hands. If you raise them to me again, I'll break your fingers."

He didn't bother with her reaction, instead striding to Kjotve's side at the high table. Immediately he stiffened in anger. Kjotve was lounging in his chair, one leg thrown over the armrest. "I see you've found a comfortable chair for yourself."

Kjotve clapped and laughed as the man on the table bowed in a circle with an exaggerated flourish. He didn't look at Hardar as he replied. "Aye, it's a fine bit of work. Just the right size, too. I think I'll keep it."

Hardar began to protest, but Kjotve chuckled. "Look at you. I joke, Jarl Hardar. I'm sitting in your chair, yes? Then I return it to you. I thought you'd be longer with your woman. I know how time at sea can make a man eager for his woman."

"Er, yes, sure," Hardar scratched his head while Kjotve stood up. The size of the man still amazed Hardar, who was himself taller than most. "But let us both sit on benches tonight. I'm eager for your news, Jarl Kjotve."

They moved to benches and Hardar's slave attended. For a while they spoke of trifles, Hardar trying to get the measure of his guest. Soon he no longer doubted Kjotve was who he claimed to be. Despite being dispossessed of his land, Kjotve called himself a sea-king. He traveled the world in search of plunder, making landfall wherever he desired. Hardar thought it sounded like a horrible existence, but Kjotve seemed pleased enough. "I'm fresh from the Orkneyjar, had a narrow escape from Hrolf the Ganger. If you marvel at my height, he dwarfs me. But long legs mean nothing on a slow ship, eh Jarl Hardar?"

Soon they were at their meal and talk lulled. Kjotve ate like a starved man and was picking fish bones out of his mouth before Hardar was halfway done. He renewed their conversation, a greasy finger probed his back teeth and marred his speech. "So you are satisfied with my tale? Now we speak of how we benefit each other."

Hardar drained his mug, then wiped his beard with the back of his hand. "It's all I've been waiting for."

The men below were drunk, and their arguing and shouting reverberated through the hall. The thin man remounted the table and started bawling out a tuneless song. Both Hardar and Kjotve watched him as they spoke.

"I picked up trading ships returning from these lands," Kjotve said as he watched the thin man struggle with his balance. "They were wise enough to pay a king tribute on his own estate. Since the traders were generous, I let them go. But they carried much gold for traders plying islands I thought harbored only poor sheep herders. How wrong I have been these years. They mentioned you as the wealthiest in the islands, but they spoke of a new power: Ulfrik. I got what news I needed from them. Seems like you've been talking up your fears of Ulfrik conquering these islands."

Kjotve turned to him with a grin. Hardar's mouth dropped open. He hadn't realized he had been so open with traders. "Why else build up so much military strength? He's totally out of line, acting like he's some sort of high king. Giving out gifts and parading his warriors, it's ridiculous."

Kjotve's smile deepened. "But your warriors are no match for his, and you know it."

"Nonsense! He has stolen my daughter, and I sailed to his land to show him my power. He has a lot to think about now."

"And where is your daughter? Did you leave her on your ship?" Kjotve leaned back and smirked. Hardar felt his face grow hot, and turned back to the thin man singing and spinning on the table. Men laughed or threw scraps and bones at him. Kjotve paused dramatically before continuing.

"Ulfrik has stolen your daughter and yet all your men did not convince him to release her. Let's be honest, his men scare you because they are warriors. Your men, I saw their faces. They are farmers who row your ships and carry spears for you. What you need are warriors, and I bring warriors."

Kjotve's hand swept over the heads of his men. Hardar looked at them anew. They were well geared and battle-scarred. "My men are not as bad as you say. But they are outnumbered and out-geared. I have been gulled into thinking my neighbor was peaceful all these years."

Kjotve gave a gusty laugh. "No neighbor is at peace for long. I have learned that lesson with my blood and the blood of my kin." Kjotve's laughter tore away and he leaned so close to Hardar that he flinched. "I want Ulfrik. He was sworn to me, and fled when his oath

112

still bound him. He could've made the difference. He could've saved my kingdom. I sheltered him when he had nothing! Now he has lands and gold and your daughter. What shall we do about this?"

"Hang his head on a pole and let birds eat it."

"Yes! I have a hundred men and six ships. Together, we would crush him and divide the spoils!"

Hardar was about to leap off the bench and shout agreement. But looking into Kjotve's eyes, he saw they darted and shifted. Something was wrong, and the doubt calmed him. "You have enough men to ruin him yourself. Why invite me to this?"

"You are the ruler of these islands. If I attack from nowhere, for no reason, you understand, then you might unite the others against me. I only want to shatter Ulfrik and take from him what is owed."

"I am not the ruler of these islands," Hardar said, though he sat up straighter at hearing the idea. "But what you say is true. Now that I know your intent, I wonder why divide the spoils with me?"

"Fair is fair, Jarl Hardar," Kjotve's eyes widened and his brows furrowed. "Besides, I know Ulfrik and I know his men. He trains them, disciplines them, and gets them experience. He served me only a short time, but his instincts for leading men in battle impressed me. I will not underestimate him, and neither should you."

Hardar nodded, but Kjotve still left him vexed. Hardar understood men like Kjotve, and greed was their motivating force. Kjotve would seize everything after battle and leave him with nothing. Hardar wanted a better guarantee of fairness than a raider's word. "I won't underestimate him. I agree with you, Jarl Kjotve. But I am not the only one with an interest in Ulfrik. He has stolen my daughter, who is promised to another jarl. Honor would dictate that he participate in the attack as well, if only to save his betrothed from that evil bastard."

Kjotve leaned back and stroked his beard. His eyes darted about as he thought, making Hardar uneasy. "So the spoils would be split three ways. I have a large crew and I doubt Ulfrik hordes enough gold to make it worth my time. Revenge is fine for me, but my men need more."

"It would be an insult to leave my friend out of this. I cannot have it another way." Hardar leaned both arms on the table and glanced at the guests. The thin man had finally been pulled down and someone dumped a horn of mead over his head, causing an explosion of laughter.

"I will discuss it with my crew, but you and your friend will need me no matter what. My only condition, and you must agree to this, is that Ulfrik be given to me. He must face justice from my hands and no other. What do you say, Jarl Hardar?"

Hardar did not hesitate. Ulfrik was a match for both him and Vermund. "It is a fair start. Let's drink to the fall of Ulfrik and Nye Grenner."

CHAPTER TEN

Ulfrik stood before every man in Nye Grenner. They assembled in the thick grass, murmuring in low voices. Concern was written in the creases of the men's faces, and vibrated in the timbre of their voices. Women and children either waited in the hall or remained at their homes. Ulfrik thought of Runa, and how she had quivered to restrain tears at hearing the news. He wished he could be with her, but his first duty fell to the people under his protection.

The sun hung fat and low in the sky, turning the high clouds pink. It would not vanish for several more hours despite the late hour. A balmy breeze shuffled the grass. In the distance, white dots of a sheep herd crossed the green slopes. Ulfrik held his arms tightly behind his back until the murmurs died, then cleared his throat.

"You all know why I've had to call this meeting. But I wanted you to hear the news from me. Halla Hardarsdottir fled to my lands, seeking protection from a man she fears. I cannot say if her fears are true. But she came to us of her own will, and Toki has offered her shelter. Now Hardar claims she has been kidnapped and demands her return. I would have been glad to do this, but he also demanded Toki's life. He refused a payment of silver instead. So now he has fled and vowed to return with allies. We are at war."

Men spoke all at once. Snorri and Toki sat at the front, and both turned to the crowd to ask their silence. Ulfrik let the initial reactions subside before he continued.

"War is all Hardar wants, and so he shall have it. Each of my hirdmen are worth three of his. He counts on allies and numbers to crush us. He is wrong. We will send his men to the feasting hall, seize his flocks and wealth, and put an end to his threat."

Men clapped or shouted in agreement, but not all did. The young and warlike seemed eager to find glory in the shield wall. But the older men, the family men, frowned or blinked silently. One voice shouted louder than the others. "You gamble all our lives for one man. Who wants war if not you?"

Ulfrik started at the accusation, and the rush of voices dropped. He recognized the man, an old farmer, and realized he had two sons in the hird. The pulse in Ulfrik's neck throbbed, even though he had expected such a rebuttal. "I know it seems an unfair trade. But if it were your life, would you feel the same? Toki did not commit the crime Hardar claims. He does not deserve death."

Toki hung his head and picked at the grass. Ulfrik felt an

116

awkward mix of sympathy for his guilt and satisfaction at his suffering. His rash action had cost Ulfrik his peace. The crowd returned to grumbling, a few voices calling out in support and others demanding to reconsider. Ulfrik's patience flagged.

"Hardar has no right to demand any of our lives without better proof than his own stories. Where does it stop if I surrender Toki? Will he then demand another life for another imagined crime? Law must rule or we will have chaos."

"Where is his daughter now? If you return her, his rage might cool, but never if you keep her."

Ulfrik paused, knowing there was truth in the claim. He glanced again at Toki, who continued to hang his head. "She is my hostage now. Hardar will not dare much with his own daughter's life at stake."

"She is Toki's lover," shouted a voice from the back rows. "You keep her for his pleasure!"

Men stood and the uproar echoed over the field. Toki leapt up and spun to curse the anonymous accuser. Ulfrik paced from one end of the crowd to the other, waving men down and begging for calm. He wished he had something to bang or a horn to blast. But he could do no more than yell over the confused voices until he prevailed.

"Silence! By the gods, stop your bickering! Listen!" The crowd grumbled a few moments longer, then returned their attention to Ulfrik. "Now, I keep her as my hostage and she fulfills that role before any other. Hardar cannot gamble with the life of his only child. I am no murderer, and I could no more kill her than I could kill a baby. But if Hardar attacks and she is in the hall with your women, will he burn it down? Does that help you understand the benefit to her presence?"

117

Ulfrik folded his arms and glared at this man. He avoided Toki's gaze, even though he felt it hot upon his own. Just as it seemed calm might prevail, another voice rose up.

"Is it true Toki broke an oath to the gods when he took in Halla?"

Ulfrik felt as if he had swallowed ice. His belly fluttered at the question. "Who asked that?" Toki's oath had only been known to Ulfrik's closest men. None of them would have spread this secret, yet one had.

Silence blanketed the group. Every expression turned stony and every face turned to Ulfrik. He attempted to assemble a response, scrambling for the right words. But Toki jumped in front of Ulfrik as if to shield him from an arrow.

"My oath is to the gods and not to you. But I will answer, since my actions have brought worry to your homes. Yes, I vowed to never see Halla again. I made a mistake, and the gods will have their vengeance upon me." Toki's head drooped and his voice became a whisper. "And they have already begun. Guilt is a worm that eats my heart."

Ulfrik placed his hand on Toki's shoulder and guided him to his side. "It is as the old sayings go: 'Nothing good can happen to a man who breaks his solemn vows.' But it is not our place to judge Toki, for many of us have broken small oaths. And many of us have not dared to take a heavy oath, and tested our own will. Let the gods deal with Toki. We must deal with Hardar."

The assembled men shifted and looked away, but many still folded their arms in dissent. Ulfrik leaned toward Toki. "Don't worry, old friend. It is easy to make accusations. I will bring them around."

Toki shook his head. "It is not for you to bring them around to me. It is my task. You focus on Hardar."

Ulfrik patted Toki's back, then addressed the crowd again. "We have much to prepare. If we suspected Hardar of raiding sheep or disputing fishing grounds before, we can plan on worse aggression. I want the levy prepared, and each man to take their flocks upland if you haven't already. We will watch from the cliffs, prepare beacons to warn us if Hardar returns. In the meantime, I will plan our attack with my war leaders. That is all for tonight."

He waved his hand in dismissal, and the crowd divided and wandered away. Ulfrik watched the two groups forming: men who were prepared to fight and those who were not. He spoke to no one in particular. "No matter what my plans, the first battle will be at home."

***

Halla's eyes and head throbbed from two days of crying and worrying. Muscles she never knew existed burned after the struggle to hold fast during the storm at sea. Even now, safely on land, she still felt the violent rocking of the ocean. When she closed her eyes, her mind replayed Toki's friend tumbling overboard with an arrow in his back, his smile incongruent with the moment of death. She knew no peace, no rest, since that moment.

She sat at the edge of Toki's bed while Dana sat on the floor, picking at her tattered dress and humming softly. Toki's home made her feel like she was in a box. The small fire pit was unlit and the smoke hole open. A watery light spilled down and outlined Toki's few possessions that hid in the dark corners. The home was uninviting and unused, a

119

place for ghosts and forgotten dreams.

One of her dresses was balled up and tossed into a corner. It had been ruined during the flight to this place. She and her mother had made it together. The thought of her mother brought shudders of sadness, but her tears were spent. She expected to never see her mother again. Everything she took from her old life was stuffed in a sealskin bag that now lay on Toki's bare dirt floor.

Dana noticed Halla was now sitting up, and leapt to her feet. Her delicate face was smeared with dirt, but her smile came through. "Lady Halla, I didn't realize you were awake. Master Toki is away, but promised to return soon."

"I never slept," Halla said, stiffly rising to her feet. "My mind is too busy for it."

"You need sleep," Dana chided. "You must look your best for Master Toki."

Halla's shoulders slumped. "He favored me well enough to risk his life. Let him see me as I am, which is tired and unhappy."

"Lady Halla, you have to charm the others too. You need friends here, if this is our new home."

Halla walked the short distance to the door, pushed it open and welcomed more light and fresh air. She didn't dare leave, as if crossing the threshold would commit her life to Nye Grenner forever. The thought of Nye Grenner being a new home had appeal, until her father had complicated that possibility. *Now I will become a hostage*, she thought while turning back inside. *I am still a piece on my father's game board, only on his opponent's side. What have you gained for all you've done?*

"What do you think of this place as a new home, Dana?"

She shrugged her shoulders and sat on the floor again. "I won't miss your father's temper. Otherwise, it's all the same for me. My home is far away from here, Lady Halla."

"How foolish of me, sorry." Dana smiled, and Halla continued. "If Toki is the man I hope he is, maybe one day you can return home. My father kept you as my slave, but I think of you like a sister."

Dana's hugged her knees and looked away. Halla sat on the floor across from her, leaning against a bench coated in dust. Halla wondered at the dust. *Does no one ever visit here? Will this lonely house become a prison?* She pushed the answers down into her mind. She didn't want to guess.

She heard footfalls approaching and a shadow crossed the open door. She didn't stir, but Dana scrambled to her feet and faced the entrance. Toki's dark shape filled the doorway. He paused, curly hair and cape stirring in a summer breeze. His hands were working the belt that held his sword. When it came free, he entered and absently dropped the weapon into a corner.

"You are awake. You must be hungry now."

Halla nodded slowly. The engaging and intelligent conversations of days past had become three and four word sentences since she arrived. She sensed Toki struggle to keep a pleasant face.

"When you are ready, I will take you to the hall. My sister's cooking is famous."

"So you've said about twenty times in two days." Halla stood, and Toki extended his hand to assist. He still smiled, and she felt her face grow warm. "I'm sorry. You didn't deserve that. I'm being terrible."

"It is a difficult time for both of us." Toki stepped back from her once she had her feet.

121

"To be honest, I don't want to go to the hall. Could you bring something back to me?"

He stared at her, his lips tightening as he did. "It's time you came to the hall with me. You will be here a long while yet, so there's no shame in going to the hall."

Halla trembled and feared she might cry again. Toki had been more patient than she had expected, but he must have a limit. She dreaded to find it, and learn what he would do to her. An image of her mother sprawled out and cradling her face as her father leaned over her popped into Halla's mind.

"I am a hostage, am I not? That means Ulfrik must hate me."

Toki laughed, placing both hands on his hips. "He does not hate you. What he must tell the people and his true heart are two different matters. He will welcome you and treat you well."

"How can you know his heart?"

"We have faced death together, many times. We are brothers, Ulfrik and me, not of blood but of the sword. We know each other's minds."

"Then did he know you would seek me after vowing to the gods you would not?" Halla asked intending to deflate his confidence. But she saw her words had struck deeper. Toki's face clouded and he turned away, walking farther into house. He unpinned his cloak and threw it on his bed, then sat on a bench. Dana stepped back, trying to disappear and not knowing where to look. Halla dismissed her with a nod. Once Dana had exited, Halla sat beside Toki and placed her hand on his knee.

"I have made a mess of things, for you and me. For everyone on this island. I was foolish to think my father would not act as he has."

Toki smiled and covered her hand with his, warm and rough on her skin. "Neither of us planned things well. I am not so good at planning, and hoped you'd be stronger at it than me. Forethought is better than afterthought, they say. I will learn that lesson one day."

They both laughed, and Toki squeezed her hand tighter. He met her eyes, his expression becoming earnest. "But we followed our hearts. Can that be wrong between a man and woman? I will make you glad for your choice."

Halla tensed at the weight of his words. She had fled to him seeking escape from Vermund. As rash as it seemed now, she did not expect to marry Toki, not immediately. But then what had she been thinking? She pulled her hand from Toki, and touched her head. She had made so many mistakes, and hoped to avoid making more. Yet she did not know what was right.

"I'm sure I will be glad, Toki. But nothing is settled. My father is at war with your lord, and so you are sworn to battle against him. Does that mean you would kill him? Would you kill my father?"

His eyes grew wide, and Halla seized on that idea. She needed to create space for herself, to avoid being rushed into marriage with a man she did not honestly know.

"If I had to defend my lord, my sister and nephew, then I would." Halla heard the iron in his voice. He gave her a hard look, then studied the floor at his feet.

"And if you had to defend yourself?"

"I would do what I must," he snapped, twisting on the bench to snarl at her. "This is an odd situation, and I understand. But what would you have me do? Allow myself to be gutted? Beg the gods it will never

123

happen, and that your father will come to his senses and accept payment for my life."

The tears finally began to run again as Toki glared at her. She wished she were back home, even with her father and Vermund. She longed for her mother, badly enough that her sorrow broke through. She had prodded Toki, at last finding his limits. Thinking of him killing her own father filled her with horror. He was a miserable man, but she didn't want her father dead.

Toki blew out a long breath and rose from his bench. Halla watched him stand through tear clouded eyes. If he disowned her, then she would truly be alone in this land. The panic began to build, and she found herself blurting out her thoughts. "I want to go home to my mother."

Toki had fetched his cloak from the bed, but froze at her words. Then he spoke and threw his cloak across his shoulders. "That would be unwise. You are under my protection here."

"So I am your hostage!" She stood now, her heart racing and a stream of worries flooding her mind. "I thought I meant more to you than that?"

Toki fixed his cloak pin, and smiled at her. "I will let you decide whether you are a hostage or otherwise." Without another glance he pushed past her and paused at the door. "I will bring you back something after I eat. I trust you will remain here if you won't come with me?"

Halla didn't answer. She sniffled instead, lost for anything to say. Toki grabbed his sword out of the dark corner where he had dropped it.

"If you plant to visit your mother, men watch this home and

watch the shores. Stay inside if you won't consider being my guest." He ducked out of the door. Halla watched the shadow grow smaller until he had gone.

She collapsed to the bench and began to sob, wishing she could undo the past two days.

***

The last of Ulfrik's men locked into place in the battle line. Ulfrik paced before them, mail flashing in the afternoon sun. He tucked his helmet underarm so he could peer into the eyes of each man as he passed. Nye Grenner's green standard with black elk antlers cracked and snapped overhead. On this pleasant afternoon full of wind and high clouds, where seals barked merrily on the rocks and the air was redolent of the sea, war would visit Nye Grenner.

Smoke from the beacon on the cliffs overlooking the northern entrance to the fjord struggled against the wind, but had given its warning nonetheless. He judged Hardar's ships to appear within the hour of the smoke appearing. He planned to richly reward the two boys manning the beacon fires. Their sharp eyes had proved as valuable as any weapon. From his vantage on the hill, he spied the first sails on the glistening water. He watched with his men, his mouth silently moving as he counted the sails.

Ulfrik called his army to attention. He held them in momentary silence, reviewing them and judging their will. Satisfied he saw no weakness, he planted himself before them and thundered out his speech.

"Make no mistake, today we are called to defend our lands. Hardar's intent is clear: to reduce our homes to ashes and tears. If you count the sails behind me now, you will see he has bent others to evil. No matter. All foes will wash away on the tide of blood before this day is done. We stand on this ground and we do not budge. We do not show mercy. We accept only victory. We fight for family, unlike Hardar and his jealous friends who fight only for pride. The gods love us and will grant us justice. We deliver the gods' justice at the point of our blades!"

Ulfrik thrust his fist into the air and his men followed, shouting in one voice. Ulfrik's heart thrummed at the grit and determination arrayed before him. Without looking back, Ulfrik knew the ships closed on the shore.

"Remember how we have drilled. Follow my command and those of my seconds. Protect yourself and protect your shield-brother. Then let your blades speak for you. Your families are safe in the hall, and Hardar will want to threaten it. He knows you will worry for your kin. Forget about the hall. If we stand here there is no way for him to reach it. You do not leave this hill; you do not leave your position! Do as I've ordered, and victory will follow. For Nye Grenner!"

The men roared back as Ulfrik joined the center of the line. Snorri gave an approving nod as Ulfrik donned his helmet, drawing the cheek plates closed. On his right, Toki gripped the banner of Nye Grenner. His stoutest warriors formed the front ranks, and many ranks back his trained hirdmen bristled with spears and axes. Behind them, Ulfrik had clustered bowmen drawn from the levy.

"Plant that banner, Toki. We are not moving from this place." Toki grunted and drove the banner pole into the soft earth.

"Well, now this is a surprise," Snorri said under his breath. "Where did Hardar raise this many ships?"

Ulfrik looked down the slope to where his docks stood empty. His own ships had been hauled away for safety. But now the dock and the tight beach of flat rocks and pebbles filled with ships coming aground. He silently counted twelve total, six beached and six still out at sea with furled sails. He could hear the invader's anxious voices calling orders back and forth as men spilled over the sides.

"They can't land them all and there's no other approach," Ulfrik replied. He snorted a laugh, as if one or one hundred ships made no difference. But this was a fleet, more than the local islands could raise in a few days. A hand tapped him from behind, and the man offered a skin of mead. Men facing battle needed mead to ease their natural fears of blood and slaughter. Ulfrik normally preferred his wits to anything that might blunt his mind, but now he seized the skin and guzzled before handing it to Toki.

"If they can't land them all, they can't fight with them all," Snorri observed.

Ulfrik grunted and drew his sword with a rasp. The blade song repeated down the line, and he felt the heat of his men press around him as they readied. The attackers were mobbing up, seemingly disordered. Ulfrik expected Hardar to raise a banner and form a block, then advance up slope. Instead Ulfrik saw him draw his blade and point. Then he bellowed and led a wild charge.

"What a fool," Ulfrik said with a smile. Then he shouted his first command. "Bows! Send them to Nifleheim!"

Ulfrik and his warriors dropped to one knee as the mass of bowmen at the rear shot. The thrumming filled Ulfrik's ears, followed by the swish the arrows overhead. He watched as the black fletched shafts

127

plunged into the oncoming mob. Men screamed and tumbled into the grass. A second volley followed fast, and Ulfrik's smile stretched wickedly. Everything unfolded as he had planned. The wide slope offered no cover and was the sole approach to his hall. Bowmen only needed to arc their shots and the landscape ensured a killing zone at the front of his line.

The second volley was as devastating as the first, and dark bodies cartwheeled down the slope as arrows pierced them. Ulfrik expected the third volley to break them. No sane man would continue into the arrow storm. He heard brave voices booming out from the enemy, demanding them to keep moving.

As the third volley hissed overhead like a flight of ravens, Ulfrik anticipated Hardar's retreat. But instead he spotted a cluster of enemy in a side pocket where the arrows were not falling. Even as more enemy toppled, Ulfrik's eyes bulged and he cried out his warning. "Shields up! Enemy arrows!"

The counter fire was not significant. But Ulfrik and his men were on their knees and shields at their sides. Before they were beneath their shields, arrows were falling among them. A wet cry came from behind Ulfrik and shrieks followed. As they scrambled to raise their shields, they ruined the shots of their own archers.

It was the break Hardar needed. Ulfrik heard him screaming. "Charge! Get up the slope! Go!"

Ulfrik leapt to his feet. "Lock shields! For Nye Grenner!"

His men reacted with practiced fluidity. Shield clacked on shield and spears lowered into the gaps between them. Hardar's men drew to the final distance, and Ulfrik read them correctly. "Watch for their spears!"

Thin bladed throwing spears flashed and sailed across the gap. The spears thumped into shields or drove harmlessly into the earth. The spear blades bent, denying Ulfrik a chance to hurl them back. Several of his own men from the rear ranks flung their own spears. It was too late to stop the enemy.

Ulfrik swallowed hard and braced his shield. The back ranks braced against him as well. Hardar guided his mob in an uneven line. The two forces clamped together in an overwhelming thud of wooden shields and the groans of the men behind them. Ulfrik drove forward, plowing with his shield and stabbing under its rim. Hot blood splashed his hand and a foeman collapsed.

Now the steady murder began.

Spears sliced down from the second ranks of both sides, like the maw of a dragon slamming shut. A shaft thrust past Ulfrik's shoulder into the gap before him. The man stepping into his companion's place caught the spear in the collar of his leather vest. He yelped as the edge gashed his neck, but it was not fatal. Ulfrik rammed his shield forward, driving the metal boss into the dazed man's face. A second stroke beneath the shield turned on something hard, probably a thigh bone, and the second foe collapsed.

Ulfrik's pulse beat to the rhythm of the fight. His heart lifted with the wild joy of battle. Many years had passed since he tasted the euphoria of the shield wall. Too often a raid was finished before any serious fighting. Now he could slake his desire for true and glorious combat.

With two men piled dead before him, Ulfrik shoved into the

space. Snorri and Toki both squeezed forward. Being on higher ground made driving back the enemy a simpler task. Spears again wove death, striking from above and between the front ranks. A spearhead clanked on Ulfrik's faceplate, dragging on the iron with a frustrated rasp. He roared back and redoubled his shove into the line. The dead at his feet nearly tripped him, and gore slicked the grass.

"Hardar, you bastard! Fight me if you have any stones!" Through the press of sweating, grunting, and bleeding men, Ulfrik spotted Hardar at the front of his lines. But Hardar's red face and white-eyed expression flickered between intervening men. No amount of maneuvering would realign them to face each other. The lines were too tight.

The banner of Nye Grenner cracked above the carnage, marking Ulfrik's position. He repeated his challenge to Hardar. But few places were more chaotic than the front rank of the shield wall. Clanging swords, battering shields, battle cries, and death shrieks overwhelmed the ears. The nose filled with the tang of blood and the cloying musk of sweating men. The mouth filled with sour fear or metallic blood, and every word was an incoherent slur from split lips and broken teeth. Hardar would not find him.

"Retreat!" Someone on Hardar's side screamed the order. The man facing Ulfrik gave a pleading look, as if to beg the chance to flee. Ulfrik punched his blade under his shield. The enemy's face tensed in pain and he pulled his hand back, several fingers missing on the bloody fist. Then he melted away.

"They're breaking! Arrows! Finish these dogs!" Ulfrik bound forward as the line broke, laughing and smiling, slashing out at anyone slow enough to catch. He shoved to his right, hoping to snag Hardar in the retreat. He couldn't see him any longer. But he located Jarl Vermund.

The bony-faced Vermund had lost his helmet. He was smeared with blood and his gray-streaked hair matted to his cheeks. Toki harried him, making retreat impossible. Ulfrik cast about for Hardar, who should have been near his ally. In the moment Ulfrik searched, not finding his prey, Vermund had fallen and Toki's foot pressed the old jarl's sword arm.

Ulfrik opened his mouth to order Vermund's capture. But Toki growled a curse and slammed his blade hilt deep into Vermund's gut. He jerked with a ghastly shriek, then died as his companions fled. Ulfrik had no more time to consider. His men had lost discipline and were running after the retreating foe.

"Hold the line! Do not get separated!" Ulfrik cursed and cuffed any man he could lay hands upon. Snorri yanked overeager men back into place. But too many had run ahead and found themselves outnumbered by desperate enemies. He watched in frustration as his men fought two or three foes at a time, and met senseless deaths.

"Cut them down! Go!" He had to counter his orders unless more of his own die from lack of support. The lapse in discipline made his fists tremble. But he still smiled as Hardar's ships hastily put to sea. The other six ships never unloaded their men.

Ulfrik returned to his banner, gore draping him like a mantle of rubies. He yanked the pole out of the grass and held it high. "Victory for Nye Grenner! The dogs are broken!"

Death had swept the grassy slope in a vicious stroke. Crumpled bodies flecked the landscape in bloody piles. Arrow shafts and spears

131

were quills in the torsos of the dead. Those enemies who failed to reach their ships turned to surrender. Some were captured, others cut down. Ulfrik surveyed all of this with a smile. He sounded his horn three times to signal the hall of their victory. It gave him pleasure knowing his preparations and training had won him the battle.

He squinted at the ships lurching away on the shimmering waves and realized Hardar would have to be destroyed. The war was not over. With twelve hostile ships still at sea, Ulfrik wondered if it would ever be over.

CHAPTER ELEVEN

Ulfrik slouched at the high table, his eyes passing over the heads of the assembled men but resting on none. A hush fell the moment Ulfrik grasped his wooden mug. The sun slanting in from the windows mixed with the low firelight of the hearth and the whale oil lamps dotting the tables. Weak shadow fluttered in the light. Many faces bore the cuts and bruises of battle, though each was grave and thoughtful. Ulfrik stood with his mug in hand.

"The price of victory was heavy. Far too heavy. So many good men, our brothers, now feast and await us in Valhalla. They were the bravest of us, beyond compare in this world. We will miss our brothers, but we shall stand with them again one day. They watered the earth with their blood to save our home. Let us drink and remember them."

Every mug or horn was raised and held in silent thought for a lost friend, brother, or father. Ulfrik swept his mug over the gathered men then drank. Ulfrik closed his eyes and drank deep. All the dead had been dear to him, but some more than others. Ari, his navigator and friend from his days under Kjotve, had died from an arrow in his neck. His gnarled face floated in Ulfrik's mind as he drained the last of the mead. Then he placed the mug down and regarded his men.

"Our fight is not done. Hardar is weakened but has crawled home to heal himself. As weary as we are, we destroy him before he regroups. His ally, Vermund, is dead. But his kin will seek vengeance. We must finish Hardar before Vermund's kin can send aid. I know you men are ready for this."

Many of the men shouted curses on Hardar and called for his death. Others frowned and looked at their feet. Ulfrik's gaze lingered on those men, hoping to catch their eyes. He could brook no wavering now, not with a chance to deal a decisive end to Hardar. The dissenters remained silent and downcast, stealing glances at each other. Then Thorvald shoved forward out of the crowd.

"Many men would be alive today were it not for Toki's lust." He snarled through his teeth and his face was taut with anger. He stabbed his finger at Toki, who stood woodenly next to Ulfrik. "He gave Hardar the excuse to make war."

Ulfrik's hands trembled and he locked them behind his back to hide it. He bored into Thorvald's eyes, putting all the finality and threat he could into his voice without courting disrespect. "That argument is fast wearing itself out. Hardar bit his tongue off in jealousy when he witnessed what we have built, and same for his friend Vermund. You were present when he accused me of wanting to conquer his lands. He has been trying to start a fight since that day. Toki was a convenient excuse for him. But he would find another even without him."

"So you admit Toki is the reason?" Thorvald appeared ready to collapse from his rage. His skin flushed the color of a man exposed to the sun for days.

"Do not persist in this, Thorvald. This is a time for unity and not blame. Hardar attacked today. It might be better that he struck earlier and had less time to prepare. I guarantee he planned to attack this summer on any pretense that would preserve his face with the other jarls."

"So there it is! You gave him the pretense. You could've returned his daughter, and gave him Toki as well. How many are dead so that you can still share a drink with your best friend? How many yet to die?"

"Enough!" Ulfrik leapt from behind the table and pounced up to Thorvald. He fell back from Ulfrik, crashing into the men crowded behind him. But Ulfrik did not care. "You insult the honor and name of your jarl. Do you intend to push further? If so, then lay the hazel branches and make the ring. I will defend my honor in combat if I must."

Thorvald clutched his hand to his chest as if he had been stabbed, shock written on his face. Ulfrik blinked, then broke eye contact with Thorvald. He had to quell the dissent or risk losing support of the majority. One voice would be joined by another, then all discipline and power would vanish. He stepped back, everyone giving way, and cast a scowl at anyone who would not meet his eyes.

"It has been a hard day, and tensions are high." He tried to sound normal, but his voice carried a rough edge. "We must bury the dead with honor and then prepare to sail. I will question the prisoners tonight and learn what I can about these other allies. Go now and rest."

The crowd broke up reluctantly. Ulfrik's closest would remain with him, which would normally include Thorvald. Instead he filed out with the others. Ulfrik shook his head in frustration. Men mumbled as they exited. Someone stopped outside the door and shouted back inside. "Toki broke his oath to the gods and we are all paying the price. Give him up to the gods and save us!"

Ulfrik started forward, but Snorri's strong hand snagged his shoulder. Ulfrik rounded on him, but his old mentor merely shook his head. "You can't beat this idea out of them, lad. Just got to hold them together long enough to take Hardar's head."

Ulfrik relaxed and shrugged as Snorri's hand dropped from his shoulder. He watched the rest of the men exit, some turning back with a supportive nod or wink and others leaving without a look behind.

**

"None of them knew much about the other ships," Ulfrik said, rubbing his face. "Other than they are raiders from Norway. They believe Hardar sought advantage in numbers over us."

"Raiders make bad mercenaries," Snorri said, chuckling.

Ulfrik slumped on the bench. All the tension of the day had left his limbs dead and heavy. The few hours of summer darkness had turned the formerly bright hall into brown murk. Smoke from the guttering hearth searched for the hole on the ceiling. Only a few whale

136

oil lamps still guttered in halos of orange light. His inner circle had changed in the space of a day. With Ari's death, Ulfrik called upon Einar, Snorri's stepson. Thorvald's defection baffled Ulfrik; he normally was as solid as the iron he hammered in his forge. But with him gone, Ulfrik invited Runa to counsel. She sat between him and Toki.

"The prisoners are terrified farmers who want to return to their homes—levies. They'll remain hostages until I can free them. I don't expect trouble. Do you all agree?" Ulfrik scanned the faces for approval. Runa nodded grimly; having been a slave herself she reviled reducing freemen to slavery.

"Good, now we should all rest. But Toki, I have one final matter to discuss: you and Halla."

Toki stared at Ulfrik. He glanced around at the others, who all looked equally surprised. "What do we need to discuss?"

"Is she my hostage or is she your lover?" Ulfrik leaned his face on his palm, and watched Toki blush. He would have found the reaction humorous if it wasn't such a grim predicament. Toki dropped his gaze as everyone waited on his reply. Ulfrik yawned. "I assume your lack of an answer means she's my hostage. I'm sorry to hear that for you, though it plays out easier for me."

"This has all happened so fast. She has never seen war before; she's frightened."

Ulfrik yawned again, ready to collapse. But he needed a solid answer and knew Toki was not going to provide it. "Bring her here and let's settle this tonight."

"But she is probably sleeping."

Ulfrik straightened himself and drove Toki back with his

expression alone. Toki's blush deepened. "I'm afraid we didn't leave off in a good place. Runa, would you go? I think she will respond better to a woman."

Runa smiled and stood. "I'll go. But if you think I'm going to be gentle with her, well, you don't know your own sister."

"Bring her alive, wife. Toki, go with her and grant me some peace while you're gone. Snorri and Einar, you two may stay or leave as you wish."

Toki and Runa threw on cloaks against the night chill while Snorri and Einar decided to return home. Ulfrik found his bed and lay down next to his son, who snored beneath a wolf pelt. He drifted into a light sleep, waking short time later to Runa's cold hand on his shoulder.

Ulfrik jolted up, automatically reaching for his sword. Runa squeezed his shoulder and shook him. "They're all waiting for you now. Gunnar is still asleep?"

Runa adjusted the pelt over Gunnar's small body. Ulfrik wiped his eyes, stood, and kissed Runa's head. "Get some sleep."

"I want to see this too. She has a woman's body but a girl's mind. I think she'd be a better hostage than future sister."

Together they returned to the hall. Toki was throwing branches into the hearth to keep the weak fire alive. Halla and her slave sat on a bench positioned to face the high table. She was wrapped in Toki's wool cloak so that only her head showed. Next to her sat a thin slave, shorn hair growing back in uneven lengths. Ulfrik's eyes glided over the slave and settled on Halla. She held her chin up and wore an expression of mock bravery. He could see her trembling.

"Relax, Halla Hardarsdottir. You are not in danger." Ulfrik sat at

138

the high table and Runa joined him.

"You have summoned me in the dark. How can I think otherwise?"

"Because if I summoned you in the light there'd be a line of people eager to seize you. Your father brought us grim business today. I've got twenty-seven men to bury and many more injured. Believe me, my word is all that prevents widows and mothers from ripping your eyes out. Do you understand?"

"I understand." She studied her feet and shifted beneath her cloak. Toki, finished rekindling the hearth, sat at the bench a respectable distance from her. Neither looked at the other.

"I'll come to the point. Up until a few days ago, the two of you risked everything to be together. Now it's all in the open, and you can have what you planned in secret. But it seems you've grown cold on Toki. If you are not his woman, then you are my hostage to your father's behavior. Is this adding up for you?"

Ulfrik let his words hang. He knew the girl was bright enough to comprehend. She appeared to think, then turned to Toki. "I have not grown cold on Toki, as you say Lord Ulfrik. I have been frightened, and I've been ungrateful. Toki has a kind heart, and I enjoy his company."

"I think you're the only one willing to say that these days." Ulfrik meant it in jest, but Toki snapped his head up and Runa elbowed his arm with a frown. "Sorry, I am tired. I'm glad to hear you say so, as I guess Toki is. But you came here seeking refuge from a man you feared. Did you know Vermund is now dead?"

Halla's eyes widened and her cloak unfolded as her hand raised to her mouth. "Dead? What happened?"

139

"I killed him in battle," Ulfrik said, shooting Toki a silencing look. Runa patted his leg beneath the table, and Ulfrik let a small smile grow. "That is what happens in battle. Men die, and Vermund was one. This time. Now here's another thing to ponder. Your father has taken arms against me. If you are promised to Toki, I can be lenient with him. But his pride is amazing, and he may yet return to fight again. If we meet on the battlefield, only one of us will survive. And I'm certain it will be me. Does this change your heart?"

Halla shrank beneath her cloak, her eyes widening and face growing pale. Ulfrik did not relent in his stare, silently demanding an answer. Panic, confusion, fear, all played out on her face. She seemed unprepared to make a decision, and Ulfrik's fist balled at her wavering. He inhaled to prompt her again, then she spoke.

"I don't want my father to die. But he makes his own choices, and if those lead to death, then I must accept it. That is Fate, which cannot be denied." She glanced around at everyone, including her slave. "I have chosen Toki and he has chosen me, also the work of Fate. All of this loss saddens me, and it cannot be for nothing. If Toki will have me, then I will be his."

Toki slid across the bench to Halla's side, eyes flashing and mouth quivering. Ulfrik shook his head and rolled his eyes at Runa, who simply smiled. Toki took Halla's hands into his own. "Of course, I will have you."

"By the gods it's late," Ulfrik said as he stood. "The last thing I need is to sit through this. So hear my words, both of you. I'm your jarl and you are sworn to obey me in all things. I am sworn to protect you and your property. Let neither side forget the duty to the other. Halla, you are no longer my hostage but part of my home. I cannot guarantee your father's life. But I demand your loyalty."

Halla's eyes brimmed with tears, not joyful ones, Ulfrik suspected. Her voice quavered as she answered. "Yes, Lord Ulfrik. My loyalty is with you now. But I beg you, be kind to my mother. If the worst happens, please allow her to join me here. She needs me."

"I make no guarantees. I will treat her fairly, on that you have my word. Now all of you leave and let me sleep."

When they had all left, Ulfrik offered his hand to Runa and helped her from the bench. "You don't agree with this, do you?"

"Where there are wolf ears wolf teeth are close."

"You think she will betray us?"

"I think she doesn't know what she wants, no matter what she just said. That can be dangerous to us."

"But Toki will keep her in line."

Runa laughed and hooked Ulfrik's arm to guide him to their bed. "Toki looks at her and sees only sunshine. I will keep her in line, you can count on that."

Ulfrik laughed, then paused to stretch. "Maybe I should give you command of a ship. I'm always looking for a strong leader."

They laughed again, and once beneath the covers of their bed, Ulfrik fell into a sleep as deep as death.

***

Hardar's hall finally emptied of crying wives and weeping children. Except the moaning of injured hirdmen laid out on the floor, the place was quiet. He slouched on his chair, fire in every joint and pain at every movement. A thick gash flamed on his inner calf where a spear had narrowly missed his thigh. His eyes throbbed and whenever he closed them he saw a bloody slope of crumpled bodies and raining arrows.

He was ruined. His best men spent their lives on a wild gambit that was doomed from the first. Kjotve had counseled against a head-on attack, cursing it as foolish and weak. Hardar slid further down his chair, shaking his head at how he and Vermund had expected numbers to overwhelm Ulfrik. He had never seen so many arrows. If he had not guided his few bows to counter-fire, they would have all died without striking a blow. The thought made him twitch with a chill.

With the bitter business of paying weregild to the families of the dead finished, Kjotve emerged into the low light of the hall. His massive shape lumbered to Hardar in his chair, pausing beside him before pulling up a bench. "It was ill luck, Jarl Hardar. Your men say you didn't offer anything to the gods before setting out. Now that's another misstep, right there."

Hardar's eye twitched, then he exploded from his chair. He rounded on Kjotve, seizing his furs in both hands and hauling him off his seat. "You fucking arrogant turd! You could've turned everything. Ulfrik was on his knees even when we broke. You have a hundred men. A hundred fucking men! And you sailed off! Why?"

He shoved wide-eyed Kjotve back to the bench, bending over him, heaving like he had just lifted an anvil overhead. Kjotve's shock twisted to a wry smile. "Did you see his archers reforming? You were too busy running to notice, eh? I want Ulfrik, but not badly enough to charge into an arrow storm."

"But we had you covered. They chased us to the water and killed us boarding the ships. You were three spear-lengths away; you could've done more than abandon us."

Kjotve rose like a glacier emerging from the frigid sea. He stared down at Hardar, whose anger cooled in the shadow of the great jarl. Kjotve's voice was low but rich with potent ire. "You call me an arrogant turd, when I gave you every warning of your own stupidity. You and that fool Vermund were so full of yourselves, so sure I'd be willing to die for your whore daughter. You wouldn't listen to me. What could a foreigner know that you kings of grass and sheep don't? Well, you sailed past as fucking beacon. Do you remember what I told you?"

Hardar recoiled as Kjotve bore down on him. He nodded, recalling Kjotve's plea to turn around and find a way to strike with surprise.

"Good you recall. Ulfrik had hours to ready himself, and he did. Look what it earned you. I told you I would not charge upslope into waiting spears backed by arrows. That you managed to inflict the damage you did is a gift of the gods. Now you are a broken man. Ulfrik will sail into your fjord, burn your homes, rape your women, plunder your treasures, and put your head on top of a pole. All because you wouldn't listen to me."

Kjotve's words pushed him back into his chair, where he collapsed with his hands covering his face. He dragged them down his cheeks, pulling his bottom eyelids. The cool air touched the exposed eyes and drew water. Everyone left in the hall hung their heads or stared into the dark corners. Hardar sensed the air of desolation gripping the hall, but then inspiration flashed.

"I'm not defeated." Hardar sat up in his chair, looked into Kjotve's shadow-painted face. "Jarl Vermund has fallen, and his body not even recovered. He has family and allies throughout these islands. They will seek revenge for him. I have kin in the north yet to unite with me. But Ulfrik stands alone, and I have struck him a heavy blow."

Kjotve nodded appreciatively. "You better hasten to send word to your allies. It may be as you say, but I wonder if you will be alive to see it. Ulfrik is only hours away while your allies will need days to assemble, if not more."

"Have you no sense?" Hardar hissed under his breath. "These men cannot hear that. They need hope."

"They need a plan," Kjotve said, without adjusting his voice. "Let me deal with Ulfrik the way I suggested. It may be easier for me, now that you've reduced his numbers."

"A nighttime attack," Hardar said flatly. "Haven't you been in these lands long enough to know that even the darkest hour is never truly dark? It's not like your battles in Norway."

"But men sleep here, in whatever passes for night. It is enough. I do not need to strike him dead. I just need to cut off his legs. He will be watching for me, as he surely counted the sails that invaded his lands. But we can move with speed he cannot match. I have done this more times than I can count. I have touchwood to start a flame, something you lack here. Fire will spread, panic will greet it, and my men will do their work and be gone. You will then have the time to assemble your allies and finish matters for yourselves. Your name and glory will be preserved."

Kjotve's smile flashed from the blackness of his face. Hardar caught himself leaning in to hear the plan. Other men had wandered close, while Kjotve's veterans smirked at their leader's words. Suddenly Ingrid broke in from behind.

"But you risk Halla's life with raging fires. Ulfrik might even kill her!" Ingrid's voice rose to a shriek and vibrated with terror. Hardar spun on his chair, his hand itching to belt her, though she was too distant. She huddled at the edge of the hearth light, hands clasped at her chest.

"Lady Ingrid, I will rescue your daughter if I can. I give you my word." Kjotve's face brightened and his voice smoothed. He stepped toward her. "I have a plan for my fires that will bring no risk to Halla. I know Ulfrik won't harm your daughter. He is smart enough to make the threats, but not ruthless enough to carry them out. Trust me."

"Don't worry about what she thinks." Hardar stood up sharply and flipped a lock of hair off of his face. "Yes, try your best with Halla. But tell me more about your plans for Ulfrik."

Hardar touched Kjotve's shoulder and then guided him back to the bench. He glared at Ingrid, who stood with her hands still gripped across her chest. Kjotve winked at her and then smiled down on Hardar. "When I am done, Ulfrik will be ripe to pluck. You may take everything you want of his lands. Just give him over to me. I am anxious to have him in my service again."

Kjotve laughed, a laugh that echoed from the mist-shrouded plains of Nifleheim, where worms gnawed the ignominious dead. Hardar shivered, feeling the chill of that frozen world brush his heart.

CHAPTER TWELVE

Ulfrik sprang to his feet, snatched his sword up from beside the bed, and dashed out of the hall dressed only in a linen shirt and pants. Then he awakened.

The horn blared again. But now Ulfrik heard the shouting and clang of swords.

The air was clammy and the twilight of summer night dyed the world a deep ocean blue. But yellow light stained the sky from where his ships were beached. Ulfrik screamed and dashed for the scene, his naked feet digging into the soft ground.

Men tumbled out of the barracks house, hauling swords, shields, or spears. They scattered without anyone to give direction. Ulfrik turned to them, shouting. "The ships are under attack. Get to the dock!"

His heart thudded as he rounded the barracks, arriving at the top of the slope. He looked across the field.

He felt like he had fallen into the ocean during the heart of winter. Two of his ships were wrapped in flames while the third sprouted ribbons of fast running fire along her rails. Flickering black shapes tangled against the brilliant backdrop. His guards battled the raiders who attacked with both spears and torches. His fourth ship had been dragged far enough away from the others to be out of danger for the moment. However, a few torches spun through the blue night to land near it.

Racing down slope, Ulfrik tore his sword from its scabbard. Men passed him and converged on the attackers from all angles. The horn continued to blast, then cut off suddenly. Ulfrik faced the water, and spotted the six ships. Two ships were beached while four bobbed further out to sea.

He took fleeting consolation from all the mercenaries on those ships being held at bay. But hot anger overwhelmed him as he watched his own ships burn to ash.

Arriving at the fight, he encountered complete chaos. His left side grew taut with the blazing heat from his ships. Men swirled about the field slashing with yellow glowing blades. A few bodies piled on the grass. One rolled over, holding his face. Friend and foe were indistinguishable in the rippling light of the fires. He feared his men fought themselves in the confusion.

"Prisoners! I need prisoners!" Ulfrik shouted to anyone who would listen. Despite the ever growing press of men, he felt desperately alone. He had no control over this brawl.

A spear flashed at him, and he skittered to the side. Ulfrik's attention narrowed to the one man. He wanted to capture this one prisoner. He was a reed thin blur of a leather jerkin and a red shirt. The spear point jabbed again, keeping Ulfrik at a safe distance. Ulfrik circled a moment, both hands on his sword and wishing he had a shield. The wicked spearhead stabbed for his unprotected thigh. Ulfrik struck down the shaft with his sword and closed the distance. But his opponent's reaction attested to his experience. In the instant it took Ulfrik to glide up the length of the spear, the enemy had drawn a long knife and plunged it at Ulfrik's ribs.

Instinct saved Ulfrik. He read the man's smile, knew the blade was coming, and twirled away at the last moment. But now both of them had stumbled out of position and were staggering to regain momentum.

Ulfrik was faster. His sword hacked into the back of the enemy's thigh. He toppled forward with a scream. Ulfrik stepped on his spear then stabbed the man's hand. He kicked aside the spear and flicked the long knife away with his sword. For now, it was all Ulfrik could do. A new threat had arrived.

Back across the slope, points of orange light bounced in a ragged line. Like glowing ants, the trail ran from a bright burning flame on the shore and pointed at his hall.

"The hall is under attack!" Ulfrik was sprinting back up the slope. Warning shouts rose among the throng of men fighting by the ships. Everyone able to break off combat ran toward the hall, their enemies slipping away.

Men still arriving to the fight now turned toward the new line of attackers. Ulfrik screamed like a wild animal, his throat nearly bursting.

148

He could not stop thinking of Runa and Gunnar trapped inside a burning hall.

The attackers resolved into view from the gloom of the night. There were more attackers than the points of torchlight revealed. The torchbearers flung their brands at anything in reach. Between them, archers put arrows on their strings.

Ulfrik dove to the ground as arrows shrieked overhead. The grass whipped his face as he slid on his belly. Several men around him screeched and tumbled in broken wrecks.

It had been a covering action for the withdrawal. The arrows shot recklessly, wastefully, into the night. But neither Ulfrik nor his men could risk facing the shooters. The enemy hustled back toward their ships. Ulfrik craned his neck above the grass to see beached ships already launched. He saw errant flashes and gleams of iron as men boarded another ship and sailed off.

Ulfrik got to his feet, ran to the man near him and found him with an arrow jutting from his chest. He crouched again, still fearing the enemy archers. He looked back toward the hall. It was safe, the torches smoldering harmlessly in the dewy grass. The threat to the hall had been a feint to extract the enemies who had burnt his ships.

He ran, bent at the waist in case more arrows came. He found men in laying the grass, either taking cover as he had or pierced with arrows. He urged those still alive to follow. Without a horn to signal his men, he summoned as much strength as he could to shout his message. "They are retreating. Quickly, to the ships! We can still save them!"

Ulfrik knew they couldn't be saved. Two had settled into a rippling flame of a long burning fire, like giant logs on a hearth. The third still flew banners of fire, and might be salvaged. At least his fourth was still intact.

Someone had located a horn and blasted three times. Men rose from the grass, looking like ghosts emerging from burial mounds. Ulfrik's run flagged to a weak jog. Finally he walked the final distance, stopping at the circle of heat and light. Others shambled over to watch the flames crackle and pop and streak up into the blue night.

Ulfrik bit his lip, closed his eyes, and imagined that once he opened them again the fires would be extinguished. But instead, the deck of the first ship collapsed, spraying sparks into the air like a swarm of fireflies.

***

The sun had risen, despite Ulfrik's belief it would never again shine on him. Fog lay thick on the land and mingled with the smoke chugging from the smoldering ruins of his ships. By the time the fires died, two were like blackened whale bones. The third appeared repairable, though its seaworthiness would be questionable. Ironically, the undamaged ship was *Raven's Talon*, Toki's ship. He wondered what the gods intended him to understand from that sign. It seemed as much an accusation as an affirmation of Toki.

More men had been killed in the raid. More mothers, wives, and children wailed as they found the dead on the field. Ulfrik joined the survivors in carrying their bodies to the side of the hall, where Runa, Gerdie, and Halla covered the corpses in sheets held down with stones. Seven more had died in the fight, while a dozen had taken injuries.

Ulfrik worked in grim silence, but felt the unspoken accusations.

150

You've offended the gods. You chose your friends over your people. You put pride and competition before the safety of your own. No one spoke the words aloud. But they nevertheless clanged in his head like an iron bell.

He sighed as surveyed men picking over the litter of the battle. The air smelled sour with soot and ash. Not even the birds called on this morning. With the blurry figures shuffling in the fog, Ulfrik thought this was what Nifleheim must look like: gray, hopeless, and dead.

"We've got a few prisoners." Snorri appeared from behind. Ulfrik startled at his words, which sounded as loud as a crumbling glacier in the defeated silence.

"Let's get to work on them. I want to know what we're dealing with." Ulfrik's own voice was ragged and hoarse. He followed Snorri past the hall toward the edge of the village. As he left, Runa's gaze followed him. Her face was creased with worry and her hair curled wildly in the humidity. She looked as if one night had aged her a decade. Ulfrik turned away, and set his mind on the captives.

"We dragged them to Thorvald's forge."

"We can use his blacksmithing tools to get the information we need."

"My exact thoughts."

A thick group of men clustered at the forge. The squat building housed Thorvald's tools and supplies, and was a place for him and his family to sleep. But his anvil and forge were outside under a wooden roof. Toki stood at the edge of the group, and broke off to meet them.

"There are two men still alive. Thorvald just started working on them."

Ulfrik patted Toki's shoulder in greeting, and pushed forward

151

into the group until he broke through the front. Two men were trussed in thin cords and seated on the dirt floor. Ulfrik smiled as he recognized the red shirt of the spear fighter he had crippled. The other was a man of average build, weathered skin, thinning hair, and many scars. If they had any valuables, those had already been stripped. Thorvald wore thick leather gloves and hovered over them as the onlookers encouraged him. He punched the crippled man in the face, snapping his head back.

"Hold on, Thorvald." Ulfrik stepped into the forge area and the crowd silenced. "We're not going to get anything out of them with broken jaws and no teeth."

Thorvald straightened up and his face turned red. He seemed on the verge of exploding but then softened. "They're not talking, anyway. I just hit them a few times."

Ulfrik smiled and looked down on the two captives. "Well, I bet you two hadn't expected capture. I hope Hardar is paying you well, because I'm going to make whatever he gave you feel worthless. I need answers and I'm getting them."

Ulfrik's eyes throbbed and his body quivered with anger. Part of him understood these two were simple men who took orders from whoever paid highest, and that he should not blame them for their actions. But that part of him was not in control. The part that raged against his losses dominated.

"Thorvald, get this one's hand on your anvil. Someone give me a hammer." Thorvald's smile grew wicked as he seized the crippled man and hauled him up. His swollen eyes pried open in terror.

A hammer fell into Ulfrik's waiting palm, and he weighed the head in his other hand. "You can start talking now or I can mash your hand. You ought to know I'm serious."

The man started sputtering his words and the other prisoner started to shout. "Don't tell him nothing!"

Ulfrik kicked the other man in his face. He snapped back and bounced his head on the anvil, then slouched to the side with bloody drool oozing from his mouth. "I only need one man to talk. One more word from you and it'll be your last."

The other prisoner moaned in answer while the one with his hand on the anvil started to talk. "Don't break my hand, please. I'll tell you what you want. Anything!"

"Who is your leader, and what is your deal with Hardar?"

"I'm sworn to Jarl Kjotve the Rich, and he has a deal with Hardar. I don't know what it is. We get a take of the spoils from sacking this place."

Ulfrik's vision flashed white. "Now that was the wrong answer. Jarl Kjotve the Rich died at Hafrsfjord. I was there."

The hammer slammed down and the man screamed. His bones crushed and his fingers splayed out. Ulfrik hammered again, until the meat of the prisoner's hand was flattened and the skin torn. The prisoner slumped and fainted from the pain. The crowd cheered at the violence. But as the white haze cleared from Ulfrik's mind, he felt revolted at his action. It was one thing to maim a man in battle, and another to maim the helpless.

His disgust only worsened his mood. He dropped the hammer with a dull thud and picked up the other prisoner. He sat him upright and grabbed his hair, pulling him so that his throat lay exposed. He crouched beside him.

"Your friend lied and you saw what it earned him. Now are you ready to speak honestly? Who do you serve?"

"I serve Kort the Gray. We are mercenaries or raiders, whatever you like to call us. Hardar promised shares in your treasure. It's all I know."

"I've never heard of Kort the Gray. Anyone else know of such a man?"

Ulfrik didn't look around but heard the confused grunts behind him. "Are you lying again?"

"We come from all lands, but founded our band after leaving Northumbria. We were last in the Orkneyjar, raiding a rich jarl there. It's the truth."

Ulfrik searched the man's desperate face. Whether it was the truth, he would never know. "Very well. How many crew your ships?"

"One hundred men. I don't know how many we lost. But we'll make them up. Maybe you should think about joining us, eh?"

Ulfrik slammed the man's head against the anvil. "How did Hardar find you?"

The man's eyes rolled as he recovered from the blow. Ulfrik shook him again, getting an answer. "We found him. We came to raid, but he offered payment and promised you were easier prey. Not so easy, we found out."

"Will Kort the Gray switch sides? Can he be paid to join with me?"

The man laughed, a noise like rocks grinding together. "Kort has honor, and has given his word. Besides Hardar has many friends here and we don't want to fight all of them. We're after the easy prey, you."

Ulfrik shoved the prisoner to the ground and stood. He looked up at Thorvald, his face a tapestry of shock, despair, and fear. He twisted to survey the equally horrified faces of the crowd. Even Toki and Snorri could not keep defeat from their faces.

"One hundred men plus more allies." Someone intoned the words at the back of the group.

"Six ships," another voice answered. "We had to expect at least that many crew."

"But more allies," a new voice added.

"Enough," Ulfrik spoke as evenly as he could. "Keep this information quiet. No need to spread panic yet. I will have council and decide what we do next."

"We have to surrender." A desperate, small voice floated up from the group. Ulfrik cringed at the suggestion. Faces turned to him, notably Snorri and Toki. Ulfrik stared back at them for long moments.

"I will have council and decide. Lock up these prisoners. Thorvald, you will come?"

Thorvald nodded slowly. Ulfrik blinked and looked at the desperate faces. There was nothing more to say. He left for the hall.

***

Ulfrik leaned beside the door to the hall as the last of his men filed inside. Now that so many had died, the main room felt expansive, large spaces separated the cliques seating themselves. No one spoke beyond simple greetings. The threat Hardar and his allies represented had become too desperate for anything more. Men wanted to know what would come next. Ulfrik wanted to know the same thing, and

155

dreaded the answer.

Runa stood beside him at the door, holding Gunnar in her arms. Halla waited with Gerdie at a respectable distance, their feet hidden in the long grass turning blue in the twilight. Gunnar buried his face in his mother's shoulder, responding to the black mood that had overtaken everyone. Ulfrik looked into Runa's dark eyes. They had argued all afternoon, but achieved nothing more than angering each other. Now as she left the hall for the night, he forgot the reasons for fighting. It only remained to make a final decision, a single choice to fight or surrender.

"Sleep well tonight. Try not to think too much." Ulfrik touched Runa's arm as he spoke. She rolled her eyes.

"No one will sleep tonight, and least of all me. We must flee, Ulfrik. Make the right choice for your family."

Ulfrik rubbed the back of his neck and shook his head. Then he gave her a kiss and tousled Gunnar's hair. "The men are waiting for me. Go on."

He watched her depart. Gunnar peeked over her shoulder as they left, and snapped his head away when Ulfrik caught his eye.

Inside the hall, men parted as he strode to the front where Snorri, Toki, Thorvald, and Einar sat at the high table. Each man nodded solemnly as Ulfrik took his place on the bench. He returned their greetings, then searched the assembly. The hearth burned brightly, obscuring men in the rear behind a yellow haze and crisply defining the rest. Every face, young and old, watched him. Ulfrik swallowed, then spoke.

"You've heard the news, and what the prisoners have said. We have decisions to make."

156

Ulfrik began with an outline of how they had come to make war with Hardar and how he had hired Kort the Gray and enlisted other jarls. He recounted the dead, gave them honor, and named them. It was a long list of thirty-four warriors. The surviving warriors bowed their head at the names, shouted oaths of revenge, and some even wept.

"The burning of our ships destroyed our ability to strike Hardar at will. The terrain prevents overland attacks, and one ship cannot carry enough warriors to attack by sea. But that doesn't mean we have no use for a single ship. I will send men to seek allies. We will need help in this fight. I know that Ragnvald will stand with me. Others might be willing to do the same for a price. It will place us in their debt, but this is the best way."

Several men chorused approval. But the number of men who remained silent and studying their feet outnumbered them. The few supporting shouts faltered as no one added their voices. Ulfrik's head grew heavy and his breath shortened, knowing he did not have his men's hearts.

"I think sending for allies is a good idea," Snorri said brightly. "We have to fight defensively and resist Kort the Gray."

"It's a pointless move now. It's too late." Thorvald stepped out of the back and walked to join those beneath the high table. Ulfrik's eyes followed him as he approached, though otherwise he kept his face closed. He knew Thorvald's mind, and knew what to expect. He was not disappointed when Thorvald faced him.

"We needed allies long ago. But you failed in securing them. This last festival was a nice start, but too late. Hardar has still managed to make us look like outsiders, and law-breakers on top of that."

Ulfrik put up his hand to stop him. "The past is meaningless here. We need to focus on a plan."

"The past is everything!" Thorvald's rage pealed over Ulfrik. His face flashed red and his nostrils flared. "You've focused exclusively on building up Nye Grenner to surpass Hardar. You've been competing with him since the day you set up camp here. All you've wanted is to build a stronger army, better weapons, better homes, better ships. Everything better! But you neglected to make us one with the original settlers. Besides Ragnvald, who will come to our aid? No one!"

Ulfrik stood to the challenge. But several men shouted in Thorvald's defense. "Let him speak! A man has a right to speak his mind."

Ulfrik realized he had no other choice, and Thorvald did have his right to speak. He sunk back to his bench as Thorvald continued, his anger cooled from the break in his shouting.

"Now that those men you prided yourself upon are dead, and the fine ships are burned, what are we left with? I can craft swords and armor for you until Ragnarok. But ghosts cannot wield them in battle."

"Are you saying we cannot fight?" Snorri spoke up. "A man will defend his home until the last if he has any spine."

"I agree," Thorvald said, though he turned to face the crowd. "But we do not have to fight. Hardar wants his daughter returned. He wants justice for her kidnapper."

"Careful with your words," Ulfrik snarled. His fist clenched and he leaned forward. But Thorvald continued.

"We do not have to fight. We have to meet the demands of justice. Thirty-four men are buried today because we have not done so."

"I warn you, Thorvald"

"Toki broke his oath to the gods. Ulfrik has supported him in it."

"Silence, Thorvald!"

"We shed our blood and risk our families for men who cannot honor their sacred oaths!"

"You treasonous whoreson!"

"Surrender, Ulfrik. Take Toki with you. The gods demand it. We follow the will of the gods!"

Ulfrik leapt from the table and grabbed for Thorvald. His mind hummed with anger. But hands grabbed him from behind, while other men seized Thorvald and covered him. Ulfrik lashed out halfheartedly. Snorri banged the table calling for order. Shouting and punches flew. Men divided against each other, and Ulfrik's rage turned inward. He had only made things worse.

Ulfrik tore free from the hands gripping him. He jumped up to the table and joined Snorri in demanding an end to the argument. The more cool-headed men broke up the few scuffles and order slowly returned. Ulfrik stood before the table, breathing heavily. Men glared at each other, at Ulfrik across the hall, at Thorvald amid his supporters. No one spoke and no one appeared ready to utter the first words. Ulfrik broke the impasse.

"As ill-put and misleading as Thorvald made his argument, I cannot refute the basics. It does not change that we can still fight. But I have asked that of you twice already. I think now we must vote to fight or surrender. I can't have men in the shield wall who will run or not answer the battle call. If you are not prepared to defend your homes, then let's find out now."

He studied the assembly. His heart throbbed as desperately as if he were in battle. In fact, he was in a battle for his life. Surrender to Hardar would likely end in his own death. "All who are willing to fight, no matter the odds, show your hands."

All the men at the high table raised theirs immediately. Slowly others floated to the top of the crowd. But by a quick count Ulfrik saw he barely had a full crew for one ship. A burning ember fell into his belly.

"Is there anyone who has not decided? Show your hands." His voice was weak, defeated. No one raised their hands to his question.

Not enough men were willing to fight at his side. He could not prevail even with allies. To resist would be folly, costing more lives with a small chance for victory. Now his last duty to his people was to negotiate fair terms for surrender to Hardar.

The hall was deaf silent. Ulfrik nodded and turned back to his bench. His people had just killed him.

CHAPTER THIRTEEN

"You can flee with us. Please, Ulfrik!" Runa was on her knees on the hard dirt floor, clutching the hem of Ulfrik's shirt. Her head flopped forward as she sobbed. Ulfrik stood like a man of stone. Tears streaked his cheeks, but he said nothing more. He searched around his room, eyes settling on his bed piled with furs. He hoped one day he would return to lie in it with his wife and his son and dream. But that required a mercy from the gods they were not likely to give.

"Fleeing will only bring Hardar and his mercenaries to the chase. And he might turn his wrath upon the innocent people left behind." Runa violently shook her head, but Ulfrik pressed his point. "His mercenaries own big ocean-going ships. We'd be caught, and once that happened, we'd all be killed."

"Then we would die together!" She looked up, her eyes red and face contorted with anguish.

"I can't abide that, Runa. I want you to take Gunnar to a safe place. Life is driven by Fate's plan, and this is what Fate has woven for me. Yet one more black strand. But not the last strand of my life."

Runa stood, her expression darkening and her voice dropping. "Do not speak to me like I'm a fool. Hardar wants you dead and you will deliver yourself to him."

"No." Ulfrik grabbed Runa's shoulders and she turned away. He guided her chin up to look at him. "My father or brother would have killed a defeated enemy. But Hardar is vain. Death is too easy for me. He wants to see me punished, degraded, vilified. Chopping my head off and hanging it on a pole is not imaginative enough for him."

"Are you comforting me? This sounds horrible."

"I have a plan. I will use his vanity against him."

Runa's eyes widened and the tight lines of worry eased on her face. "It's a daring plan, then?"

"The most daring plan I've ever made."

"The gods love a daring plan. It's what you've always said."

"Because I know it is true."

Runa's eyes searched his. A tear dangled from her chin, then splashed onto his arm. "You cannot die, Ulfrik Ormsson. And you cannot leave me. Ever."

"After this, I never will. But for a time we must be parted."

Her face contorted and tears flowed again.

Ulfrik drew her to his chest as she wept, stroking her ample hair. He inhaled the sweet smell of her, tried to impress the soft warmth of

162

her body into his memory. Such memories would help him remain alive over the coming weeks. She quivered in his embrace and he pressed her harder into his arms, wishing he could squeeze the fear from her. His plans were daring, desperate, uncertain, but he could not let her fear failure.

"Please, escape with us to a new land," Runa said, sniffling. "We can start anew. I don't care as long as we are together."

"The gods would not love that. No, Hardar has won. For now."

***

Ulfrik sat at his high table for the last time, aware even if his plan executed perfectly, life would forever change. The brief summer of the gods, the five years of prosperity he had grown heady over, now turned to winter. He journeyed into uncertainty, and his life was entirely entrusted to Fate.

Runa sat next to him, wrapped in a plain woolen cloak pinned with the deer antler pin she had carried from Norway. She had stripped herself of adornment, and stared straight ahead, expressionless. Beneath the table she crushed his hand in a cold, trembling grip. They both watched the hall door, waiting for it to open.

All the windows were closed, but the smoke hole let in gray sunshine. The door at the end of the hall revealed a rectangle of dull light before Toki entered. Halla followed him, and Snorri and Einar came close behind. The four shuffled to the front where Ulfrik noted their care-worn faces. He tried to force brightness into his voice as he addressed them.

"We have a few more things to plan before I leave. But first, how has my boy been?"

"Gerdie has him playing with his friends," Snorri said. "He's as happy as ever."

Ulfrik smiled and nodded. "I hope he will always remain so carefree."

The words crashed like dropped pottery. Ulfrik studied the table in embarrassment and Runa withdrew her hand. He cleared his throat and asked them to sit. Only Halla moved to a bench, but stopped when no one else budged.

"Many still support you," Snorri offered. He smiled but his voice crumbled as he spoke. "They wait for you outside, came to send you off. No one here wants to do this."

"Least of all me. But we are done with that discussion. I gathered you to discuss my plan. Snorri and I plotted all night, and it's the best we can do." Ulfrik glanced at Runa. She held her chin up and stared at the back of the hall. "Hardar will not kill me, not outright. He will enslave me, make me tend sheep or row on his ships, something he considers humiliating. He will parade me around the islands to make certain everyone knows I'm fallen and disgraced."

Ulfrik fixed his eyes on Halla. She kept her head lowered and hands locked over her lap, a study in modesty. "Hardar is an over-proud fool, saved only by luck. His pride will be his undoing."

Halla met his gaze. For a moment she appeared just like her father, and Ulfrik worried she would betray them. His eyes drew to slits. "What I plan next cannot be shared. Halla, my life is hostage to your loyalty. My plan might lead to your father's death, especially if he fights. It can't be easy for you to hear this."

"It is not easy. I never wanted his death or harm to come to my family."

"You witch!" Runa shouted. Everyone jumped at her outburst. She slapped her palm on the table. "What do you want? Your family is our mortal enemy. You've twice chosen us over them."

"Over my father."

"It's the same thing. Now, you have no choice. Your loyalty or your death!" Runa's voice cracked and she glared at Halla, who wilted at the tirade. Ulfrik placed his hand on her shoulder to calm Runa, but she jerked it away.

"My loyalty is to Toki and Lord Ulfrik. But I was promised my mother would be cared for."

Ulfrik sighed and shrugged. "If I am ever in position to offer her hospitality, I will. For now, I go to certain slavery. Let's refocus on the plan."

He reviewed the group again. Halla stood chastened. Einar and Snorri stood together, arms folded and faces set hard. Runa looked at no one. Finally, Toki turned away and held his face in one hand. His leg pumped nervously and he seemed ready to burst. Ulfrik empathized, also wanting to end this horrible experience.

"I surrender myself to Hardar today. I will go alone on the *Fjord Runner*; it is ruined from the fire and can probably make it to Hardar's shores. The rest of you, along with a small crew, will take *Raven's Talon* and sail away in secret."

"No!" Toki stepped forward, fists balled at his sides and his eyes alight with passion. "I will go with you. This is my fault, the price for breaking my oath to the gods."

"Toki, no. You can't leave me after all this." Halla grabbed his arm, but he pulled away.

"All this destruction, it's because I made an oath I failed to keep." Tears began to flow from his eyes. "I should pay the price and not you."

Ulfrik shook his head. "It was only a matter of time, old friend. Do not judge yourself. Leave that to the gods. If you do them honor, they may overlook what you have done. If you accompany me, Vermund's relatives will put you to death. Your place now is with Halla, and with my family. They will need you, and I demand you do this for me."

Toki nodded and Halla finally latched onto his arm and drew him close, as if he might disappear. Runa continued to stare at nothing, keeping her face empty of feeling. Ulfrik realized she had been pushed beyond her limit, but could not think of how best to help her cope.

"Once Hardar has received my surrender, he will come to seize my wealth. His mercenaries will be paid and will move on. At least that is my hope, since remaining here makes no sense unless they find more plunder. That is always possible. Still, while this goes on, you will be seeking aid. Go to Ragnvald. We are not so close that he might fight for me. But he may still be swayed by Hardar's aggression, or at the proposition of wealth."

"If we take your treasures with us," Snorri said, "then Hardar will know something is amiss. We have to leave a good portion behind."

"True, and who besides me knows how much wealth I truly possess?" Ulfrik spread his hands wide. No one answered. "So we leave him enough to see that I've been trading my wealth away all these years.

Besides, in flocks and property he will have enough to satisfy himself."

"What about the people left behind?" Einar asked. "Won't they be mistreated or enslaved?"

"Maybe so. I can only ask for mercy. They did not want to fight, and so have chosen the loser's path. Hardar will do what he wants with them. Fate decides in this as in so many things."

"Too many things." Runa broke her silence, finally facing Ulfrik. "What if Ragnvald joins? We still have the same problem, only worse since you will be a hostage."

"Do not stop with Ragnvald. Keep looking among the islands. Hardar does not have everyone's love. Make sure the other jarls see the threat to their lands. He hired a massive fleet and destroyed me. What about them? A smart jarl will understand what happened to me could happen to himself. If a few act, there is hope. Hardar will have to release me, and swear an oath of peace."

Runa frowned, but her stare faltered and she lowered her head, hair falling over her face.

"Ulfrik, this plan is dangerous. Even if Hardar doesn't execute you, he might mistreat you badly enough to kill you. It could take too long to gather allies. We might even be caught at it. Isn't there another way?" Toki pleaded.

"I know the danger. But if I flee with you, then those mercenaries will catch us."

"The ocean is vast and the world wide," Toki countered. "One ship can hide easily. We've hid all four of our ships many times."

"Then truly those left behind will suffer. Hardar will destroy them out of rage and spite. He will torture them for information. My honor and name would be forever destroyed. You know this, Toki."

The two men stared at each other in long silence. Then Toki shook his head. "I wish there was another way."

"So do we all," Ulfrik replied. "But the gods will have blood before they have mercy."

CHAPTER FOURTEEN

Hardar felt nearly out of breath, such was his excitement and his rush to don his linen cloak and sword. Ingrid sat on their bed as he fumbled with the belt of his sword. She slumped forward with both hands cupping her listless face. The pin Ulfrik had given as a gift was fixed to his cloak. "Gods, woman, you look like something dredged from a fishing net. We must look like victors."

Ingrid stared at the wall as she replied. "He didn't come with Halla. Why do I care about looking better? There's nothing to celebrate."

Hardar yanked her off the bed. She flopped around like a drunk; he actually thought he caught a scent of mead from her. He pawed at her hair and brushed down her dress, attempting to make her presentable. "Let's get out there. Hurry."

Bounding into the hall, he faced a group of men in neat rows of threes assembled before the high table. At their front stood Ulfrik. Hardar's warriors flanked them, weapons drawn. *This is really happening*, he thought. *Kjotve's word was true!* He strode to the edge of the short earthen rise to stand in front of Ulfrik. A smile exploded across Hardar's face.

Ulfrik stood ragged and limp, like seaweed washed up on the beach. His hair was lank and his cheeks sunken. Hardar gleefully took in every sign of Ulfrik's defeat, from the forced way he tried to stand tall to the way the corners of his mouth trembled. His eyes were couched in blackened bags of flesh. But the icy gaze peering out from them stilled Hardar's rising excitement. Purpose showed in that gaze, as well as a flash of threat.

Turning to his other captives to break Ulfrik's arresting gaze, he counted a dozen other men, all unarmed and dressed in plain clothing. No sign of status on any of them, no arm rings or gold. Hardar smiled, knowing he would uncover their wealth despite their efforts to hide it. The rest of the hall was filled with the remainder of his men and a part of Kjotve's. The fearsome Kjotve was absent, which pleased Hardar.

"I hear your ship barely made it to shore. My men had to tow you the distance." Hardar folded his arms across his chest, careful to let the hand with his gold rings show on top.

"Your mercenaries did what you could not. Don't gloat over your ability, which lacks in every detail. You couldn't piss your own pants without someone to point your cock."

Ulfrik's men laughed, and Hardar's face grow hot. He opened his mouth to curse, but drew back. *Time enough to beat that arrogance out of him, one broken bone at a time.* "And all your ability washed you up on my shores. So much for the high and mighty Jarl Ulfrik Ormsson of Nye Grenner." Hardar flicked a hand as if shooing a mosquito. "Our lives are in the hands of Fate, and Fate has placed you in mine."

"I sailed here under a sign of truce, which your men recognized. If you had any honor, you would do the same."

"You came here in a sinking ship. You came to surrender. So let's not pretend anymore, Ulfrik." Hardar spit the name like a mouthful of fish bones.

"I demand terms first. You see I've not come with all my men. There are plenty more willing to fight you, and we will fight until death. Be wise and you can have what you want without further loss. Without mercenaries, you are helpless. Without pay, your mercenaries will abandon you. Maybe they won't want to pry at my hall as long as you think."

Ulfrik smirked as if his logic were infallible. Hardar conceded he would be correct in any other circumstance. But Kjotve wanted the pearl inside the shell, and Ulfrik did not realize it. Yet.

"Then what are your terms? Don't leave me quaking in fear." Hardar exaggerated a shiver, eliciting laughter from his warriors.

"I surrender myself, my wealth, and you will accept my people and lands as your own. Treat them as your own, and they will serve you well. No slavery, no hall burning, no more killing. My people desire peace."

Hardar tapped his foot as he considered. Ulfrik was only a few feet away. A plain cloak pinned with a bit of bone or wood hid most of his body. His own men flanked him with spears leveled, but they seemed

171

lulled by the safety of numbers. Despite the defeated posture of his captives, their blades pointed at their bodies, he suspected Ulfrik laid a trap. "You don't hide any weapons under that cloak, do you? You're not going to drive a blade up my throat?"

Ulfrik unpinned his cloak and dropped it at his feet. "Search me if you must. I have nothing more than my clothes. I am yours, Hardar. My men have foolish notions of following me into death. But I ask you send them home."

"Death? But that would be too generous of me!" Hardar unfolded his arms and began to pace. He noticed Ingrid had followed behind and now stood next to him. She looked like a spirit faded into the half-light. "No, Ulfrik, you should be made to understand the pain you've caused my people, the ill will your scheming has brought to these lands. The others jarls must see the price of arrogance."

A faint smile seemed to flit across Ulfrik's face, drawing a scowl to Hardar's. "Do you think I'm a fool? Is this a joke to you? You will not be smiling before the day is done."

Suddenly Ingrid stepped forward, her voice shrill and screeching. "What have you done with my daughter? Why did you not deliver her to me?"

"She remains with her people," Ulfrik stated.

"Her people?" Ingrid's voice threatened to pierce Hardar's eardrums. He leapt to her side, gripped her thin arm and hauled her back. She wrested herself free as Ulfrik explained.

"Toki and Halla are betrothed. She has freely entered into marriage with him, making her one of my people."

Hardar's laughter came automatically. Ingrid regarded him as if

172

he had bitten her ear. "Your arrogance is endless. Without my permission, Halla's marriage means nothing. She was betrothed to Jarl Vermund, whom you slew. As I see it, she will return to me and the rat who stole her from my hall will be executed. But not before I've flayed every inch of flesh from his body."

Ulfrik shrugged. Such a simple gesture, but it kicked Hardar in the gut. He lunged up to him. "I'm going to enjoy carving that spirit out of your heart. You want to mock me, even in defeat? Have fun at it. It won't be much longer before those teeth are falling out of your rotten mouth."

Ulfrik pierced him with his gaze, but Hardar did not flinch. The two bristled a hand's breadth apart. Hardar watched a fly land on Ulfrik's cheek, parade in a circle like a victory dance, then twirl away. Not a muscle moved on his face.

"Until my daughter is returned, I will accept none of your terms. You and your men are prisoners until she and her so-called husband are standing on the ground you occupy right now. Where is she?"

Ulfrik flinched for the first time, a darkness passing across his features that pleased Hardar to see. "She remains in my hall."

"If she is not, then your wife and little boy will help me locate her. Do you understand?"

"I was not about to deliver them all to my enemy. Go fetch them from my hall. But my wife and son, they are to be left alone."

Hardar's frown melded into a grin. "They will be my guests, hostages to your behavior."

"Then we have an agreement?" Ulfrik asked. Hardar paused again.

"I expected more fight from you, even in defeat. Why are you so eager to surrender?"

Ulfrik spit in Hardar's face, spraying him in the eyes. "Does that suit you better? If you want a fight, I'm ready any time."

Hardar pawed at the wetness as one of his men rammed his spear-butt into Ulfrik's side, collapsing him to one knee. The man raised the spear for another blow.

"Enough! We'll get to the beating later." Hardar wiped his hand on his pants as Ulfrik recovered from the spear strike. "So we have an agreement, Ulfrik. You and all of these men are my prisoners until Halla is returned. I will take all that you possess, and rule your lands as my own. Your people will swear oaths to me, and send hostages. Those who refuse will die where they stand."

Ulfrik bowed his head. "So be it."

Hardar laughed, deep from his soul. He had pulled victory from certain destruction. The gods had sent Kjotve to strengthen him. This victory confirmed he was true spiritual leader of these islands, and now his one challenger lay crushed beneath him. A warm glow wrapped him as he lorded over Ulfrik.

"Now I get my pay." The booming voice echoed across the hall. Hardar looked over the heads of the others, spotting the huge and shaggy shape of Jarl Kjotve framed against the light of the open door. He flickered into shadow as he entered, men parting to allow him forward.

"Not as of yet. My daughter is not returned."

"Not my worry." Kjotve lumbered forward. Hardar watched Ulfrik twist around, then stagger back. Kjotve chuckled. "Seeing ghosts,

174

are you, Ulfrik? Someone left for dead, surrounded and cut off on a little island, has now returned to see all debts paid."

"You died at Hafrsfjord. Everyone said so. The island was surrounded, cut off." Ulfrik's voice diminished. Hardar enjoyed watching Ulfrik stripped of all bravado. He was like a frightened boy, and Kjotve's hulking size made even the statuesque Ulfrik appear child-like.

"No thanks to oath-breakers like you, I lived. And I've rebuilt. There's much catching up for us to do."

"There is no Kort the Gray." Hardar didn't understand Ulfrik's dejected statement, but Kjotve and his followers roared in laughter.

"But there is. He's just not me." Kjotve now turned to Hardar, his voice becoming a low threat. "I take him and this crew as my payment. Then I'm done here."

"But we agreed just on Ulfrik. I need hostages to ensure my daughter is returned."

"Do you think my services were not worth the price?" Kjotve's yellow and black teeth showed in his smile. His followers stood forward, reminding Hardar how desperately he was outnumbered. He shook his head and looked away, but Ingrid flew at Kjotve like a gull to a fish.

"My daughter was kidnapped and still hasn't come home. You can't do this!" Ingrid snatched a mug from the table, but Hardar clamped his hand atop hers. Kjotve smiled at the whole scene.

"You will find her, Lady Ingrid. But Ulfrik and his crew have been long in tracking down. The gods granted them to me, to see justice done. So I will be taking them now."

Hardar shoved Ingrid behind him. Halla didn't matter now that her chastity had been compromised and Vermund killed. He wanted her returned as a point of pride. "Then take the lot of them, Jarl Kjotve. Well worth it for the help you've given me."

Kjotve growled in pleasure. "Wise choice. And you, Ulfrik, might recall a time when my son took you as a slave to save your life. Well, that happens once in a lifetime. I'm making you slave and plan to whip the skin off your back while you row my ships. How does that sound to you?"

Eyes wide, Ulfrik did not answer. His jaw moved in wordless shock. Hardar shuddered thinking what the monstrous Kjotve planned, though his largest regret was missing the chance to witness it.

***

Ulfrik's plan went awry at the first step. Everyone had come to send him off. Somber faces surrounded him. Many begged him to stay, others said nothing. He suspected a few came merely to see the spectacle of leaving his family. The throng of observers prevented him from secretly launching his family in a ship. Instead, he had to devise a ruse to cover.

Heavy clouds filled the skies, appearing as plowed fields of ash. The sea lay flat and gray, waves lapping as if the ocean had lost its strength. *Fjord Runner* and *Raven's Talon* swayed placidly at dock. At least his treasures had been loaded to *Raven's Talon* before the crowds had gathered. Now people formed a line down the slope to the ships. He noted how many were middle-aged women, their head covering flapping in the breeze. This brief, brutal conflict had created an abundance of widows. He faced the burial mounds in the field behind the hall. He gave silent thanks for the bravery of the men interred within, then started down the line.

Runa and Gunnar awaited him at the end. With every step he grew more numb. His hands grew cold and his eyes watery. He trembled with fear and sorrow. An image of Runa's face from the first time they made love came to mind. They had owned nothing, nothing more than hope. But their love had been fierce, and the years had only increased their passions. They had given so much to each other. Now, a thread of hope was all he was leaving her.

People touched him as he shambled down slope. Some thanked him, others merely nodded, some turned askance as he neared. The faces filed by in a blur. As he passed, they fell in behind and followed him to the ships. At last he arrived at the end, where Runa and Gunnar stood. They both stared at him, both keeping emotion off their faces. A weak smile trembled on his lips, realizing they were better at hiding their feelings than he was. Toki and Halla, Snorri and his family also came forward, along with the crews for each ship. He turned to address the gathered people. Rows of sullen faces spread up the slope, and hardly a sound above a lone bird call was heard.

"I will surrender to Hardar and demand the best terms for all of you. I cannot guarantee you what he will do. He could kill me and burn all of your homes. Whoever will lead you now, my advice is to stay ready. My family will accompany me as will those still sworn to my service. What happens next is for Fate to decide."

Ulfrik's words created the stir he had intended. He knew no one had thought of a replacement leader. They started to mumble. He took the moment to whisper to Toki. "You will have to follow me for a while, but then break way. The men aboard my ship, I can only hope they will be loyal once they return."

Toki gave him a sad smile. "The men on your ship have no intention of returning without you."

Ulfrik began to protest when Thorvald emerged from the crowd. He squared off with Ulfrik, jaw set and face inscrutable. Then he embraced Ulfrik. "I am sorry that it has come to this. I am your man, if ever you return."

Ulfrik pulled away and said nothing. He wondered if Thorvald was excited for the chance to lead Nye Grenner. He didn't care anymore. Instead, he approached Runa and took her hand.

"Trust in my plan. Turn the others against Hardar, then come with haste. We must endure time apart."

She tried to look away, but failed. Her eyes glittered as she groped for words. Ulfrik pressed his finger to her lips, sparing both of them the pain of good-bye. She kissed his finger, as tears pressed out of her closed eyes.

Ulfrik knelt down to Gunnar. He met his son's flinty eyes. As much as he resembled his mother, the resolve he saw in Gunnar's face resembled Ulfrik's father. His chest filled with pride. "I will be gone a while. You must obey your mother. Time for play is over. Now you are on an adventure, and must be brave. Can you do that for me?"

Gunnar nodded. Ulfrik smiled and ruffled his son's hair. He wanted to say more, but had to stand before tears overwhelmed him. Breaking down before Gunnar would not help anyone. He unhitched his sword and offered it to Runa. "Keep it for Gunnar. It's not the best I've ever owned, but it's a good weapon."

"I don't plan to give it to him." She hesitated a moment, then snatched it from him. She unpinned her cloak, and held out the antler pin on her palm. "It's poor enough that even Hardar won't want it. I've owned it since we met. Take it."

Accepting it, he pushed it into his own cloak. There was nothing left but to leave. Snorri stepped forward and guided him down the dock to *Fjord Runner*. "Get aboard and let's get this started."

Ulfrik turned to watch Runa and Gunnar board their ship on the opposite side. Toki assisted Halla aboard. Einar and Gerdie waited for Snorri. Once Ulfrik was aboard, a crew of twelve men joined him. Some were young and others old, but all had followed him from Norway, the last of his original crew. Ulfrik's tears flowed anew at their loyalty.

The ship lurched as it pushed away. The crowd gathered at the end of the dock were as still as lichen-covered standing stones. The dismal sky and thin fog painted the world gray. Ulfrik watched Snorri kiss Gerdie and hug Einar before helping them aboard *Raven's Talon*. Then his gray-haired friend made a running leap onto the deck of *Fjord Runner* as it was about to leave the dock.

"Damn you, Snorri! You're to be on the other ship!" Ulfrik felt his head grow hot. "Who is going to lead them?"

"Your wife," he said as he regained his balance. "Toki and Einar, plus the other men with them will do her fighting. But she'll be in charge, no doubt."

Ulfrik's ship lurched away as men dipped their oars into the thick water. He looked past Snorri to see Gunnar watching over the rails, Runa standing behind him. "I cannot allow you to do this." Ulfrik cast around to all of his men. "You all should turn back once I'm ashore.

Hardar's battle is with me alone."

Snorri shook his head, a smile tugging his grizzled beard. "We serve our lord to the end, as honor dictates."

"What about Gerdie and Einar?" Ulfrik flung his hands up in exasperation. "They've already lost their family once."

"Gerdie is a strong woman, and Einar is a man now. They know I must keep you alive long enough for this plan to work."

The two men stared at each other for long moments. A bird screamed above, providing Ulfrik an excuse to look away. He went to the tiller and grabbed it. "I'm sorry to admit, but I'm glad you will be with me."

Snorri laughed. "I serve until the end, Ulfrik. May that end be long in coming."

CHAPTER FIFTEEN

Toki gazed after *Fjord Runner* as it shrank and vanished over the horizon. He swallowed, then noticed Runa leaned against the rails, watching the same spot. Her cloak pulled tight and her hair flew in the wind. Her stony silence was louder than the slashing of the waves breaking across the hull.

The sail snapped full above his head and two men adjusted the rigging. Totally the ship held ten people, with only four fighting men. Not many had been willing to sail with Toki the Cursed. Since hitting the open sea, no one had interacted much, each one wrapped in their own thoughts.

Halla and Dana shared a seat on Toki's sea chest. Dana spoke quietly while Halla merely nodded. Despite her proclamations, Toki had not experienced a deeper connection to her. The frantic planning for Ulfrik's surrender had not allowed time for them to strengthen their bond. Being at sea and traveling to other lands, he doubted their relationship would improve.

"The wind favors us." Einar approached, wiping his hands on his legs. "We will make good time and can sleep on dry land tonight. How far to Ragnvald?"

"We will arrive tomorrow morning, if he will have us. Did you pack provisions like I asked?"

"My father and I loaded what we were able to on short notice. Some mead too, in case we can't make landfall for a day or two."

Toki dropped his head when he recalled Einar's father, Snorri. Toki would miss him, especially his experience and wisdom. "I'm sorry for your father, Einar. This is all my fault."

"We've talked about that," Einar placed his hand on Toki's shoulder. "My father made his choice and was not sad for it. So neither am I, and neither should you be."

"Does your mother feel that way?"

"Well, she's not happy. But she's strong, like me."

Einar smiled, a young and naive smile that Toki wore not long ago. Bright and innocent, Toki could not help but match it. Yet the smile died when he caught Runa's eye. She glared at him as she wrapped her cloak around Gunnar. Toki felt the cold penetrate his core.

"Man the tiller for me, Einar." He approached Runa. *Raven's Talon* was not a large ship, and afforded little space for people to speak privately. But he had to try.

They both studied the sea gliding past them. Gunnar stood on his toes to peer over the rails, sticking his hand out to catch spray. Runa did not acknowledge Toki, though he noted her knuckles were white from gripping the railing.

"Do you blame me for this?" Toki knew no other way to get through to his sister besides a direct assault. She remained as if she had not heard him. "Do you think this is punishment for breaking my oath?"

Sighing, she shifted her weight but did not answer. Toki stole a glance over his shoulder. Both Halla and Dana looked on. Gerdie sat alone while everyone else appeared not to hear. So Toki leaned on the rail and kept quiet for as long as he was able, which was not long. "I feel responsible for all this. It would ..."

"Toki, not now," Runa snapped. "We are not one hour gone from home. I'm not ready to talk about this."

"I'm sorry. I just feel ..."

"Are you not listening?" She faced him, her brows drawn tight. "This is not a time for feeling. What are you, a woman? There are enough women on this ship. My husband is trusting his life to you. Do you feel bad? Then focus on what we must do to help him. That will make you feel better and be more useful as well."

Toki stood back, shocked at the power of Runa's words. She continued to stare out to sea, and Gunnar withdrew beneath her cloak. She started to blink, then tears began to run. "I will sail to every island, I swear, and I will make them see Hardar's threat. I'll do anything to get help. I will not rest until I'm sailing back with a fleet of my own. So that's what you must help me with, Toki. Stop worrying about how you feel and lead this mission."

"You're right," he admitted, returning to lean on the rails. "My mind has been full of trifles. Ulfrik is still my lord. He spared my life when he shouldn't have, you know. He gave me a family again. I promise you, I will dedicate myself to freeing him."

Toki imbued his words with emotion, but Runa simply nodded and brushed tears from her eyes. He reached to place a consoling arm on her but she recoiled. "Why don't you go make things right with your woman. She thinks I can't hear her complaints, but she may as well shout in my ear. If she carries on, I'm going to stave in her head with an oar."

Halla's head snapped away as Toki faced her. She and Dana both fell still and silent. "I hadn't realized they were upsetting you. I'll speak with her."

The few steps to Halla was like traveling miles uphill. A sudden wave lurched the ship and Toki and others stumbled. Dana tumbled off the chest and Halla toppled as well. But Toki caught her, and gently set her upright. She gave a light laugh, and thanked him. But her smile was short and false, and she paid more attention to helping Dana back to her seat.

"We should talk," Toki said, trying to keep his tone neutral. Halla shrugged and fixed her skirts. Toki clasped his hands behind his back, glancing about the small deck. "I'd prefer to talk alone."

"Well, then, let's take a walk." She flashed a sharp smile. Before Toki responded, Dana stood and stumbled away toward Gerdie in the bow. Toki let his breath draw out, grateful Dana understood what he wanted. He sat in her place.

"Runa says you've been complaining. Is it true?"

"Why would I be complaining? I'm just sailing away into

184

nowhere, hoping to find someone to kill my parents. It's really nothing to complain about, right?"

"We're not trying to kill your parents." Toki spit the words out so harshly that he did not even believe them. He would take as much pleasure in gutting Hardar as he did in gutting Vermund. But admitting it would only worsen Halla's disposition. She looked at him, tears standing in her eyes.

"There's more than one smart woman on this decrepit old boat. So let's not pretend. Your mission, as you're calling it now, is to raise an army against my father."

"Simply to force him to free Ulfrik and the others and swear an oath of peace."

"Men go to war with murder in their hearts, not for something stupid like oaths of peace." Halla grunted a laugh and flipped a strand of hair out of her face. "You will promise them glory and gold, and they will dream of battle. Once their swords are drawn, they will not put them away until their thirst for war is quenched with blood. Tell me I'm not right."

Toki studied his feet and scratched the back of his head. She was correct, of course. Only flippant replies bloomed in his thoughts and he bit those back as he searched for more affable words. The pause grew awkward and his desperation mounted, so he trusted inspiration.

"This is difficult for you. It is a hard time for us all. I wish things could be otherwise, but they are not. My heart is loyal to you, Halla, and will always be so. If I can find a way to settle with your father, I will. But I doubt he wants to make peace. There was a time when I thought your father's threats empty. Now it is a real possibility that he will have my

185

head. But for you, the risk is worth it."

They fell into silence again. The ship swayed and mast creaked as the sail filled, driving the ship over the foamy sea. Toki waited patiently for Halla. After several moments, she placed her delicate hand on his knee.

"I'm sorry, you did not ask for this. I first sought you as a way to escape Vermund. I wasn't sure what else I wanted. You are a good man, and I have no other to turn to now. It's just hard to accept what is happening. I have the same guilt that you do. Your sister hates me and blames me for this."

"That is untrue," Toki said. It was yet another statement lacking conviction but one he thought necessary. Halla withdrew her hand.

"You know it is true. I hope your sister can accept that I am not my father." Frustration infused her voice as she touched her head, shaking it. "But I did choose you, and I still believe it was the right choice. The time we spent together in secret gave me the fondest memories of my life. We spoke to each other like I never imagined two people could. Be patient with me on this mission. I understand how my father has brought this upon himself. I know he sought any excuse to make war with Ulfrik. I know he thinks me tarnished and useless now that I've left with you. But it still does not mean I wish to see him dead. Can you understand that?"

Toki nodded.

"Good, I will need your support in the coming days. I want to start a new life, one where we control our destinies. But so much seems uncertain today."

Toki took her hand again and squeezed it. He glanced around, and everyone was absorbed in other duties, real or feigned. His face heated up at the thought of displaying his tender side. Rather than deepen his embarrassment, he merely stood with Halla's hand in his own.

"You will have my support. But remember your speech is for all to hear on this ship, even when others pretend they are deaf. My sister worries for her husband and her son fears for his father. Your words must be soothing ones in their presence. Save other thoughts for when we can be ashore and alone."

"I will. I'm sorry to have been so thoughtless." She withdrew her hand, a sincere smile widening on her face. Her hair gleamed white with a ray of sunlight poking through the gray clouds. Toki felt calmer now, having navigated those treacherous emotional currents without a wreck.

Feeling the tension in his neck and shoulders abate, he returned to the tiller. As Einar handed it over to him, Toki caught Runa glaring at him again. He smiled, but it was like smiling at a wolf. She would rip out his throat if he gave her cause. He pulled hard on the tiller, hoping his sister and his future wife could share this ship long enough to find help for Ulfrik.

***

The morning of the next day, Toki conferred with Einar and the two other men. Toki had camped them on shore for the night, and woke to discover a square sail on the horizon. Fortunately they had not started a fire, and the ship sailed past. Toki had actually held his breath as he watched the ship vanish into the morning fog. *Raven's Talon* with a cargo of gold and women would be a plump target for raiders.

"Could it be more mercenaries drawn here by Hardar's offer?" Einar asked.

Toki frowned and shook his head. "We'll never know. It could be anyone. But I saw it filled with crew, and even a peaceful crew might make slaves of us. We must skirt that ship."

The two other men were brothers and close friends of Toki's. The older brother was near Toki's age, broad shouldered and stout. He was called Njall the Tall. His younger brother wore an innocent face ruined by a lazy eye, and was called him Thrand the Looker. Together with Bork they had been the core of Toki's friends.

Njall studied the point on the horizon where the unknown ship had disappeared. "What if they're headed to the same place? Wouldn't want to sail in on whatever business they're doing?"

"So can't we try somewhere else?" Thrand's sideway gaze landed on Toki. "Just go find another jarl to persuade."

Toki spit on the sandy grass. He heard Runa shouting. His stomach lurched and his hands went cold. But when he spun around she was yelling for Gunnar to climb down from a pile of high rocks. Toki's shoulders slumped in relief. The three others gave him worried looks. "I thought she was warning of danger," he lied. He had feared Halla and Runa were at each other's throats. "You've got a point, Thrand. But Ragnvald is our best hope and if we can gather him to our cause, we will have more influence on the other jarls."

No one appeared to have any better ideas and they shifted around rubbing their hands or stretching and delaying. Toki hated the absence of Snorri and Ulfrik. One of them would have taken his ideas and make a real plan from them. But now he was on his own, and the obvious leader. Then an idea flashed and he started to put it together as he spoke.

"What if we were to hire our own mercenaries? We can offer some gold up front, and promise a take in whatever spoils they can capture from Hardar." Toki's eyes widened in excitement at his new idea. The others seemed less favorable.

"Wouldn't have Lord Ulfrik thought of the idea himself?" asked Einar.

"Yeah, it sounds dangerous," Njall said. "Why not just kill or enslave us and take all the gold we carry?"

"Let me think this out." Toki clapped his hands together and rubbed. "We only want to bring more men to the cause. If we have more men, the other jarls will be encouraged to join us. Why join a single ship of desperate women? A ship of fighting men will give them confidence enough to join."

"But Lord Ulfrik said we should hurry. Where are we going to find mercenaries?" Einar asked.

"The islands to the east are filled with the remnants of the armies that faced Harald Finehair at Hafrsfjord. Among those lands are men ready for battle. Bork came to us from those lands, you'll remember." Toki's excitement began to overtake his judgment. "We could seed the word along the shores, hire those who seek adventure and be back to persuade Ragnvald. My ship can hold twenty men or more. A filled ship is more likely to attract another filled ship."

Einar frowned in thought while Njall and Thrand looked to him for a response. Toki believed in the superiority of this idea. Ulfrik had planned in haste and under a tremendous burden. But this type of daring plan seemed more like the cunning Ulfrik loved. Even if only Ragnvald joined them, he could still bring three ships full of men to Ulfrik's aid.

"So your silence means you haven't a better idea?"

Njall folded his arms. "I'm just trying to think this out. It's two days sailing with good weather. Then we need time to find men willing to join us. Once we get back to Ulfrik it could be weeks gone."

"It was going to be weeks anyway," Toki insisted. "How fast do you think the other jarls will act? What if one of them decides to side with Hardar? We will have no men of our own for protection. Ulfrik would be truly lost then. But with a larger crew, we can deal more safely. I think this is the right plan."

Njall and Thrand both appeared to accept Toki's reasoning. Only Einar seemed to still debate the idea.

"There's an ill cloud over this plan. But I can't say what it is."

"That's only because the plan is new to you. Give it time and you will see it makes sense." Toki looked to Njall and Thrand for agreement, which they gave. "Besides, we need time for Hardar's mercenaries to depart and that strange ship to pass through. So let's get back to sea and take advantage of this wind."

Einar begrudgingly nodded. Toki scanned the distant sea, seeing nothing but gray fog obscuring the horizon.

CHAPTER SIXTEEN

The ships appeared as flat water bugs stretched out on the sea. Oars formed their legs, pulling across the sparkling azure surface. Inside the ships, flesh colored dots swayed back and forth in unison with the oars. Each dot was a man and each ship held twenty men at ten oars to a side. Other men walked between the rowers or leaned on their tillers. Some sat idle in the prow.

But the men at the oars labored, as they had for a full day. Their grunts were audible above the splash of the water and the creak of the hulls. They sat on sea chests, and some had their feet bound with seal skin rope. Those with free legs sang songs. Those with bound feet grunted or kept silent.

Ulfrik had not spoken since being dragged aboard Kjotve's ship.

His arms and shoulders burned from the strain of rowing. His back and chest felt tight and heavy. He kept his head down, focusing on the seawater sloshing around his bound feet. Though others sat before and behind him, he was alone. The foolishly brave men who had followed him into slavery were seeded throughout the other ships. The few on his ship were seated behind him. He hadn't dared turn around.

Ulfrik's mouth was filled with paste. His throat constricted so even spit popped his throat when he swallowed. His hands and feet were cold, not from the ocean temperatures, which were mild, but from fear. The cold seeped into his chest, and were it not for the constant friction of rowing, Ulfrik would have felt like a naked man in a winter gale.

But for all the physical symptoms, nothing matched Ulfrik's inner suffering. This was not how the plan was to work. Hardar was supposed to have shamed him in front of the other jarls. Toki and Runa would have had time to find allies, to build a resistance to Hardar. Kjotve should have been dead. Now Ulfrik was a slave to a blood-thirsty raider, rowing to an unknown destination. How would anyone find him again?

For the first time in his life, Ulfrik knew fear. He had survived trials and battles that had left better men dead. He had faced the evil of his brother's schemes. He had been driven from his home to be chased by wolves and dark-hearted men. He had walked away from all of it.

But this fear was different.

Unlike everything else he had faced before, his actions now affected many. Thoughts of Runa and Gunnar filled his mind, envisioning them lost at sea or falling into enemy hands. His beautiful family, those he loved and swore to protect, were now on a hopeless

192

mission. Their lives were ruined. He had caused it. He blamed his hubris, short-sightedness, and foolishness. He cursed his arrogance. What had he been thinking? Why had he refused to flee with his family? How had he made this terrible choice? How had so many people put faith in him, only to be ruined? These questions seized his mind and clenched out anything else. Worry turned the scraps of food he had been given to tasteless leather. Fear and worry refused to leave him, and enslaved him as well as Kjotve had.

"Oars in! Raise the sail!" A voice boomed behind Ulfrik, and the rowers hauled in their oars with grateful moans. The wind had steadied at their backs, and would give them better speed to wherever they traveled.

Ulfrik yanked in his oar and let it thud to the deck. He slumped to lean on his knees, but a heavy hand cuffed his head. "Don't drop it on the deck. Rack it, you stupid dog!"

Ulfrik hoisted himself off the chest, dragging the oar from the deck. The man moved past him, finding other slaves to cuff. Ulfrik shuffled to the rack beneath the mast and flung the oar onto the pile. Others did the same. He met one of his former crewman's eyes as they stared at each other across the rack. Ulfrik had to turn aside, his stomach knotting at the hopelessness he read in his follower's expression.

He slouched on the sea chest and stared down at his feet. Kjotve's crew stood and stretched while others hoisted the sail. The ship tugged ahead as the wind filled it. Someone handed him a wooden cup half filled with water. He took it, stared into the reflected sky in his cup, then drained it. When he finished, he found Kjotve seated on the chest across from him.

"How are you enjoying life aboard my ship?" His thick forearms were folded across his belly as he smiled. "Nothing like a good day of rowing to renew a man. Don't you think so?"

Words fled Ulfrik. A croak bubbled out of his throat, making Kjotve roll back with a laugh.

"Never thought I'd find you without something to say. How far you've fallen, boy. Anyway, you've been boring me. I've been expecting a little more spirit out of you."

Ulfrik stared at Kjotve's lusterless eyes. Years before, they had sparkled with passion, but now were like two nubs of old wood. Ulfrik's pasty mouth produced rough, dry words. "Your eyes say you died at Hafrsfjord."

Kjotve laughed again, but false and short. "I lost everything at Hafrsfjord, if you didn't know. I lost my son, my ships, my fortune, my home. I lost my kingdom, and all with no small thanks to men who fled me rather than honor their oaths."

"I thought you were dead. Harald had you cornered on an island."

"You fled while I lived. The sheep herders on these islands might call you a hero, but I know you for a coward. I survived and learned who was true and who was not." Kjotve leaned forward on the sea chest and jabbed a finger at Ulfrik. "You broke your oath to me! After I took you in and gave you land!"

"I gave my oath to your son, Thor. My duty died with him."

"I was the Jarl of Agder, and that oath was mine as well. You destroyed your honor when you fled."

"I thought you dead," Ulfrik mumbled. He dropped his head,

feeling numb.

"So you had hoped." Folding his arms again, Kjotve leaned back on his seat. "You know oath breakers should be killed out of hand. If a man can't honor his oath, then what's he worth?"

Ulfrik met Kjotve's eyes and sneered. "I suspect you will tell me. You didn't kill me, and so must see some value."

"You're value at market will tell me what you're worth," Kjotve said, his voice low and hissing. "You and your fool crew are going to the slave markets of Dublin. I'll recover some of the gold I wasted on you, and justice will be served."

Ulfrik's heart leapt at the shock. He had suspected as much, but to hear his fate uttered aloud hit him as hard as an actual blow. Yet Kjotve's smug face turned his fear to anger, and he experienced a surge of strength. "Justice? Not even a chance to speak on my behalf, nor any other man to support your claims, and you call that justice. You took one too many hits on your fat head if you believe yourself. Don't waste your breath convincing me of justice. You're just a ruined man, pretending to greatness."

Kjotve rolled back on his seat and guffawed. "Now that's the spirit I expected from you. Hope you can build it up, since it will be so much more fun to beat it out of you. Oh, but Fate has been kind to bring us together."

A vision of strangling Kjotve flashed through Ulfrik's mind. His body nearly reacted to the thought. He was an arm's length away, his thick neck lay exposed. Ulfrik's palms itched to clamp around it and squeeze. But no sooner had the beguiling thought arisen than it yielded to reality. Ulfrik knew he would be run through a dozen times before he could harm him. The hateful power drained from his limbs, and Kjotve carried on oblivious.

"I came here to raid, hearing that men lived on these barren rocks who paid traders in gold. When I learned that Ulfrik Ormsson was one of the wealthiest, I knew I had to come. I honestly considered sailing straight to your hall and gutting you right there. But Fate and bad information guided me to your enemy instead. That's where I found how much more fun things could be. These islands are filled with men grown dull from tending sheep. They are led easier than lambs."

Other of Kjotve's crew gathered to hear his bragging. Ulfrik, though wearing a scowl, was also interested to know what Kjotve had plotted.

"While Hardar was away fighting you," Kjotve again stabbed his finger at Ulfrik. "I got his fool wife to tell me everything. There's a lot of fighting men here, as I had guessed with so much gold changing hands. So I realized that your little war would help me whittle down their numbers and aid me in my original purpose in sailing here. And was I wrong? Here you are rowing my ship while half of these islands are without men to defend them!"

Kjotve laughed again, joined by his crew. Ulfrik's eyes drew to slits as he began to understand the real danger that had been growing while he and Hardar feuded.

"So before we head off to Dublin, we're sacking Vermund and Hardar. Thanks to your warring, their lands are wide open. Let no one say Kjotve passes up opportunities to increase his wealth."

Kjotve lumbered to his feet. A swell rocked the ship and he had to grab the rail a moment. Then he laughed along with his crew. Ulfrik sat glowering at him. The shame and fear he had been feeling was now giving way to a fierce anger. He agreed that Fate had brought them together, but not for the justice that Kjotve thought. Fate placed him next to Kjotve so that he might save these lands from the predations of this so-called sea-king.

"Rest, Ulfrik," he said as lightly as if they were old friends. "Once these winds die you'll be at your oar again."

"When ill seed has been sown, so an ill crop will spring from it."

Kjotve paused at Ulfrik's words, turned with a frown on his face. "And so it is with your broken oath. Now still your mouth or I'll bind it too."

Kicking the puddle of seawater at his feet, Ulfrik followed Kjotve as he returned to the prow. A nascent smile formed on his face. He was going to fight and win. Now he understood Fate's purpose for him. "The ill crop is not mine to harvest," he whispered to himself. "But it is yours and Hardar's. So Fate will show you both."

***

Ulfrik watched the sacking of Hardar's lands unfurl in the same way as Vermund's. Kjotve drove his ships aground and his crew leapt the rails with battle-maddened howls. They streamed inland waving swords and spears, and fell upon anyone they encountered. Ulfrik stood on the shingle, in full view of the carnage. Hardar's hall and surrounding homes were laid out in a large basin surrounded by lush green cliffs. Orange bursts of flames from the buildings snapped at the sky. With Hardar and most of his hirdmen gone to subjugate Nye Grenner, Trongisvagur fell without resistance.

The raid on Vermund's hall had yielded a dozen captives and piles of loot. Sheep were herded aboard one ship; Ulfrik guessed these would be traded within the islands. Sheep fared poorly on open sea. This meant at least one other jarl was aware of Kjotve's plans.

Since now more slaves had to be guarded and sheep corralled on ship, the guards remaining behind herded all the slaves in a single mass. Vermund's people held to themselves, staring at their feet or else looking vacantly ahead. A mother and daughter clung together, their faces smeared with blood and dirt and eyes wide with terror. None made a sound or otherwise indicated they were alive. Kjotve's men had more trouble herding the sheep aboard their ship.

Kjotve had left eight men on guard duty. They were outnumbered two to one, but Ulfrik understood no one had heart to fight. Bound feet made running impossible. So instead he gathered his men, whispering for them to pull closer while the guards watched the spectacle of Hardar's kingdom burning away. A distant roof crashed, sending a flurry of sparks twirling skyward. The guards laughed and hooted. Ulfrik used the moment to speak with his men. Snorri stood beside him; though haggard and tired, his stalwart presence bolstered Ulfrik.

"We don't have much time to speak," he whispered. "Kjotve was a bad turn of luck for us, and my plan needs adjustment. But I am not defeated, even if you see me weaponless and foot-bound."

Some nodded and smiled, a few held their expressions flat. Ulfrik pressed on, watching for the guards to catch him planning.

"Fate has put us with Kjotve for a reason, and that's to rid these lands of him. Look at what he's doing now. If he had more room on his ships, he'd carry away everything in these islands. We're the only ones who can stop him."

He scanned the tight circle of faces and read their doubt. "It seems impossible now; but who better than us? We are trained warriors, not sheep herders. Kjotve has forgotten that in his rush to claim victory and spoils."

"Ulfrik," Snorri said, his voice low and tired. "You're right, but we're also underfed, overworked, and bound at the feet. Once in open sea, what can we do? We can't overtake six ships."

"But we can overtake one, and we have twelve new captives to help. I just need a weapon, anything. We all have oars. The short oars for working the shallows are fine weapons."

"I've never heard of battles being won with oars," Snorri said and laughed. A few other echoed him, and even Ulfrik smiled.

"A skull will break from a hammer or a heavy shaft of wood. I'm just saying we are not without options. Look, I don't have the plan laid out, but it will have to happen when we are gathered like this. Kjotve was canny enough to put us on different ships. So he must fear we could overtake him. We must figure out what he fears and build off that."

The others began to nod, and Ulfrik's spirits buoyed. He did not need them to be screaming mad and ready to run, but just latch to a strand of hope.

"I'm also going to use what chances the gods provide. So I may be acting fast and you will all have to make your best judgments. We want to get our own ship, and have a head start on pursuit. Capturing a ship is something that will come easily. But the gods are with us, even if they seem distant. They want us to work for this, to entertain them with our cunning and bravery. If we can do that, then the gods will reward us with freedom."

Kjotve's guards finally turned and caught them huddled. One called out for them to stop, while others shoved apart their group. Satisfied that nothing strange was transpiring, they turned away again. But Snorri remained close. He leaned into Ulfrik as he spoke.

"Do you really have a plan, or was that just a talk to keep our hopes up?"

"I don't have a plan, but I believe what I said." Ulfrik spoke without looking at Snorri. A guard eyed him, but then resumed watching for Kjotve's return.

Groups of men like swarms of beetles emerged from the ruins of Hardar's lands. Kjotve's men were retuning, carrying their loot and driving their captives ahead of them. Ulfrik and the others silently observed the procession of destroyed lives. Only the young and strong were taken, driven at spear point. Ulfrik imagined the old maimed or dead among the collapsing roofs of Hardar's village. A young man tried to flee. Ulfrik stifled a warning shout. Without a thought, one of Kjotve's marauders speared him as he ran. The young man toppled with a shriek. The first strike had not killed him, and the marauder stabbed him repeatedly until the screaming ceased.

Kjotve led the group, and was in great spirits. Ulfrik could hear his ragged laughter over the wails of women and their children. He had a woman thrown over his shoulder who kicked and screeched, though the giant Kjotve seemed bothered no more than if a fly circled his head.

"Get aboard the ships," ordered one of the guards, emphasizing his command with a flash of his spear. "Make it fast."

Ulfrik turned and shuffled toward the ship. His foot binding had enough slack for a curtailed stride. He hissed a whisper to those nearby. "Try to stick together as much as you can."

Guards grabbed a few of his crew and shoved them toward other ships. But Snorri and most the others boarded Kjotve's ship. The guards' interest lay in learning what they had missed rather than herding captives.

"More slaves, and I'll suppose you will want to save them too," Snorri quipped as they took seats by the starboard oars. He sat directly in front of Ulfrik.

"I will do what I can; these are mostly farmers and their families."

"Whatever you plan, it better work the first time or we're all dead."

Ulfrik grunted, then decided not to think any more on it. "I'll look for the gods to give a sign."

Men clambered aboard, throwing sacks of booty onto the deck or shoving captives aboard. Captives cried for mercy and their captors laughed or roared curses into their faces. Heavy bags of loot thudded as they landed on the decks. Men laughed and bragged. Some groaned at wounds given by others strong enough to fight back. From another ship the stolen sheep bleated in despair. Above it all Kjotve's voice carried as he ordered his crew.

Though he knew his family was safely away, Ulfrik could not help envision Runa and Gunnar as these captives. A short man with red hair dragged a woman up the gangplank and dumped her on the deck. Her son, only a few years older than Ulfrik's, ran crying to her side. The red-haired man kicked the mother aside and he measured out rope for her bindings. Ulfrik swallowed and looked away, his hands and feet growing cold with fear.

He scanned the fjord, trying to block out the sounds of defeat. Out there Runa searched for help to defeat Hardar and win his freedom. He wondered what would happen when they arrived and found nothing but ash. *How would I even find them again*, he worried. *As long as they remain within the Faereyjar I can find them. But I beg you, wife, stay long enough for me to escape.*

"Now you're a spirited bitch!" Kjotve's shout broke his thoughts. He bounded up the gangplank with the kicking woman still on his shoulder. He let her down as lightly as if she were a child. As soon as the woman's feet alighted on the deck, she stood back and slapped Kjotve. But he blocked her with a muscled arm and laughed. "I hope you fuck like you fight!"

The laughter of the crew was dull in Ulfrik's ears. He focused only on the woman: tall, fair-haired, and noble. She was Ingrid, Hardar's wife. She stood straight though her hair flew loose and wild over her face and her fine green dress was spattered with mud and torn at the shoulder. She struck him again, and Kjotve parried with his thick arm.

"You troll! You promised you would find my daughter." Her shouting died beneath the laughter of Kjotve's crew.

"Come now, I'm not all that bad. I've caught the bastard who stole her from you." He pointed at Ulfrik. "That ought to be worth a kiss at least."

Before she could follow his finger, he seized her arm and yanked her to his mouth. She shrieked and finally landed a slap over his eye. But he jammed his face into hers and kissed her as the crew laughed and clapped.

Ulfrik looked away, unable to watch without imagining Runa in the same position.

Once Kjotve had bound Ingrid, he spun her around for his crew to leer and laugh. Ingrid's head dropped and her fight drained. Someone handed Kjotve a skin of mead, and he guzzled from it. Then he shouted for the ships to push off.

CHAPTER SEVENTEEN

Toki's prayers to Thor and all the gods he could name went unanswered. By the second day at sea, he watched the storm forming, everyone did, knowing they were trapped in a landless expanse of water. Though the summer sun would not set until the heart of night, the sky had grown thick with darkness. Sparse rain drops pattered on the deck, driven slantwise by an increasing wind. Each drop felt like a punch to Toki. Without being issued orders, Thrand and Njall unstepped the mast and stowed the sail.

"Einar, speak with me a moment." Toki beckoned him over. "This storm will be fierce. The angle of the wind ..."

"Is bad," Einar finished for him. "We all know it. We have nothing to sacrifice to please the gods, but for ourselves."

Toki put up his hand. "The gods seek their vengeance upon me alone. You and the others will be safe. But let's be sure of it. Tie the women to the rails and Gunnar too. Tie yourselves if there's enough rope left. Better to break an arm than drown."

Einar nodded and started to turn, then paused. "Toki, don't make the gods work easier than it need be."

He laughed, the sound awkward in the tense atmosphere. "I swear to you I will not."

Einar and the others tied off the women and Gunnar. Halla and Dana were pale and trembling. The wind pulled their clothing tight and set their hair dancing. Halla looked at him blankly, in stunned horror. The sea had begun to churn and footing became treacherous. Njall stumbled toward the gunwales, grabbing the rail before falling overboard. Toki's heart pounded and everyone froze, as if to move would condemn him to the sea grave. But Njall landed on the deck.

Runa shielded Gunnar from the wind by covering him within her cloak. She had the most sailing experience of any of the women. But Toki knew she had never experienced a storm like the one approaching. Lightning flashed and Thor's mighty roar boomed across the water. "Spare these people, Thor," he muttered under his breath. "I am the one who offended you."

His arm grew heavy wrestling the tiller. Now the wind and rain had strengthened, gusts driving the ship. The current was not his to command, and rather than lose the steering board, he and Thrand stowed it beneath the deck where the sail lay. All that remained was to wait. He huddled beside Halla, drawing her trembling body close.

At the heart of the black clouds, the wind and rain exploded.

Raven's Talon crested its first swell, and crashed down the trough with a shudder. Halla screamed and her hands clawed Toki's sides. They all slid down the deck, seawater and rain drenching them. Their travel chests, heavy with treasure and gear, slid faster and one clipped Toki's side.

"Hold tight to me," he shouted to Halla. The roar of the storm filled his ears. Her arms winded tighter and she cried. He endured what seemed hours of sliding over the deck as waves bashed the ship and thunder broke. He finally chanced to look up over Halla.

Everyone was screaming in the darkness. Waves scoured the deck and pounded the sides. The wind and rain were the roars of angry Fate. But still Toki could hear voices screaming in the mayhem.

"I don't want to die!"

"Thor spare me!"

"I can't hold on!"

Their cries beat on Toki as hard as the waves flailed his ship. He balled up over Halla again, lashed with rain and doused in seawater. He had tied himself to the railing as well. His wrist burned and flowed with blood.

A wave punched down on the deck, slamming them in cold water that turned all sound to the muddied gurgle of water.

Toki was utterly powerless to help anyone, even himself. The gods had tired of him. He had defied them, and now they would fling him into the sea. Down to Rán's Bed at the bottom of the ocean. He was sure of it. But as the water sloshed away, he tossed his head back to check the others. Halla was screaming and sobbing, clenching herself against him.

The storm had stolen all the light from the world. Only flashes

206

of lightning revealed anything. In those stark scenes of black and white, he saw the lumps of bodies huddled to the deck. Runa's hair flowed out from beneath her hood, the only person Toki could identify. Everyone else had slid and shifted and were so bedraggled they all looked the same. But there were six of them, and Toki felt mild relief that no one had been lost yet.

He embraced Halla tighter as they slid once more. The rain and wind sawed at him. Despite the futility of it, he again begged the gods to let them survive.

***

Toki realized the rain had calmed and the ship no longer shuddered. Halla still clung to him, and she resisted as he tried to stand. He gently but firmly unlatched her arms. His sealskin cloak dumped water as he stood, his knees popping with the effort. He wiped water out of his eyes.

The others were rousing as well. He heard Gunnar calling his mother's name beneath her cloak. Runa pulled back her own sealskin and peered out. The others began to follow. It was still night, the sky dark but for patches of deep blue twilight poking holes in the clouds. A dull bluish light filtered down to outline shapes on the deck. Lightning flashed, now in the distance, and the thunder followed long after. The sea was blood-dark and choppy, but no longer raked with storm winds.

Toki smiled, then laughed. *Raven's Talon* had lost sections of railing and spots of decking had loosened. Otherwise, she had survived. He did not believe his old ship had come through such a storm without becoming swamped or capsized. He squeezed his eyes shut and silently thanked Thor for the mercy, grabbing the silver hammer hanging about his neck. Without looking, he knew the others were doing the same.

"Is everyone alive?" he called out. "The storm has passed us."

Einar was the first up, then pulling his mother to her feet. Gerdie sobbed and hugged him. Toki turned back to Halla and raised her up. "You are fine. See? We have survived."

Halla's clear eyes were wide in terror and she merely looked at him, clumps of wet hair hanging over her face. Toki smiled, but she stood mute. He took a knife and cut the rope tether from her arm, then did the same for himself. Dana stood under her own power, and offered the tether for him to cut.

Toki checked each person to reassure them and check for injuries. Gerdie's shoulder had twisted and her arm was numb. Otherwise, bruises and rope burns were the worst damages. Runa nodded wearily and waved him away when he tried to help with her tether. Instead he knelt down to Gunnar. His face was serious and stern. Toki held his breath a moment; he swore Ulfrik was looking at him from Gunnar's eyes.

"You were a brave man," Toki said, bracing Gunnar's small shoulder.

"No I wasn't. I cried."

"We all did, Gunnar."

"Father told me not to cry and to obey my mother. She told me not to cry, too."

Toki shook his head, glanced up at Runa who seemed oblivious. "I think he'd make an exception this time. It's natural to be scared when death is near. Just don't let the fear rule you. You did well today. Now

208

continue to take care of your mother. You'll do that, won't you?"

Gunnar nodded with the sober solemnity of a child. Toki patted his head and stood, now addressing Runa. "You're not hurt?" She looked away and shook her head. Toki continued, "I've been in worse storms, but I didn't think this old ship could take it. She really took the beating well."

Runa now fixed him in her gaze, her brow drawn tight. "If we had stayed in sight of land, we could've avoided the storm. Now we are in the middle of the ocean, and you don't know where we are."

"Of course I know where we are," he said, his stomach sinking. He had vague idea, but the storm had buffeted them for what seemed hours. Without stars in the sky or land on the horizon, he was only guessing.

"You looked away when you said that," Runa said gently. "You could never hold my eyes when you lie, not since we were children."

"Well I'm not lying now," he lied. "I marked our heading before the clouds covered the sky. When the sun is out again, I will pick up the course."

Runa stared at him, her eyes flinty and her jaw flexing. He thought she would strike him, but her shoulders fell and she exhaled. "I hope so. I hope the gods didn't spare us only to have us die lost at sea."

Gunnar suddenly interceded, pulling Runa's sopping skirt. "Uncle Toki is the best sailor in the world. Father said so. He can sail to the edge of the world and back. Don't worry, Mother."

Toki laughed. "Listen to your son. When the sun is up, we will get a bearing and make up the lost time."

A dim smile played on Runa's face. She lightly brushed Gunnar's

209

smooth cheek and looked out at the black water.

Toki focused everyone on recovery. They worked stiffly to clear debris and account for damage. At first the sea fought them, rocking *Raven's Talon* and making the slick deck treacherous. Soon the waters calmed and the sky lightened to an exhausted gray. The water flattened out like an iron pan beneath a heavy cover of clouds. After several hours there was nothing more to do. Without work to focus on, worry set in.

He scanned the skies constantly, finding it gray and the sun hidden behind thick clouds. The other men began to do the same, and Toki realized how vexing it was to see them checking the skies. The women started to do the same, though he knew none of them understood navigation.

"I don't know where we are. There's nothing to show us the way." Thrand looked expectantly at Toki; even his lazy eye seemed to pierce him.

"These clouds won't last forever. Let's just give it time."

"But the wind is blowing us somewhere."

"Gods! Do you expect me to blow the ship back to shore myself? Give the weather some fucking time to change!"

Toki's outburst drew everyone to him. He felt like a lone man in the center of an enemy attack. Faces were flat and expressionless. He felt lines of anger pulling down his cheeks. He shook his head, and rubbed his face briskly.

"Toki, we are lost, aren't we?" Halla's voice was small and fragile, but it tinkled like a silver bell in the stillness of the sea. She stepped forward, her hair matted and her clothes clinging to her body. "Aren't we, Toki?"

210

"We are not lost, but we might be off course. There's a difference. I just need the sun or a landmark to show me where I am." He smiled, but Halla did not. No one did. Toki felt his chest tighten. "Well, look for yourselves. Can anyone say where we are right now? It's all the same until the clouds break or we get some other sign. Listen, have you ever known clouds to last forever? They'll break, and then I'll reset the course."

"We're lost," Halla said quietly. She hugged herself and looked at the others. Then her lip began to tremble and her voice grew shrill. "We are lost at sea. Like in the stories of men who sail away and never return. We are going to die out here."

"Don't be foolish," Toki shouted. "You're just scared. Don't speak like we are doomed."

"Foolish?" Halla's voice hit a new height, setting Toki's teeth on edge. "Then where are we? Where are we headed? You don't know! No one knows! We could be heading deeper into the ocean, and we've got nothing to eat nor enough water to drink. It's a disaster!"

"Be quiet, Halla!" Toki stepped toward her, felt his hand itching. Halla reacted as if he had struck her. She leapt back, screeching, and then tears started to flow.

"You led me away from home to kill me at sea! How could you? How could you think of hitting me?" Dana, her slave, grabbed her arm and whispered to her. But Halla tore her arm away. "I'm going to die, and for what? Nothing!"

Toki did not see Runa coming. She flashed beside him, then she strode to Halla. Her blow thudded on Halla's face. She collapsed to the deck with a yelp, holding her cheek. Dana moved but Runa flashed her

211

eyes at her, and Dana stood down. "Your screeching is not helping us either. Calm yourself and mind what you say. You are on this ship because you chose to run away with my brother. This is Fate, so accept it."

Runa turned and faintly smiled at Toki, who stood bewildered. Runa then swept her gaze around to everyone. "Toki does not control the wind or the skies. But he is the best sailor any of you know. So respect him, listen to him. Let no one blame another for this. It is the work of the gods alone. If we are lost, we are lost. We must discover where we are and where we can find help. Until the sun or stars shine again, be silent." She looked down at Halla. "No one is interested in opinions. We all want facts, which can't be had until there's more to see than clouds."

Runa massaged the back of the hand that had struck Halla. She smiled broadly and then rejoined Gunnar who stood behind Toki. As she brushed past him she spoke in a near-whisper. "It felt good to shut her up."

Toki rubbed the back of his neck. He looked at his sister, with Gerdie at her side and patting her back. Then he looked at Halla, struggling to her feet with Dana helping her. The three men stood in between, faces red with embarrassment. Finally, Toki faced the sky. It had not changed.

Another storm was brewing, but this one on the deck of *Raven's Talon*. He again sent his silent prayers to the gods, entreating them to calm this storm as well.

CHAPTER EIGHTEEN

Signals passed from ship to ship as Kjotve revised his heading. The wind that had filled the sails now grew too strong and it lathered the ocean white. Ulfrik had enjoyed the reprieve from rowing. But now he and the other slaves had to slide their oars back into the water. The crack of a lash emphasized the orders, and he needed no more encouragement.

"Black skies and rough seas," Ulfrik muttered to Snorri still seated before him. "Do you think the gods will drown us instead of letting Kjotve row us to death?"

Snorri coughed a laugh. "My arms are going to fall off, and I think my back would feel better on a bed of knives."

A crewman shouted at them to shut up. Thus far Kjotve seemed oblivious to the concentration of Ulfrik's men on his own ship. After sacking Hardar's homeland, Kjotve spent his time singing songs or drinking. He boasted of his victories and his battle prowess. He thought himself invincible.

"Row, you dogs! Stay ahead of the storm," Kjotve hollered from his position at the tiller. His exhortations were unnecessary. One look at the mass of black clouds crawling over the water on legs of lightning and every man pulled hard to flee it.

Still within the Faereyjar Islands, land was not far. Kjotve had sailed north after sacking Hardar. He sold his cargo of sheep to Jarl Hermind the Fat. He traded many slaves, mostly women or girls. Ulfrik remembered the jarl from the festival. He had loved his mead. If Ulfrik ever returned, he swore to drown Hermind in it.

Eventually Kjotve located a beach he favored enough to pull ashore. Because Ulfrik and the other slaves were bound at the feet, they were spared the work of pulling the heavy ships up the shingle. A fat raindrop hit Ulfrik on the nose, and he instinctively drew his cloak tighter.

Once the gangplanks thumped to the ground, men gathered spears and weapons, then ordered all the slaves disembark. Ulfrik assembled with others on the rocky beach. The land was flat and grassy, like every island in the Faereyjar. He hobbled over to Snorri as the crew organized themselves, Kjotve alternately laughing or roaring curses.

"This could be our chance," he said, fighting with the wind to keep his voice low but audible. Snorri squinted at him, and he repeated himself. "The storm would be good cover for a chance at escape."

"Are you expecting Thor to send lightning down on Kjotve?"

214

Snorri shook his head, his gray hair lank and flat. "We're going to pull these ships overland; you know that. We can't stay by the water. Are you planning to carry one of these ships in your free hand while you escape?"

Ulfrik paused and bit his lip. "I suppose that's true. But keep your eyes open for a chance. I might still form a plan. This storm feels like something sent to us by the gods."

"Isn't every storm?"

Ulfrik left Snorri to his defeatist thinking, instead focusing on finding a way to exploit the unexpected storm. If the island were large enough, they could escape overland. It would still be desperate, far from certain, but it would be a chance. Ulfrik lost himself in planning while the storm gathered force.

As expected, they were forced to carry the ships onto higher land. But the storm moved fast and they soon realized that not all six ships could be ported to safety in time. So they carried away their treasures and supplies, abandoning two ships as far up the slope as possible. Ulfrik and his fellow slaves stood in the rain on shore as crewmen scurried around the beached ships and threw over whatever they could find. Ulfrik and another man had to carry a heavy box up the slope.

The storm winds now flattened the grass and rain pelted their faces. Four of the six ships were safely up the slope, and Kjotve pulled his sails over these to make a place for his crew to shelter. The slaves, except for Ingrid, were to fend for themselves in the wind and rain. Lightning burned the sky white and a boom so terrible followed that men cried out. Kjotve hastily ordered a few unlucky spearmen to remain

215

with the slaves, then ducked into the ship.

"This is a bit of bad luck," Snorri screamed over howling wind. "I think we're going to die out here."

But Ulfrik's heart beat with anticipation. Four hapless men were accepting sealskin cloaks from their fellows hiding on the ships. They clung to the hulls and faced their backs to the wind and rain. Four men. At least twenty other slaves, more than half of which were his own crew, clumped close to the ships. He smiled.

"Snorri, the gods do love us."

"What?" The wind drove at them, and voices died beneath its roar.

"We're escaping tonight!"

Snorri hunkered in the grass and jabbed a finger at the sky in frustration. Lightning streaked overhead and Thor's roar nearly flattened them.

People crowded toward the ships to find relief from the wind. Ulfrik watched the guards huddle, oblivious to their approach. The ferocity of the storm threatened to sweep men away, and everyone outside had a single concern to survive the wind and avoid lightning.

Ulfrik crouched and yelled in Snorri's ear. "There are only four of the bastards. They're not even watching us. We kill them and get to the ships left by the shore."

Snorri's eyes widened, and Ulfrik smiled. Then he pulled himself to Ulfrik's ear. "You're fucking crazy. This storm would drive us into the cliffs or swamp us. And we don't have any weapons."

"Of course we do. Look under your feet."

Snorri scrabbled back and looked down. "We're going to choke

216

them with grass?"

"No, you old fool. Rocks. Bash their heads open with rocks. Look!" Ulfrik pried up a fist-sized rock. "Time to crack some hazelnuts."

Ulfrik hefted his muddy rock and smiled as Snorri dug up his own. Ulfrik stooped low against the wind, going from man to man and instructing them to find a rock. He monitored the guards as they huddled against the ship with their backs turned. He crawled closer and waited for his men to join him. He glanced back. Lightning flashed and painted the land white and black. His men inched across the grass like giant snails.

Ulfrik struck in time with the lightning. His rock slammed into the skull of a guard who crumpled as thunder shuddered the earth. One guard turned in time to catch a rock in his face. Two other men beat him down, his howl inaudible over the hiss of wind and rain. Ulfrik fished a knife from the man at his feet. The guard lay face down in muddy water, but Ulfrik took the knife and thrust it into the man's throat for good measure. He did not trust his plan to a rock, but cold iron gave him heart. Then he cut away his bonds.

The other men huddled over dead bodies, stripping them of anything useful. Rain bounced violently off their backs. In moments, eight of his twelve men were armed either with long knives or spears. The other slaves, captives from Hardar and Vermund's lands, hung back. When lightning struck, Ulfrik saw the whites of their terrified eyes.

Snorri scuttled over to Ulfrik. "Now what? We're armed. Do we attack?"

Ulfrik shook his head. "Let's get to the ships. We can be ready to launch once the storm eases up. Kjotve won't come out before then, not in this weather.

As if to emphasize his point, a gust of wind flipped his sodden cloak over his head and caused him to stumble onto Snorri. They laughed a moment, then Ulfrik stood straight above all the others who still hugged the ground. He circled his hand in the air, then pointed toward the shore with his spear. Without delay, he put his head down and ran.

Wind fought him, and more than once he fell into the thick muck. But he reached the two ships, and threw himself against one's hull. Others tumbled after him. He wiped mud and water from his face. The storm had not abated, but he had seen storms like this often enough in these lands. They would rage a few hours then pass. Patience would be repaid with a change of weather.

"I think this is going to work," Snorri hollered. "By the gods, we're going to get away with a ship!"

"I told you he was over confident. Let's pick one of these ships and wreck the other one. Steal the rudder, ropes, oars, anything he could use to steer it. That will give us strong lead."

"Good idea. Where are we going?"

"To find help. Ragnvald or anyone else who will listen." Ulfrik shared his plan with his crew, and they jumped to the work. The other captives, mostly women and children, watched silently and huddled together like a black lump in the gloom. Ulfrik shook his head and inwardly cursed them for being no braver than the sheep they had once herded.

After the rudder and oars of one ship were aboard the other, Ulfrik decided the storm had subsided enough to chance the sea. Snorri disagreed, but Ulfrik insisted. "If we wait until it's completely safe, Kjotve will find us. We have to brave the storm. You know I can do this. Let's move!"

Ulfrik's heart throbbed with joy. Escape was as easy as walking away. He only had to steer the ship clear of hazards and then his crew would row them to safety. Kjotve would give chase, but the ocean swallows all trace of man's passing.

Though sore and weak from his days in captivity, he put his shoulder to the cold strakes of the ship and pushed. The ship sank into the mud as he and the others shoved. He groaned with the exertion. Rain and sweat mixed on his face.

Then a man stumbled. Wind still filled his ears, but he thought he heard screams. He looked back.

At first he saw only flashing silver eyes in the night. They might have been elves come searching for mischief. Then he realized they were the flashes of weapons in the storm gloom. Kjotve's roar became clearer.

"Push!" Ulfrik screamed. The rocks of the sea were already at his feet. But strong waves rolled them back. "We are so close!"

Another man fell, and Ulfrik realized that despite the angry winds, Kjotve's men still hurled spears or axes at them. Ulfrik felt tears streak down his face. "Push!"

But the ship thudded to the rocks, becoming as unmovable as a mountain. He felt a sharp point jab his back, and he put up his hands. He had thrown his spear on the deck of the ship, but a fight now would be his death.

The man spun him around and yanked him forward. He landed

on the rocks, and as he tried to raise himself, something butted the back of his skull. His head slammed forward onto a heavy stone and his world snapped to soundless darkness.

***

Ulfrik felt the cold rain of the storm blast him full in the face. He awoke with a shout, a blanket of sullen gray clouds filling his sight. Then someone kicked him and he heard angry voices. The water in his mouth was salty, not rainwater. He felt a deck beneath his hands, and he raised his head.

His vision swam from the blow, but he instinctively sensed the rocking of a ship at sea. The he remembered what had happened, and realized he was aboard Kjotve's ship. He was laid out in the stern, facing Kjotve as he glared down on him. He heard oars splashing the water.

"Oars in! Time for a demonstration!" Kjotve ordered. Ulfrik's head fell to the side. He saw people seated at their oars, hauling them in. The mast was up and the sail furled. He saw Ingrid with her hands tied before her, staring at him from beneath tangled, platinum hair.

Someone hauled him up, then smashed him face-first into the mast pole. Another man jerked his hands around the pole, while the man behind him kicked Ulfrik's feet into position on both sides of the mast. Then they bound him, and lashed him to the mast with heavy coils. Kjotve inspected, circling around as they did.

Kjotve tested Ulfrik's bindings. He had some tightened and others loosened. "We don't want your hands to go cold and dead. I won't get much sale value if you don't have limbs, though I've a mind to hack them off anyway." Kjotve's breath was hot on the side of his face.

Ulfrik's cheek pressed to the smooth mast pole, blocking vision from his left side. On his right, he saw Kjotve and beyond his shoulder he saw Snorri. Tears filled his old friend's eyes.

Kjotve shouted orders and signaled the other ships in his fleet. The ship drifted under the slate sky, a watery light rendering the world plain and dull. He waited for the other ships to pull in closer before he stood in the prow and shouted.

"You killed four of my men. Four! Were I not such a greedy bastard, I'd have your balls cut off before I drowned you. But you owe me repayment, and I can't get that from a ball-less corpse. So you go to the slave block still. If your plan had worked, it would've been a tale for the skalds. Yet you failed. So punishment is necessary, and someone has to be an example. Who else should bear the punishment, but the leader?"

Ulfrik squeezed his eyes shut. Every muscle tensed and he trembled. He didn't have to hear Kjotve speak the words to know what he planned.

"Forty lashes is light punishment! This hardy young man probably won't even feel it. That's how generous I am in these matters. But if anyone tries or plans another escape, I will have that person lashed to death."

Ulfrik gritted his teeth. He had heard stories of men dying under the lash. A stray hit to the head instead of the back could kill. He prayed Kjotve had good aim.

The mast obstructed his sight, but he heard Kjotve approach from the prow. He appeared at Ulfrik's side and brandished a lash of sealskin, just like the ropes used to bind him. "It was an admirable attempt, worthy of you, Ulfrik. But you've got to bleed for it."

Rough hands stripped his tattered shirt and the cold air washed his back. A moment of refreshing sea air hung before the first lash. Then he heard the whip inhale and crack.

His vision exploded into a bright white field. Then pain came, thunder after the lightning. He felt the line of hot agony from his shoulder blade to his hip. He gritted his teeth and determined not to cry out. The next stripe came fast on the second. Kjotve was practiced with his whip and landed close to the first. More pain bloomed, but Ulfrik could withstand it. The whip snapped and struck, repeatedly the crack broke across his back. He squeezed his eyes tight and stifled his cries. His back was crossed with lashing. Errant blows hit the backs of his calves. He did not know if Kjotve counted those. He did not know if anyone counted at all. His back softened, the pain intensified. He thought he would pass out, but instead he forced his knees to lock and stood.

The lash stopped. Only the creaking deck or slapping waves made any sound. He heard Kjotve's lash dragging on the deck as he gathered it to his hand. It was over.

Someone doused him with seawater. The salt on his back made him scream at last. It was all he could take. The fiery throbbing intensified with the sea salt. He thrashed against his bindings, blind with pain. Kjotve again appeared at his side. "Seawater is good for the wounds. You'll live, at least long enough to sell your hide at a fair price."

Ulfrik hung limp, the pain of his bindings incomparable to the agony inflaming his back. Even the breeze, so refreshing moments before, felt like dragon's breath. A vague awareness of Kjotve shouting orders and the lurching of the ship penetrated his haze of suffering. He held his eyes closed, and used whatever strength he had to keep himself from crying.

CHAPTER NINETEEN

Clouds hid the sky and refused to dissipate. Toki had waited for a break, and receiving none he chose to sail rather than drift. He had often traveled beneath hidden skies, but never after becoming so disoriented. He had no landmarks to follow, and the only signs were the lack of birds and seaweed that indicated he was still far from land. He had picked a southern course based off the bright patch of sun seeping through the cloud cover.

They rowed south and east, but it was slow travel with only three men to row. Dana took the fourth oar, being a slave accustomed to manual work. She rowed surprisingly well, but did not last. Reluctantly, Toki raised the mast and fought with his steering board to guide them to where he guessed to find land.

But by the end of the day, the expected coastline did not emerge on the horizon. No one spoke more than necessary. Only Gunnar's voice broke the monotony of rowing oars or billowing sail, and he only spoke to his mother. The men rowed and Gerdie tended them like a nursemaid, bringing mead or wiping their brows. When the sail went up, she had nothing more to do and paced the deck in silence.

Halla sat deep in the forecastle, disappearing into the shadows as if she wanted to leave the world. Toki's head ached when he thought of her. He tried to be understanding, but had no patience for it. Ulfrik, for all his fierceness in battle, could effortlessly summon patience and understanding for others. *How I wish I could be like you, old friend*, Toki thought. *You would know how to speak to her. Look at how you tamed my sister!*

By the onset of twilight, land still eluded them and the sky still withheld its secrets. Exhausted, he gave the steering board to Einar, who had already rested, and stretched out to sleep. "The wind wants us to go east, and we must head south."

"Odin's Wagon hides from us. Without the north star, I cannot know where I steer."

Toki patted Einar on the shoulder and left him. "Wake me if the skies clear."

He checked on Halla, now curled asleep with Dana in the prow. He considered resting with her, but thought better of it. Instead he tightened his cloak and lay under the mast pole.

Toki awakened in what seemed no time at all. He rolled over, facing a light blue expanse with a faint speckling of stars. The sails bulged with strong wind, but the clouds were gone. The thought jolted him. He shot to his feet in excitement. Thin morning light painted

225

everyone as lumps of rosy gray. Toki turned to Einar and his stomach dropped.

He was asleep at the steering board, slumped over the tiller as if he were dead. Toki rushed to him, shook him violently. "Wake up, you fool! How long have you been asleep?"

Einar snapped awake, batting at Toki as he came to his senses. Toki snarled in his face as realization bloomed in Einar's expression. "I don't know. I was exhausted."

"I see that. The clouds cleared and the sun is up. We can get a heading now. But who knows how long you've steered us in these winds. You should've taken in the sails!" Toki silently cursed himself, knowing responsibility for the sail laid with him. He let go of Einar. "Forget that. There's still no land in sight, and we're lost. From here we need to take a new heading, for Norway."

Einar straightened out his shirt and rubbed his face. "Norway? Are you sure we're that far off?"

Toki shook his head. "But we sail straight east and we will find land. Any other direction and we could be at sea longer than we can survive. Landfall in Norway will let us resupply at least. The wind has been blowing in that direction anyway. We can't be south or we would have found the islands we sought. So we are probably halfway to Norway now. We'll just finish the journey."

"And what about Ulfrik?" Toki jumped at the sudden question from behind. He turned and found Runa seated with Gunnar in her lap. The child still fought with sleep, but Runa's eyes were awake and sparkling.

"He will survive while we find help in Norway. What do you

226

want me to say? We can't help him if we're dead. I don't like this any more than you, but there's no choice."

To his relief, Runa nodded and stroked Gunnar's hair. "Ulfrik is strong. He might even escape without our help. Don't think he needs us to succeed."

Toki smiled. "Half of me believes we're on this journey to get out of his way. I bet he will be waiting for us in the hall back at Nye Grenner, a stupid smile on his face."

Runa laughed faintly, though Toki could see the glimmer of tears running over her cheeks. A teardrop landed on Gunnar, and he fussed with an annoyed cry.

He left his sister to her thoughts, then roused Thrand and Njall to share the plan. He let the others remain asleep, hoping they would awaken with shores in sight.

***

Landfall occurred later than Toki had expected, but in time to avert disaster. They had lost precious rations during the storm, and casks that held mead were now ruined with seawater. First birds had appeared, lifting spirits, then a purple stripe showed on the horizon which they greeted with cheers and shouts.

But a successful landing proved more challenging. Other sea traffic increased with their proximity to land, and Toki feared square sailed ships plying the distant waters. If any turned toward him, he headed the opposite direction. Once he had arrived at the craggy islands splattering the coastline, Toki found it easier to hide. He managed to

227

catch two fishing ships unaware, and while the crews brandished spears, they were not warriors.

Toki hailed them in peace, though the fishermen were wary of such ploys. He maintained distance as he called from the prow. "We were blown off course in a storm. We only want to find a town to resupply. Where are we?"

The men conferred with each other, until a white-haired man shouted back to him. "You've found More; Jarl Rognvald the Wise rules here. Follow the coast, you will see where the trading ships go."

Toki thanked them and then banked his ship north. The names told him everything he needed. After a short time, he pulled into an inlet where the waters were calm and the shore flanked by high cliffs topped with dark evergreens. He and the men dragged the ship onto the fine sand beach, so unlike the rocky shores of the Faereyjar, then assisted the women down the gangplank.

Halla accepted his hand but did not look at him as she trotted down the plank. Toki gritted his teeth and forced a smile, reminding himself he had others who needed him to focus.

Everyone delighted in setting foot on land. Gunnar spent his youthful energy running along the shore under Runa's watchful eye. Toki gathered everyone together with a whistle. Only Gunnar refused to heed him, continuing to run and scream with joy.

"I know exactly where we are now, and this place is not friendly to us. Not if they knew we fought Harald Finehair at Hafrsfjord."

"We didn't fight him," Njall said. "Only you, and your sister if the stories are true."

"The stories are true," Toki said. Runa's lips twisted in a wry

228

smile. "But fortunately, we're not the famous ones. I think it's best if we don't tell anyone we are from the Faereyjar Islands. Many of the high king's enemies fled west, and we would be suspect. Let's use my accent to advantage and be Danes. Let me and Runa talk and no one would know better."

"What if someone talks to us?" Thrand asked.

"Then answer; don't act strange. We're not going to be here long. The rest of the plan is to get supplies and get back to sea."

"What about help to rescue Ulfrik?" Runa folded her arms. Toki noticed that behind her, Halla looked away and rolled her eyes at Dana. The gesture irritated him, but Runa misread it. "Sorry if you don't like my question, but that's the whole point of being at sea. We can't delay any longer."

"Agreed. But as I said, the men here will likely side with Harald. I do not trust them. We will go to the Shetlands as originally planned. Men there will be more reliable, and more willing to travel the shorter distance."

"And as I said, we need to get help for Ulfrik. Gods, Toki! You have us sailing everywhere and getting nothing done. First we will find men here, then we won't. Then we go home, but then we sail to the Shetlands. We need to do something!"

Runa's voice echoed off the cliff faces. A flock of birds shot into the air out of the trees as if irritated. Gunnar finally stopped laughing and stared silently at his mother.

"We are doing something," Toki said, steadying his voice. "We are getting back to our plan. The storm delayed us."

"Praise Thor it didn't kill us," quipped Halla. "This whole trip has been a fool's errand."

Runa rounded on her. "Fool's errand? You little whore! We wouldn't be on this errand if you stayed at home like a proper daughter!"

Halla staggered as if she had been punched, backing into Dana. Toki froze, not knowing how to calm two fighting women. But he knew his sister, once loosed, would not quiet easily.

"Are you shocked? Yet you admit you wanted to escape marriage to Vermund. Toki was just a handy excuse. And now look at all that has brought to us. My husband is enslaved to your shit-eating father. I will gut that bastard myself and make you watch!"

"Enough, Runa!" Toki had come to his limit. "Should we kill each other on this beach? Will that help Ulfrik? We are past the time for blame. But if you must blame anyone, then blame me. Strike me if you think that will help your husband. Go on!"

Runa's face was clouded with fear, twisted with frustration, and red with anger. She barred her teeth like a wolf with a leg in a trap. Toki saw how the stress was turning her into someone else. She shrieked in frustration, then snapped for Gunnar to come to her. He trotted to her side, his head bowed as if he had done something wrong. Toki felt the worst for him. He had to see the adults in his life become scared and angry trolls.

Runa yanked him up into her arms, gave Toki a scowl, then bounded back to the ship. Toki let out a long sigh, scanned the expressionless faces of the others, then turned to Halla. He stepped toward her, but she shook her head. "No, stay away." She put out her hand. "Just stay away from me and don't speak."

He stopped, wavered and looked at the others. Gerdie and Einar boarded the ship while the other two drifted away. "Halla, I am sorry for my sister's words."

"No!" She shook her head, then hugged Dana and started to cry. The slave gave Toki a confused look, as if she wanted to help.

"Halla, listen to me. I cannot ask you to forgive or accept what my sister said. But her life has been hard. She was once dragged away into slavery, and Ulfrik saved her from that life. She fears the future, and fears that she will return to that slave's life, but this time bring her son into it with her. Try to understand.

"I am being as patient as can, because I know how hard this is for you too. We are raising arms against your family. I get it. This is easy on no one."

Halla began sobbing, shuddering as Dana awkwardly stroked her hair. Toki looked away, deciding he could do no more. "Bring her aboard when she is ready. We will find a small village to buy what we need and then go."

Dana nodded and Toki left her with Halla wailing like a child.

***

Toki skirted the large villages of More, fearful of sour luck turning worse by being named fugitives from High King Harald. So when he spotted the fat ocean-going trading ships and their sleeker escorts angling into a wide fjord, he did not follow as the fishermen had advised. Instead he bumped along the coast to find the smaller settlements he knew would be close.

The mood on his ship was as taut as a sail in a storm. Runa and Halla brooded at opposite ends of the ship. Everyone else found

231

something to engross themselves. No one made eye contact. Toki experienced the frustration as a knot in his chest and a lump in his throat. He hoped resupplying and returning to their mission would ease the tension. He strained to think of another way to soothe nerves but failed, lacking the tact and ingenuity of Ulfrik. Again he found himself wishing he shared his lord's talent with words.

The coastline was flat and welcoming, unlike the brash cliffs of the Faereyjar. He eventually found a strip of beach where he saw ruts leading to the water. Men had launched small boats here and their homes would be near. A sparse woodlands of pines speckled the near distance.

Once *Raven's Talon* was secured on the beach, Toki stretched and inhaled the fresh scent of the trees. "Now there's a fair scent, one I've not enjoyed in many years."

Both Gerdie and Runa smiled, and Gunnar sucked the air into his nose with a snort. "It smells like wood."

Toki laughed and patted Gunnar's shoulders. "Your mother and I grew up in a world filled with these trees. You've never seen one, have you now. Today you'll get to walk among them, even climb one if you like."

Gunnar's face brightened and he peered toward the tree line. His excitement gave him an idea. "Halla, have you ever seen trees like these? You've never seen a forest before, am I right? You will enjoy walking in one." Halla remained aloof, staring at the distance. "Dana, do these trees remind you of home?" She nodded, looking as if she had been asked to jump into a fire.

Seeing he would get no further, he shrugged. "We are better off trading here. We can get what we need, then be away before greedy men hear of a small group of travelers carrying gold. We should also offer a sacrifice here, to help with the rest of our journey."

He scanned the faces and everyone seemed agreeable. Again he felt a momentary pang of emptiness for not having Ulfrik at hand to lead. Toki had always considered himself an able leader, until he found he had relied so often on Ulfrik that much of what he thought had been his own talent was borrowed.

"Well, good, then we need to find the locals. There's a track leading through the woods, and probably enough homes nearby to get what little we need. Freshwater is never far here. We will be quick." Again more agreeable faces nodded, though Halla had already drifted to the back of the group and was watching the woods. "Right, so, well, then someone should stay with the ship, just in case."

"Thrand and I will stay. One is not enough protection, but two men with swords will discourage opportunists." Njall patted his sword.

Toki agreed and decided the rest would be under his care. So he picked a handful of silver bits from the box of treasure, and followed the path through the woods into a large clearing of six homes and their adjacent buildings. It was a peaceful scene Toki had long forgotten in the barren harshness of the northern islands. The slant-roofed homes were made of wood and thatch, and pleasant ribbons of hearth smoke flowed from the smoke holes. Chickens and pigs caroused in their pens. He had lived in a similar place for many years, but had long been removed. Seeing this place brought a smile to him.

A dog began to bark, an unfriendly warning sound. This drew a man out of his home, an older man with a bent back and sparse hair. He jumped back at seeing Toki. But Toki, not finding a hazel branch, had instead prepared a thin branch of pine to signal peace. As soon as the man spotted them, he held the branch overhead and stopped walking.

The dog continued to bark, and several others dashed outside, mostly all were women. Their men were likely at sea in the fishing boats Toki had seen in the gray distance before landing here. One younger man ran outside, a sheathed sword in his hand. He was tall, copper-haired and built like a man who used to be strong. He fixed his eyes instantly on Toki, who merely waved his branch and shouted, "Peace! We are lost travelers."

He put the women and Einar behind him. The young man strode forward as the older man followed. Toki watched the sword anxiously, and was glad the man lowered it carelessly to his side. Toki kept his branch high as he walked forward to the men. They met halfway, and now Toki could see the dog barking. A square-built girl held it at bay with a rope.

"Hail, friends. My name is Toki the Black." He manufactured the name on the spot. "My ship was lost at sea, sailing from Denmark. We sought Kaupang to do trade there."

The copper-haired man laughed. "You are far off course, Toki the Black. You are traders? This is your crew?"

"Most of the crew was lost at sea; their families survived." He lowered the pine branch. "Two more remain with my ship. We saw where you launch fishing boats, and I picked this place to land."

The man smiled, but the older man frowned and rubbed his scraggly beard. Toki trusted their down-trodden appearance would convince the men to be hospitable. The old man, despite his distrusting looks, welcomed them.

"It's a sad tale, but not an uncommon one. Living by the sea brings us these stories often enough. I am Isleif, and this is my son Sigvid. My other sons you will meet when they come home with their catches."

Toki bowed low, offered the names of the others. Gunnar proudly proclaimed himself Ulfriksson, which made Runa smile but Toki wince. He knew he overreacted; Ulfrik was not so widely known or so pursued.

They gathered into the main hall, swept in to a welcoming hearth with fat, square women tending the stew leftover from the morning. They welcomed Toki's group to be seated along the wall benches. The once-barking dog now ran among them, tail wagging and snout pushing into everyone's legs. Light from the open smoke hole placed a large square of white at the center of the hall, and it filled the rest of the single room hall with a pleasing glow.

Isleif assured safety for their ship, and that the local Hersir who King Harald installed had eliminated banditry. "I don't much care for the high king's tax, but we are loyal to Jarl Rognvald. Been on these lands since Odin made the world with Ymir's flesh. So we do what we must to stay."

Eager for news from the world, Isleif and Sigvid pressed for details. Toki had to invent more news, to cover his story. But somewhere he must have given a conflicting report, as he noticed Isleif and Sigvid exchanging confused glances. So he hurried his point. "Truth is we want to be back at sea as soon as we can and return to Denmark. We need supplies. Food mostly. There's little left to trade, but I carried some silver bits with me to buy food. If you can help us, I would appreciate it."

"We can help," Isleif said without delay. "Silver is good in summer, so they say. Can't eat it or burn it in winter. But what is the rush? Certainly you want to refresh yourselves. Stay for a meal."

"We couldn't impose like that. We are simple traders and must be gone soon. Families in Denmark must know their husbands are lost to the sea."

"But yet their families are here," Isleif said, his face smiling but his voice carrying the accusation.

"All right, I will be honest with you." Toki looked at Einar then Runa, and both nodded. The other women huddled together, frightened. "We come from the Faereyjar Islands. Our lord is enslaved there, and we seek fighting men to aid us in freeing him. But we were blown off course, and we do need supplies. The men we seek are far from here. I will pay generously for food fit for sea travel. Then we will be gone and never heard from again. I promise this is the truth."

Isleif's face creased in a smile. "That hardly seems something worth lying about. But it sounds a good deal more like the truth. Most of what we can spare will last you at sea. But still you must at least eat one good meal. My wife and daughters should cook for the gods. And you should meet my other sons. Share your news with us. Fishermen can take your words far, and maybe bring more help to your cause. Plenty of men in these lands are looking for a good fight now that King Harald has conquered everything."

"It's true," echoed Sigvid. "I know men willing to sail for the right price."

236

"I can offer some silver upfront," Toki said. "But there is not much, and they would be fighting for a take in the spoils."

"If the spoils are rich, then at least a few might be interested in joining."

"He's speaking of himself," Isleif shouted. "He's long been a widower, and his last child died in winter. He's also useless in every way. Why not take him?"

Toki's pulse quickened, excited to find potential crew. "There is gold in the north, and the enemy we face has captured much of it."

"Good, I'll think on it. But stay for a meal. We will need time to arrange for your supplies."

Toki scanned the others in the room. Runa seemed appeased to make some progress, while Halla and Dana seemed uninterested. "Then we will accept your offer of a meal. Such generosity is unexpected but much appreciated."

They began to discuss the details of what Toki needed for the return journey. He liked Sigvid and Isleif. Their homes were simple communities, innocent of any concerns beyond making a living for their families. He hoped Sigvid would make good on his promise to persuade other men to join them. Toki felt like his luck had begun to turn.

**

Halla kept away from the others, using Dana like a shield between her and Toki. She could not face him, not with what she planned.

She was leaving at the earliest possible moment.

Isleif's hall was overcrowded with his multitudes of family.

Thrand and Njall had returned with other fishermen. Isleif summoned all his sons, daughters, grandchildren, and daughters-in-law. They all joined a raucous feast proclaimed as a welcome. Halla appreciated hot food again; after a few days of rations, even leather would taste sumptuous.

Sigvid was loudly bragging of his old life, then inexplicably offered a toast to Toki. Halla was not interested in them. She only considered the exit an arm's length away. Unfortunately the door was shut or she could have already sneaked away. Dana pressed against her right side, while her left side hung at the edge of the bench. The table where the remains of dinner now lay locked them in place.

"Lady Halla," she whispered. "You are not serious?"

"I've already told you. There's a larger village to the north. The women say the jarl there is stern but fair. We just follow the road a short while."

Dana remained silent, then crunched a chicken bone in her mouth. "It's dangerous to travel roads alone."

"You will protect me." Halla had never seen Dana fight, but her father had insisted she was a good brawler. Thinking of her father summoned a wave of anxiety. This whole trip, everything was bent toward killing him. He was not a good man, she knew. He beat her mother, beat her, and treated them like possessions. But he was her only father. It felt wrong to be aiding people set on killing him, even if he had earned their hatred.

"What about Lord Toki?" Dana asked. They both glanced at him with the mention of his name. He was laughing with Runa and Isleif.

Halla's face crumpled to a frown. "His sister rules him, and his sister is a witch."

"But don't you love him?"

Halla elbowed Dana and she dropped her head in silence. Halla did love him, or had loved him. She no longer knew; everything had become overwhelming. He was a patient man, gentle with children, brave and smart. He had confident and strong features. But so much had happened. In his heart he must blame her for his troubles. He might say otherwise, but surely he knows none of this would have happened without her. One day that knowledge would turn against her. One day, he would drink too much, dream of all he could have done, and blame her. Then the beatings would begin and a life of misery ensue.

She could not let that happen. Starting over elsewhere was her only hope for a better life.

The sun set early in this land, so that by the end of their feasting twilight fell. She heard Toki informing Sigvid he would sail the next day.

"Our hall is crowded," Sigvid said. "But you are welcome to sleep in the barn."

Toki shook his head. "We should sleep with our ship. Thank you for the fine meal."

As they returned to the ship, Toki attempted to speak with Halla. She limited herself to a few nods and no words. She dared not speak, fearing she would abandon her plan to leave. Toki gave up once they arrived at the ships, drawing a thin sigh of relief from her. Sigvid and Isleif, who had guided them, said farewell and promised to return at first light.

Halla knew she had to flee this night, and shared a wide-eyed stare with Dana.

They slept aboard the ship with the sail drawn over for cover. Each man would take watch. They had all drank too much and Halla expected they would fall asleep. She thought Einar looked the most hopeful, and he had the second watch after Toki.

She lay curled on the deck as if asleep, Dana next to her. Halla marveled that her slave had actually fallen asleep. It seemed hours before Toki slipped aboard the ship and roused Einar for his turn. Halla waited longer still, then nudged Dana awake.

They slipped off the ship one at a time. A bright moon filled the sky, spilling light onto the beach and the path leading back to Isleif's home. They lingered a moment, in case anyone heard them leaving. Only muffled snoring and the lapping of waves on the beach made any sound. Einar, as expected, lay asleep by a dying fire. The women slipped past him like two elves fleeing into the woods. Halla turned back once, staring at the covered ship. She felt her hand start to raise as if to say good-bye, and her eyes began to mist. Dana hissed at her, having gone ahead, and Halla spun around and followed her away.

***

They found the track that the women of Isleif's home had promised. It was well-traveled and coiled through the purple gloom of the woods. Halla clung to Dana, who did not appear any braver than herself. But the two kept moving down the track, pausing at every hooting owl or snapping branch in the underbrush. Despite their delays, they found the outskirts of a large village before sunrise.

The moonlight revealed silver rooftops of long houses and squat buildings. The track led straight into the heart of it, though Halla could not see where it ended. She guessed it must lead to the mead hall that

240

poked above the other buildings. Deciding a nighttime arrival would invite trouble, Halla planned to wait until dawn before presenting herself to the jarl.

They settled into the darkness beside the road. Halla felt crowded and overpowered by so many trees. Their branches looked like ugly claws and the pungent scent of them assailed her nostrils. She and Dana huddled together in silence, listening to crickets.

"Lady Halla, what are you going to tell the jarl of this place?"

"The truth. I am a jarl's daughter taken here against my will. I am fleeing those who took me here."

Cricket song filled the gap. Halla looked at Dana, who was barely visible now that they were out of the moonlight. She could see a faint gleam on her forehead.

"Did you bring any silver?"

"Just a few of my rings. We can cut those down to trade for what we need."

Again Dana nodded and fell quiet. Halla shifted around to square off with her. She was looking into the middle distance and seemed worried.

"Tell me what you're thinking."

Dana smiled and shook her head. "We're not really running away, are we? You just want to get back at Lord Toki."

Halla slammed the damp earth with her fist. Her voice was raspy low. "Of course we are running away. We have to start over somewhere else. If we stayed tonight, then we'd be stuck on that awful ship tomorrow. What else could we do?"

Dana nodded, and it did nothing to satisfy Halla. "Well, I asked

241

you a question. What else could we do?"

"We could have taken silver, planned a little more, then fled when we reached those other lands."

"Well, I suppose that's true." Halla twisted away from Dana again, folding her arms. "But I could never be sure if a chance would come, unlike tonight. So this is better."

They sat for a long time, watching the sky turn deep blue with the first hints of sunrise. Halla stewed on Dana's presumption. She was only a slave, after all, and could not be expected to understand the nuances involved in this situation. That is what Halla told herself. But eventually the silence overwhelmed her.

"You don't think we'll get away?" Dana shook her head. "Then what do you think? We've been together forever. Just tell me everything you're thinking."

Dana chuckled. "Lady Halla, you've never wanted to hear truth. Why start now?"

Halla sucked her breath. "You're horrible!"

"I'm sorry. I was wrong to say that. But I'm not worried about getting away. I'm worried about the jarl and the people of this place."

"What for? The jarl has a good reputation."

"A good reputation among strangers. What do we really know? We're two girls walking into a foreign place, no silver, no weapons, no one to protect us. Lady Halla, you will make a terrible slave."

Halla put her hands to her neck, as if a slave collar had already been clamped around it. "But look at this place. It's civilized. Why would I be made a slave? I've done nothing wrong."

"Neither did I," Dana whispered. "But men from a village just like this killed my family and dragged me across the ocean for no other reason than that they could."

Halla suddenly felt cold and her stomach tightened. From within the village a cock crowed and she jolted at the sound. The sun was rising and already from the edge of the tree line Halla could see people emerging from their homes.

"Do you think we should go back, then?"

Dana nodded.

They carefully emerged from their hiding spot, stepped out onto the path while watching the village behind them. Then they turned and faced a man standing in the path. Halla screamed and the man jumped back, drawing a knife.

Dana immediately leapt in front of her, dropping into a crouch and throwing her hands wide. The man regained himself, smiled and lowered his knife. He was tall but thin, a fringe of hair circling his bony head. His gap-tooth smile was friendly, even silly. He held up his other hand in peace.

"I thought you were elves come to kill me or worse. What are two strange women doing on the road at dawn?"

"Stay away from us," Halla warned. She ducked behind Dana. Her heart throbbed, feeling like it would burst out her throat. "Get off the road and let us pass."

The balding man laughed, dry and hollow. "I'll not be hearing orders from you two. You look like you rolled up with the tide." He started to approach. Halla heard sounds coming from behind. The man's knife glinted in the thin light. "Where are ..."

"Go, Dana!" Halla shoved Dana forward. She pounced on the

man, her fist colliding with his face before Halla could start to run. The man yelled in surprise and pain. Dana left no time for the man to react. She swept him at his left knee, yanking him to the ground with both hands. Then she stamped on the man's crotch.

The man shrieked now. His hand sought the knife he had dropped. But Halla swooped past, scooping the knife as she ran. She did not look back, but heard Dana pounding the track behind her. "Keep running, Lady Halla!"

Dana caught up to her, nearly passed her, but slowed to keep pace. Halla ran with all her strength. The man's screaming was already fading into the distance. *I don't want to become a slave*, the thoughts poured through her mind. *I should have never done this. I was a fool.*

They sprinted away into the ever-brightening distance. She hoped Toki was ready to sail when they returned. She hoped the man would leave them alone. But in the distance she heard an angry, frustrated roar.

CHAPTER TWENTY

The six ships fled across the emerald waves, harsh voices booming across the water, struggling to rise over the splash and swish of oars.

"Row or die, you dogs!" Kjotve growled from the stern. "Those ships are headed straight for our hearts!"

Ulfrik wished he could row. Anything was preferable to remaining tied to the mast. Every stroke of the oars jarred the ship and his bindings bit deeper. His knees ached from remaining locked. His back tingled with strange sensations, like ants crawling over and biting his skin. Kjotve had ignored him on the mast for three days. He loosened Ulfrik's bindings so his hands and feet did not die. But Ulfrik could not sleep except when exhaustion swept him into dreamless black.

His face mashed against the smooth wood of the mast, Ulfrik struggled to turn to either side. Only piles of high clouds and blue skies broke the expanse of the sea. Kjotve's ship led his others in this race against pursuers. Snorri sat across from him, something Kjotve either allowed or overlooked. They could not speak often, but Ulfrik drew comfort from the physical closeness of his mentor and friend. Now, Snorri heaved on his oar. His thin hair was flat and matted to his head. Sweat flung from him with each gyration.

"Snorri," Ulfrik called, his voice weak. It sounded like another man's voice, even to himself. "Snorri, what's happening?"

Snorri glanced at him, then put his head down again. Kjotve repeated his command to row harder. Finally, Snorri chanced speech. "We're halfway to Dublin. Picked up sails on the horizon."

"When?" Ulfrik had lost his sense of time. He might have been asleep and not known it.

"Feels like a week ago." Snorri grunted as he kept the frenetic pace. "But just a few hours ago."

Ulfrik heard the crack and boom of the sail above his head. He had not realized it had been lowered. He immediately grasped Kjotve's plan: to disappear over the horizon then make a heading change, preferably toward fjords or islands, and lose the pursuers. Ulfrik had done as much himself in the past. Not many options existed to lose pursuers at sea.

"Rowing is a desperate gamble," Ulfrik shouted to Snorri, who shook off streams of sweat as he nodded. Ulfrik guessed a large fleet had to be at their backs, or Kjotve would have fought. Rowing to add speed to the sails aided evasion but exhausted his crew. If the pursuers caught

246

up, tired crews would make poor fighters.

Ulfrik locked his knees again, relieving the stress on his legs. He did not care what happened now. Becoming another's slave would be no worse than being Kjotve's. He considered slavery to another might be better. He closed his eyes and tried to swallow, his mouth dry.

He thought of Runa and Gunnar, remembering them in better times. He could see Gunnar flitting over wide, green fields with a pack of other children. They danced in laughing circles, found excuses to tumble into puddles of mud, and threw handfuls of dried grass into the wind. The scene shifted, and Ulfrik saw his son as an infant. He was swaddled in a gray wool blanket, tucked into his mother's arms. Runa looked at Ulfrik and smiled. "He has my hair," she had told him, and pulled back the blanket to reveal the proof. Ulfrik had laughed then. He found himself nearly laughing now, his face still pressed against the mast.

Kjotve roared again. Ulfrik wondered if he would be finally cut down and forced to row. He was no help to anyone tied to a mast.

"Snorri," he called again. "We're halfway to Dublin?"

"At this pace we should be halfway to fucking Asgard."

Ulfrik's mind began to clear. Since his lashing, cogent thought was hard won, wrung out of waves of pain and delusions. But as he hung against the mast, plans began to form. If Snorri had spoken true, the Orkney Islands were close. If so, their pursuers were likely from the same place.

"Those ships," he shouted to Snorri, "there are many more than ours, yes?" Snorri shrugged, saving his breath for the rowing. "They must be Harald Finehair's men."

Snorri shot him a grave look, but did not reply. Ulfrik was convinced he guessed correctly. Harald had persecuted his rivals as far west as he could, straight into the Orkneys. Ulfrik had heard the stories from witnesses, men who had fled the attacks. Kjotve's fleet was large enough to fear no summertime raiders. But the organized military might of Harald Finehair would set him running. If Harald scented blood, he would not be put off the trail until he had tasted it as well.

"When the time comes, fight for Harald."

"What?" Snorri looked at him with wide eyes. Ulfrik realized he was shouting for anyone to hear. His world had shrunk to the left and right of the mast. He had forgotten Kjotve's men rowed aside Snorri, or one could be standing behind him. But no one appeared to have noticed, each man trapped in the hellish nightmare of rowing at top speed.

Row the men to death, Kjotve, Ulfrik thought. *You will be caught. Harald won't miss such a fat prize.* Ulfrik remembered a rhyme from his youth, heard in his uncle's hall. The rhyme told of a small fish that was eaten by a bigger fish, that was then eaten by an even bigger fish, until finally the biggest fish of all had eaten. The biggest fish did not care for small fish, or even consider them food. At the time it was a funny rhyme to his childish mind. But now, it was reality, with the biggest fish in pursuit of them.

He hoped Harald would catch Kjotve. If given the chance, he would fight for Harald. If he fought well, he might earn freedom. He was the small fish.

***

248

Ulfrik still remained tied to the mast, flopping with the rocking waters. Kjotve ordered the men to stop rowing. They slumped forward in exhaustion, moaning with one voice of agony. Ulfrik's heart dropped at the order, realizing Kjotve had evaded pursuit. But he had to know for certain.

"Snorri, do you see anything on the horizon? Have they really dropped off?"

"Would we stop otherwise?" Snorri did not look up from hanging over his oar.

Ulfrik twisted his face to the opposite side. A wall of green-topped cliffs sped past in the distance. The coastline extended as far as he could see, which was not far with the mast in the way. But he recognized these as the Orkney Islands. The time at sea and the stars he had seen the night before informed him. These lands looked much like Nye Grenner. The islands were walled castles, encircled with their brown, shadowy cliffs occasionally opening to small beach.

The pang of loss struck him with that thought. So much water now separated him from his family. He believed they would never be reunited, not in this life.

Kjotve guided his ships through treacherous waters. Many rocks and strange currents guarded these shores. Men began shouting when one of Kjotve's other ships became caught in a current that threatened to wreck them. The ship pulled out, though Ulfrik could not see it. Eventually all the ships arrived safely at the beach. Once their ships had been pulled ashore, the crews and slaves gathered in a noisy crowd. Kjotve's men were pleased at having slipped pursuit, and they boasted loudly with one another.

Ulfrik expected to remain hanging on the mast. He imagined gulls would settle on his shoulder to pick at his raw flesh. Then he heard heavy footfalls behind him, then felt their presence.

Two men cut him free. He staggered, his legs weak and used to the rocking of the sea. He crashed backward into another man, and his back lit up with fire as he hit. Then he was shoved forward, bouncing off the mast pole. One of the two men caught him and yanked him steady. He spun Ulfrik to face Kjotve, who stood with his thick arms across his chest.

"Tell me your legs still hold you up," he growled. "If they don't, you're no value to anything but sharks."

"Bend down and I'll kick in your rotten teeth."

Kjotve's laughter exploded, spittle catching the evening light as it flew from his mouth. "Good to see your spirit isn't broken yet. I'm saving that for the slave block. Maybe you'll go to one of those dark men from the south, where it never snows. They buy men slaves for lovers. They pay well, too, but you're a little older than they usually like. Maybe I'll go back for your boy. Now he'd fetch me a good price."

Again Kjotve laughed, his two companions following his lead. They flanked Ulfrik and secured him each by an arm. Ulfrik pulled against them, if only to show he defied them. But the effort was halfhearted and they only laughed harder.

"Your dispute is with me, Kjotve. I'm the one you claim broke your oath. These other men are innocent. You disgrace yourself by taking them captive and selling them to slavery."

Kjotve doubled over in laughter. Tears sprouted from his eyes. Ulfrik felt his knees tremble, knowing he had come to his last chance to reason with Kjotve. "You should sell me, but free the others. Return them to their homes. It is the honorable thing to do."

Kjotve straightened himself and wiped his face with a meaty hand. As he choked off his laughter, he placed his hand on Ulfrik's shoulder. "I will admit that you've made a fine attempt for your men. Your argument, however, needs more work." He burst out laughing again, as did the others.

"I still have treasure buried in my lands. You know I wouldn't keep it all in my hall. If you free them, I will show you where it's buried. It will compensate for them, and you still keep me as your slave." Ulfrik expected more laughter, but instead Kjotve grew serious. His eyes darted back and forth as he thought. Ulfrik knew he had captured his interest.

"You probably do have treasure stuck away someplace," Kjotve said thoughtfully. "But the only twist in this story is that you're willing to show it to me for the lives of your men. Everyone else in your position always has hidden treasure to show me, only they promise to reveal it for their own freedom."

Kjotve smiled, a deep crease of shadow spreading across his face in the gathering darkness. Ulfrik did have treasure hidden, and no one but he and Toki knew its location. He would have done everything he promised, and hoped some chance for escape would show itself. He sagged between his two captors, his last plan played to no avail.

"I'm not a man to gamble, not with gold. I like the sure thing of sending all these strong-backed men to the slave block. They'll fetch me a good sum, as good as what you've dumped in a hole on your island of grass and sheep." Kjotve glanced out over the sea and rubbed his face.

"We're nearly to Dublin now. I cut you down so you can heal.

You need to look healthy on the block. So starting tonight you'll be fed well and get rest. Bright eyes and a straight back will help sell you for the best price. Now get down with the others and no tricks. If you risk my investment, I'll have you skinned. I've got a man who can keep you awake the whole time he's peeling off your flesh. You don't want to find out what that's like, do you?"

Ulfrik shook his head. They dragged him down the gangplank and deposited him among the other slaves. Snorri and his other crew huddled around him. He looked up into their faces, a mixture of hope and resignation showed. Ulfrik swallowed hard, then closed his eyes, whispering, "I've tried all I know. I really tried."

***

No food tasted good to Ulfrik, though it was an improvement over the gruel impatient hands had spooned to him while tied to the mast. He sat in a circle with Snorri and the others, which now included Hardar's and Vermund's people. Divisions held no meaning. They were all captives, all frightened, all worried for the future. They ate in silence. The night had turned ugly blue before darkness settled.

Beyond their ring, guards kept spears leveled at them. Kjotve had taken Ingrid and several of the better looking women and raped them. Then his men had their turns. Some of the men slaves, who had probably known the women, tried to rescue them. They were beaten down, but one persistent man ended his life on the point of a spear. While the rape continued unabated, Ingrid and the women screaming beneath one man after the next, the waiting men savaged the corpse. He was hacked into pieces and his head placed atop the spear that had slain him. His head overlooked the slaves now, ensuring no one moved.

Ulfrik closed his eyes as he chewed. Ingrid's screaming jabbed at him, setting him on edge. He tried to blank it out. Undoubtedly Kjotve had been serious about flaying him if he caused trouble. Ulfrik wondered if Kjotve might change his heart at the last moment and flay him anyway.

Once Kjotve had slaked his lust as many times as he could, the women's screaming stopped and turned to whimpering. It filled the night, a terrible comparison to the jovial talk and laughter of Kjotve's crew. Despite knowing Dublin was near, Ulfrik fell asleep easily. Exhaustion pulled him into the blackness of dreamless slumber.

The next morning they were herded aboard the ship. Kjotve ensured all were tied securely, but gave no order for rowing. They were to remain seated on the deck, bound to each other by seal skin ropes. Ulfrik and his crew were placed on Kjotve's ship, along with Ingrid. He observed Ingrid, her clothes dirty and torn, hair flying wildly in the sea breeze. She folded her arms over her chest, as if she wore nothing, and hunkered down against the gunwales with a few other women. Her expression was blank, as if she had no thoughts in her head. Ulfrik had barely known her, and she was the wife of his bitter enemy, but pitied her condition. She had seemed a decent woman to him, undeserving of this horrid fate. But so it was for all the others in captivity.

Once the ships had launched past the incoming tide, Kjotve ordered one to scout the way ahead, with the other ships following.

"Do you think he still expects trouble?" Snorri asked. He sat across from Ulfrik.

"The way to markets are always lined with thieves and pirates. I'd do the same." Both men drifted into silence as the ship swayed beneath the blue sky. Gulls cried merrily above them, as if mocking their captivity.

"Do you think Einar and Gerdie will be all right?" Ulfrik asked Snorri. The thought came to mind as soon as he had asked.

"Yeah. Gerdie is strong and Einar smart. I was just a man to fill the hole in their lives for a while. They don't need me now."

"Don't say that, Snorri. You are a great man, and they needed you."

"It's better to forget the past. We'll be in Dublin tomorrow morning, and probably on the slave blocks a few days later. No use thinking about whatever went before."

The men nearby grumbled their agreement with Snorri. He looked at the others and smiled. "Maybe we'll find a home with a kind master who needs help milking his cows and tending his flocks. I wouldn't mind it, to be honest. As long has he doesn't try to beat me. If that happens, I'll be hanged for strangling the bastard."

"We won't be tending pigs," said another. "We're too strong, too good for it. We'll row a trader's ship all across the world, then be captured and resold. It'll go on until we die."

No one argued the prospect. Everyone silently accepted the prediction, fearing the worst. Ulfrik felt a lump growing in his throat. He cleared it, scanning the men as he waited for their attention.

"I am honored that you followed me to this fate. No one could have asked for more loyal men. Fate is strange and still hidden from us. If ever there is a way for me to repay you, I will do so. No matter how we die, it will be how we lived that matters. Each day lived, even in slavery, is proof of your honor and bravery. Your battles will be fought with your hearts, and not with swords. The gods know it, they see it now, and will welcome you to the feasting hall when you die."

Heads bowed and nodded, a few attempted to conceal their tears. Ulfrik met Snorri's gaze and his old friend smiled. "You have never let me down. Not since you were a boy. I am proud to have kept my oath to you."

Ulfrik did not know what to say. He flashed a quick smile, then studied the deck.

Hours passed. The worry among the captives kept them pensive. The crew were at their tasks, ever scanning the horizon. The constant sway and gentle winds lulled Ulfrik into drowsiness. His head bobbed several times as he fought to remain awake.

He glanced around, seeing they were passing an island close on the starboard side. Over the port side, the stern faces of the Orkney cliffs frowned in the noontime sun. The sails were full and snapped in the wind. Their pace was steady, inexorable he felt, ever drawing them south to Dublin. He craned his neck and saw the lead ship ahead.

"Enemy ships!"

Ulfrik heard the call from another of Kjotve's ships. Suddenly everyone, crew and slaves, were on their feet and seeking the source of the warning.

Fearsome, high-sided ships streamed out from behind the small island on the starboard side. Their crews rowed furiously, the oars flashing manically as they stroked the waters. The lead ship had a dragon's head on the prow, and dark figures bristled in the forecastle.

Kjotve roared. "Man the oars! Hurry!"

The crew leapt to action. They snatched oars off the rack, fitted

255

them to their holes and rowed. The ship jumped forward and Ulfrik had to steady himself on the man whose foot was bound to his own.

"The dogs caught us after all," Snorri said, a hint of admiration in his voice. "Bastards knew we'd pass this point. Probably rowed all night to get here first."

"They own these waters," Ulfrik said. He watched the ships glide across the sea like gulls skimming the water. He counted eight ships, five large enough to hold fifty or more men. The smaller ships raced to encircle Kjotve's while the large ones plowed an unerring straight line toward them.

"It's not Harald Finehair's ship," Ulfrik observed. Kjotve was screaming for speed, looking over his shoulder at the ever-nearing enemy. "At least not the one I remember. But it's the same trick that fooled Kjotve at Hafrsfjord, though he's not getting away today."

He felt calm, at odds with the crew who strained against their oars. He knew Kjotve's attempt to flee would fail. The size of the enemy sails alone would let them outstrip him, never mind the extra speed the oars provided. He expected the battle; even weaponless and bound at the feet, he anticipated the fight. The battle song began to beat in his heart, flowing with his pulse through his body.

If he had any chances of freedom left, this would be the last one.

The large ships were already nipping Kjotve's rearguard and the sleek, fast moving ships were herding Kjotve on the port side. Ulfrik recognized the precision and practice at work in the enemy's movements.

"Listen to me." Ulfrik addressed the slaves openly, knowing Kjotve and his crew were preoccupied. "We are going to be caught.

Some of you might not be familiar with a sea battle." He looked at several of the scared men and women who were not his own people. "First they're going to sweep the decks with arrows. If you want to live, tuck yourself into the gunwale closest to the firing ship. You will have the best chance there. Kjotve's crew will try to use us to shield themselves. Fight them if they do. Fight for Kjotve's enemy and hope he will recognize it and reward us later."

Kjotve's roar broke Ulfrik's speech. "Fate be damned! If they want a battle, then let the Bear of Agder teach them how it's done!"

Ulfrik shuddered at the name Kjotve gave himself. His son, Thor Haklang, had been a berserker. If even half of that came from Kjotve, then the enemy would have a difficult fight. Ulfrik saw two ships were already caught and the enemy ships lashed to them with hooked ropes.

"Tie up the slaves!" Kjotve ordered. He abandoned the tiller and opened his sea chest, pulling out a mail coat.

Men rushed to the chore, roughly shoving Ulfrik and the others into a group and hastily tying their hands. When it came to Ulfrik, the man pulled the bindings painfully tight. "Don't need you leading a fight against us," he added as he checked the bonds.

When the man turned away, Ulfrik shoved against him and sent him sprawling to the deck. "You couldn't fight me with both my feet and hands tied off. I bet you couldn't even get your cock up with the women last night."

Snorri intuitively got the idea and head butted the man tying his hands. In an instant, discipline vanished and the crew were fighting with Ulfrik and the other slaves. The brawl lasted only a moment, in which

257

time Ulfrik had taken two solid punches in his face. But it was worth it.

Finally donning his mail, Kjotve waded into his crew and slammed them back. "What are you doing, you sheep-fucking fools? Get ready to be boarded!"

Kjotve's face flushed red and his eye were as wide as a maddened horse. He shoved Ulfrik away, and his back flared in pain as he struck the mast, but he only laughed. He had succeeded. The enemy ship now glided alongside and Kjotve and his crew were not prepared.

"Arrows!" Someone shouted the obvious. A line of men on the enemy ship lowered their bows. They were close enough to pick their targets. Ulfrik saw men twirling hooked ropes, ready to snare Kjotve's ship and draw it in.

He dove forward as bow strings thrummed and arrows screamed across the short gap. The shafts plunked into the wood of the deck and mast, and many plunged into the flesh of men. Ulfrik pressed against the gunwale. Bound hand and foot he felt more like a bale of hay than a warrior.

But the gods had awarded him his final chance. They desired more entertainment, more surprises from Ulfrik. He expected not to disappoint them.

***

Bodies collapsed to the deck inches from Ulfrik. Black feathered arrows jutted from their corpses. He had reacted swiftly, as did his men, practiced in battle unlike the farmers. They hesitated and arrows impaled them alongside Kjotve's stone-footed crew. They died one atop the other.

Ulfrik squeezed tighter to the gunwale. The second volley hissed across the gap and more shrieks preceded the thud of bodies on the deck. He heard the grappling hooks biting into the ship, felt the sudden tilt as men hauled alongside.

A counter volley streamed overhead. Across the deck from Ulfrik, over the port gunwale, another of Kjotve's ships had lashed to Kjotve's while archers neutralized the enemy's shooting. Ulfrik recognized the battle platform, three ships tied together for the two enemies to fight. Already Kjotve's other crew were leaping the rails to reinforce their companions.

Overhead, the enemy jumped aboard. Kjotve's bear roar went up, and for a moment Ulfrik saw the giant man raise his ax. He looked like he would cleave the ship with one strike. He disappeared behind others joining the fight.

Then chaos. The enemy passed overhead, colliding with waiting defenders. Grunts ended in cries. Iron clanged on iron. Blood flowed to the deck, running in streams toward Ulfrik.

He struggled against his bonds. A body wedged him into the gunwale. It was one of the other slaves, weaponless and useless to Ulfrik. He growled in frustration.

Then someone grabbed his hands and pulled them up.

Ingrid hunched over him, hair hanging in clumps over her face. Blood smeared her dress and a rend revealed a gash in her thigh. She brandished a knife.

Ulfrik swallowed and met her eyes. For a moment he saw the eyes of his enemy, the man he would kill if the gods allowed. Then he blinked. She became a worn, tired woman who grimaced in pain. "You will kill him?"

He nodded, not knowing if he agreed to killing Hardar or Kjotve. He was relieved at her smile. Bringing the knife to his hands, she sawed at his bonds. "Make him suffer. Avenge me."

The bonds snapped away, and she cut the rope at his feet. He shoved aside the body that had blocked him, searching for others of his crew. Snorri was already loose and freeing others.

Enemies still leapt from their ship, forming a mass that pressed toward the forecastle. Ulfrik saw Kjotve, a giant among his crew, clad in bright mail and wielding a bloody ax. He was a man of legend, Ulfrik did not doubt. But as Ingrid released him from his final bond, he paused before standing.

The enemy leader now joined at the back of his men. He made Kjotve small in every way. He stood two heads taller than any other man. His build was slender but powerful. His mail and sword blazed in the high sun. The man commanded by sheer presence alone. His hirdmen held close to him, guarding his flanks. But no one challenged him as he melted into the center of the battle.

Snorri dragged Ulfrik to his feet, put a sword into his hand. "Already the deck is full of shields and weapons. Let's join the fight and die as warriors!"

Scattered in twisted piles lay Kjotve's crew, swords still in their sheaths and shields just out of reach. Arrows poked out like quills on their corpses. Ulfrik snatched a plain shield and pointed his sword at Kjotve. "For freedom and vengeance!"

Battle was thickest in the fore, where Kjotve roared and his picked men hewed their attackers like fire wood. But the aft swelled with fighting men. Ulfrik chose to lay into these men first.

The weariness of fear and the pain of his wounds no longer burdened him. The battle song pulsed through his body and he became lithe and free. His blade darted into the gaps between shields, returning blood slicked. Men screamed when he slashed. He roared his frustration, seeking the familiar faces of his tormentors.

An enemy clashed with him, but Ulfrik caught the blow on his shield. "I'm with you!" he screamed, but the man was mad with battle lust. Ulfrik slashed beneath his shield, his blade turning on the man's mail coat. Ulfrik slammed his shield into the enemy's face, then stabbed down into his thigh below the hem of the mail.

The man skittered away into the mayhem. Snorri emerged from the throng, his white hair matted with gore and his face wild with joy. He howled and threw himself back into the fray.

An arrow thumped into Ulfrik's shield, and he instinctively ducked. A sword passed through where his head had just been. Ulfrik rammed his sword into the body that had leapt in front of him. He did not see his enemy's face, but heard him scream as he crumpled to the deck. Blood sloshed like foamy red water. Bodies flopped as the ship rocked and men struggled to stand and fight.

Kjotve had fought his way out of the forecastle. The slain piled around him and his hirdmen like a tide mark. The enemy king, for that is what Ulfrik knew he must be, fought with skillful ferocity. Kjotve, it seemed to him, wanted to avoid the king and escape to his other ship. But the enemy had pinned him and his hirdmen to the gunwales.

Ulfrik grabbed the men beside him. They were not his own, but they responded to his command. "Get to the other ship and cut off his retreat. He will back into us and be doomed."

The enemy men exchanged glances and then followed Ulfrik. He bounded over the rails, landing on the opposite deck. He slid on the blood clinging to his feet. One of Kjotve's crew charged him as he struggled to keep his balance. Seeing the threat, he let himself fall back. The attacker stumbled past, and Ulfrik kicked into his feet. His legs entangled, the attacker tumbled and the others following Ulfrik skewered him to the deck. One paused to help him stand.

Now Kjotve's men were escaping over to where they expected no resistance. But Ulfrik and his small crew stood prepared to cut them down. Kjotve was effectively trapped between both ships. His roar of frustration rose above the thunder of battle. Men stumbled screaming into the water to be swallowed below.

Now the enemy king and Kjotve clashed. Ulfrik burned for revenge. Hot anger at the enemy king flashed through Ulfrik's limbs. Kjotve was his alone to kill. He deserved it. With a battle cry, he jumped back upon the rails. "For Nye Grenner! Kjotve, your death is come!"

He hovered on the rail, heedless of falling into the water. The two ships bucked together as men fought across the ships. Ulfrik stood above the combat, shield feathered with arrows and sword dripping with gore. The two giant leaders battled at the center of the knot of warriors. Kjotve had discarded his ax in the close fight, now slashing with a short blade. Breaking away from the enemy king, he cleared the rails and landed on the opposite deck.

Men sawed at the ropes to cut free. The enemy king, his face pulled tight with rage, stepped onto the rail to follow Kjotve.

The aft of the ships broke free. Ulfrik shifted back to the rail on

Kjotve's side. The king stumbled forward.

He sprawled on his face. Kjotve, despite his brutish stature, reacted swiftly. The king flipped over. Kjotve raised his sword to strike.

Ulfrik sprung from the rail, holding his shield before him. He collided with Kjotve, deflecting the killing strike. The impact crushed both of them to the deck in a tangled mass. Kjotve's foul breath blasted Ulfrik's face as he screamed curses. Ulfrik recovered first, straddling Kjotve and bringing a blade to his throat.

He imagined pushing the cutting edge through the flesh, biting deep to the bone. He could hear the gurgle and see Kjotve's eyes pop in horrible realization of death. But he held the blade. He pushed only hard enough to draw blood.

"Yield to me or die!" Ulfrik roared. Kjotve flexed, his arms pinned to his sides. Ulfrik sawed the blade deeper and blood flowed readily. "Yield or die!"

Kjotve howled in pain. "I yield! You pig fucking son of a troll!"

An incredible lightness enveloped Ulfrik in that moment. Kjotve wrestled, but now more sword and spear points tagged him. He ceased. Ulfrik heaved with the exertion, the pure joy of victory. Kjotve's dark face snarled and he spit curses like a snake spits venom. But all around, his men yielded as well. The fight ended with the fall of Kjotve.

A hand rested upon Ulfrik's shoulder. The voice that spoke was deep and powerful, like rolling ocean waves. "Stand and surrender your blade."

Ulfrik's sword remained where it stayed. He twisted around to face the king leaning over him. "He is my captive. By rights battle known to every man, he's mine."

The king nodded, but his grip tightened. "Surrender your blade. The battle is done. You are hurt."

Ulfrik jumped in surprise, looking down at his torso but finding no wound. His mind reached out to the rest of his body, and he felt the blood running down his back. The lashing wounds must have re-opened. He slumped with relief.

One of the enemy firmly took Ulfrik's arm and removed his sword. Ulfrik did not resist. The king himself helped raise Ulfrik to his feet. "For now you are my prisoner."

"I saved your life," Ulfrik said as he was lifted off Kjotve, who was still ringed with spears and swords.

"I know. Give me time to settle matters. I will not forget."

Ulfrik scanned the results. These three ships were surrounded by the enemy, and other of Kjotve's ships had already been cleared and captured. He smiled when he found Snorri begrudgingly turning over sword and shield. He saw other of his crew, but not all. Ingrid was lost to him in the battle.

"The great sea-king Jarl Kjotve the Rich!" The giant king clapped his hands together as Kjotve was hauled to his knees before him. "You have much to pay for. That you should return to these lands again is either the most foolish or most brave thing I've seen in a long while."

"Fuck you and your High King Harald." Kjotve spit at the king, a weak effort that sprayed bloody spit on the deck. But a man kicked his side for the insolence.

"Yes, fuck the high king. I agree. But such sentiments buy you nothing with me." The king ordered Kjotve bound, and then he raised his sword and proclaimed victory. The enemy shouted and stabbed their swords in the air.

Ulfrik felt the impulse to cheer, but remembered he was still a captive and nothing had changed.

CHAPTER TWENTY-ONE

"Why would Halla and Dana go off on their own?" Toki asked Gerdie the question, since he had asked everyone else enough times for them to tire of him. Gerdie shrugged as she helped him fold the sail.

"They left everything behind, so they will return," Gerdie said with a yawn. Her face said she did not care if Halla remained away.

Toki bit his lower lip. He understood the last days had been trying, and Halla needed time alone. He sometimes needed the same for himself. She had left obvious footprints, making no effort to conceal where she had gone. He hoped when Sigvid arrived, she would accompany him.

"She didn't make any friends in Sigvid's hall. Why go there? It makes no sense."

Gerdie met Toki to complete the fold of the sail. He took the bulky cloth from her and stowed it. The others prepared the ship for sailing. Runa monitored Gunnar as he practiced climbing trees. Halla's absence elicited no concern.

Halla, you have not made friends here, he thought to himself and grimaced. Einar had been the only one who seemed worried, and Toki felt it due to guilt he bore for sleeping on his watch.

Toki stood in the forecastle of *Raven's Talon*. He braced himself against the long neck of the prow. The dawn had broken, slashing a pale pink stripe along the horizon. The wind blew steady and strong, good sailing weather. He hoped Halla would return soon and Sigvid would deliver the promised supplies. Then he could seize the good weather to make up lost time.

As the sun came up, Gunnar shouted from his tree. "Ma, the witch and her raven are back!"

Halla and Dana flitted out of the shadows of the track. Toki's heart lifted, though Gunnar's innocent repeating of what must be Runa's epithet distracted him. Neither woman seemed to hear. They trotted excitedly toward Toki. He smiled, but it vanished from his face. He read fear in Halla's countenance.

"Where have you been? What happened?" he shouted as they approached. Gerdie, who sat heavily on a flat rock by the campfire watched with mild interest. No one else stopped what they were doing to greet her.

She drew up short, as if surprised by the question. She exchanged glances with Dana, then gave a smile so false that even a dog could not be fooled. "The air under the sail made me ill. I went for a

267

walk."

"For this long?"

"Well, I wanted to rest again when I got tired and then I fell asleep. Dana didn't want to disturb me until now. Isn't that right, Dana?"

"Yes, Lady Halla. You just lay down and fell asleep. You seemed so tired, I couldn't disturb you."

"So are we ready to sail? I'm ready to sail. We should be leaving soon."

Toki frowned at Halla's overeager expression. She lied, but he hesitated to call it out. He searched her clear eyes, and could hear her voice in his head: *please do not ask me anything more*. He shifted to Dana, also uncharacteristically eager.

"The supplies have not arrived. Once Sigvid comes with them, we will leave."

"Will that be long?"

Toki folded his arms. "I don't know. What really happened while you were gone?"

"Nothing! I fell asleep." Halla mirrored Toki's stance. "Fine, I was just concerned I delayed us. Take as long as you want. I'll wait aboard the ship."

She stalked past him, her head held back in a mockery of indignation. None of what Halla had said or did fooled Toki, but he judged he should leave her alone. He looked at Gerdie and she shrugged. "At least she's speaking to you again."

"There's that." Toki turned himself to other preparations.

Once the morning sun had climbed higher, Sigvid and Isleif emerged from the track. A brown fjord horse lugged a cart, and Toki

268

waved in greeting. He palmed the small sack of silver bits he planned to trade and met the men as they came down to the shore.

"Fine sailing weather," remarked Sigvid. "We've got everything you asked for and then some. If I'm going with you, we'll need good mead to keep me happy."

"If you let him drink, he will start singing." Isleif slapped his son on the back. "Don't let him sing or you'll want to throw yourselves overboard. Now let's get these provisions on your ship."

Toki thanked them for their help. He dropped the bag of silver into Isleif's hand. The old man weighed it in his palm, peeked inside, then threw it into his cart. Toki gave him a puzzled expression. "Why not check it? Maybe I filled the bag with rocks and covered them with silver."

Isleif frowned. "I'd know. And Sigvid would have his dagger to your throat faster than you could pull your own. Besides, we drank on our deal last night. You're not an oath breaker, I don't think."

Toki smiled weakly. "Of course not."

They formed a line starting from where the horse would go no further. "She's afraid of the ocean," explained Isleif. They worked swiftly to move the boxes of food, new coils of rope, and casks of mead. Halla stood on the rails of the ship, helping where she could. Even Gunnar carried supplies, bearing his loads as if he carried golden treasures.

Toki stood on the deck, the wind tugging at his shirt and refreshing him. From the track, he saw a group of people emerge. At first he thought they were Isleif's people. But then someone pointed and the group began to stride with purpose.

Sigvid followed Toki's gaze. "Who told him we were here? By

269

Odin's one eye!"

Isleif dropped his head and cursed. Toki immediately turned to Halla, and she smiled nervously. "Don't look at me."

A tall, balding man led the group like he dragged a pack of unwilling hounds behind him. His pointing finger wagged at them and as he neared Toki heard him shouting. "There they are, on the ship. Two witches, I tell you!"

Runa, also aboard the ship nervously beckoned Gunnar to her side, then glared at Halla. "Taking a nap in the forest, were you?"

Halla looked as if she would faint. Toki returned Runa's glare, then drew Halla to his side. She clung to him willingly. "Stay by me and do not fear."

He picked up his sword from where it lay sheathed by the steering board. He gestured to the men and Gerdie to join him on deck. Once aboard, he pushed the gangplank into the sand. The men stood before the women, in line with Toki.

The crowd now clustered around Isleif and Sigvid, blocking their cart. The thin man raved frantically, shouting in an older man's face. The older man wore fine clothes of green and brown. His cloak was fastened with a gold pin, and he wore an armband of silver. Toki understood he was the jarl, and he had taken five hirdmen with him, all armed with swords but no armor. A sad faced woman stood behind the bald man, goading him on whenever he paused.

"This man keeps pointing at my ship," Toki shouted over their heads. "I would like an explanation, and a chance to speak." He fastened his sword belt, so that he would be equal to the others. But the jarl and his hirdmen both frowned at him as he finished.

"Those two witches worked a spell, then robbed me!" the thin man's voice cracked as he shouted.

"Now that's a wild accusation." Toki's eyes drew to slits as he regarded the man. "One that should not be made falsely." The iron in his voice cowed the thin man, though the woman behind him hissed in his ear. He waved her away like a fly. However, the iron in Toki's voice drew out the jarl and his men.

"Calm yourselves, both." He pointed at Toki. "If you wish to speak, then come down off your ship."

"I am a freeman. I speak from my ship while all I see below is an angry mob." Toki felt Halla clench him tighter. He put his arm around her. "You accuse my wife and my slave of evil magic."

"This is still my land," Isleif said, raising his arms over the crowd. "And he has been my guest since last night. Let's speak like reasonable men."

The jarl grumbled but nodded. Isleif waved Toki down. "I vouch for your safety. Jarl Orlyg is an honest lord, and his word is true."

"Come down and be safe," Jarl Orlyg said in a weary voice. "Let's discuss what has happened."

Toki leapt down and approached the group. He smiled at the bald man who returned a frown.

"Runolf," Jarl Orlyg gestured to the bald man, "tell your story."

The woman behind Runolf whispered a flurry of words into his ear. He hunched like he was in a rainstorm, then snapped at her. "I will tell my story, woman! Now, I was on the forest track at dawn. I wanted to get to Isleif early and arrange to buy his catch today. I planned a celebration tonight for friends. I was strolling along the path." Here

271

Runolf mimicked walking, which to Toki looked like a man limping with a broken leg. "I heard voices all around. The woods were still dark and I couldn't see anything. I drew my blade." He dramatized pulling a knife from his waist. His woman jumped; Toki yawned. "The voices grew louder and lights started flashing." Runolf squinted and blocked imaginary light from his eyes. "Then these two witches leapt out of the bushes and started dancing around me. My head was spinning. I fell and hit my face on a rock." He pointed to a line of bruises beneath his eye. Toki had thought it dirt. "Then they rolled me over, took my purse and dagger. They ran off towards Isleif's home and left me blinded and helpless on the track. Sif found me."

"I did!" His wife, Sif, had a voice like a screeching raven. "I found him laid out on the track. A pox on me if I'm lying."

Runolf smiled triumphantly, his face brightening. "I went to Isleif's home, found him gone and his sons already at sea. But his wife told me about these visitors. That's when I knew I should inform you, Jarl Orlyg." He bowed his head, then looked up at Toki with a smirk that begged to be punched.

Jarl Orlyg rolled his head to Toki with a look of long-suffering patience. "Do you have a claim to dispute this?"

"Well, I claim that my wife is no witch, and my family and crew will vouch." He looked up at the others lined against the ship rails. He paused at Runa, who gave an imperceptible nod that bolstered Toki's confidence. "Has Isleif or Sigvid witnessed anything suspicious?"

Isleif and Sigvid both shook their heads. Sigvid smiled without mirth. "Are you sure you were just not drunk again, Runolf? Last time you showed up naked and covered with bee stings."

"Who's talking about drunkenness? You piss yourself every night, Sigvid, and cry about your wife."

"Enough of this!" Jarl Orlyg's arm barred Sigvid from lunging at Runolf. "If they stole your purse and dagger, then they should have it still. Which one took your dagger?"

He pointed to Halla. Toki held his expression blank, but now suspected what happened while she was away. "My wife has no dagger or purse. If you accuse her, then she must tell her story. She was away this morning, true. But more has happened than this liar is willing to say."

"My husband does not lie!" Sif's arms flapped as if she could fly.

"Then your wretched voice has scrambled his mind," Toki said. One of the jarl's hirdmen laughed. "The accused should speak her story."

Jarl Orlyg waved Halla forward. "Let's settle this quickly, please. It's only morning and my head hurts already."

Halla let herself down and Dana followed. The two sheepishly came to Toki's side. Halla trembled and looked Toki in the eyes. He smiled and put his arm over her shoulder. "Just tell us the truth of this morning."

She sighed and paused, then started to tell how they left at night and found the edge of the village. She described her fears of slavery and their decision to return. "I was so childish. I should not have run from my husband. He is too kind to me." Sif clucked her tongue and Runolf rolled his eyes. "When we got on the track, this man blocked our way. We told him to stand aside, and he said he doesn't take orders from us. He came at us with his dagger. I feared what would happen. So my slave defended me. She hit him in the face and tripped him. Then she stomped on his stones. I took his dagger so he couldn't use it on me. We ran back here. There was never a purse, but I threw the dagger in the bushes by the track up there."

"Do you see what liars they are? Could two scrawny girls do that to me?" Runolf folded his arms as if his logic were irrefutable.

Jarl Orlyg smiled. He pointed to two of his hirdmen. "Go search the bushes for a dagger. You, slave, show me the hand that struck Runolf."

Dana held out her hand. Orlyg grabbed it, roughly flipped it over. He rubbed the red, scraped knuckles on Dana's hand. A low laugh grew from his belly. He folded Dana's hand into a fist and gently guided it to Runolf's face. He ducked away but Orlyg snarled at him. Dana's knuckles fit the line of bruises. In only a few moments, the hirdmen returned with an unsheathed dagger.

"It's a fine dagger," Orlyg observed. "Was that one picked off a defeated Frank too?" He and several others laughed at the joke Toki did not understand. "I'd check your stones, but I think there's enough proof to bear out the woman's story."

"This is an outrage, Jarl Orlyg!" Runolf's face twisted in shock. "These are strangers. You don't even know their names. How could you side with foreigners over your own people?"

"They are witches!" Sif began flapping her arms again. "They've caught you in their spells!"

"Not another word." Jarl Orlyg's voice registered no anger. "Not a single word. Or I will become very angry. Very angry."

Sif stopped flapping and Runolf bit back whatever he was about to say. Jarl Orlyg turned to Toki. He asked for his name and his homeland.

"I am Toki Sveinson from Denmark. You must have heard of me?"

"I've not heard of you. Not really interested. You're leaving, for good?"

"As soon as I have your permission to sail, I will be gone with no intention of ever returning."

Orlyg nodded appreciatively. "But your wife did steal his dagger."

"Which has been returned."

"Let me finish." Orlyg's voice held a hint of ire. "Your slave also assaulted and injured Runolf." Runolf began to protest, but Orlyg's scowl silenced him. "So you will pay him seven bits of silver for his troubles. This is the fastest way to settle and get you off my land. Can you pay?"

Toki agreed that he could, and asked Einar to bring the silver from the ship. He came with it cupped in his hand, and showed it to Orlyg. He judged the pieces to be a fair size. Runolf took the silver with a trembling hand. Toki could not resist teasing the fool. "Use the silver to buy yourself a codpiece."

"This will not be forgotten," Runolf said as he clutched the silver in his fist, shaking it at Toki. "You and your witches will pay."

"Forget it," Orlyg snapped. "You've been compensated for your troubles. And you forgot about your stolen purse?"

Runolf staggered like he had been struck. Orlyg and his hirdmen laughed.

"Make up better lies when you get me out so early. Toki Sveinson, be on your way before nightfall." Orlyg patted Isleif on the back and nodded to Sigvid, then left. Runolf and his wife followed.

Toki watched them go. As he expected, Runolf turned once he reached the track. He pointed his dagger at Toki before vanishing into the woods.

***

They launched *Raven's Talon* by early afternoon, after a final meal and farewell at Isleif's home. Toki worked the tiller as he guided his ship along the shore, seeking mercenaries Sigvid promised lived along the coast. The winds had remained strong and sea spray misted the deck. He inhaled the salty air, excited to renew his mission. Runa stood in the prow leaning forward as if she could force the ship to travel faster. The others scattered along the rocking deck, biding time until the next landing.

Toki called Sigvid to join him. He asked about their route, which Sigvid detailed for him.

"So what was the joke about Runolf and the Frankish knife?" Toki asked.

Sigvid chuckled. "Runolf is mad. All I know is he spent many years away. He claimed to have gone a-viking everywhere: Ireland, Anglia, Frankia to name a few. He says he went as far south as Micklegard, and has a coin to prove it. He constantly brags of treasure gained while a-viking in faraway lands—always after picking it off the body of a warrior he killed."

"He doesn't seem like much of a fighter to me."

276

"He might have been once," Sigvid said with a shrug. "I didn't know him then. But your two women took him out, could've slit his throat had they wanted. Doesn't much credit him as a warrior."

"The slave's Irish, and a good fighter for a woman."

Sigvid gave a gusty laugh. "No matter, these days Runolf is a drunk and a fool. But he married well, even if it doesn't seem so, and only Jarl Orlyg is richer. He has many friends, too. Not all of them good men. We did well to leave before he caused more trouble."

"He got all those riches while raiding? I think you don't believe that."

"Doesn't matter what I believe. He's been rich a good long time and people like rich men."

They spoke of other things for a while. Toki outlined the general plan and the goal of killing Hardar. He kept his voice low, and explained Hardar and Halla's relationship. Sigvid winced, and both looked at Halla.

"That will explain running off," Sigvid said. "Plus I've been watching your sister, and she wants to hang your woman and dance under her corpse."

"No need to be so blunt," said Toki. But he looked past Sigvid to Halla and Dana seated together with their heads bowed. Gerdie and Gunnar sat opposite, now joined by Runa who at least smiled again now that they were back to the mission.

"Well, I'll check the sails again. You should've caulked this ship before we left. Water is coming from five different places." Toki merely nodded at Sigvid's excuse to leave. His mind had drifted to Halla.

He was beginning to feel used, as if his only purpose for her was to remove what she disliked. The heady glow of protecting a beautiful,

277

innocent woman had faded. Now he felt detached. *Why shelter someone who doesn't recognize the effort*, he thought. *Others need me just as much, if not more.*

As if his thoughts were a beacon, Halla looked at him. He had been staring and not in a friendly way. A smile trembled on her face, fading before it could show. She looked at Dana, said something, then approached Toki. She staggered as the ship rocked, but came to his side and held the ship's rail.

"We should talk," she said in a small voice.

Toki nodded, resolving that he was not going to crumble. She had to understand words cannot solve all problems, and he planned to teach her that lesson. They stood together in silence as Toki wrestled with the tiller. He watched the pale green stripe of the coast, seeking the landmarks Sigvid had described. Halla followed his gaze.

"I am sorry for what I did, Toki. I behaved like a foolish child. I caused so much trouble for everyone."

He glanced at her, trying to act unimpressed. He glimpsed the pain on her face as she watched the coast. He felt a visceral reaction to it. His hand itched to draw her near. But he fought it and kept silent.

"My worries have burdened me, beyond what I can carry. Your sister hates me and so does everyone else. They all blame me for the problems. I guess they are right."

"There is truth to that," said Toki. "But it is only half-truth. I must share in the blame."

Halla smiled, then dabbed her eye with her sleeve. Toki saw tears beginning to roll down her cheeks. "But they don't want to blame you, and so blame me for all of it. I understand why; I'm the stranger here.

But enough of that."

She turned to Toki, placing her hand on his. Toki stiffened, felt his heartbeat strengthen. He glanced past her at Runa, who watched them with a bland expression. "Halla, I know you've suffered. But running away was foolish and dangerous. In this land, you would have soon been made a slave or worse."

"I know," Halla whispered. She withdrew her hand and rubbed her face. "I've always run away when things become difficult. I will change that. I've learned my lesson now."

"So easily? It may be as you say, but I will need to see the truth of it."

"You will. I've done so much thinking about myself. My fate has been strange, but I've been gifted with you. You are unlike any other man I've known. I will remember that, and I hope you will forgive me."

"You never ran away, so there is nothing to forgive."

He continued to study the coast. Ahead he saw the large cluster of high rocks indicating the first landing was close. Halla stood in silence. She at last sniffed and drifted back to sit with Dana.

He swallowed hard. His heart pounded and he felt himself wanting to call her back. His mouth even opened. But he could not let Halla assume tears and fine words paid for all. She needed to doubt herself a while longer, even if it pained him to leave her so distraught. He told himself it was for the best, and he needed to focus on saving Ulfrik. His own problems must wait.

He guided the ship around the rocks, keeping a wide margin. Gulls dotted the highest rocks, staring down impassively from their high roost. Suddenly they rushed into the air, screeching in anger.

Toki's stomach dropped. Something had scared the gulls. So far off the water, gulls would not flee seals or dolphins. That left only men. *Raven's Talon* could not turn sharply enough, and it glided past the rocks. "Danger behind the rocks! Get down!"

He shouted before he saw the small, dark ship sliding out from its hiding place. Despite his warning, everyone only paused in confusion.

"There shouldn't be any danger this close to ..." Sigvid stumbled back, hit the mast, and slid to the deck. A gray fletched arrow vibrated in his chest, a dark red bloom forming on his wool shirt.

Nearly ten men stood in the small ship that had launched from behind the rocks. It was no warship, with only space wide enough for one man to a bench. The dark figures were swathed in gray robes, cowls drawn and faces covered in cloth masks. They fumbled to keep their balance as several of them leveled bows.

The women screamed. Runa grabbed Gunnar and draped herself over him. Dana did the same for Halla.

"Hard to port!" Toki shouted. The men took to the rigging and Toki slammed the steering board. If he could cut the angle to the bowmen, he would spoil their shots, and then out-pace pursuit. But as Toki struggled to turn, the attackers had the broadside of the ship.

Arrows plunked into the deck, or hit the water. Njall screeched as a high arcing arrow landed in the soft flesh of his neck. He plunged overboard, the rigging he held snapping free. Thrand wailed as his brother vanished over the sides. Einar dragged his mother to the gunwale, then took up Njall's place.

The ship creaked and moaned as it veered toward the coastline. The aft of the ship dragged across the current, and Toki glanced behind.

The enemy blocked each other in their narrow boat and shouted curses as they arced their shots into the air. Arrows clattered onto the deck. One pinned Runa's cloak. She did not cry out, only tightened around Gunnar.

"We have to get Njall!" Thrand had tied off his rope and now pointed at the water.

"Get on an oar and row. We can get away."

"He's my brother!"

Toki shook his head. He hated leaving Njall behind, but the arrow wound had been mortal. Sigvid's body fell flat on the deck as the ship leaned, as if to emphasize the danger.

Einar took an oar but Thrand ran to the port side to search for his brother. Two more arrows hit the deck. Toki again glanced back, and found the enemy rowing.

"Get back to an oar, Thrand! We have to escape or we'll all join Njall."

Thrand raged but finally obeyed. With Thrand and Einar rowing, Toki felt confident he had speed enough to slip the enemy.

Then he saw they were fast heading for the shore.

With a curse, he fought to turn the ship parallel to the coast. In just moments they would become beached and easy targets. The enemy had been falling behind, as if they intended not to pursue. But again Toki had no choice but to expose his side to the enemy. They stopped rowing and took up their bows.

"Row for your lives," Toki screamed. In moments they would be past the danger and *Raven's Talon* would shoot away.

An arrow hissed past Toki's head. He could feel the air, it had

281

come so close. He laughed.

Then he staggered back.

He was looking at the blue sky. The frightened gulls glided in circles. He realized his hand still gripped the tiller. But his waist burned hot and wet. He raised his head.

A shaft had bored into his side. *Only half a thumb's width and it would've missed me*, he thought. His mind was strangely calm and clear. He looked around. He met Sigvid's empty eyes staring at his across the deck. He heard Einar and Thrand grunting with effort. He did not hear any more arrows falling.

"That's good," he said to the gulls high above. "I think we're away."

Hot wetness expanded beneath him, and he began to grow cold. "So now the gods claim their price. I should've have lived to do more." His voice trembled low and weak. He realized he could no longer see anything. In moments, neither could he hear. Then he drifted into a cold sea of silent darkness.

CHAPTER TWENTY-TWO

Ulfrik sat on the dirt floor of the small house. Watery light filtered from the smoke hole, infusing the space with a cold glow. The house had been lived in until recently. The hearth still contained warm ashes, a striking steel shaped like an entwined serpent sat next to it. Wool blankets and furs piled on a bed as if thrown aside by whoever had slept there. A ruddy brown cloak hung on a peg. A knife impaled a chopping block.

Once the king had led his fleet and Kjotve's captured ships back to his docks, Ulfrik had been dragged away to this home. The man who shoved him inside said to wait and not come out. He was not a prisoner, but had been separated from the others. Hours had passed and restlessness tempted him to peek beyond the door.

Creeping up to it, he stretched out a tentative hand.

The door swept in, nearly slamming into his hand. Ulfrik recoiled, his face warm with embarrassment.

Framed in the rectangle of yellow light stood a bulky man. He filled the space. He wore a wolf pelt across his shoulders, making it seem as though he had no neck. A gleam of mail shined from the tears in his gray tunic. Shadow filled the man's face, turning him into an unruly black shape of lanky hair and fur.

"I'm sure you weren't thinking of leaving after you'd been told to stay inside." The man's laugh was coarse, as if the sound hurt him. He pushed into the room, backing up Ulfrik while speaking to someone out of sight. "You two stay outside. We'll be done soon."

The light from above splashed down his face as he entered. His head was broad, his hair and beard shot through with gray. A white lump of scar crawled over his left cheek up into his brow and forehead. A pale nub of skin filled the eye socket. He smiled, a genuine gesture unexpected from such a stern seeming man.

"Gunther One-Eye. Welcome to my home."

"Ulfrik Ormsson. This place seems too small for you."

Gunther sat on a bench, wincing and holding his leg as he did. He moaned. "Old wound acts up this time every year. As for this place, I hardly come here. At sea mostly, or sleeping in Hrolf's hall. I keep a woman or two, or my slaves might stay."

"And am I to be one of your slaves?"

Gunther shook his head, then stretched his pained leg and rubbed vigorously. "You go before my lord, Hrolf the Strider. He'll decide your fate. You'll meet him soon, which is why I'm here."

Ulfrik noted the gold and silver armbands, and the heavy rings he wore. "Does Hrolf send his best men to fetch prisoners?"

"No, you're my guest. Besides, you saved Hrolf's life. He'll reward you and let you go, most likely. I don't always know his mind. He's a true lord's son; you've heard of him?"

Ulfrik shrugged. "What about my crew and the other slaves? They are all my people."

"Their quarters are a little less comfortable. But nothing like Kjotve and those scum. Your people fought against him, which is not surprising. We've caught him before and the same thing happened. He doesn't ever learn, the oaf."

Ulfrik cocked his head. "But you let him go? You were waiting for him this time, though. Why?"

"First time he had people to ransom him. He had raided in the Orkneys, which are now all under Jarl Rognvald of More. High King Harald Finehair awarded him these lands. Hrolf's his son, and here to settle things. Can't have fools like Kjotve running amok. We heard news he traveled to Dublin for the slave market. So we ambushed him. And here we are."

Ulfrik turned to the bench behind him and sat. The two of them stared at each other across the short space. Gunther stopped rubbing his leg and pulled it in. The silence stretched until Ulfrik's curiosity bubbled over.

"Why am I your guest, Gunther One-Eye?"

"I saw how you led your men in battle. You led my men! You've got a spark, a voice of command. I've been a warrior all my life, and men like you show up once every ten years. So I'm saying you're interesting to

285

me."

"And I hope that your lord will find me equally interesting." Ulfrik laughed and Gunther smiled. They spoke at length, Gunther explaining how the islands would prosper under Hrolf and his brother. Ulfrik knew the kingdom of More, one of the few that willingly absorbed into Harald's ultimate control. Hrolf was nobility, explaining his kingly presence. But Ulfrik worried that his connection to Harald might prove dangerous.

A voice beyond the door summoned them. Gunther stood and gestured for Ulfrik to go first. "The hall is nothing much to see. But it's where we going. Hrolf is ready to decide on you."

Outside, three more warriors fell in as they passed through the village. Chickens and dogs ran between buildings. A scattering of villagers were about their business, though they stopped to stare as Ulfrik passed. The long mead hall came into view. It was twice as big as any he had ever seen, though the construction was simple and unadorned. The doors already stood open, probably to let in the breeze.

They stopped at the entrance where two other men relieved everyone of weapons. Gunther took Ulfrik's arm and guided him inside. The hearth filled the hall with amber light and threw a wide circle of heat. A pot simmered over it, and mouth-watering scents wafted across the hall. Rows of tables pointed straight down to the high seat, where Hrolf the Strider sat.

He overflowed from the bench, such was his size. Two women sitting next to him seemed doll-like in size. Ulfrik had forgotten how imposing he was and it must have shown on his face. Gunther whispered to him.

"They call him the strider because he's too tall to ever ride a horse. He has to walk everywhere."

"Come up here!" Hrolf commanded, patting the table beside him. The two women backed away into the shadow. "Share a drink with me. I bet Gunther hadn't the hospitality to feed you."

Gunther chuckled and encouraged Ulfrik to thread his way to the high table. Hrolf rose to meet him, clasping his arm in a gesture of friendship. He felt his own grip lame compared to Hrolf's. They sat, Ulfrik waiting until both Hrolf and Gunther first took their places. The women who had disappeared now returned with horns filled with mead. Each man took one.

"You saved my life," Hrolf said as he raised his horn. "Never have I needed it, but for this time. I was too hasty in my attack. The gods sent me your sword and preserved me to make mischief again. I thank you for it."

Hrolf and Gunther both drank, and Ulfrik followed. After so long with nothing more than sour water, the mead tasted like pure honey. He guzzled it, turning the horn upside down on the table next to the others. "You honor me, Jarl Hrolf. We have a common foe in Kjotve the Rich."

"That we do. He's ruined now, of course. He is tied to a post in a barn, where he shall remain until ransomed. Or he can show me where his treasures are hidden."

Ulfrik smiled. "So you have taken him as your own hostage."

"Of course. I captured him and all his crew. I know you expect to claim him as your own. Perfectly understandable for a man in your situation. But that moment would not have happened if I had not

287

waylaid his ships."

"And what is my situation, Jarl Hrolf? Gunther has told me I am his guest."

Hrolf laughed. "And so you are, as well as mine. You saved my life, Ulfrik Ormsson. You were a slave then, but a freeman now. Let us eat before speaking further. I am sure Kjotve fed you fish tails and bones. Time for something better."

Serving girls returned with wooden bowls of hot mutton stew. Ulfrik's mouth flooded as he waited for Hrolf to eat first. Gunther grunted and nudged him with his elbow. "Eat as much as you want."

Halfway through his first bowl, he felt a burning shame. His men and the others were still so-called guests somewhere else. *What have they been fed*, he wondered. *I have already filled myself with meat and mead and never a thought for those who followed me. I am a disgrace.*

"What's wrong?" Hrolf asked. "Too accustomed to fish tails and bones to eat anything else?"

Ulfrik sat up from his bowl, wiping his mouth on his sleeve. "I have forgotten those who serve me. Until I know their fates, how can I feast and drink?"

Hrolf replied with his mouth full of stew. "I'm as cruel as a shark, and as ravenous as a wolf. But for my friends, I am a seal pup. Ask Gunther. It will be my undoing one day." He paused to swallow, then met Ulfrik's eyes. "All those who we freed are being cared for. Some of your men were wounded. Some died. The other slaves, if they are yours, are kept together, comfortable but not free. Until we know each other better, I will keep your group separated. You understand."

"I understand. I would like to see them soon."

"You will, but eat first. Then tell me more of yourself. You are an interesting man, quite a force in battle even in your terrible condition. Gunther thinks you are something special. It's quite a compliment, as I consider Gunther something special."

Ulfrik finished his meal, then pushed his bowl aside. "Jarl Hrolf, I will tell you the whole, long truth of my story. When it is done, if you can abide what I tell you, then I will ask a favor."

Hrolf nodded slowly, giving a careful look over Ulfrik's shoulder to Gunther. "I will hear all there is to tell, then if the favor is in my power you shall have it."

With a long sigh, Ulfrik started his story. He began from his childhood in Grenner. He hoped the telling would not bore Hrolf. He told it quickly without embellishment. Hrolf asked questions, smiled at the mention of certain names, laughed when he learned of Ulfrik's relationship with Kjotve and Thor Haklang. The battle of Hafrsfjord did not even elicit a raised brow. Ulfrik feared Hrolf's commitment to the high king, but also felt Hrolf's commitment was lax. Finally, he ended with Hardar and how he became Kjotve's slave.

"The mead has made me careless of time. But that is the whole truth of my life." During the telling, Ulfrik had stood and paced the behind the high table. Recounting every injury and defeat, every fleeting joy and victory, filled him with restless energy. Hrolf and Gunther twisted around on their bench, now leaning back on the table.

"I have a skald who must hear this story," Hrolf said.

"Such a tale should not be forgotten," agreed Gunther. "Fate has woven a strange destiny for you."

"Not so much strange as it is frustrating. How many times must

I start anew?" He immediately felt foolish for showing his bitterness. His father would have been more in control. Ulfrik could not stop thinking of him, now that he had summoned the ghost of his memory.

"Start anew as many times as it takes," Hrolf said with mild surprise. "If you can stand, you can fight. If you can fight, then you must."

"True wisdom, Jarl Hrolf. So my role in Hafrsfjord does not bother you?"

Hrolf stared blankly as if waiting for more. Finally he looked at Gunther with a bemused smile. "My father is sworn to High King Harald, yes. I have no need for high kings, least of all Harald. He's a blood-thirsty, ambitious snake. A crafty war leader, too, unfortunately for us."

"But your father's oath ... I am Harald's enemy ..."

"And the mead has clouded your mind," interrupted Hrolf. "Do you see Harald here? I obey him when I see him. Otherwise, we are all freemen. We settle the land, raise farms and families. Since the day Odin made the first man from a branch of ash we have been free. We make the kingdom, not the king. Piss on Harald and his taxes."

Gunther slapped the bench in agreement. "Besides, more than half of everyone here is a fugitive from him."

Ulfrik exhaled and laughed. "Then we are agreed. Now there is the favor I would ask." He paused for Hrolf's response. He extended his hand to prompt Ulfrik. "I ask freedom for all the people taken in slavery with me, my men and the men of my enemies."

"That is not a favor, but a decision I've already made."

"Thank you, Jarl Hrolf. The favor I seek is transport back to the

Faereyjar Islands for all of us. Kjotve took our weapons and mail. If you find these among his possessions, then I would appreciate their return. I will have my revenge on Hardar and end his curse upon my lands."

Hrolf and Gunther exchanged knowing glances. Ulfrik felt his chest tighten and his neck tense. Hrolf met his eyes, and spoke softly. "After hearing the story you told, I don't suppose you will be persuaded to stay with me? I could make it worth your while."

"Nothing would persuade me. My wife and son await me."

"Understood. This is such a simple favor, that I'm almost insulted. I owe you this much for what you did. But, it will fulfill my obligation to you. My life repaid with a return of your own. I will give you fine weapons and mail, better than whatever you had. I will put a gold armband on you and send you to anywhere my ships sail. Once this is done, no debts are owed. Agreed?"

"Agreed." Ulfrik stifled his smile. He could see Runa and Gunnar now, standing on the shore to greet him.

"But," Hrolf interjected, then paused. He gave Gunther a sly look before continuing. "I think you would be mistaken to take that offer."

"There is no mistake in returning home and seeking vengeance for myself." The words rang defensive in his ears, but he did not care.

"Following your request, you will have to raise your own fighting men. Your enemy, Hardar, was weakened and Kjotve gutted his allies. But do not underestimate what has happened since you left. Maybe he has new friends now. Maybe he took credit for destroying the other lands, and cowed other jarls to ally with him. Point is, you may not find it easy to take back what you lost. I think I can offer you a chance to do to Hardar what he did to you."

Ulfrik felt tension mounting in his neck. "And I suppose this offer of assistance will end my freedom."

"Hardly. You swear an oath of service to me. We become allies. I now offer you more than an escort, but men to fight by your side. Two of my ships, and you have all the men Kjotve took plus whoever else you can rally to your cause. You will crush Hardar and anyone fool enough to stand with him. Victory is assured."

"How will you hold me to my oath? Hostages? My son?"

"Your word is your word, is it not?"

"Kjotve thought not."

Hrolf exploded into laughter, surprising Ulfrik. "You were sworn to his son, who died, and he seemed ready for the same fate. No, I will not take a hostage, not for what we are discussing. The men I send will want spoils and rewards. You will give them the pick of the battlefield. Captured ships make excellent compensation. Long term, I would like an ally in a faraway land whom I can trust. If I call on you for hospitality or to support me in battle, you will answer. That is all I ask."

Ulfrik looked at Gunther then at Hrolf. "Would Gunther lead one of those ships you promised?"

"I can't stand waiting here while he whips the skin off Kjotve's back. So, I'll go."

Hrolf smiled as if he knew the answer to his offer. Ulfrik studied the floor. *Only a fool would pass up this chance*, he thought. "Is there a battle you already have planned for me? But you wouldn't tell me that now, would you."

"No and no. But battles spring up all the time, and you will be too far to reach for an emergency. I would only call you for something big. The remoteness of your home is attractive. Let us say sometimes I find it prudent to be not found, especially when I shit on Harald's laws."

Ulfrik smiled. "Then you will have my oath, Jarl Hrolf."

"I never doubted you would see the sense in it. Drink deep of your revenge, and reclaim all you have lost."

Ulfrik smiled as the two men chuckled. His mind was already awash with imagery of bloody vengeance.

***

Ulfrik sat in Hrolf's wide and empty hall. The sun had set, much earlier than expected, a reminder of how far from home he had traveled. The low hearth fire cast a wavering light against the encroaching dark. Distant voices of villagers came from outside.

Snorri stood from his bench. "Are you sure you don't want me here?"

"No," Ulfrik waved his hand as he leaned heavily on the table. "This talk must only be between the two of us. Go and rest."

Snorri nodded, touching the cut on his face. His cheek had been nicked in the fight with Kjotve, but he was otherwise unscathed. Still, he and all the others were soul tired, and needed all the rest they had taken and more again. He pulled on the gray cloak that Hrolf's people had provided, then left.

Ulfrik waited a few pensive moments before the door to Hrolf's hall opened once more. Ingrid stepped inside, soundlessly closing the doors behind her. She stood, pale and thin, with her back pressed to the doors. "No one else is here?"

"This business is ours alone. Please, come sit. Hrolf has lent us this hall for a short time." She remained at the door. Ulfrik stood and spread his own cloak to show he was weaponless. "You are safe, Ingrid."

She swept across the floor. Ulfrik had never paid her much attention. She only ever appeared with Hardar, and then she only fluttered in the background. Despite her gaunt features and bruised chin, she was beautiful. Halla looked much like her, only Ingrid's eyes shimmered with a haunted sadness. She sat across the table from him.

"You promised to kill him, to make him pay. But he lives."

"The heads of Kjotve's crew line the shores. Food for gulls and flies now."

Ingrid frowned, shifting to face the door. "But he still lives. You had the chance; it's all anyone talks about."

"Kjotve's future is little better than his men's. He lives at Hrolf's pleasure. He is destroyed, Ingrid."

She squinted at him, her lip curling. The expression seemed so foreign to his memories of her. They sat in uncomfortable silence, Ulfrik wondering if she had survived her ordeals with her mind intact. He tried to divert the tension with conversation.

"I have not seen you here during meal times. Is this your first visit?" She nodded, keeping her silence. Ulfrik kept his patience. "It is a bigger hall than any I've seen, though plain. Hrolf seems to be very sensible about these things. I like him."

Ingrid's head snapped around to him, an eyebrow arched. "What deal have you made with Hrolf? I've seen you practicing with sword and mail. Are you sworn to him now?"

Ulfrik cleared his throat at the pointed question, having expected a more circumspect discussion. "We have agreed on an alliance."

Ingrid coughed out a laugh, swiveling both her legs under the table and leaning across. "Then you are a bigger fool than I ever thought. Mighty jarls don't ally with slaves. You are his pawn or his slave, which one?"

"You're much different without your husband present." Ingrid sat back, blinking in surprise. "For years I've heard only a handful of words from you."

"My father was a jarl of great fame. I grew up learning his business, watching him rule. My husband married me for that reason, and hasn't had a use for me since."

"Your husband is a fool, through and through." Ingrid relaxed her posture but rewarded Ulfrik with nothing more. "This is actually the matter we need to discuss." He waited for her to react, but when she only stared at him as he licked his lips and continued.

"I have sworn to serve Hrolf when he calls for me, and to provide hospitality whenever he comes to my lands. In return, he sends me back home with two crews of fighting men. Do you understand me, Ingrid?"

"You plan to renew the war with my husband."

Ulfrik slowly nodded. He searched her face for a hint of her thoughts, but she remained impassive. He wondered if she realized how many men two crews were, and that Hardar stood no chance. But something fluttered in her cloudy hazel eyes, a look of appraisal.

"You have a few choices, Ingrid. You are free in Hrolf's land. You could make a new life among the people here. I would ensure your daughter visits you."

She was already shaking her head before he finished. "My other choice is to be your prisoner, a threat to my husband."

Ulfrik stared at her. "So you see why remaining here is a better idea."

"No, Hardar's land was my father's land. He had no sons and left everything to me, which my husband and the rest of the people seem to have forgotten. Fame is a fast burning thing, Ulfrik, gone when life's flame is no more. But some will remember and stand for my claim. That land is mine."

Ulfrik rubbed his chin, considering where Ingrid was leading their talk. "Your husband's doom is at hand. I bring too much against him in his weakened state. I will claim that land."

Ingrid threw her head back and laughed. The emptiness of the hall made it seem as loud as thunder. "You think he is done? By now, mark my words, he has sent word to his filthy cousins in the north islands. They will come to help him rebuild, to carve a piece for themselves out of the ruin the two of you created. By now, he has refitted his men and sent a call for more recruits further afield. You are not sailing back to an easy victory. Like you, I guarantee, my husband has been restored."

The thought had never occurred to Ulfrik. He thought of Runa and Gunnar, fearing they might have been captured or worse. Ingrid shook him away from his worry.

"But I have a better idea. As Hrolf helps you back to your land and accepts your loyalty, so you will for me. My daughter is married to your wife's brother. We are now extended family, yes?"

Ingrid's brow arched again, and Ulfrik now recognized what

swirled in her eyes. Ambition. "You are right. So you hold your family lands, and swear loyalty to me."

"An alliance, as you like to call it. My daughter will live in your hall, and is the most precious person in my life. You could have no better hostage. But I will be free and rule my own land, as my father before me and my daughter after."

Ulfrik stood and extended his hand. "Then we are agreed."

They clasped arms, Ulfrik suppressing his smile. He had never expected to do this with a woman.

"The Jarl Ragnvald, your friend, will remember my father and my claim. He, among others, will support me."

"You win either way, Ingrid. If I fail, I die and you resume your life with Hardar. If I prevail, you have your home and hall returned. I assume you have no care for your husband's life?"

She hesitated, a darkness passing over her face. "If it could be any other way, I would prefer it. But Fate has led us to this choice. As things are now, it would be better for all if you prevail. I just don't want to see it."

Ulfrik closed his eyes and nodded. When he opened them, Ingrid was already fleeing the hall.

***

The skies were heavy with dull, gray clouds. The crisp air heralded the end of summer. Seals barked complaints at the passing ships, seated indolently on flat rocks that dotted the coast. But Ulfrik's heart still beat with anticipation. Never had such formidable, fog shrouded cliffs seemed so welcoming.

297

"I had despaired of seeing this again. Isn't it beautiful?" He leaned over the rails, smiling at the pale cliffs that shot past them.

"Islands in the fog," Gunther mumbled, steering his ship to Ulfrik's directions. "Cold and damp air. Impossible cliffs and strange currents. That's what passes for beauty here?"

Ulfrik ignored the jibe. Snorri and his six surviving crew joined him at the rails. Each man was absorbed in thought. Only Ingrid remained aloof and stood wrapped in a heavy cloak with her head hidden beneath its hood. Ulfrik could imagine Runa and Gunnar waiting for him on the shore. The tight ringlets of Runa's full hair splashed over her shoulder, the breeze catching it. Gunnar stood at her side, barely to her waist, acting as reserved as a little boy could. Then he explodes into a run as Ulfrik jumps into the surf. He sweeps him into his arms, and trudges forward to Runa. She smiles and they embrace as a family.

"That's the inlet," Gunther shouted, bringing Ulfrik back from his reverie. Ulfrik confirmed it as the entrance to Jarl Ragnvald's shores. Gunther's ship led, and the second ship followed in line. The ships had taken down their dragon heads to signal peace. But to be certain of no tragic misunderstandings, Ulfrik asked to leave the second ship at sea until he had spoken with Ragnvald.

Their approach was not unnoticed. Men hurried down the slope to form up on the small beach of rocks and sand. Gunther expertly navigated to the shore and moored his ship on the beach. Ulfrik jumped into the surf with him, taking all his effort not to run up the slope. He did not want enthusiasm mistaken for hostility.

"Jarl Ragnvald, it is Ulfrik Ormsson." He kept his hands up and left his sword on the ship. He was confident of his reception. He searched for Ragnvald, but hoped for Runa.

Ragnvald stood directly before him, neatly blending in with his men so Ulfrik's gaze swept past him. But when they set eyes upon each other, both men broke into a smile. Ragnvald strode forward with both arms thrown open. "Were it not for your smell, I would say a ghost made landfall on my shores."

They collapsed together in an embrace. Ulfrik felt a hot dampness at his eyes. Ragnvald was not a dear friend, or even a particularly close friend. He was a reasonable man whose company he had enjoyed and who seemed to feel the same for Ulfrik. But after everything that had happened, to Ulfrik it was like meeting a lost brother. They pulled back and Ragnvald sized him up.

"You're thinner, hungrier looking than when we last met." He swept his gaze over Ulfrik's shoulders, regarding the men and ships behind him. Snorri already appeared at Ulfrik's side. "There must be a story worthy of a song for what I see."

"More than can be told standing here. The other ship stayed back to put you at ease. Truth of it is, we are without a home and must beg from old friends. Runa would've told you as much. May we pull up on your shores for a while?"

Ragnvald's brow furrowed but he agreed. Gunther waded out to wave his other ship forward. The ship already on the beach dropped a gangplank, and Ingrid appeared atop it.

"Is that your wife?" Ragnvald asked, his eyes fixed on Ingrid. Hrolf had treated her well, dressing her in fine clothes and gifting her with a silver chain. She had regained a measure of composure since she and Ulfrik had reached their agreement. She had become more regal, and despite the ravages of slavery, more beautiful.

Ulfrik laughed at Ragnvald's joke. "She is a wife, but not mine. That story is maybe the strangest of all. She is Hardar's wife, Ingrid. She will no doubt speak better of her tale than I could."

Ragnvald's expression was incredulous. "The day grows stranger still. And these other men, they are not yours? Rumors said you left with only a handful of men."

"Take us to your hall and I will reveal everything. But, no, these are not my men. They are part of the story I must tell you."

"Then let's not waste time." A smile renewed on his face, and he clapped Ulfrik's shoulder. Ulfrik, Ingrid, his crew along with Gunther and his hand-picked men followed Ragnvald and his hirdmen to his hall. He spoke animatedly of all the rumors surrounding Ulfrik's fate. Most of what he told had predicted Ulfrik's demise. "But I knew you would return, and many others did, too. And now here you are."

"Has my family given you much trouble?" Ulfrik asked as they entered the hall. Though a large size for these lands, it felt much smaller after the spaciousness of Hrolf's.

"I have not seen your family, Ulfrik. Last word was they vanished along with you."

Ulfrik stopped just inside the door. Snorri bumped into him. "I sent them here before I went to Hardar's trap. They were to seek aid from you. Did they never arrive?"

"No, and I've heard no more of them."

Snorri put his hand on Ulfrik's shoulder. "They may have went elsewhere first. It does not mean they are lost to us."

"But summer is nearly done. Surely by now they would have

been here, or Jarl Ragnvald would've heard news."

He saw Ingrid waiting beyond the door. He realized she could become difficult if she knew Halla was missing. So he agreed with Snorri and decided to not speak of his fears within her hearing. He followed Ragnvald further into the hall.

Once they had settled into the hall and mead and cheese served, Ulfrik shared his tale with Ragnvald. He omitted nothing, including his plans to strike back at Hardar. Throughout, Ragnvald and his household sat in rapt attention. He stole glances at Ingrid at each mention of Hardar's name. Ingrid sat in stony silence and betrayed nothing.

"I came here directly, in hopes Runa and Toki had come to you first. But I see they must have traveled elsewhere." Ulfrik felt a burn in his stomach as he spoke, doubting their situation was so prosaic. Ingrid's gaze turned cold, for she had been expecting a reunion as much as he had. "I'm sure I will catch up with them. You've heard no news at all?"

"None, but we stay close to home now. Men don't dare travel when war is near. So we hear little news; it is possible they could've went even further north. Though they would find less sympathy there."

"So you've heard nothing of Hardar, I assume?"

Ragnvald spread his hands wide and smiled. "I know more about that. Ill news always finds an audience. He has taken your home for his own. Not long after his mercenaries left, more men came to him from the north. Cousins who are rebuilding his hall. He even sent ships out that have but recently returned with more men."

Ingrid gave Ulfrik a sharp look. It was as she had said it would be. The loss of family and home seemed to have not slowed his ambition. "He has no shame."

"I have often wondered what held him back," Ragnvald said.

"He must be bought to account. His attacks on me are only the start. He is sending for more men. What purpose can he have in that? Which one of the jarls are next, you Ragnvald?" Ulfrik's eyes flashed with anger. Ragnvald's hand reflexively covered his chest.

"I know he has been unkind to your people, Ulfrik. Many have been put to death."

"He broke his oath to treat my people as his own!" Ulfrik slammed the table, his voice a snarl. "You must join me in putting him down. We must wipe his threat from the land."

Ragnvald shrank in his seat. He did not roar back agreement as Ulfrik expected. Instead, his eyes faltered and he looked aside.

"What is this? You do not agree, or is there something worse yet to reveal?" Ulfrik glanced about the table; every face seemed as confused as he felt.

"Hardar's attack on you was wrong. But he has not threatened anyone else."

Ulfrik sputtered his laughter. "Of course he hasn't. Once he is certain of victory he will sweep out and attack. He's hiring foreign swords. What else do you need to see?"

"I see you have done the same." Ragnvald suddenly no longer seemed small. He sat up, crossing his arms. "You bring the warriors of a foreign king, who is allied to Harald Finehair even. When you finish Hardar, who will rule those lands? You? And what have you traded for your new allies if not an oath of loyalty?"

Gunther chuckled deep in his throat. He leaned over to Ulfrik. "You promised the men of these lands had fight in them. I can tell you this one does not. Let's be gone and see Hardar's army for ourselves. My warriors would equal ten of his, and are hungry for battle."

Both Ulfrik and Ragnvald open their mouths to speak. But Ingrid spoke sooner.

"Calm yourselves. We are here as guests, and Jarl Ragnvald has been kind. Let not our doubts strain the bonds of friendship, which have been long and true."

"Lady Ingrid is right," Ulfrik said, his head lowered. "I have been a poor guest."

Ragnvald waved his hand dismissively. "Times have been difficult. It makes a man wary of everything, even his friends."

"But your question is fair," Ingrid continued. All turned toward her, and she smiled delicately at the attention. She pushed a lock of hair over her ear as she spoke. "Lord Ulfrik and I have an agreement. My husband has proved faithless. He did not even attempt to rescue me, but rather looked to himself first. I am finished with him. Lord Ulfrik proposes to destroy Hardar. Those lands are mine by birthright, and I will rule them. Lord Ulfrik and I will be allies, not enemies. No foreign power will rule here."

The room fell silent as Ragnvald searched Ingrid's face. "And Ulfrik is still sworn to Hrolf the Strider. But still, Hardar is the immediate threat." He softly shook his head. "I need to consider all of this."

"Jarl Ragnvald," Ulfrik spoke carefully. "If you cannot commit to battle, I understand. It is not your fight. But will you at least support us? I have not done all that I should have to befriend the jarls of these islands. You are the closest to me. Allow us to shelter on your land while we plan."

He sighed heavily, puffing out his cheeks. "You are welcome on my lands, but do not drag the battle here. Do not entangle me before I am decided."

"You have my word."

The tension dissipated, and Ragnvald's expression brightened. "Then tonight we shall celebrate your safe return. On the morrow, you will no doubt go to seek your family."

Their agreement made, talk shifted to trite conversation. Eventually Ragnvald excused himself to make preparations, leaving Ulfrik with Ingrid and the others.

"That did not go as well as I had expected," Ulfrik admitted, after checking no others listened.

"My daughter had better be safe," Ingrid hissed. "I thought Toki was to protect her, Lord Ulfrik."

He stared at Ingrid, rubbing his arms. "I thought so as well, Lady Ingrid. I know Ragnvald is honest, and they never came this way. It could be they decided on another plan. But we cannot seek them now, at least not too widely. Our strike on Hardar must be a surprise."

"I don't trust Ragnvald," Gunther interrupted. "He's wormy, can't make a decision. An enemy is half a day's sailing distance and he won't move. You don't need that kind of ally, Ulfrik."

The words felt right, though Ulfrik did not want to accept them. He looked to Snorri, who had remained pensive throughout the afternoon. The disappointment of not finding his family had weighed on him as well, Ulfrik guessed. "What do you say, old friend?"

He shrugged. "Hardar must die. It must happen first and happen fast. If we can't persuade Ragnvald, then we haven't much chance with others."

Ulfrik put his hands to his temples, nodding agreement. He closed his eyes and silently asked the gods to show him the way to victory. But for the moment, he stood alone on a path shrouded in fog.

CHAPTER TWENTY-THREE

Fog rolled across Nye Grenner, wiping color from the land. The turf roofs of the huddled buildings floated within it. Summer was ending and the air remained cool long after sunrise. Shadows of people moved within the fog as they began their daily routines. Yellow light still shined from the central hall, a wide square of it pushing through the fog as someone emerged.

Hardar stood with arms folded across his chest. He stood at the top of the grassy slope where months ago he had led a desperate charge. From this vantage he understood how cleverly Ulfrik had laid out his dwellings. The placement of buildings, rock formations, even the grade of the slope all worked to channel attackers one way. The defenders only had to stand in the correct spot and dominate the approach with bow fire and spears. Hardar supposed the gods had loved him that day, for he should have died in the trap.

He heard the grass swishing, but remained studying the slope as he felt the presence stop behind him.

"Are you refreshed, Skard?" Hardar's voice shook with irritation.

"Much better now that I've eaten. I departed as soon as the messenger arrived. Didn't even stop to eat."

"Yet you stopped to eat from my table." Hardar turned and faced his cousin. Skard was older than him, but his beard was still black and hair full and spotted with crumbs of his last meal. "Now let's get to our discussion. Thorod is ready?"

Skard nodded and both men returned to the hall. Nye Grenner's hall had seemed much grander to Hardar before he took it over. Now it seemed like a child's attempt to imitate a man's hall. Even this high table did not rise suitably above the others. Yet Hardar had endured it, as his own hall was nothing more than a black skeleton buried in ash. One of the local girls, thin and sleepy-eyed, fed the hearth fire dried twigs of heather. She smiled at Hardar as he entered. He could not remember her name, only having recently taken her to his bed. Ignoring her, he found Thorod guzzling from a mug and seated at the high table.

Plodding through the hall, he dropped himself onto the bench at the high table. His cousins, Skard and Thorod, stared at him with expectant expressions.

"Ulfrik has returned." Hardar spoke as if describing the weather. Both cousins drew a sharp breath, but he did not look at them. He stared at the young girl keeping the fire alive.

"That's not possible," Thorod said. "A hundred men led him

away as a slave. How do you return from that?" He laughed, a thin and nervous laugh that caught on with no one.

"But he did. Word came that strange ships entered these waters, headed for Ragnvald's lands. I sent a spy and he returned last night with confirmation." Hardar watched as the girl finished dropping twigs into the fire. She closed the box of dried branches, then began to collect the remains of the last meal off the tables. She was a good girl, he thought. Maybe one to keep this time.

"You are certain of this? How long has he been here?" asked Skard.

"Nearly a week. He travels with foreigners who are camped on Ragnvald's land. About ninety men or more, all in good war gear." He finally regarded his cousins. They appeared to shrink underneath his gaze like frightened children. "They form Ulfrik's war band."

They all sat in long silence. Hardar returned to staring at the girl. She was maybe as old as his daughter, even resembled her. He had not thought much about Halla or Ingrid since they had left him. He was glad to be rid of Halla. Having whored herself on common scum, she was worthless. Ingrid, though beautiful, had outlived her purpose. He owned her property and men had forgotten her father. Each year made her more shrill and defiant. Kjotve had done him a good turn when he carried her off.

Hardar leapt in shock at a touch to his elbow. Skard and Thorod recoiled. His heart thumped as if he had run up a mountainside. He resisted an urge to strike one of them.

"You were not listening," explained wide-eyed Thorod. "We have to act quickly."

308

"Which is why I dragged the two of you here. Forget rebuilding my old hall for now." Hardar stood and found the girl he had been watching was now staring at him. He shooed her with a flip of his hand. "Get out of here, woman. This is talk for men."

He paced with his hands locked behind him as he waited for the girl to exit. Then he resumed with his cousins. "Your men will fight?"

Skard and Thorod looked at each other. Skard answered for both. "If they are paid well, they will fight."

Hardar's fist slammed into Skard's cheek. The thick crack echoed in the vacant hall as he crumpled to the floor. Hardar seized him by his shirt and hauled him up to his face. His spittle dappled Skard as he screamed. "They will fucking fight or die! This isn't about thieving my last piece of gold, you scum! This is about destroying Ulfrik. If I don't pay, then what will they do? Sail off? Ulfrik will hunt them, you fool, and then they die!"

He shoved Skard back to the floor. Thorod had leapt clear and reached for the hilt of a dagger. Hardar bellowed at him. "Fight me, and I'll show you why I'm the greatest jarl in all these lands. You won't be alive to know, but you'll teach your brother. Now sit down, both of you, and let me hear no more about payment. This is about duty."

Skard's reddened cheek had already begun to swell. He scowled at Hardar, but sat as directed. Thorod's hand melted from his dagger, and he also sat. Skard spit on the floor. "They will fight, but they will expect something for risking their lives. This is not their home. It's all I wanted to say."

Hardar grunted and continued to pace. "How many men do you have in total, about forty?"

Thorod shook his head. "Forty including whoever remained from your men. I bought you back twenty more men from the Hebrides."

"Sixty men is not enough!" Hardar yelled, punching the air. "At least twenty more must come, and I'd want twenty again to be sure. Where can I raise forty more men?"

Skard and Thorod stared at him. He stared back. In one summer of fighting he had reduced his army to a paltry forty men. Kjotve had stolen most of his wealth and Ulfrik had hidden his own treasures. He could scarcely afford the men he had already employed.

"We need allies," Hardar said. "The two of you will go north and promise thirty pounds of silver to any jarl who will come to my aid."

"You have that much?" Skard frowned, still holding his bruised cheek.

"I will have that much by the time you return. Each of you take a ship, bring men, and I will give you silver to pay the jarls a portion in advance. You will leave immediately. Ulfrik is not going to launch his attack any day soon."

Thorod and Skard sat with their brows furrowed and mouths agape. Hardar saw the disbelief in their eyes. He was lying, of course, but not entirely. He swallowed the angry curses he felt rising in his throat, and smiled.

"I will give you silver, as well. For your service to me. This I will give you today."

"So you've kept a secret from us?" Thorod said with a sly grin. "There's more in the stores than you want us to believe."

The stores had nothing more, but Hardar smiled sheepishly.

310

"Every man keeps something for himself. But now I cannot afford to withhold it. As for the rest of the promised silver, more is hidden on this land than Ulfrik took with him. There are still those loyal to him who should know where it is."

Thorod and Skard smiled, though Skard's vanished as quickly as it had appeared. "You don't know that. You're just guessing. If we go out and promise silver you cannot pay, you will be making new enemies."

"Be ready to sail as soon as the fog lifts. I will have your silver ready, and you will do as I've asked."

Thorod and Skard eventually rose from the table and left the hall. Hardar searched around, as if he had overlooked a secret hiding spot where mounds of silver and gold lay. He licked his lips. Prevailing against Ulfrik was his highest priority. The other jarls would hopefully die in battle, or could be helped to that fate once victory was assured.

He exited the hall, stepping into the milky light of the morning. He set out for the barracks where the mercenaries passed their days drinking and playing dice, waiting for the promised raids to begin. They would not hesitate in breaking bones or cutting off noses from the local people. One of Ulfrik's circle still lived here, Thorvald the blacksmith. He planned to start with him. He hoped the smith would still have the use of his hands once he confessed the location of the hidden treasure.

CHAPTER TWENTY-FOUR

Ulfrik awoke with his face on a dirt floor. He scratched at it, and fear flashed through him. He flipped over, expecting Hardar's pug-nosed face to appear above him. Instead he saw tendrils of smoke inching along the ceiling, entwining the rafters. He heard a few low voices, and remembered where he was.

"There's the great drinker!" Gunther One-Eye's voice hit his head like a hammer. "You and your friend together couldn't put me under. What did I promise you?"

Ulfrik's mouth was stiff and dry, a burning thirst consumed him. "You promised I'd regret challenging you."

"But you couldn't resist!" He chortled and his companions joined him. "Ragnvald can throw a feast, I'll offer you that. If he can fight like he can drink, then maybe we should try harder to get him on our side."

More laughter made Ulfrik's head ring. He stood, brushed down his shirt and hair. He pulled away bits of straw caught in his beard and pants. Snorri slouched over a bench, gave a bleak smile over his shoulder. "My age is showing."

Ulfrik moved stiffly. Ragnvald's feast had been the first good thing he had experienced in months, and he had overindulged. Now, in the unforgiving clarity of the morning, he felt ill physically and mentally. His wife and son were lost, maybe even dead. He hit his head to clear his mind, but also to chastise himself. He shuffled to the bench and seated himself.

Ingrid sat across from both of them. Her pale eyes flashed cold disdain, her face a mask of snow. She perched on her bench, making Ulfrik think of a hawk. He knew the talons were ready to strike.

"Lord Ulfrik, you are causing me great doubt. My family, all of our families, are relying on your plans. Getting drunk and falling into a puddle of your vomit is no way to help anyone. You know there is no time to waste. How clear are you this morning? Could you defend yourself if Hardar surprised us here?"

Ulfrik stared at her. She was right, and he hated it. "I've got to piss."

He shuffled away, leaving Gunther and his crew snickering. Rather than pissing inside, as he often did, he fumbled outside and let go on the wall beside the door. Steam rolled of the wetness pattering on the wall as he considered next steps. If Ragnvald would not assist, neither would anyone else. He had to learn the situation at Nye Grenner for himself, which meant sending spies or handling it on his own.

He ambled back inside, where no one had moved and Ingrid sat in frigid anger. Returning to Snorri's side, he cast around at the expectant faces. "Someone needs to see what's happing at Nye Grenner. Who can we send?"

"Didn't Ragnvald tell us everything we need to know?" Gunther asked. "He's hired some farmers to supplement his own men. We only need to kill them along with Hardar."

Gunther's crew laughed but Ulfrik shook his head. "I value Ragnvald's insights, but I need to know what is happening today. This is my one chance, one I cannot treat lightly. Someone must go to Nye Grenner."

Ingrid cleared her throat. Ulfrik ignored her, still suffering the embarrassed sting of her words. "Would not the best person for this be you? Who knows the land better?"

"I'd lose my temper the moment I set foot there. I'm the worst choice. But someone should be sent immediately. Gunther, someone from your crew would do. One of my own men will guide him."

"I've got a boy on my crew who's like a shadow. I can send him if your man won't give him away."

"I'm sure Ragnvald would lend a small boat, or someone could spare one for the right payment."

Gunther frowned. "I'm supposed to grow wealthier on this adventure. Whatever I spend is coming out of your take."

"I'll take my share in Hardar's teeth." Laughter rippled across the gathered crew, but Ingrid winced. Ulfrik fell silent. The shame only lasted a moment. "Come now, Lady Ingrid. He's no longer your

314

husband. You're planning this attack with us, you'll remember."

She waved her hand before her face, her own blush forming. Satisfied, Ulfrik turned to Gunther and explained how to best approach Nye Grenner and where to hide. Men came and went as he detailed the plan. Ragnvald later joined and agreed to help secure a small boat for the job. After most of the morning had passed, all was ready and Gunther's man rowed off with his guide.

Ulfrik and several others joined Gunther to wish them luck as they departed. If the gods were with them, they would make landfall by night, or so Ulfrik had planned.

"I hope the sea remains flat," Gunther said absently. "Or that leaky barrel you claim is a boat will capsize."

"Ragnvald said it was all he could get us on short notice. We have to trust to the gods." Ulfrik heard the insincerity in his own voice.

"You'll pay the man's gold price too, if he doesn't return. So you better make good with the gods."

Once the small boat disappeared from sight, they headed back toward Ragnvald's hall. Ingrid blocked Ulfrik's path, stopping him and Snorri. Gunther smiled and continued on with his men.

"So we just wait?" She shifted her weight to one leg and folded her arms. Though Ingrid grew more beautiful as bruises faded and flesh refilled the bony spaces of her frame, Ulfrik found her less attractive each time he saw her.

"I don't expect to wait more than three or four days. Once we know the situation, we attack."

"What about our families?" She looked between Snorri and Ulfrik, her eyebrow arched.

315

"As I've said, we can't search for them now and risk announcing ourselves."

"I know where they could be, or might have been."

Ulfrik's eyes widened. "Then why not say something earlier? Where do you think they have gone?"

"The Irish monks. They keep a monastery not too far north."

"I know it, the only holy place of the new god without any riches. Why would they go there?"

A breeze caught Ingrid's hair, blowing it across her face. She tossed her head, and looked north. "My hus ..., I mean Hardar, tried to marry my daughter to a man named Erp. She was very young at the time, but even then headstrong and prone to running from trouble. She stole a golden broach from me, traded it for passage to the monastery. She begged the monks to hide her."

"Did they?"

She smiled, wistful and distant. Her voice dropped as she answered. "For a short time. But they knew better than to anger her father. The monks wanted her to become a Christian. We found her before the monks could work their spells to bind her to their god."

"So why go there now?" Snorri's voice was a gruff intrusion on Ingrid's dreamy tone.

"Because no one else will help her. The monks help those in need, as that is the sacrifice their god demands along with taking no women to their beds."

"Now that seems more of a danger," Ulfrik said. "How long can even a holy man resist a beautiful woman?"

Ingrid smiled strangely at him. It caught him so unexpectedly that he felt a chill. She laughed lightly at his discomfort.

"We could check the monastery while we wait for the return of Gunther's spy," Snorri said. "It's a short journey, and worth it."

Ulfrik agreed. The three of them resumed their walk to Ragnvald's hall. The silence felt awkward, and Ulfrik could not resist another question. "What happened to Erp?"

"He died." Ulfrik and Snorri stopped, but Ingrid continued a few paces before turning with a wry smile. "Of fever, of course. Halla was so plain about her dislike of Erp that he gave up on her and I agreed the marriage deal was best abandoned."

"And Hardar didn't force her?"

Ingrid shrugged. "Erp was my idea, not his. He felt she could marry higher, and bring him better connections. My father still lived then, if only in body and not in mind. He respected me more when my father lived."

They returned to the hall and shared plans with Gunther, who agreed to take them to the monastery. Ulfrik started preparations, hoping that Runa and Gunnar awaited him there.

"You really think you're going to find you wife and son?" Gunther asked as he helped Ulfrik aboard his ship.

"There is no harm in trying, and it sounds like it could be true." Ulfrik leapt the rails to land on the deck.

Gunther shook his head. "Maybe you should sacrifice to the new god to be sure. Burn some fish. I hear that's what the new god likes, besides gold and silver."

"The new god is like any other god. If we entertain him, he will reward us. If we don't, he will forget us."

Ulfrik stretched his back, the healed lashes still tender and sore. Gunther scratched his nose, then spit.

"From the looks of these lands, nothing but grass and rocks covered in bird shit, I'd say all gods have forgotten this place."

Gunther laughed at his wit, but Ulfrik gazed over the beach and did not disagree.

***

Hardar knew no hidden treasure existed. The torture would have wrested its existence from Thorvald. Now his head monitored the docks, freshly severed and placed on a spear. But better news had arrived, and Hardar now waited outside the blacksmith's forge. It was already splashed with blood from the last interrogation, and so became Hardar's slaughterhouse.

The day was uncommonly humid, and Hardar fanned himself as he waited. The whole village was silent, not even a gull squawked. He heard the struggling men long before they arrived down the dirt lane. His second, Dag the Sword-Bender, shoved a young man at spear point. An older man followed, held between two other hirdmen. They deposited the two before Hardar.

"You're spies for Ulfrik." Hardar did not need to ask, only to confirm. The two men looked up, the younger one nodding.

"Don't say anything," snapped the older man. Hardar felt his stomach burn with anger.

"When is the attack coming? Tomorrow?"

"You'll get nothing from me." The older man raised his jaw and scowled at Hardar.

"That's fine. You can still help." Hardar picked up the hammer that he had used to break Thorvald's hands. "You two, put his head on that anvil."

The man scrabbled back, but the hirdmen held him tight. He sounded like he might be babbling about Ulfrik. Hardar did not care, as the younger man would reveal everything. The hirdmen shoved his head down to the anvil and Hardar smashed the man's skull. He screamed and flexed, but Hardar slammed again until the head flattened and blood and fluid plopped to the dirt floor. The body slipped to the base of the anvil and more gore gushed from the broken head.

He pointed the dripping hammer at the young man. "That was a mercy. You'll be tortured for days unless you talk now."

The young man's mouth fell open, and a stain bloomed at his crotch. Hardar laughed and lowered the hammer. The words flowed out like his urine. "Gods, I'll tell you anything. I'm not Ulfrik's man. I belong to Gunther One-Eye. He'll ransom me good, anything you ask. He likes me, he does. Plenty of gold in it for you."

"Tell me everything and I'll consider it."

The young man told Hardar about Ulfrik and all he knew. Hardar stopped him at the mention of Ingrid. He could not believe she cooperated with Ulfrik. The thought made him quiver and bite his lip. The man continued to detail the fighting strength of Gunther's troops. When he finished, Hardar gave a solemn nod to Dag.

Dag rammed his spear through the young man's back. He fell forward, blood rushing out of his chest where the spear tip exited. Dag let go of the shaft as the man died with a whimper. His body plopped alongside the other dead captive.

Hardar left the others to clean up, with an order for Dag to join him at his hall when finished. His cousins had also returned, though without the fleet he had hoped to see. He strode into the hall, everything black as his eyes adjusted to the darkness. "Someone open the smoke hole and let in some light."

His order bounced around the hall. Everyone had fled him shortly after Thorvald had begun screaming. He jumbled around for the draw rope and opened the smoke hole himself. The bright light splashed the room, and lit his high table. He seated himself there to await his cousins, who joined him just as he began to grow bored.

"How many?"

"Enough," said Thorod.

"Twenty more men," said Skard. "And they expect good pay. Did you find the rest of the treasure?"

"Twenty? Who sent them?" Hardar wanted to avoid mention of payment. His wealth had vanished.

"They come from all over," Thorod said as he seated himself. He picked at his fingernail as he continued. "They are desperate men. That you've been sacked and ruined is well known. The only men to come were those who will take any chance to earn silver. Otherwise, no one believes you can pay for anything."

"And neither do we," Skard said and folded his arms. Hardar began to stand, anger pulling his neck and face tight. But Skard leapt forward, his fist in the air. "You had us believe you could pay. We left our homes to help you, brought our men here to find glory. You can't fucking pay us, can you? It was a lie."

Hardar sank down. He could not deny it any longer. His voice was a low grumble. "I can pay you, but not all your men. Nor all the other men. I am without gold. For now, though. Once Ulfrik is defeated, there will be no more threat to the land. We can go a-viking, raid for treasure in Frisia or Frankia, anywhere in the world. I can make us wealthy again. My family, our family, will be the greatest the Faereyjar ever knew."

The hall door opened and Dag entered. Hardar welcomed the distraction. Skard's and Thorod's gazes followed Dag as he joined Hardar at the high table.

"You cannot delay paying these men," Thorod said, continuing where his brother left off. "We are family, and we are sure of being repaid. But these others, they might rebel. They might flee the battle if they doubt you, and they do."

"What my brother is saying," Skard raised his voice over Thorod's, "is that you have lost this fight with Ulfrik. His return has marked your end."

"Never!" Hardar shot to his feet, his face hot and eye twitching. "He stole my daughter and my wife. He overstepped his bounds. He'll never be equal to me, never. I will fight and I will win."

"You won't," Thorod whispered. "You're paying men to fight for you, and your poverty has become famous. If you can't pay, the men will disappear."

"Then I won't pay," he shouted. Both his cousins exploded in laughter at the statement. Hardar paused, wondering what he was thinking. The words came from somewhere, but not him. Then, a plan began to form.

"I won't pay, that's right. I won't need to pay. I will finish this pup myself, like I should have done before."

Everyone regarded him with sideways gazes. Hardar, however, began to smile.

"When Ulfrik comes, we will be prepared. The men only need to look ready to fight. But they won't have to fight. This place is a fortress, and Ulfrik knows it. We stand where he stood when we last fought, we dominate the field. He won't want to make the charge we did, knowing how deadly it is. But I will give him an out. I will offer him single combat, to the death."

Thorod and Skard exchanged glances. Skard tilted his head. "Why would he be so fucking stupid? He's got a better army."

"He's got mercenaries, too. They'll see that slope and know what Kjotve knew. What can Ulfrik offer them that would drive men to their deaths? If I offer him single combat, he'll take that bait. He has no other way around us."

"When his spies don't return, he'll know we're ready," Thorvald said, continuing to pick his nails. "Doesn't he know his own land better than you? Are you sure there's no other way to attack us?"

"He can only fight us where we stand. It will work." Hardar could already see it unfolding in his mind: Ulfrik's mercenaries balking at the steep slope and the threat of arrows.

"And what if you're fucking killed?" asked Skard.

"I won't be, and Dag will make sure of it." Dag sat up at the mention of his name. "Dag, you put an arrow through one of the men kidnapping my daughter. You did it in a storm, barely a moment to aim."

"The arrows had the gods' hands upon it, lord," he said with a

322

falsely modest nod of his head.

"You've won every ax throwing or archery contest I've ever held. You get up in the rocks, have your bow ready. You'll be there from the start. Stay hidden, easy enough in those rocks. If I signal you, put an arrow through Ulfrik's throat."

"That breaks your word. It will start the battle you want to avoid."

"His army will retreat. Who's going to pay them when he's dead? There'll be no fight." Hardar looked expectantly, both Thorod and Skard frowning. Dag shrugged as if the matter made no difference to him. He took their silence for agreement. "There will be no fight, only Ulfrik dead at my feet."

CHAPTER TWENTY-FIVE

Toki stared at smoke-blackened rafters. A vague light struggled with the shadows above. He did not know how long he had stared. He felt as if he had staggered out of a fog, the remnants of which still clung to the edges of his vision. He shivered, then realized he was covered in furs though naked but for pants. He lay on a wooden pallet softened by straw under a linen sheet.

He tipped his head to one side, facing a wall of stone no more than an arm's length away. A stone wall made no sense. Something important had happened. He had been hurt. Why?

Strange singing emanated from beyond the wall. Male voices sang in a language he did not understand, though Toki considered the wall might have distorted the sound. He reached for the wall, placing his palm against the chill hardness.

"You're awake," came Halla's excited voice from beside his bed. Toki felt a flush of happiness at the familiar sound and turned to her.

She was dressed in a simple gray robe that could not depress her beauty. Her hair had been combed and brushed so that it shined. Her clear eyes were wide and sparkling, tears welling. She had been seated against a wall in this cell, but now rushed to embrace him.

"I knew you would get better," she said as threw her arms about his shoulders. Her hair splashed across his face, smelling sweet and clean, and her body felt warm and soft. Wet tears dripped onto his neck. "The brothers have brought you back to me."

Toki stroked the back of her head. Then he began to remember. "An arrow pierced my side. I fell to the deck. We were fleeing something. I can't remember."

Halla shook her head next to his. "No, don't think of those terrible days. They are done, and you will be well. The new god has placed his hand on you. You will live. Your fever is broken. Your blood price to the old gods was paid."

"Old gods? Where am I? Where are the others, my sister and Gunnar?" Memory returned from the mists of his fevered sleep. He remembered the ambush and the deaths suffered. "How did we escape?"

"Einar and Thrand rowed us away from danger." Halla pulled back, her tear-stained face looking into his. "Toki, I am so sorry. It was again my fault. We think those men were sent by Runolf, for the embarrassment I caused him. I thought you were dead."

She hugged Toki again, sobbing. He now felt the hot wound at his side. His hand sought it, finding bandages wrapped tightly about it.

"But I did not die. It was not your fault."

"Everything is my fault," she hissed in his ear. "I was so foolish, so childish. I caused so much suffering for you. Will you forgive me, Toki?"

He pushed her back, her face hanging inches from him. Her hair fell like a veil around them, a secluded and warm place. He breathed in the fragrance of her, the sweet taste of her closeness. Then he gently tugged her forward, and she responded, joining her lips to his. The kiss filled Toki with strength. He tightened his grip on her shoulders, and funneled passion into their embrace.

When they parted, Halla's eyes remained closed and she smiled. He whispered to her, "There is nothing to forgive."

She opened her eyes and they stared at each other for a long moment. Then she pulled back to stand at his bedside. He began to rise to his elbows, but a sudden flash of pain in his side made him cry out.

"Lie still," Halla said. "The wound went bad after the brothers removed the arrow from you. They've used the last of their willow bark to ease your pain. So you must be careful now."

"That hurt enough to not try again. But where are the others? What happened after we got away?"

"I insisted we come here, back to the Faereyjar Islands. The Irish monks help those in need. This was the only safe place I knew to take you. That's them singing."

"I thought the monks wanted to be left alone." Toki looked about the cell, which was fitted with his pallet, a stool, and a desk with a candle. A high window let in sunlight and a breeze, the hide shade flapping against the stone.

"Toki, you were dying. Christ asks us to do for others what we would have done for ourselves. For so long, I thought the brothers could not save you, that nothing could."

"But they did, and I am grateful."

"It was the god Christ who did."

Toki paused, then caught sight of Dana hovering just beyond the door. For a moment he hoped the others were still with him. "Is Runa here?"

"They have all gone," Halla said, returning to her stool beside the door. "Lord Ulfrik visited here not long ago, looking for us. He left word with the brothers that we should go to Jarl Ragnvald's lands like originally planned."

Toki felt his face grow hot, and he looked at the ceiling. The pain in his side still throbbed. "So he freed himself, and depended upon me to be where he expected. I failed him. He will not have the men I promised to find."

Silence filled the room. Questions crowded his mind, but the answers would do him no good. He thought of Njall who had given his life to this quest. He thought of the suffering Runa had endured, knowing her husband was a prisoner without help. He had only wasted time, and done nothing for anyone. He felt tears pushing beneath his eyelids.

"Lord Ulfrik had found men of his own, a large ship filled with warriors, or so the brothers said. I expect he has gone on to fight my father. I would lie to say I am unhappy to miss it."

"Well, I am unhappy," he said, frowning at her. "Ulfrik is like a brother, and I should serve him until death. I should be at his side when he fights, holding his battle standard. It is my duty, and I have failed."

"You have kept his family safe. He entrusted you with that duty, too." She hesitated, and Toki considered the truth of her words. But before he could reply, she started anew. "Toki, there is one other thing I must say."

He looked at her expectantly. She bit her lower lip.

"The brothers, they are poor men, only surviving here by their own hand."

"As do all men who live here." Toki's stomach tightened, heightening the throb from his wound.

"There are only five brothers left, and three are very old. They will soon be gone and nothing left of them. They asked, in return for their help, that I accept their god, Christ. I told them if you lived, then I would."

Toki laughed, then began to cough. His abdomen pained him with each hack. "Gods, woman, you had me worried they wanted you to live here. That's all, then?"

Halla smiled, then giggled. Toki reached out for her, and pulled her close for another kiss. Adding to the list of gods he had to placate was hardly a matter worth considering.

"Now you must take me to Jarl Ragnvald. I have to know what has happened. Who has *Raven's Talon*?"

"Einar and Thrand are the only ones who can work the sails, though they showed us all how to do it. But you've just got your wits back, Toki. Last night you were still babbling."

"I will go to Jarl Ragnvald. The brothers have no ship?"

Halla shook her head. Toki again tried to sit up, a sharp pain flattening him instantly. A drowsy weakness was already overcoming him. He understood Halla was right, and he would have to miss the one battle in which his lord and brother would most need him. He asked the gods, both Odin and Christ, to guide Ulfrik's sword in battle and to behead the poisonous snake, Hardar. He could do no more.

CHAPTER TWENTY-SIX

The sun flared over the flat line of the eastern horizon. Gunther's two ships bobbed in the shallows, their crews bristling on the decks, joking and boasting as men do before battle. Loud talk soothes the nerves of even battle-tested warriors. Ulfrik left his few surviving followers in Snorri's care.

"You won't change his mind," Snorri said, standing in the blue shadow of a ship.

"One last try. Tell Gunther to wait a while longer."

Snorri shook his head. "I'm in no hurry for battle, not at my age. I'll tell him, but he's losing patience."

Ulfrik patted Snorri's shoulder, leaving him to board the ship with his men, then climbed the slope to where Ragnvald and his hirdmen watched. The sun at their backs turned them to gold-lined shadows. All he could see was Ingrid's platinum hair fluttering in the breeze as she stood beside Ragnvald.

"Gods grant you victory today," Ragnvald said in a way that sounded like he had asked Ulfrik to leave and never return.

"I've worn out their ears with my pleas." Ulfrik closed the distance, then clasped arms with Ragnvald. "I wanted to thank you one last time. If I do not return ..."

"Your family will be safe if they find their way to me. The Lady Ingrid will be welcomed here as well."

Ragnvald inclined his head to Ingrid, who smiled demurely. Ulfrik wondered if Ragnvald's wife welcomed her, but then pushed aside the thought.

"If I do return, it will be in victory, and I will repay you for your kindness." Ragnvald held up his hands and shook his head, but Ulfrik continued. "I must ask one final time, why not join me? Hardar has obviously captured my spies, and knows you've supported me. If I fail, you will be next. Why not ensure I do not fail?"

Ragnvald dropped his gaze and his shadow-darkened face grew deep lines. Ingrid astutely wandered into the open field behind her, while Ragnvald's hirdmen pretended they did not hear. Ulfrik searched Ragnvald's face, hoping one last word would change his mind.

"I have agreed with you," Ragnvald said slowly. "Hardar has been aggressive and irresponsible. You were a victim and a friend, and so I have given you hospitality. At no small cost for the number of men you brought here. But this does not make us allies in war. My people look to me for a stable and safe land. They fight for their homes, but

331

they are not warriors or raiders."

"This is a fight for their homes. Don't you see that?"

"What I see," Ragnvald said, raising his eyes to meet Ulfrik's, "is a battle between two ambitious men that has cost much in lives for little in return. Your war has brought so much grief to the families under your care. I would not add the names of my people to that list."

Ulfrik blinked, his mouth open. Ragnvald's eyes bored into his own.

"Count the cost, Ulfrik. When Hardar is dead, what have you won?"

"I will have won safety for the people of the Faereyjar," Ulfrik said in a growl. "Hardar's ambition is exposed now, and I was his biggest threat. He sought to remove me, and pick away at others like you."

Ulfrik's voice echoed over the rolling fields. Even Ingrid turned back to look at him. But Ragnvald did not slacken his stance.

"Until he attacks me, Hardar is merely a poor neighbor to be watched carefully."

"If it were your land destroyed, you would do the same." Ulfrik's fists balled, and he forced them to loosen. He saw the flame of anger growing in Ragnvald's eyes.

"If I were you, I would forget this battle. What are you promising these warriors behind you? You've sworn off your lands, made yourself a thrall to a distant lord. You are not fighting for your home. You are fighting for your pride. You've given your home to a foreigner. And you'd ask me to aid you in that? Who is really thinking of the people?"

"Nonsense," Ulfrik shouted. "I fight for my home and for the people who still live there. I will be their lord, and no other. My family must have a hall to return to, or am I to wander the seas in search of them?"

"It may be better for all if you did," Ragnvald said, his voice low. "But I cannot change your mind. So go. Settle this war with Hardar. I pray you find victory. Otherwise, your allies may turn to other lands for their promised spoils."

The two men exchanged hard looks. Ulfrik then stalked down the slope, calling over his shoulder. "Thank you for your kindness, Jarl Ragnvald. Let us meet again in happier days."

He strode through the grass, tramped across the rocky beach, then splashed into the knee-high surf. Gunther met him at the rails and helped Ulfrik aboard. The crews drew up their anchor stones and struck their sails. Ulfrik squeezed out the water from the legs of his pants.

"A lot of yelling, and nothing to show for it," Gunther said, then spit on the deck. "We don't need a man like him with us. He's no warrior, no killing instinct in him. I wonder if he worries about how loud he should fart?"

"What did Ragnvald say?" Snorri asked as Gunther laughed at his own joke.

Ulfrik watched the thin line of Ragnvald and his hirdmen standing in the waving grass. He thought of standing stones, like those left by the old people. Ragnvald was one of those lichen covered giants, sunk into the earth and never to be moved.

"He told me I'm proud and that I waste the lives of my people for it." Ulfrik waited for an answer. The deck rocked as the ship hit deeper waters. When no reply came, he turned behind and found Snorri

333

had left to join others in getting the ship on course.

"So you say the same, old friend," Ulfrik muttered to himself. The shore rapidly fell away, all while the black line of Ragnvald's men stood watching. "If the gods would grant me another way, I would take it. But Fate draws me to this doom with Hardar, and only one of us will live."

***

Ulfrik stood in the prow of Gunther's ship, hand resting on the fearsome dragon head fixed to it. He glimpsed small boats frantically rowing over the horizon. He smiled grimly, final confirmation Hardar knew the time and direction of attack. Those boats had probably been manned in shifts ever since his spies had been caught. He drooped his head and stepped down from the prow.

The sail formed a belly in the wind, and sea spray flew over the deck and flecked him with cold water. Gunther steered his ship, singing a song about a dragon-slaying hero who won gold and glory. Such battle songs gave men heart. With Hardar warned, the men would need heart to climb the slope that formed the only approach from the sea.

A thin fog clung to the islands where the cliffs dampened the winds. He spied milky blue outlines of the mountains surmounting the fog on the horizon. Snorri appeared at his shoulder.

"Never thought we'd have to take that slope ourselves."

"It was your idea. I wanted to build further up."

"No, it would've cut into pasture land. We built in the best spot."

They stood at the center of the deck. The others were already wearing their mail and readying weapons. No one rowed, saving strength

334

for the battle ahead. A group of men were dividing arrows into sheaves. Ulfrik swallowed hard.

"If I fall, flee the field. Look for my family and if they still live, care for them."

"If you fall, I am already dead. Ask someone else to flee."

As they closed the distance to Nye Grenner, men passed skins of mead to steady their nerves. Ulfrik normally would not bother, but this day he gladly took the skin and guzzled until his belly warmed with drink. He handed it to Snorri who likewise drank. Gunther called his men to prepare for landing, then gestured for Ulfrik to join him.

"If this slope is the Valkyrie home you claim it is, you better have a plan to lead my men up it." Gunther's fixed his single eye on Ulfrik. "We're expecting easy work here. I don't have another eye to feed to a spear."

"It will be glorious. I will lead the charge, and Odin's hand will sweep away the arrow storm. Then we will smash their shield wall with the might of Thor's hammer. Nothing but death will be in our wake."

"Better come up with something besides bad poetry if you want me to follow."

"Once we start moving, don't stop. That was Hardar's failure. There is a dip where we will drop out of sight. Get there fast, then it's a sprint to the top. You are always safer going up than going down. Besides, arrows are costly and both Hardar and I spent most of ours already."

Gunther frowned at him. "I hope I wasn't wrong about you."

"I will lead the way, and if I die and you were wrong, then don't follow."

Ulfrik now donned his mail, strapped his sword and long knife around his waist. He took a throwing ax, smiling at Snorri as he did. His old friend was also his battle mentor during his childhood, and had emphasized the value of throwing axes. Snorri stuck two into his belt. "Seems like Gunther has plenty, and you know how useful they are."

The ships bumped and glided across the final stretch. He returned to the prow, where many warriors now crowded, shouting curses and laughing at the distant shadows of the enemy. They boasted of the easy killing, and spoke of what plunder they hoped to find. Two men worked to fix Gunther's battle standard to a pole. It was a wolf's head with open maw that dripped blood. It was faded and worn, flown many times in hard weather. They raised it up with a joyous shout from the crew.

Ulfrik's standard lay trampled in his hall. His eyes drew to slits, thinking of flying it once more. For now, he reached into his bag and withdrew his helm. It was the nearest thing he had to a standard. Gunther had recovered it from Kjotve's spoils and returned it to Ulfrik. He slid it onto his head, drawing the cheek plates over his face. His brother, Grim, had once worn this helm. Now he wore it and remembered all the struggle it represented. It bolstered his resolve. He closed his eyes a moment, summoned memories of his father and his uncle, of his wife and son. He gritted his teeth and felt his arms tremble with power. When he opened his eyes again, the shore had drawn near.

Hardar had sensibly pulled his warships onto land, though the boats that had been picketed at sea were hastily beached. At the top of the grassy slope, in the swirling vestiges of fog, stood Hardar and his men. They formed a block, dark and solid. Overhead Hardar flew his

336

banner of a running stag with blood tipped horns.

Gunther's two ships glided to the shore, almost jauntily, and disgorged the men. One hundred snarling warriors assembled on the beach, crowding into a mass of glinting iron and clacking shields. Gunther stood large and proud at the center of the line, as did Ulfrik. Snorri was to his left and the rest of Ulfrik's men filled the front ranks. The wolf head standard went up, and the men roared. Hardar and his men did not waver.

"Seems like the old fool learned some sense," Snorri muttered.

"We outnumber him," Ulfrik scanned the spear tips blinking at him in the evening sun. Then he scanned the rocks to on either side, detecting nothing hidden. He noticed severed heads had been posted at the empty docks. Ulfrik could not identify them, but knew they were his people. His pulse quickened.

"The barracks might hide more men," Ulfrik said to Gunther. "Either inside or behind. If you try to flank those rocks on our right, the buildings will funnel you into bow fire. The straight path up the slope is safest still."

Gunther nodded. "Is the fat one Hardar? Why doesn't he do something? What is wrong with the jarls of these islands? No one loves action?"

"Hardar, you oath-breaking turd," Ulfrik screamed, sliding his blade from its wooden scabbard. "Ulfrik Ormsson is here. I am the blade of the gods, come for vengeance. Stand down and face justice."

A ripple went through the front ranks. Ulfrik could not see Hardar's reaction. As he was about to bellow another taunt, Hardar and two other men came forward. He held a dried branch above his head.

337

"We've got to fucking talk about this?" Gunther said, slamming his sword back into its sheath.

"Come with me to the parley, and you too, Snorri."

"That can't be a hazel branch, so we don't have to honor it," Gunther said.

"It's not, but it's the same meaning. Let's discover what shit will drop from his mouth."

Ulfrik climbed the slope with as much careless ease as he could muster. A war leader's every action was a signal to the men who followed him, and he wanted to communicate strength and certainty. Hardar descended carefully, angling his way down so as not to slip. His motions looked clumsy and afraid, which Ulfrik relished.

The two groups met in the middle. Gunther and Snorri flanked him, their expressions stony. Ulfrik looked Hardar over as if estimating a trade horse. He was still fat, his eyes flinty. Coppery gray hair flowed from beneath his iron helmet. His mail, however, had patches of rust in the deep links. Ulfrik did not recognize the two men with Hardar, but they all shared the pug noses that ran in Hardar's family.

"So the dog returns to sniff his shit," Hardar said, a sneer creasing his face.

"You're standing on my land. Surrender or die. What's your choice?"

Hardar exploded in laughter, though the other men remained unimpressed. "I don't need to make a choice, Ulfrik. You do. You stole my family. Not content with my daughter, you took my wife too. So I am justice and vengeance, not you. I offer the same choice: surrender or die."

338

"You're outnumbered," Ulfrik pointed past Hardar. "And these men look like farmers playing at warrior. See the men I bring to battle, fierce warriors every one. You are finished."

Hardar shook his head. "I'm not coming down this slope. You can send your men into my arrows. They're not fighting for you, but for the easy victory. They'll run to their ships when they taste of the arrow storm." Hardar looked directly at Gunther. "Am I wrong, One-Eye? You're not sacrificing men for this foggy island of rock and grass."

"Wasn't planning on it until I found out what a fucking maggot you are. Now I look forward to pissing on your entrails."

Ulfrik jabbed a finger at Hardar's chest. "I'll meet you at the top of this slope. When I get there, you die."

He whirled away and began to return to his lines. Then Hardar called his name.

"There is another way to settle this."

Ulfrik stopped, but did not turn. "There is no other way. You've brought this on yourself."

"Single combat, you and me to the death. Let the gods decide who is just."

The offer hit Ulfrik like a rock. He turned slowly, confusion written on his face. Snorri and Gunther appeared equally surprised. Yet Hardar and his cousins stood resolute. Hardar stepped forward, raising his voice. "I challenge Ulfrik Ormsson to single combat to the death. Will he accept?"

The decision had to be swift. He looked to his companions, whom he could not read. He did not fear declining the challenge, for despite his poor positioning he had an advantage in experience and numbers. But Ragnvald's words came back to him. He thought of Hardar's men, as strange as it was to consider the enemy. He padded his ranks with mercenaries, but otherwise he mustered the locals, maybe even people from Nye Grenner. Ulfrik would be killing local people. Gunther's foreign men would be killing local people at his command.

"I will accept."

"Ulfrik," Snorri stepped toward him. But Ulfrik held up his hand to stop him.

Hardar smiled, and instantly Ulfrik realized he was led into a trap.

"But only if we fight on the ground of my choosing."

Hardar's face flinched. "We are all assembled now. We fight here, and end this struggle."

Ulfrik took two strides toward Hardar, and his cousins reached for their blades. He stopped short, now certain of the trap. "I choose the ground or nothing. There is nothing special about this slope unless you've laid a trap here. Decide now."

Hardar and Ulfrik squinted at each other. Then Hardar's eyes faltered. "You choose the ground," he said.

"The field where we held the summer games, just behind the village. We fight there. You bring your men, and allow my men through to the place. Then let the gods decide who is just."

They parted, Hardar tramping back up the slope while Ulfrik walked lightly down to his lines. Snorri caught his arm. "What are you thinking? You're not afraid of taking this slope? We've got him beaten."

"This is between Hardar and me. No more people die for our quarrels."

"My men aren't afraid to die," Gunther said. "And not many will. We've faced tough charges before, you know."

"It's not your men I care for."

Snorri released his grip. Ulfrik pulled ahead. He knew death shadowed him now. He looked skyward for a sign, but the gods withheld their auguries.

CHAPTER TWENTY-SEVEN

Ulfrik prodded the ground with his foot, smiling at the mud clinging to his boots. "Rain and fog, never have I welcomed you as I do today."

He studied Hardar, who spoke hurriedly with men. His cousins shouted at him and his face grew red. A hirdman stood behind, carrying a large shield with an iron boss and rim. Red and white adorned the wood, Hardar's colors. He shoved one of his cousins away, then took the shield, and donned a new helm, one similar to Ulfrik's. His hirdman leaned into him, speaking in his ear and grasping Hardar's hand. They parted with a nod, then Hardar lumbered into the center of the field.

Ulfrik scanned the expanse. Hardar's men formed a tentative line. He noted some betting, reflecting their lack of discipline and loyalty. He hoped they also lacked a will to fight. To his right, Nye Grenner sat empty and silent. He had searched for familiar faces, and had found none. He prayed they were not in Hardar's battle line.

"This is madness," Snorri stated. "But I should have expected it from you. It is in your family."

Ulfrik gave a wan smile, then handed his sword and knife to Snorri. He removed his helmet and dropped it into the grass with his shield. "Gunther, help me out of my mail."

"I was only joking," Snorri said, his eyes wide. "What are you doing?"

"Making myself lighter and faster than that lump of iron and fat standing across from me. Feel the ground; it's muddy. It'll hinder his footing with all that weight." Gunther laughed as he helped Ulfrik out of his mail. Snorri kicked the ground and frowned.

"You've made it so he only need hit you once."

"He won't hit me once." Ulfrik took back his sword and knife, then scooped his shield from the grass. Gunther slapped his back.

"Gods guide your sword," Snorri said. "And come back with that pig's blood on it."

Ulfrik winked, then stepped into the field to meet Hardar.

***

Ulfrik walked across the field toward Hardar, wary of traps, but Hardar merely came straight forward with his giant round shield in front and sword out to the side. At nearly a dozen paces, Ulfrik saw the smirk behind the cheek plates of Hardar's helmet. He gave no smile of his own, though felt the satisfaction of knowing Hardar considered him an

343

easy mark.

He charged. The gap closed. He feinted a strike at Hardar's sword arm. Then he broke hard to the opposite side, gliding past. He ducked, feeling the swish of Hardar's blade over his head. Ulfrik spun around, nearly slipping in the boggy ground, and thrust at Hardar's back.

The point of the blade pierced the mail, and struck flesh. But he had only hit Hardar's shoulder. He grunted and twisted, pulling the blade out. Ulfrik had only scratched him. Hardar slammed forward with this shield, causing him to skitter backward. He slashed with a roar, but the blow clanged off the iron boss of Ulfrik's shield.

They both regained their footing, circling at arm's length. Hardar's smile had vanished. He pulled his shield tighter to his body. Ulfrik heard sporadic cheering and laughter. He screened the voices from his mind, looking for the next feint. He planned to tire Hardar, keeping him moving and circling in his heavy mail until he faltered and created a gap for the killing blow.

He stepped forward and Hardar charged with his shield out. His sword flashed as Ulfrik danced away, parrying the strike. He felt the crash of weapons shiver up his arm, and the blades screeched as they dragged apart. Ulfrik shuffled right, and Hardar swiped again.

He continued sliding right, Hardar chasing him with a flurry of pointless blows. He heard someone jeering Hardar, who pulled back breathing heavy and sweat blowing off his mustache.

"You are old and fat," Ulfrik said, baiting him. Hardar simply hunched behind his shield, protecting himself while he recovered. "Ingrid was a fine lay. She was glad for it, since you never satisfied her."

Hardar charged again, and Ulfrik barely pulled his shield in front.

The collision of shields sounded like ships ramming each other. Ulfrik had hit the tender spot he had sought. "She's waiting for me to return. Her legs ..."

Ulfrik found himself stumbling back and slipping to the ground. Hardar had pummeled him with his shield. He screamed his rage and drew back for a killing strike. Men on both sides of the field cried out in surprise.

Ulfrik flipped aside and sprang to his feet. Without mail to weigh him down, he was nimble enough to recover. Hardar's sword thudded to the dirt, though Ulfrik was out of position and unable to take advantage. He swiftly righted himself, dropped into a crouch behind his shield and kept his sword low. He expected to strike a lethal blow.

Hardar rolled his injured shoulder then cracked his neck. He huffed and blinked, but remained still. Not wanting him to recover, Ulfrik pressed the attack. He sprang forward as if to bowl him over. Hardar braced, and then Ulfrik fell to his knees. He stabbed up under the shield, and his blade sank into Hardar's arm. Ulfrik was rewarded with a splutter of blood and a screech.

He twisted the blade, but Hardar tore back. More blood splashed to the ground, and Ulfrik jumped upright. Despite the injury, Hardar managed to thrust down. He caught Ulfrik's shirt, slashed it along his arm and nicked his thigh. Ulfrik grunted at the burning pain, but the wounds were superficial.

As the two staggered away from each other, Hardar's shield arm drooped. He shook his head like a bull, tossing the shield to the side. Ulfrik saw his handiwork. His thrust had traveled beneath the cuff of Hardar's mail sleeve and the blade had impaled the meat of his forearm.

345

His hand was slick with blood, fat drops pattering on his boot. He pulled the wounded arm close to his side.

"Do you yield, Hardar?"

"Not if I'm still talking, maggot."

Ulfrik lunged, screening himself with his shield and striking for Hardar's undefended side. Mid-stride he saw Hardar slip his foot forward. Ulfrik jinked left to avoid the trip. He looked up, and Hardar smiled.

His bloody hand shot forward, and a cloud of glittering dust exploded in Ulfrik's face. Reflexively he pulled up his shield, but the dust was mixed with iron filings. The heavier filings washed across the shield into Ulfrik's face. Without cheek plates and nose guard to deflect them, the filings shot into his eyes. Pain and terror from sudden blindness ruled him. He staggered away, dropping his sword and shield, clawing at his face and rubbing his watering eyes.

Something hard pounded his head, dazing and toppling him into the mud. Though both eyes were still tightly shut, he saw white flashes. Sounds became muffled. Time slowed.

His heart beat wild and strong, a dull thud in his ears. He searched for the reason he lay on his back in the grass. He could think of nothing. Then he felt the tears, the rush of snot from his nose, and the fire in his eyes.

He remembered. Fighting the impulse to shut his eyes against the gritty junk filling them, he looked up.

Hardar held his sword over head in both hands. One of his arms drained blood over Ulfrik's body. Hardar's fierce eyes were wide behind his helmet.

"Now you die, Ulfrik," he roared.

He pulled back and then began to swing down. Ulfrik, still addled from the head blow he had been dealt, could not react in time.

A throwing ax spun across his vision, sinking with a meaty chop into Hardar's chest. He pitched back, the ax blade protruding from beneath his left shoulder. He screamed, dropped his sword and grasped the ax handle. Then he turned and collapsed.

Battle cries filled the air. Still on the ground, Ulfrik heard the thud of footfalls from both sides. He felt the ground shudder as the two forces charged, the duel having ended in dishonor.

His head still swam; the sides of his vision were crusted white as if he looked through ice on a frozen lake. He knew he had to stand. A man on the ground during battle was as good as dead. He would be hacked and stabbed before he could rise again. So he climbed to his feet, fell around in a circle rubbing his eyes desperate for relief. Forcing them wide open, he saw Snorri and Gunther leading the charge. He whirled around and found the opposition closing the distance.

Galvanized by the impending clash, he snatched his shield and drew his long knife. Hardar lay in the grass with arms splayed out, his chest heaving and his breath a labored sucking noise. Ulfrik stumbled forward, then dropped to one knee beside Hardar. He put his blade to Hardar's neck.

"Yield and you might yet live." He watched the ax rise and fall with Hardar's breath. Blood poured out from the mail, running back over his neck and staining his hair red. Hardar's eyes met his.

Pain bloomed in Ulfrik's hip. He snapped his head down. Hardar had driven a knife deep into his flesh. Seeing the wound increased the

347

pain. Hardar then drove his elbow into Ulfrik's chin. He bit his tongue, coppery blood springing into his mouth, and he fell astride Hardar.

Snorri and Gunther had arrived, and formed a screen around the two. But the attacking enemy clashed with them, and the horrid cacophony of battle filled the air. Ulfrik could count on no other help from them. He flipped over and threw himself atop Hardar. He held down Hardar's good arm and raised his knife to finish him.

Hardar's free hand gripped the knife still in Ulfrik's hip and yanked. A streak of fire flashed through his leg and side. Ulfrik's strike faltered and Hardar rolled away. Tears streamed down Ulfrik's face, from the pain and from the grit in his eyes. Through the mess of his vision, he saw Hardar sit up and pull out the throwing ax.

They struck together. Hardar, his face a rictus of pain, chopped down at Ulfrik's exposed head. Ulfrik, teeth clenched and face smeared with blood and tears, stabbed for Hardar's throat.

Coming together, Ulfrik ducked beneath the blow. His knife plowed into the soft flesh under Hardar's jaw. He felt the ax drop across his back. He continued forward, landing atop Hardar. The two embraced like lovers.

Ulfrik scurried back. Hardar clawed at his neck. Blood gurgled from his mouth, bubbled like a spring from the gaping, torn wound on his chest. He gripped the knife wagging from his neck. Ulfrik crawled back to kneel over him, looking into Hardar's eyes which desperately searched an invisible landscape. Ulfrik imagined Hardar was seeing the other world now. His hand hesitated over Hardar's, thinking to pull it from the knife and deny him Valhalla. Warriors who died without weapons in hand had no chance to feast and fight for eternity.

He laid his hand atop Hardar's. The touch seemed to bring his vision back to this world. He looked into Ulfrik's eyes. Regret, sadness, defeat all glittered within. Then the light of life dimmed and died.

Men struggled in a circle around Ulfrik. Blades clanged on shields, spears crunched into mail shirts. Men fell screaming, holding shut gaping wounds or clawing at the blade that impaled them. Those who collapsed were chopped and hacked until blood and flesh leapt into the air. Such was death on the battlefield. Ulfrik, his leg already growing numb and stiff, flopped onto the grass. Gunther's men prevailed, driving foemen to their knees and reaping them like hay. Some surrendered while others fled. Everywhere men shouted or wailed. Ulfrik no longer cared what else happened.

Snorri found him, his face blood splattered and sweaty. "You live?"

"I do, but will I walk again?" He pointed at the knife in his hip.

Snorri grimaced, scurried to Ulfrik's side and touched the handle. He shook his head, and looked plaintively at Ulfrik. He sunk back on the grass and watched the sky. Tears still leaked and his eyes felt like rocks had been stuffed beneath his lids. Without Runa and Gunnar, it mattered little what happened now. He had claimed his victory over Hardar, and it tasted like blood and dust.

***

Ulfrik lay on his bed, feeling hot beneath the stack of blankets and furs Runa had piled atop him. Beads of sweat formed upon his head. A rooster cried and he realized it had awakened him. Runa had slipped from the bed, leaving a warm emptiness at his side.

Boosting the heat beneath the blankets was Gunnar pressed to his side. Ulfrik smiled at him now. Only months ago he would have cursed the boy for being so weak. But having come through the empty death of believing him lost, Ulfrik could not suffer to let his son from his sight. He would never forget the moment Gunnar and Runa entered his bedroom. Ragnvald had been true to his word, delivering them immediately to Ulfrik's hall. Though Ragnvald stayed only long enough to wish Ulfrik a good recovery, it mattered little to him. His family had rejoined him and tears and joy flowed in a torrent unlike anything he had ever experienced. Any concern, any thought, any other feeling flooded away in that reunion.

The morning darkness lingered now that summer had fled. A lone candle guttered on a small table, freshly lit. From the hall beyond he heard Runa's murmuring. It grew louder as she returned to the door. Stepping inside, she placed a second candle on the table along with a bowl of water and pile of bandages. The room bloomed with an orange globe of light from the dual flames.

"Every time I look at you, I remember why I'm alive." His voice filled the room, and Runa started at the suddenness.

"Get well so I can kill you for all you've put me through." She moved to the bed, perching on the edge and careful not to disturb Gunnar. He snored lightly, seeming tiny next to Ulfrik. Runa stroked her son's dark hair. "He was brave, Ulfrik. For a child, he never cried or fussed. He wanted to be strong for me."

"He's my true blood." They both admired the sleeping boy for a few moments. "Who were you speaking with?"

"Gerdie. She is worried about Einar taking so long to return."

Ulfrik yawned, rubbed his still swollen face. "He has a full crew

350

with Gunther's men. He'll be back with Toki and Halla today, I expect. Tell her not to worry."

"She only tells her worries to me. Doesn't she have a husband for that?"

"Snorri doesn't listen to worries." Ulfrik and Runa laughed, and drew together over their son. They kissed, and Ulfrik's skin tingled. Her scent was as intoxicating as the strongest drink. Gunnar grew fitful and Ulfrik pulled back. "I had never hoped to kiss you again."

Runa's expression became serious. Her eyes flashed in the low light. "Never again, Ulfrik. We will not part again. I would rather fight and die next to you than be parted."

Ulfrik laughed, but Runa held his gaze. He recognized her resolve, and he felt a pang of shame for the terror he had bought to her. He leaned forward to kiss her again, but the pain in his leg flared and he cried out.

"Let's have a look at that wound. I have to change bandages. But Gerdie should be here for this." Runa stepped around the bed to work on his leg.

After the battle, Gunther had men with the tools to remove the knife and stitch the wound. Were it not for his swift work, Hardar's knife would have remained stuck. Ulfrik had known men to die from bits of iron left in their wounds, or from the lockjaw that followed the cuts of some blades. He originally feared the blade had ruined the bones of his leg. But astoundingly he was able to move it and stand, for a short time, following the treatment. Now Runa and Gerdie tended his wounds and were far more gentle and skilled in it than Gunther's man.

As she unwound the bandages, the cool air felt wonderful on his

351

hot skin. He spoke to keep his mind off the pain as she washed injury. "Gunther took good care of my leg."

Runa grunted as she patted down the wound with a damp cloth. A cloud passed over her face, and he understood what it represented. He voiced her concern.

"He also took every bit of silver we had. I'm not sure what is worse, being unable to walk or being poor."

Ulfrik flinched as Runa pushed too hard on his wound, closing his eyes and laying flat.

"Don't be foolish," she chided. "You can make silver anytime, but you can't get your leg back."

"True. But a poor lord attracts no men."

"Well, it seems like Gunther is happy to remain longer than anyone would like. You have no worries with men."

Ulfrik groaned. It had only been a week, but Gunther was already an issue with Runa. His men consumed food and drink Nye Grenner could hardly supply. "Without his aid, Hardar would be lying here instead of me."

"And now Gunther should leave with our thanks. There are one hundred men on his ships. They are eating away our winter stores. Doesn't he know?" Runa put down her cloth, and Ulfrik opened his eyes. Her brows were knit. "I'm not ungrateful. But if he cannot do more to care for his own men, he will end up killing us over the winter."

Ulfrik fell into silence. He knew the words were true. "When Gunther returns, I will speak to him. He will be reasonable."

Runa continued to work, and the morning passed with Ulfrik resting. Soon Gunnar awakened and wanted to go see his friends. Ulfrik gave him permission, but he seemed hesitant to leave. "Will you need me to help you walk?" he had asked. Ulfrik struggled to match his son's seriousness when he declined; he laughed when Gunnar trotted out of the room.

By midmorning word had come that Gunther's ship had returned. Ulfrik insisted he stand and greet Toki in the hall. It was an effort to reach the high table, but it was an improvement. Everyone else had gone to greet the ship, only Snorri remaining with Ulfrik. The two shared a companionable silence as they waited. He heard them approaching long before they entered. Ulfrik shoved to his feet, bracing against the table.

The group swept into the hall. Halla and Ingrid's brilliant hair caught Ulfrik's attention. He saw Runa, tears glittering in her eyes. Only then did he realize Toki stood between Runa and Halla, each woman holding one of his arms. They stopped at the far end of the hall. Toki's gaunt and haggard face told Ulfrik of all the suffering he had endured. The gods had clawed him, dragged their price out of him in blood and soul. Their eyes met, and Toki immediately forced out any hint of his pain. He pulled his arms from the women at his sides and straightened his back.

"Gods, it's killing me to stand. Come here, Toki!"

Toki ambled as fast as his wounds allowed, and stepped onto the high stage where he and Ulfrik hugged.

"Ulfrik, will you forgive me?"

"For saving my family and friends?" He pulled back, a quizzical look on his face. "I'm afraid I must remain grateful for the rest of my days."

"No, for failing you, Ulfrik. For breaking my oath. For lying on a bed while you fought for your life. For not following your plans and endangering your family."

"Be silent, Toki, and be welcomed. We are brothers, and there is nothing to forgive." Ulfrik turned to the small group of familiar faces. The remainder of people filling the hall belonged to Gunther One-Eye. "With Toki and Halla returned, my home is whole again. Let us celebrate."

Men cheered and shouted agreement. Runa shot him a frustrated look, but Ulfrik merely smiled. He had a duty to provide entertainment and generosity to his people, especially after all that had happened. So he sat gingerly on his bench, and laughed.

***

Later in the day when the sun mounted the top of the sky and the last of the fog had rolled off the plains, Ulfrik and the remnants of his hirdmen gathered by the sacred stone. Snorri had lent his support to Ulfrik's weakened stride. Pain seared his leg, but he believed exercising it was better than allowing it to stiffen and wither. He now leaned against the rock, restraining his agony behind a straight face and tight clamped lips. He needed to appear strong and confident.

Ingrid and Halla arrived with men who had once served Hardar. Despite her travel-worn clothes, Ingrid still cut a dignified and elegant figure in the sharp shadows of noontime sun. Toki ambled behind, leaning on Halla and Dana. Ulfrik at least did not feel alone in his suffering.

Gunther attended with a few of his closest, standing to the side as an outsider. But his single eye fixed Ulfrik with a mischievous glint, as if he approved of the children at play.

Ingrid stopped a distance away from Ulfrik, waiting to be summoned. He straightened himself, clasping Snorri's arm in a shaking grip for support. "Come forward, Ingrid of Trongisvagur. Stand before me and be recognized in front of this assembly."

She swept across the grass, uncommon confidence and a flair of arrogance in the lift of her brow. Ulfrik forced himself to recognize her strength, but still had come to like her less since their return home. But he needed allies, and he needed peace.

"Kneel and place your hands upon my blade." Ulfrik unhitched his sheathed sword with his free hand and tipped the hilt for her. Ingrid glided to her knee and placed her blue veined hands upon it. Eager to be finished, he drew a deep breath before speaking. "As the price of defeat, I claim Hardar's lands and belongings. But in recognition of the long held traditions of the people of Trongisvagur, I award Hardar's property to his wife, Ingrid, whose father ruled those lands in old times. Ingrid, you must swear your oath of loyalty to me, to serve as my bondsman, to provide warriors for the hird and the levy, and all other duties of a bondsman. Before this assembly of freemen, make this oath and be joined with me."

Ulfrik watched her downcast eyes search an invisible scene before her. At the moment when her silence would become strange, she spoke. "I swear loyalty to Ulfrik Ormsson and accept his generosity with the heartfelt thanks of all the survivors of Trongisvagur." She lifted her fierce eyes to his, and Ulfrik startled at the resolve he saw within their pale depths. But she smiled, and Ulfrik withdrew his sword.

"Rise, Ingrid, and be welcomed." He offered her his hand, which she took gently and stood. Men cheered and Ulfrik even felt a lightness, for now truly a peace had been restored and rebuilding could start.

"You buried my husband," she said in a low voice. "But I wish his body returned to my lands."

Ulfrik nodded, but frowned at the request. He did not expect she held any love for Hardar, but perhaps he had misjudged. He turned to address the others. "We have peace again, but the enemy has still survived. Hardar's cousins have gone north and may one day return. Our union with Trongisvagur will make us strong, and keep them off our shores. Yet we must remain vigilant."

The talk of renewed war drew sour looks and damped the celebration. Ulfrik regretted his poor timing. "But tonight we will feast and celebrate victory! Already my wife is preparing the evening meal, a last feast before winter visits us again."

Cheers renewed and a positive murmur rippled through the crowds. Ulfrik dismissed them to their duties, though he still had a few matters to settle. Before his own hirdmen departed, he called Thrand the Looker to him.

Thrand plodded to him like he carried a stone over his back. White sea salt stained his clothing and when he drew near mead stench flowed from his mouth. Ulfrik felt the pang of guilt at his appearance. Even Thrand's good eye did not meet his.

"Thrand, Njall's death was noble and brave. He is with Odin now, feasting and fighting and drinking."

"Noble? He pitched into the ocean and drowned. He's in Rán's Bed now."

Ulfrik bowed his head to the stubborn sorrow. He wanted to do more for Thrand, who had lost the last of his family while protecting Ulfrik's. But such was the duty of sworn men, and while a good lord tries to avoid it, Fate often had other designs. Ulfrik gestured to Snorri, who passed him a heavy leather purse.

"This is Njall's blood price, and more for your service to me. I will not forget it, Thrand. This gold is not enough for what you did."

Thrand regarded the proffered purse, then shook his head. "Keep it for rebuilding. You're right, though. It's not enough."

Ulfrik forced the purse at Thrand, but he already turned and stalked away into a lonely field.

***

The celebration was modest compared to the feasts of days past. Were it not for Gunther's men, Nye Grenner's hall would have been half empty. Many had fled or perished under Hardar's rule. Deaths of hirdmen had further thinned the population. Yet still families gathered to celebrate a return to peace and the memories of the dead. They told stories of Hardar's villainy, cursed his name, and proclaimed Ulfrik a hero. Ulfrik, still unable to stand but healing better than expected, sat at the high table with his leg propped on a bench and raised his drinking horn to every toast. Runa and Gunnar sat beside him.

"Mead dulls the pain," he explained to Runa.

She smiled, placed her hand upon his, then adjusted Gunnar who slept in her lap. "Time for your son to get to bed. You will do what you promised tonight?"

Ulfrik rolled his eyes. "As I promised. I've just been waiting for the right time."

Runa laughed, then stood. Laying sleepy Gunnar over her shoulder, she leaned to kiss Ulfrik's head. He watched her leave for their room. Looking back on the hall, hearth smoke laid white over the drowsy guests. Ingrid and Halla, knitted together since their reunion, still chatted among their drunken hirdmen. Toki, with a long suffering look, caught Ulfrik's gaze and raised his mug to him. Ulfrik laughed. Men who had been enemies only weeks before now shared benches in his hall.

Fate, Ulfrik had decided, was unknowable.

He judged it time to keep his promise to Runa. Gunther One-Eye and his men, valuable as they had been, now burdened him. Winter approached and supplies dwindled. Some murmured the foreigners planned to occupy Nye Grenner.

Gunther had swilled a lake of mead and still appeared unsullied and cogent. Ulfrik beckoned him over, and Gunther left his small group to sit beside him.

"You've held a fine feast for such a small place. Your mead is made for the gods."

Ulfrik laughed politely. "I think you have drank the last of it."

"Then make more." Gunther doubled over in laughter, slapping the table.

"Gunther, I have to speak to you about your men."

"Don't say it. I know. We are leaving tomorrow."

Ulfrik's mouth hung open. "It's not that I'm ungrateful."

"Of course not, but you're poor and we've got all we can from you. You've shown me a good time here. I'm ready for something new."

"I would offer you to stay, but with all the chaos we have not prepared for winter. I'm sure we will meet again, though."

Gunther roared laughter once more. "Plan on it. Hrolf the Ganger is one to keep his men busy. Once that leg is better, you're going back to war."

"War?" Ulfrik sat up straighter. "What are you saying?"

"Give it time. Fill your ships with swords and men, and make ready. You have promised Hrolf to answer his call. And he will call."

Ulfrik swallowed and blinked. Gunther, laughing, rose and slapped Ulfrik's back. He staggered away, finally showing a hint of drunkenness. Ulfrik sat alone at his bench, presiding over the mass of people falling into drunken slumber. He glanced at the door to his room, remembering his oath to never again separate from Runa.

The gods, it seemed, still found him entertaining.

Author's Note

The Faeroe Islands are a grouping of eighteen islands in the middle of the North Atlantic, halfway between Iceland and Norway and northwest of Scotland. A rugged land of cliffs and emerald fields, the islands would make a good setting for a fantasy world. Proximity to the Arctic Circle means daylight varies by season. For two months of summer the sun never completely sets, and in winter the sun barely creeps over the horizon. Temperatures are surprisingly mild for such a northern climate, thanks to the Gulf Stream. The original settlers must have felt they had arrived in another world.

Norwegians settled the islands in the early ninth century, taking residence in the north, though recent evidence suggests Celtic people may have been there earlier. Then as now, sheep outnumbered the human population. In fact, the original name of the islands, *Faereyjar*, means Sheep Islands. By 900 CE, Vikings were settling in larger numbers. The predation of Harald Finehair is considered the driving force of this migration. After the Battle of Hafrsfjord, Harald's enemies felt safer living somewhere besides Norway, many moving west to the Shetland Islands or Orkney Islands as well as the Faeroe Islands. Again, this view is challenged by some scholars.

The Vikings brought their traditions and social structure with them. Odin, Thor, Freya, and a host of other gods arrived with the settlers, even though Christian Irish monks maintained a monastery on the islands for hundreds of years prior to the Viking arrival. Jarls still ruled their communities, and freemen had voices in public assemblies that met regularly. While survival must have seemed tenuous to them, the Vikings were hardy people and laid down solid roots that exist to this day.

Most of the characters and place-names in this book have no historical counterparts. The exclusions are Kjotve the Rich, who was a leader of the failed alliance against Harald Finehair, and Hrolf the Strider. Hrolf has an interesting history, and while his name is not something every child learns in school, his legacy is well known to many. Since to reveal more would betray too much of Ulfrik's future stories, I will leave it to the industrious reader to research Hrolf on his own.

Hardar Hammerhand was loosely based upon Hafgrim from the Faereyinga Saga, the saga of the settlement of the Faeroe Islands. The saga described him as a chief over half the islands, and a quick thinker who lacked in wisdom. I took great liberties with Hafgrim's story, letting it inspire Hardar's character rather than dictate the story. Hardar is most similar to Hafgrim in the conflicts he had with other settlers. It should be noted that the Faereyinga Saga is not a historical document as much as it is epic story-telling. It is a good resource for inspiration and insight into a grouping of foggy, remote islands during the Dark Ages.

The size and scope of the conflicts described in this book are grander affairs than what reality must have been. Many conflicts and battles fill the pages of the Faereyinga Saga, but these were mostly fought between individuals or small groups. To the best of my knowledge, no great numbers of Viking age weaponry have been recovered on the Faeroe Islands, suggesting that while men armed themselves, it was not with mail coats and professional armies. However, several caches of Viking treasure have been unearthed. I have chosen to imagine wherever great treasure is found armies will be found as well. Hopefully, readers will have enjoyed reading about larger, more "epic" clashes.

The Vikings have left an indelible mark on the Faeroe Islands, as they did almost everywhere they settled. Ulfrik has had luck in carving a small part of that history for himself, but he is young and full of dreams. More lies ahead for him.

Two people have been instrumental in the writing of this book. First, I could not have done this without the support and understanding of my wife. Second, I must also thank my father for reading this story and pointing out inconsistencies, problems, and all the other things a writer can't see in his own work. My heartfelt thanks to both of them!

Printed in Great Britain
by Amazon

79154243R00210